DEATH ROLL

Dr. Hawley Crippen:

He poisoned his wife, dismembered her body and buried it in the cellar. His fate: death by hanging.

Ruth Snyder:

She got her lover to help murder her husband for his insurance money. Her destiny: death in the electric chair.

Albert Fish:

the madman who waylaid children, killed them, then calmly sliced up and ate their bodies. His punishment: the electric chair.

Henri Landru:

the middle-aged Frenchman who strangled ten women, then cut up and burned their bodies. His end: the guillotine.

Murderers infamous and forgotten . . . their vicious deeds, the legal retribution.

Murderers Die

Denis Brian

ST. MARTIN'S PRESS/NEW YORK

MURDERERS DIE

Copyright © 1986 by Denis Brian

Published by arrangement with the author.

Printed in the United States of America

ISBN: 0-312-90465-7   Can. ISBN: 0-312-90467-3

First St. Martin's Press mass market edition/December 1986

10 9 8 7 6 5 4 3 2 1

CONTENTS

Special thanks to:

Criminologists: Kimberly Joyce Budnick, James Sewell.

Attorneys: Robert R. Bryan, David T. Wilentz, Alan Dershowitz, Duane West, Craig Barnard, Victor Africano, and legal secretary Mrs. Emily Matthews.

Judge: Marvin Mounts.

Psychiatrists: Karl Menninger, Joseph Satten, and the late Frederic Wertham.

Reporters: Ed Montgomery, Arthur Hoppe, Leslie Tusup, and the late Truman Capote.

Philosophy Professor: Hugo Adam Bedau.

Sociologist: Michael Radalet.

The man who enjoys his coffee while reading that justice has been done, would spit it out at the least detail.

—ALBERT CAMUS

Whether or not you can be brave at your own execution depends on your sphincter muscles. These muscles, which you may not know you have, control the body's most private voluntary actions. If they fail you, you can make an awful spectacle of yourself.

—JACK LESLIE in *Decathlon of Death*

Part of me says Ted Bundy shouldn't die. The other part of me is the police officer who saw those victims, who dealt with the two injured women, who had to notify the parents that their daughters were dead. That part of me wants to watch Ted Bundy die.

—JIM SEWELL

"They murder," said the guard, "they rape, they stuff babies into furnaces, they'd strangle their own mothers for a stick of chewing gum."

—JOHN CHEEVER in *Falconer*, his based-on-fact novel about Sing Sing

How Murderers Die
Then and Now

Of thirty-seven American states executing murderers, Florida leads the pack—with sixteen killed since 1976.* And has the most waiting their turn. Two hundred and forty men and one woman—a cop killer—simmer in six-by-nine-foot cages, all condemned to death.

Lawyer Joan Wollin hopes to be Florida's next governor, and if she has her way Sunbelt citizens will be able to watch executions on TV. A former prosecutor and prison lawyer, Wollin believes an execution "makes everybody feel good, and makes sure the guy isn't going to get out and do something horrible again." She says she's willing to pull the switch herself. It could be a record-breaking TV series; a real sizzler.

Psychiatrist Karl Menninger is all for it, but not as an alternative to sitcoms and soaps. A lifelong abolitionist, Menninger thinks if the public saw one execution they would be so appalled they'd demand an immediate end to capital punishment.

Would they? Are we so different from our European forebears in the seventeenth and eighteenth centuries? Then, public executions were *the* great spectator sport that gave the crowd what it wanted to see—a chorus line writhing, kicking, and choking to death.

In England, some 100,000 drooling yokels and yuppies of those days frequently gathered at Tyburn, now Marble Arch, to see death by torture. Murderers were often hanged seven at a time on the same wide gallows, and the jeering, cheering Londoners jostled one an-

---

*As of May 20, 1986. By July 2, 1986, sixty-one murderers had been electrocuted, gassed, injected with poison or shot in the U.S. overall.

other for a better view. And if the hangman goofed and the rope was too short, or the prisoner's neck was too tough, so much the better: it prolonged the entertainment.

On those occasions the victim slowly strangled to death for as long as a quarter of an hour, squealing like an hysterical pig being slaughtered. And he frequently urinated, defecated and ejaculated as he died.

Attempts by British executioners to ease their victims' last moments at times failed, becoming instead a sadist's dream.

For instance: When someone found a man's head in the mud of the river Thames, a magistrate gave the order to display it atop a pole in a nearby graveyard, where a visitor might identify it. Friends of the dead man did recognize it, and his widow, Catherine Hayes, was found guilty of murder and sentenced to death. Hayes himself was no angel; he was suspected of killing his two children.

Instead of the customary hanging, the punishment for murdering a husband was to be burned at the stake. The law, however, allowed the executioner to shorten the agony by strangling the victim first.

The usual crowd gathered for the kill. Protesting her innocence, Catherine Hayes was tied to a stake by the executioner's assistants while he put a noose around her neck and held on to the other end. The moment the dry branches piled around her caught alight, he intended to tug the rope and quickly choke Mrs. Hayes to death.

But the unpredictable British weather let him down. The wind suddenly shifted, a flame scorched the hangman's hand, and he dropped the rope. Instead of a quick death, Catherine Hayes was slowly burned alive. The crowd went wild. That's entertainment!

Writer Thomas Hardy recorded in his diary an account by a descendant of a man who had seen a woman executed in Dorchester, England, in 1705. Again, the attempt to kill humanely failed. The diary entry reads:

"1919. Jan. 25th. Mr. Prideaux tells me more details of the death of Mary Channing, burnt for the poisoning of her husband . . . He said that after she had been strangled and the burning had commenced she recovered consciousness (probably owing to the pain from the flames) and writhed and shrieked. One of the constables thrust a swab into her mouth to stop her cries, and the milk from her bosoms (she had lately given birth to a child) squirted out into their faces and made them jump back."

VIPs, of course, had special privileges. Small invited groups watched prisoners hanged at Newgate Prison, then went for a leisurely breakfast and returned to see the lifeless bodies cut down.

In those good old days in Europe, confessions were often tortured out of suspects in open court. For them, it was a no-win situation. Confessing was the only way to save themselves from dying under torture. And for what? To be boiled in oil, or to watch their own intestines being ripped out by the executioner. Another popular variation was for teams of muscular horses attached by ropes to the victim's arms and legs to gallop off in four directions, tearing those limbs apart.

The French preferred beheading to hanging, as Marie Brinvilliers found to her cost. Marie had an outsize appetite for men and money. To support her male harem, she needed to inherit in a hurry, so she poisoned her father, her husband, and her two brothers. When her crimes were discovered, she fled France and hid in various convents for three years until she was arrested and returned. She didn't escape torture even though she immediately admitted to her crimes. Sentenced to death in 1676, she was driven in an open cart to the courtyard of the Church of Paris. There a gaping crowd watched as she first confessed her sins and was then tortured by having many gallons of water poured through a funnel into her stomach. For the *coup de grace,* the executioner chopped off Marie's head.

Executions were also a great spectator sport in the United States, with standing room only, and the overflow hanging out of windows and climbing poles for a clear view.*

But in the late nineteenth century, humane Americans agitated to abolish capital punishment altogether, or to find a less barbaric method of killing the condemned. An active leader in this movement was a Buffalo, New York, dentist, Alfred Southwick.

One night he happened to see a drunk stumble into a live electric wire and die instantly as if poleaxed. Impressed by the man's quick and apparently painless death, Southwick advocated harnessing electricity to replace the hangman's rope.

Spurred by the dentist, a New York State–appointed committee investigated alternatives. Its members agreed that hanging was horrible. They opposed current methods partly because prisoners often

---

*One of the most gruesome public executions took place in 1825 when a South Carolina man convicted of rape and murder was chained to a stake, soaked in turpentine, and burned alive.

got a shot of liquor before their executions, and "The gross impropriety of sending a man into the presence of the Maker intoxicated is too obvious to require comment." Crazy with terror, apparently, was okay. And atheists got no consideration.

Not unexpectedly, the committee scorned foreign practices. They considered garrotting—the favored Spanish method of gradually strangling the victim to death in an iron collar—too slow; the French guillotine, too bloody; and the firing squad so favored by revolutionaries, too undemocratic.

The dentist's idea of shocking a man to death intrigued them. It seemed somehow to give a scientific seal of approval to the subject. Every high school student knew the human body was mostly water and that water was an excellent conductor of electricity.

Called as experts to testify before the committee, Thomas Edison and George Westinghouse were not disinterested; both had mercenary motives. Edison had patented an electrical device that used direct current; Westinghouse had patented one that employed alternating. They were rivals for the huge potential profits.*

Hoping to scare the public into boycotting Westinghouse's product and buying his, Edison spread the word that AC current was deadly and his DC comparatively safe. His method was literally shocking. Edison sponsored a nationwide road show in which stray cats and dogs and even a horse were killed, electrocuted—and all by Westinghouse's alternating current.

So it was naturally AC current that Edison plugged before the committee and that they bought. When members for The Society to Abolish Capital Punishment attacked him for supporting the death penalty, Edison replied: "If we must kill criminals, the use of electricity is the best way. Society is still barbaric and so poorly organized that it cannot find any better way to protect itself than by the stupid method of killing its criminals."

The committee voted for electrocution, and after several years of experiments with an electric table, technicians came up with an electric chair. On New Year's Day, 1889, New York State made it official by adopting the committee's recommendation to stop hanging and start electrocuting.

William Kemmler, a poor illiterate who had killed his mistress with an ax, was the first human guinea pig to test the chair.

*They later agreed to share their patents.

His attorney protested that the state constitution outlawed cruel and unusual punishment.* This proposed shocking new method was obviously unusual, he said, because it had never been used before. It was cruel because, unless death was immediate, the victim might suffer untold pain. What proof is there, he asked, that electricity kills instantly?

Kemmler waited in his Auburn State Prison cell for 448 days—during which time he learned to read and to write his name—as Supreme Court justices listened to It is cruel, It isn't cruel arguments. They finally ruled it wasn't cruel because it didn't involve torture or a lingering death.

A partly literate Kemmler read that he was destined to put the Supreme Court's opinion to the test. But the decision caught the prison authorities napping, and the night before Kemmler's execution he was kept awake by the hammering and sawing of workmen trying to finish building his death chamber.

It was a bright morning, August 6, 1890, when Kemmler was brought into the room. The workmen were still at it. So Kemmler obligingly sat in one of the chairs for witnesses until they were ready for him.

A new capital punishment law restricted press coverage of executions to merely stating that they had taken place. By muzzling the press, the authorities obviously intended to keep secret from the public whatever atrocities occurred. A vain effort, because among the witnesses about to see the first man legally electrocuted were two reporters.

While Kemmler was strapped in the glistening, never-used-before chair, the unrehearsed and overanxious executioner made a big mistake. He forgot to wet the sponges under the electrodes attached to Kemmler's skull and ankle.

He was also working with far from state-of-the-art equipment. Westinghouse, who financed futile legal appeals to reprieve Kemmler had refused—from either moral or mercenary principles; perhaps both—to sell his AC dynamos to Auburn Prison. So the

*The U.S. Supreme Court ruled that cruel and unusual punishment included drawing-and-quartering, pressing, and burning. The phrase "cruel and unusual punishment" first appeared in the 1689 English Bill of Rights, and was adopted exactly a century later in the Eighth Amendment of the Federal Bill of Rights.

authorities were forced to import cheap, secondhand equipment from Brazil.

To compound the problems, the executioner was to throw the switch in another room out of sight of the death chamber guided by signals from the warden.

When the executioner got the first signal, instead of a massive, knockout charge, he sent a weak, fluctuating current into Kemmler, at times as low as seven hundred volts. Then he shut it off.

Guards beginning to unstrap Kemmler suddenly stopped. He was still breathing. They hurriedly strapped him back in. Officials held nervous, whispered conversations. Guards hurried to and from the room where the executioner waited in shock. The no less shocked witnesses watched the fiasco drag on for almost an hour while the dying man slumped against the straps.

After the equipment had been checked and rechecked, a panicky voice ordered the executioner to try again. This time he overcompensated, sending such a massive charge and keeping it on so long that he began to burn Kemmler alive. Had he remembered to wet the sponges, they would have made better contacts and avoided the burning.

A New York *World* reporter who saw the botched execution defied the gag law, and his paper headlined his account: A ROASTING OF HUMAN FLESH IN PRISON—STRONG MEN SICKENED AND TURNED FROM THE SIGHT. The doctor who examined Kemmler's corpse confirmed that parts of his body had been charred black. Westinghouse said it could have been done better with an ax.

No newspaper mentioned that the smell of Kemmler's burning flesh was mixed with the stench of his emptying bowels and bladder. Today's death row inmate facing electrocution suspects—not without reason—that the last indignity will be to have a tight rubber band fixed around his penis and a wad of cotton stuffed up his rectum to protect the sensibilities of witnesses.

Despite a public outcry aroused by the report, and the decision of some states to retain the rope, the electric chair was here to stay and to spread. Sing Sing soon had one in place.

Word of Kemmler's ordeal reached the four Sing Sing prisoners next in line for the chair. Prison officials exacerbated their fears by hiring Warden Durston as technical advisor. He had supervised Kemmler's death by torture at Auburn.

A crowd gathered outside Sing Sing shortly before dawn in July

1891. They were told a flag would be raised after each man's execution. Someone had thought to create a festive air by using colored flags. To probably everyone's surprise, the first three killings went off without a hitch. At thirty-minute intervals, a white, a blue, and then a black flag was raised.

The fourth and final man, Shibuya Jugiro, a Japanese, kept the crowd and the flag raiser waiting. When guards went to get him, he put up such a desperate fight that they debated whether to sedate him or to call for reinforcements to overpower him and carry him to the chair.

It wasn't necessary. One guard, called in to help, knew just what to say. "You wouldn't want to join your ancestors like a coward, would you?" he asked. Jugiro wouldn't. He stopped fighting and walked head high to his death.

But his resistance had gained him an extra ten minutes of life. The red flag was raised forty minutes after the black one.

Six months later Sing Sing stopped the flag raising, because too many rubbernecking motorists outside the prison caused traffic jams.

Death by electrocution was still uncertain. Several men were alive some hours after they'd been put through it. So, to make sure, autopsies immediately after execution became mandatory. No one survived those.

Ohio followed New York State and converted to the shock method. But it wasn't until nine years later, shortly after midnight on April 21, 1897, that Ohio's first electrocutions took place.

The Columbus *Enquirer* reporter who witnessed them became an enthusiastic advocate, as the gleeful headlines proclaimed:

SEARED

INTO THEIR VERY SOULS
PENT-UP LIGHTNING KILLS A MURDEROUS PAIR
BLASTED AS THEY SAT IN DEATH'S ARM-CHAIR
THE ELECTRIC CURRENT AVENGES TWO SLAIN
WOMEN
OHIO'S MAIDEN ELECTROCUTIONS PROVE A
DECIDED SUCCESS

The report that followed seemed to recommend electrocution as a great way to beat insomnia. It read:

Hanging is now a relic of barbarism in Ohio. There can be no doubt that electrocution is now to be the method of executing those whom Earth is well without their presence.

The new method of inflicting the death penalty was well tested tonight and found to be all that it was promised. Within less than the passing of a moment, two men, in perfect health when they took their seats in that fatal chair, had gone to the great beyond.

Formerly it required much more time to take the life of a first-degree murderer. Twenty-seven minutes was the period some of them struggled, and others suffered more than half that time.

Tonight, the deaths of both William Haas and William Wiley were encompassed without any mishaps and without any suffering on the part of either. It was as if each took a chair for a rest and instantly fell asleep.

Warden E. G. Coffin who threw the switch is impressed with the simplicity and the certainty of the new method and pronounces it the greatest innovation in the criminal history of the state.

Pennsylvania changed from rope to electricity in 1913, and two years later John Talap was the first of 350 (so far) to die in the state's electric chair.

Talap had killed his wife in a jealous rage. He had emigrated from Hungary and had no relatives in America. His attorney wrote to Talap's brother in Hungary informing him of Talap's death sentence, but got no reply.

At dawn on February 23, 1915, sixteen witnesses watched Talap enter the death chamber with two guards and a Greek Orthodox priest. He looked scared. His eyes were wet. He whimpered as the guards sat him in the high-backed wooden chair and strapped him in. The priest knelt before him with a crucifix, which Talap kissed and then said, "God have mercy on me. Christ have mercy on me."

Standing behind the chair, the executioner waited for a signal from the deputy warden and then turned on the electricity. There was a sharp crack, like splitting wood, and Talap seemed to be making frantic efforts to break his bonds by flinging himself forward. His fingers opened wide as if in surrender. The floor under his chair was soaked with his urine. With a sizzling sound, and the sight of blue-gray smoke rising from the electrodes, came the odor of burning flesh, of urine, feces, and vomit.

The current was applied four times in all for a total of ninety seconds, then the prison physician put a stethoscope to Talap's still heart and said he was dead. Counting intervals between the shocks, it had taken six minutes to kill him.

Since then, Talap has been followed to Pennsylvania's electric chair by 347 men and two women. During those seventy years, the phone linking the governor's office to Rockview State Penitentiary has always been kept open until the last moment in case of a reprieve. It rang only once—a wrong number.

Minnesota was among those states retaining the hangman. But in 1906 a gruesome hanging occurred there in, in which the man slowly strangled on the end of a too-long rope. A newspaper headline, DISPLAYED HIS NERVE TO THE LAST, was followed by a graphic account of death by slow torture. Five years later, Minnesota abolished capital punishment altogether.

Almost anyone who'd seen several hangings could tell horror stories. Jack Brennan, records officer for San Quentin, recalled: "My God! What a noise that trap made! Everything was so still you could hear the guy breathing, and then *bang!* went the trap. It sounded like a cannon going off. No matter how often I heard it, it always shocked me out of my skin. Then in the dim light we would see the poor bastard plunge out of sight. Sometimes the drop wasn't enough, and the guy being hung would thrash around under the scaffold, choking. Then somebody would have to get in there and grab his legs and pull so that he wouldn't take forever dying. But if the drop was too long, the guy might be decapitated."

It happened in New Mexico in 1901. Murderer Tom Ketchum was in such a hurry to get it over, he helped adjust the noose around his neck, saying to the hangman, "I'll be in Hell before you start breakfast!" The hangman underestimated Ketchum's weight and the long drop ripped off his head. The same thing happened to wife killer Frank Myer, when he was hanged in West Virginia in the 1930s.

When California's San Quentin converted in 1938, it chose lethal gas.

That same year, the first woman was executed in Ohio. A German immigrant, Anna Hahn befriended and then poisoned for profit five lonely old men. She screamed in terror when led to the electric chair but was calmed by the prison chaplain. Her last moment was poignantly out of character. As she sat in the chair, she warned the chaplain to let go of her hand, saying, "You might be killed too, Father."

With the country's highest murder rate, it made sense for Mississippi to go for a traveling executioner with a portable electric chair. An ex-con got the job. He had tried and failed to make a good living as Dr. Zogg, a stage hypnotist. He had resorted to robbery but was soon caught and jailed. Mississippi's governor pardoned Jimmy Thompson, alias Dr. Zogg, and offered him a steady occupation as the state's first mobile executioner. The man who once put people into a trance now put them away for good.*

Still the showman, Thompson exhibited the death chair on the grounds of the state capitol. His audiences agitated for a live demonstration, but when he called for volunteers there were no takers.

Mississippi eventually switched from electricity to lethal gas. For almost twenty years no one was executed, then Jimmy Lee Gray went to the gas chamber on September 2, 1984. While on parole after murdering his high school sweetheart, he had suffocated and raped a three-year-old girl. Gray had delayed his execution eighty-two times, appealing for his life to twenty-six judges. The U.S. Supreme Court declined to consider his eighty-third appeal.

Nevada had been the first state to use lethal cyanide gas, on February 8, 1925, and Gee Jon the first man to cooperate in his own execution simply by breathing. Originally, the plan was to gas the prisoner without warning while he slept in his cell until someone asked, "How do we stop the gas from killing others in nearby cells?" So that idea was scrapped and a gas-tight chamber built, hailed by a Nevada newspaper-editorial writer as "a step further from the savage state where we seek vengeance." He didn't explain why gas was more benign than the rope or electricity.

Nevada switched to lethal injection in December 1985.

San Quentin's warden Clinton T. Duffy had seen eighty-eight men and two women hanged or gassed, and was moved to advocate an end to all executions. He said there was "extreme evidence of

---

*Wife killer Willie Mae Bragg was its first victim in 1940.

horror, pain, and strangling. The eyes pop. They turn purple. They drool. It is a horrible sight."

Kentucky crowds were made of sterner stuff, and flocked to see men executed. Kentuckians used to say with a smirk that if a Negro killed a white man it was murder; if a white man killed a Negro it was unfortunate; but if a white man killed a white man it was self-defense—unless there was an argument over a woman, in which case death was from apoplexy.

Given that attitude, it's no surprise that the last man publicly hanged in Kentucky was black. Twenty thousand spectators crowded the gallows in Owensboro in August 1936 to watch him die. Some stared from second-story windows; others climbed a utility pole to get a clearer view of his last moments. So many officials shared the gallows platform that there was barely room for the hangman and his victim.

That was the last public execution in the United States. Two years later, Kentucky made it official by prohibiting all but official witnesses from attending.

Texas has led the way in the most recent attempt to execute quickly and painlessly, by introducing lethal injections.

France followed the other West European countries by abandoning capital punishment; the last beheading there of a man (who murdered a child) was in 1977. It officially stopped in France in 1981.

The United States was execution-free for almost ten years while the Supreme Court considered evidence that the death penalty was unfairly applied, especially to blacks. As violent crimes soared and grisly serial murders were reported across the nation, there was strong public clamor to restore capital punishment. In 1976 the Supreme Court decided by a 7–2 vote to reinstate the death penalty, saying that it does not violate the Constitution if a state provides strict guidelines for a judge and jury to exercise mercy in a murder case.

That same year, murderer Gary Gilmore asked to be shot by a Utah firing squad, and was.* There was one execution in the U.S. in 1978, two in 1979, one in 1981, two in 1982, five in 1983, twenty-one in 1984, and eighteen in 1985.

In January 1985, in a 7–2 vote, the U.S. Supreme Court made it

*His death was apparently swift and painless but in 1951 Utah marksmen fired at murderer Elisio Mares and missed his heart. Mares slowly bled to death.

easier to exclude people who express doubts about the death penalty from juries in capital cases.

"Capital punishment," said a Tennessee prison chaplain, "is back with a vengeance."*

There were the inevitable appeals against the Supreme Court's unleashing of the death penalty and their making it easier for a prosecutor to get a death verdict.

That was fine with Frederick S. Baldi, M.D., who felt that especially those who preyed on children should be imprisoned or executed and he didn't much care which. Baldi was a man of enormous experience. As medical director and prison administrator of Philadelphia's Holmesburg and Moyamensing prisons and warden of Rockview State Penitentiary, for forty years he had been responsible for the custody and medical care of some 750,000 men and women prisoners.

To people who called legal executions inhumane, Baldi replied that those he witnessed were carried out in as humane a fashion as possible; that once the trap was sprung or the switch pulled, they "never knew what hit them." Their deaths, he said, were doubtless much faster and more merciful than those of their victims. "The true punishment," he said, "is not so much death itself as the hours just before it, when he [the prisoner] is left alone in his cell to contemplate the final moment of horror drawing constantly nearer for him. That, unless he has been given sedatives, is the part of any execution that smacks of inhumanity. Yet it also constitutes one of the best arguments in favor of retaining capital punishment, if we look upon it purely as a deterrent. The death penalty, when enforced, also has the merit of ridding society of a man or woman who may be a thoroughly bad specimen."

Baldi knew of sex offenders who "could not be stopped by anything this side of the electric chair. We got men leading normal married lives nine-tenths of the time but going out on periodic abnormal debauches—I helped hang such a man in the early days of my prison experience, because he killed a young boy who refused him."

The cruelest sex criminal in Baldi's experience was a Texas cowboy named Morgan "who picked up two little girls so young that

---

*Though nothing like in the past: in 1935 alone 199 death row inmates were executed. And in the 1950s there were 717 executions.

his attack itself killed one of them. Morgan tossed the dead girl in Neshaminy Creek. The other child he returned unharmed. Morgan was perfectly sane and totally heartless. I didn't expect him to show remorse; killers rarely do, certainly not sincerely. But he might have shown alarm at his forthcoming electrocution. He didn't. He was the coolest condemned man I have had in custody.

"He ate heartily, slept well and felt no anxiety. He was a little afraid he might pass an uncomfortable night on the eve of execution and asked for something to help him sleep.

" 'You're going to get a big sleep,' I told him angrily.

" 'Don't then,' he said cockily. 'And I'll come back to haunt you.' I don't doubt that he would if he could."

It isn't only lawmen or the fearful who support the death penalty. A recent survey among Texas prison inmates showed that nearly two-thirds of them favored it for murder, child abuse, and sex crimes.

An unlikely advocate was Thomas E. Purvis, son of a policeman, sentenced to death for killing two women. His sentence was commuted to life in San Quentin, but he still takes a hard line, saying, "Men on death row bought their own one-way ticket to hell. For me booze and women didn't mix. I loved the women I killed in a jealous rage. Even when I paced my cell unable to sleep because I dreamed of the choking death of the gas chamber, I believed in the death penalty.

"People say only the poor go to the gas chamber. It usually is only the poor who commit the vicious crimes. The wealthy usually have good records. They don't rob and rape and kill like the poor do."

Purvis shook hands with thirty-five fellow inmates on their way to the gas chamber—or the "Smokehouse," as they called it. "Not one of those men believed it would happen to him," says Purvis. "Each man thinks a miracle will save him."

The miracle happened for five men on Tennessee's death row. The State House of Representatives had just rejected Governor Frank Clement's plea to abolish capital punishment by a 48-47 vote. On March 19, 1965, the governor arrived at the Tennessee penitentiary where five prisoners—all blacks—were to go to the electric chair the following morning.

The three to die at dawn were together in one cell; the two others in another nearby. Governor Clement stood in the corridor where they could all see him and said, "I respect everyone's opinion on this matter, but I personally have studied and prayed over this and I hereby commute your sentences from death to ninety-nine years."

"Praise the Lord," Rube Sims called out fervently. "Thank you, Governor, God bless you and bless all your family and your lovely wife." Sims had expected to die within hours for a murder during an armed robbery.

After the other reprieved prisoners had expressed their gratitude, the governor said, "I can and I have saved your lives, but I can't pardon you for your crimes and sins. Now try to do something for the good of mankind so that when you meet your Lord you can have forgiveness for your sins."

Reprieved killer Thomas Purvis shared Governor Clement's faith in the Almighty, saying that when he faced execution, "I believed in a judge higher than any who sits in a human court. I put my case in the hands of that Highest Judge and was prepared to accept whatever came."

But Purvis has little faith in the reformation of his fellow prisoners. "Nearly all the men on death row wouldn't hesitate to kill and rob and rape if given the opportunity again," he said.

In Canada, capital punishment—except for treason or piracy with violence—was abolished in 1976, although no one had been hanged there since 1962. Recent especially brutal murders spurred a demand—led by the Canadian Association of Chiefs of Police—to rehire the hangman.

A similar reaction occurred in France. In 1984, three years after the guillotine had been outlawed, nine elderly women were murdered in Paris in one month. Seven of them had been tortured, and the unknown torture-murderer was at large. Although the ruling Socialists were unlikely to repeal their own sponsored abolition of the death penalty, a poll taken soon after the torture killings showed that sixty percent of the French people wanted it brought back.

With an average of fifty-five murders a day and some twenty thousand a year, America is the murder capital of the world. With five percent of the world's population, we have three times as many serial killers as the rest of the world combined. We have been terrorized by at least 120 serial killers in the past twenty years; the rest of the world by forty. In 1983 alone, some five thousand Americans were victims of mass murderers, says the FBI.

Almost daily, Americans read newspaper accounts of vicious murders that provide a constant supply of ammunition to death penalty advocates. And until escape-proof prisons are built and life sentences for murderers mean literally that, the opponents of capital punishment are likely to remain a minority.

Most executions now occur in Florida, but only after years of appeals have been exhausted. Then this is what happens:

One month before his execution the prisoner knows—barring a last-minute stay—that his days are numbered. He is moved from death row to one of two deathwatch cells in another wing of the prison about twenty-five feet—the length of a large room—away from the electric chair. He can carry his entertainment with him— a TV set and radio, for example—which are set on a stand outside his cell. Now he is watched around the clock by guards. They make sure he doesn't beat the system by killing himself or going to the chair doped up on drugs.

One week to go. The governor has decided this is the prisoner's last week. The warden has picked the day and hour. The prisoner is told the time and date, and within reason his requests are granted—for magazines, playing cards, cigarettes, newspapers, a phone call, a visit from the chaplain. Guards, who keep him company as well as under observation, are free to discuss anything with him, with one exception—his execution.

Three days left. An electrician protected with rubber gloves plunges two electric leads from the Westinghouse equipment behind the electric chair into a tub of salt water. The salt water offers a similar resistance to that of the human body. Then he throws the switch on the control panel behind the chair, closing the 2,250-volt circuit. It's working. The water between the two leads begins to churn just short of boiling. That's what will happen to the condemned man's blood. The team that will execute the man goes through a mock execution with a volunteer who is about the same build as the prisoner sitting in the chair. At the macabre dress rehearsal everyone takes part except the executioner and the doomed man, and everything is tried out—except for the shaving of skull and calf and the final throwing of the switch.

That same day the prisoner is asked to submit written instructions for his own funeral. And he is measured for a suit. He'll wear the pants for his execution and the jacket only after he is dead—in his coffin.

Two days before the event, the electrician checks that the emergency generator is working. To avoid the awful mistake of the first electrocution in the U.S., when Kemmler was roasted alive, he double-checks that the sponge is thoroughly soaked in ammonium chloride. This ensures that when the sponge is placed between a copper plate and his shaved skull, the prisoner will receive the full impact of the electricity.

Now that all possibilities of a reprieve or commutation are spent, Deputy Superintendent Hamilton Mathis visits the deathwatch cell to tell the prisoner in detail what to expect in the next twenty-four hours. "There are no secrets kept from him," Mathis says. "I don't like surprises. I don't think many people do."

One day to death day, and the warden hasn't yet chosen the executioner. Superintendent Richard Dugger keeps the names of volunteer executioners in his head. Their names are not written down anywhere so that no investigative reporter can come across the list and publish it. The warden decides on one and phones him to make the arrangement. The executioner will be met before dawn at a spot away from curious eyes. A prison van will take a circuitous route —in case it's being tailed—to pick up the executioner. This one is a slim man of thirty-eight. The driver of the van glimpses his face but doesn't know his identity. In the back of the van the executioner puts on a black hood and robe and is driven to the prison.

Meanwhile, after seeing any family members he requested and his chaplain, the prisoner is eating his last meal. At one A.M., the guards have been joined by an independent witness to see that the prisoner is not mistreated—an innovation since 1979, when there were reports that guards had been cruel to John Spenkelink at his execution. He watches the prisoner eat his last meal with a wide spoon.

One hour of life is left to the prisoner. The executioner has arrived. Mathis and other officials arrive at the cell. Someone hands the prisoner a white shirt, dark pants and socks. He won't need shoes. A barber joins them and shaves the prisoner's head and his right calf. The prisoner takes a shower.

Half an hour: It will soon be dawn. Small groups of those for and against what is about to happen gather in a nearby field, carrying simple placarded messages. The warden joins the group in the cell; and if the prisoner wants to talk, he will talk. The witnesses are waiting in their seats, staring mostly at the empty oak chair ahead of them.

Five minutes: First official in the death chamber is the hooded executioner, only his eyes visible. He now stands hidden behind a partition near the red switch on the control panel.

Three minutes: Time to go. The prisoner stubs out his last cigarette. He is escorted the twenty-five feet to the death chamber and strapped into the oak chair. Mathis and the electrician attach a leg cuff to the man's shaved calf. He is asked if he has any last words. If he has, they are usually short and to the point. Forgiving, a plea of innocence, a proud defiance, or obscenities. A black leather helmet with electrodes attached is put over his head and secured with a chin strap. Forty witnesses watch, separated from the electric chair by a glass partition, seated in chairs with heart-shaped backs.

One minute: Warden Dugger phones the governor. Yes or No? If there is to be no last-moment stay, the Governor—Graham—says, "God save us all!" Dugger signals the decision to Mathis and the electrician, who close the switches. The current is now ready, on tap.

One second: The hooded executioner moves the switch a quarter turn to the right, and from 1,800 to 2,250 volts hit the prisoner in automatic sequences, instantly destroying his brain and then his lungs and heart. Two surges are usually enough, and two doctors confirm the man is now a corpse.

It's over. The still-hooded executioner leaves last. He is given his $150 fee and driven back in a prison van to his car.

Two hundred and forty men are waiting their turn to die in Florida, over two hundred in Texas, over 180 in California, 115 in Georgia and over nine hundred elsewhere in the United States.

Executioners keep in training even when there's no prisoner to execute. None has been executed in Idaho since 1957, but six volunteer members of the firing squad, all state policemen, practice before a dummy target once a year. In the days when they had a live target, the members of the firing squad had a psychologist available to them for twenty-four hours after the executions to ease the trauma of killing.

Although no one has been gassed in San Quentin since 1967, guards go through the drill several times a year in anticipation.

Even some experienced, perhaps hardened guards and wardens are sickened by the barbaric ritual and join those who oppose the death penalty. On the other hand, so many criminals guilty of horrifying murders literally get away with murder or, because of incompetent judges, receive inadequate sentences.

Attorney Alan Dershowitz recently lampooned one such judge in England who thought it not unreasonable for a man to kill, cut up, and cook his spouse, . . . and decided a fitting punishment was six years behind bars.

Hawley Crippen, an American doctor working in England, also killed and dismembered his wife, though he stopped short of cooking her. Crippen then tried to escape back to North America with his mistress, to start a new life—and almost got away with it. He aroused tremendous sympathy, but *his* British judge was much less lenient.

1

Dr. Hawley Crippen
He Died Like a Gentleman

Michigan-born Dr. Hawley Crippen was a shrimp of a man. Even his mustache resembled two shrimps climbing his upper lip. He stared at the world through thick-lensed glasses as if in an aquarium —and moved, dressed, and spoke unobtrusively, as if hoping to go unnoticed in the sea of humanity.

Crippen and his wife Belle, also an American, had moved to England and settled in the Holloway district of London in the shadows of a women's prison, but within easy reach of the bright lights.

And that's what appealed to Belle, a whale of a woman with appetites to match. She craved parties where she was the center of attraction with her resonant laugh, strange accent, and sparkling jewelry. If she ate and drank too much, she could always depend on Hawley to see her home safely. After all, he was a doctor, with a degree from the Hospital College of Cleveland to prove it.

Belle's biggest craving was to belt out arias as an opera star, and neighbors soon realized that the sounds coming from Belle's house were not those of a battered wife or an animal in distress. It was just Belle at it again, rehearsing *Aida* or giving *Madama Butterfly* the Belle Crippen treatment.

She got her big break: an appearance on the vaudeville stage. During the days leading up to it, Dr. Crippen behaved as if his wife were in intensive care. He hushed all visitors and muted his own already *sotto voce* remarks because Belle needed quiet to rehearse. She also needed constant reassurance from her meek little spouse that she wasn't too fat and that she sang like a bird.

Unfortunately, the vaudeville audience agreed—but they had a parrot in mind. The derisive, largely cockney audience also gave her the bird. Belle, born in a Brooklyn slum, the daughter of a Polish father and German mother, knew it as a Bronx cheer. A slap in the face in any language.

She was in shock for a while. Her big break had almost broken her spirit. When she recovered, she blamed Hawley for not being more supportive.

Her friends in the theatrical crowd urged her not to quit and to set her sights higher than vaudeville. She was easily persuaded and began to rehearse, almost in a frenzy, for a comeback.

Although Dr. Crippen's career was floundering, Belle still lived like the star she longed to be. She began drinking to excess, and splurging on flashy clothes. To pay the bills, Crippen was reduced to promoting a quack medicine and even to pulling teeth. Belle helped a bit by taking in paying guests, but she saved on servants by badgering Crippen into washing dishes and cleaning the lodgers' shoes.

It was evident their shaky marriage was on the rocks when Belle flaunted her multiple adulteries—one of them especially, with a retired boxer touring the vaudeville circuit as a one-man band.

Crippen moved into the spare bedroom and sought solace in his secretary, Ethel LeNeve, a slightly built, caring, and considerate woman. He hoped to start a new life with her, but he was almost broke and his prospects from touting quack medicines looked pathetic.

He planned to dip into Belle's private bank account, swollen with cash gifts from male admirers. Sensing his intentions, she made sure he couldn't touch her money.

When he discovered this, the shrimp turned shark.

After a dinner party with two friends, Crippen waited for them to leave and handed Belle a nightcap. It was her last drink. He had spiked it with poison.

Crippen spent the predawn hours at a gruesome task, even for a physician. He cut up his wife's corpse, mutilating it so the sex would be hard to determine, and buried the pieces under the cellar floor. How he disposed of her head is still a mystery: it was never found.

He told Belle's friends, who missed her, that she had run off to America with her ex-boxer lover.

They believed him until Ethel moved in with Crippen. But they did nothing about it until they saw Ethel wearing Belle's jewelry. Then they went to the police.

The henpecked, cuckolded, inept little doctor received Scotland Yard's Chief Inspector Dew with his customary polite manner. The two men chatted calmly about the weather, football, and Mrs. Crippen's "departure" for the United States while her dismembered, decaying body lay ten feet below them.

Though palpitating and pale around the gills, Crippen remained superficially calm until the detective left, when he panicked and told Ethel they must escape abroad.

"Why?" she asked. "You're not guilty of anything."

He stuttered that Yes, he was innocent, of course, but the law sometimes miscarried and punished the innocent. Ethel took the hint.

They left in a hurry, crossing the English Channel to a Belgian port. From there they booked passage on a ship to Quebec, Canada. They'd start a wonderful new life in the New World, Crippen promised her. For him, it would be like going home again. After all, he had been born in Coldwater, Michigan, and his father was living in San Jose, California.

Ethel even went along with his theatrical plan to escape detection if the police were really after them. Crippen cut her hair short and disguised her as a boy in one of his jackets and in a pair of his pants taken in at the waist. He shaved off his mustache and began to grow a beard; by the time the leisurely S.S. *Montrose* crossed the Atlantic, he expected to have a respectable face-fungus camouflage.

Spurred by Crippen's disappearance and his wife's suspicious friends, police searched his home, dug in the cellar where the floor had been recently disturbed, and unearthed Belle's butchered remains. Newspapers soon informed the public that the little doctor and his mistress were wanted by the police.

One such newspaper landed on the desk of the captain of the S.S. *Montrose* before his ship left for Canada. His curiosity already had been aroused by the odd couple that had boarded his ship. Mr. Robinson and son, as they called themselves, stood out among the 280 passengers. In a pathetic attempt at disguise, they had made spectacles of themselves. Father and son? They acted more like lovers. And the "boy's" table manners seemed to the captain curiously ladylike. So was his shape, his voice, and his walk. Sure, he wore pants, but they were narrowed at the waist with safety pins: obviously Crippen's hand-me-downs. To complete his attempt to travel incognito, Crippen had removed his thick, rimless glasses. Now he really looked like a fish out of water, colliding with fellow passengers, crew members, and parts of the ship.

When the ship was under way, the captain found a few moments to read his newspaper, and shortly after sent a wireless telegram to Scotland Yard. It read:

> HAVE STRONG SUSPICIONS THAT CRIPPEN LONDON
> CELLAR MURDERER AND ACCOMPLICE ARE AMONG
> SALOON PASSENGERS. MUSTACHE TAKEN OFF,
> GROWING BEARD. ACCOMPLICE DRESSED AS BOY.
> VOICE, MANNER AND BUILD UNDOUBTEDLY A GIRL.
> BOTH TRAVELING AS MR. AND MASTER ROBINSON.

Perhaps he thought of Robinson Crusoe when he chose his false identity; and escape to a desert island.

Chief Inspector Dew responded quickly to the ship-to-shore wireless telegram, the first ever used in a murder case. He boarded a fast ship for Quebec and was waiting on the dock when the slower *Montrose* arrived there. Dew had arrest warrants for both Crippen and Ethel.

When they arrived at Liverpool, Inspector Dew already felt sorry for the little American doctor. Dew lent Crippen an overcoat— several sizes too large for him—with a high collar so that when he descended the gangplank in handcuffs he could hide his face from the gawping onlookers.

The attention Belle had craved she got at last, though she wasn't alive to enjoy it. The murder trial at London's Old Bailey had world press coverage and was attended by droves of theatrical celebrities, as if in belated recognition of Belle's star quality.

But Crippen upstaged her. It seemed so incongruous that such a cool, polite, and seemingly gentle man should have committed the awful crime with which he was charged. And he never lost his professional manner. Even when pieces of Belle's skin were handed to him in a soup plate, Crippen examined them with the detached air of a physician inspecting a wart.

Throughout the trial he insisted that neither he nor Ethel had anything to do with Belle's death. Why then their futile escape attempt? He gave the answer he had given Ethel: Innocent men have been punished for the crimes of others.

The jury found him guilty and the judge sentenced him to hang. He took the grim news with his customary calm, only showing emotion—relief—when told Ethel had been exonerated.

The mousy, earnest, unassuming little murderer aroused tremendous sympathy. Fifteen thousand people signed a petition for his sentence to be reduced to life, and an old soldier offered to be hanged in Crippen's place, because "a medical man's life is more valuable than mine."

Even Chief Inspector Dew—an unlikely fan, now that he knew all the grisly details and could hardly doubt Crippen's guilt—said, "There's something almost likable about the mild little fellow who squints through thick-lensed spectacles, and whose sandy mustache is out of all proportion to his build."

The guards at Pentonville prison also felt respect and affection for Crippen as they watched him around the clock writing letters to Ethel, reading her letters, and finally writing to Winston Churchill, the Home Secretary, asking for a reprieve. He broke down and wept for the first time when told Churchill had rejected his appeal.

Now, he told Ethel, when he appeared to be reading books, he wasn't. The pages became a blank screen on which he played and replayed scenes of their happy times together.

Four days before his execution date, he wrote his last letter to Ethel, repeating his claim to innocence and adding,

> I have no dread of death, no fear of the hereafter,
> only the dread and agony that one whom I love best
> may suffer when I have gone. . . . In this farewell
> letter to the world, written as I face eternity, I say
> Ethel LeNeve loved me as few women love men, and
> that her innocence of any crime, save that of yielding
> to the dictates of the heart, is absolute. . . . Why do

I tell these things to the world? Not to gain anything for myself—not even compassion. Because I desire the world to have pity on a woman who, however weak she may have seemed in their eyes, has been loyal in the midst of misery, and to the very end of tragedy, and whose love has been self-sacrificing and strong. These are my last words. I belong no more to the world. In the silence of my cell I pray that God may pity all weak hearts, all the poor children of life, and His poor servant.

Not a word about Belle Crippen's poor heart, or her missing head.

Crippen may have guessed that the man who glanced in his cell briefly the day before the execution was weighing him up. . . . literally. It was the hangman, J. Ellis. He needed to judge Crippen's height and weight to do a good job. That done, he checked in his notebook the distance a man Crippen's build would have to fall to break his neck and render him instantly unconscious. Too short a drop, and poor Crippen would be left to choke to death for many agonizing minutes; too long, and the little fellow would lose his head. And this was England, not France or Belgium where decapitation was customary.

To make sure, Ellis filled a sack with stones approximating Crippen's weight to simulate the hanging. The rehearsal was flawless.

That night, the prison governor visited Crippen and handed him Ethel's farewell message. Crippen thanked the man for his compassionate treatment and, tears wetting his cheeks, gave him as mementoes a rosary and a ring shaped like a crucifix. The governor agreed to Crippen's request that after his death Ethel's photograph and letters to him would be buried with him.

Later that night, with only a few hours left, Crippen got a guard's permission to leave his cell for the washroom. There Crippen broke one of the metal earpieces from his spectacles and hid it in a seam of his pants. The guard waiting outside heard the noise of the breaking spectacles, and when Crippen came out, searched him and found the piece of steel. He took it away and the rest of the spectacles.

Now there was no chance he could beat the hangman by opening an artery and bleeding to death.

Most Londoners were at their work or about to start it when, at nine on the morning of November 23, 1910, Ellis the executioner entered Crippen's cell, wished him a brisk good morning, asked him to stand, and when he did, tied the frail little doctor's hands behind his back.

The hangman led the way to the gallows, followed by Crippen with two guards flanking him. Closely behind walked the Roman Catholic chaplain, reminding Crippen that God was also in attendance.

Without his glasses Crippen needed to be guided to the chalk mark that indicated where the trapdoor divided. He stood there, still and silent while the hangman's assistant tied his legs together. Before such precautions were taken, other doomed men had kicked and punched the hangman.

Ellis put a white hood over Crippen's head and fitted a noose around his neck, carefully drawing the knot tight on the lower left jaw.

It all happened very quickly—though doubtless Crippen thought different.

The hangman stepped back a few paces and pulled a lever. It released the bolts that held the trapdoor rigid.

And Crippen fell to his death.

No bell tolled to announce a hanging, as usually happened. Three others awaited execution, and the authorities decided the bell would have been a sadistic reminder to them.

At the inquest, the prison surgeon said Crippen did not put up a fight on his way to the gallows—a peace-loving little fellow to the end—and that he had died immediately from a broken neck.

Newspapers reported how Crippen's 83-year-old father in Los Angeles had died the same week as his son. The old man had been delirious, half-starved after Crippen's allowance to him had stopped. In a coherent moment he had murmured, "It will not be long before I go. But my son is innocent. He was a good boy."

What the newspapers didn't know was that at almost the moment Crippen died, the woman he loved boarded a ship at Southampton to start a new life in New York. Her face was veiled and she had changed her name to Allen. Years later she married a man not unlike Crippen, and she confided to a friend that she never stopped loving the man who had died for her.

This was true: He had died for her. He gave his life to protect her reputation.

Crippen had been told by a famous attorney, Sir Edward Marshall Hall, a defense was available to him that would probably save his life.

Crippen was to admit he had killed his wife, but to claim that it was an accident. Hyoscin was sometimes used in mild doses as a sexual depressant. And this was the purpose for which Crippen was to say he had given it to Belle—because even though they were estranged and had separate bedrooms, and despite her other affairs, she still made sexual demands on him. He was to testify, suggested Marshall Hall, that he wasn't capable of satisfying both Belle and Ethel. So he had used hyoscin to diminish or eliminate Belle's sexual desires, accidentally gave her an overdose, and inadvertently eliminated Belle.

Should a doctor of homeopathy have known better than to administer a fatal overdose of hyoscin? Not necessarily. It had been several years since Crippen gave up his faltering practice to tout quack medicines, and so he was out of touch with the latest information on dangerous dosages.

But Crippen refused even to entertain the idea of a defense that might have saved him from the gallows. He said that such an explanation would incriminate Ethel, and he could not bear the thought of her suffering any more on his account.

Raymond Chandler, an expatriate crime novelist, gave Crippen the highest accolade an Englishman can give an American: "You can't help liking this guy somehow. He was one murderer who died like a gentleman."

On the day of the execution, actor-manager Sir Herbert Beerbohm Tree had moped about London sighing, "Poor old Crippen!" No one seemed to give a damn about the poor desexed, decapitated Belle.

But sympathy for Crippen was not unanimous. Home Secretary Winston Churchill celebrated his execution with a champagne breakfast. Criminologist William Le Queux, a realistic writer of mystery and detective stories, believed Crippen was one of the century's most dangerous criminals.

And there was the little matter of Crippen's first wife, an Irish nurse named Charlotte Bell who died in her early twenties, reputedly of a stroke. An unusual death for a young woman.

Crippen killed and died for love of another woman. Our next murderer, Ruth Snyder, killed for love and larceny, and it's not clear which was the more compelling motive—the other man who was also her accomplice, or her husband's $96,000 life insurance.

Where some who could stretch a point and had Shakespeare in mind pictured Ruth Snyder as Long Island's Lady Macbeth, others saw Crippen as a martyr and hero of romance.

But there was this fundamental difference; despite the comedy of errors, especially in Crippen's escape plan, with its transparent disguises and his stumbling into furniture, he sacrificed himself.

When caught, Ruth Snyder and her corset-salesman accomplice turned on each other. The murder and their trial often descended to farce. In fact, writer Damon Runyon dubbed their crime "the dumbbell murder."

2

Ruth Snyder and Judd Gray The Dumbbell Murder

Judd Gray had an advantage over other men looking for romance. He could ask a woman stranger to take off her clothes and never get his face slapped. Because Judd was a corset salesman, willing to fit clients on the spot. Oh, he could joke about traveling in ladies' underwear, but he normally approached his work with religious intensity.

One potential customer, Ruth Snyder, was also open for romance as well as shopping for a corset. Judd fitted Ruth and Ruth fitted Judd in the otherwise empty office of the Bien Jolie Corset Company on Fifth Avenue. For both it was obviously bien and jolie, for they immediately consummated their relationship on the office floor.

Ruth was a solidly built Nordic type with pale blue eyes and a commanding chin. Judd was slight, earnest, bespectacled, fine-featured, and cleft-chinned. He had a sensitive mouth, warm hands —essential for his work—and a precise manner. He was a cross between a Sunday School teacher and an income tax inspector.

The problem was, they were both married to others.

Most frustrated Long Island housewives sublimated their long-ings with booze, radio soap operas, or lightweight literature in which lean Lotharios and mustachioed military men pleasured their ladies—in top boots. They'd once satisfied Ruth, too.

Now she wanted the real thing: mouth-to-mouth dancing, cocktails for two, and a man who understood her needs and would do EXACTLY as he was told.

Judd knew a good thing when he felt it. He and Ruth were soon enjoying many a stolen hour sleeping together in the Waldorf-Astoria.

She quickly tired of dreaming up phony excuses to explain those adulterous liaisons with Judd to her stop-at-home husband, Albert. So she decided to get rid of that problem by getting rid of Albert, or "that old crab" as she called him. But first, to ensure her financial future, she tricked him into taking out double-indemnity life insurance for $96,000 by folding back sheets of paper so he thought he was signing for only $1,000. Now if Albert died accidentally or was killed, say, in a burglary, Ruth would get a small fortune.

Albert, a stolid workaholic whose idea of the high life was to go bowling once a week and sailing once a year, was art editor of *Motor Boating* magazine.

He was obviously not too attentive. Ruth made several attempts to kill him and he hardly noticed a thing. She put knockout drops in his prune whip and he asked for more. While he was snoozing on the sofa with the windows shut, she turned on the gas without lighting it. He woke just in time and staggered out for air. He accepted her excuse that she must have accidentally tripped over the gas pipe and turned it on. When he was working under his car with the engine running, she closed the garage doors and the carbon monoxide fumes nearly finished him off. To cure his hiccups, Ruth gave him poisoned whiskey. It, surprisingly, did the trick. It also, as expected, made him sick, but he recovered.

Albert told his brother he suspected something odd was happening, but he couldn't put his finger on it. Just in case, he bought a revolver and kept it loaded and under his pillow.

Ruth's murder attempts having failed, she turned to her lover for help. Judd resisted manfully, but not for long.

One evening when Ruth, Albert, and their nine-year-old daughter, Lorraine, were partying at a neighbor's house, Judd let himself into the Snyders' home. He had the murder weapons with him: a five-pound sash weight, chloroform, and piano wire. He hid in a guest bedroom upstairs and waited nervously for more than one reason. To give himself courage, he'd consumed a bottle of bootleg booze; and now an urge to stay hidden fought with an urge to go to the bathroom. The trio returned just in time.

Albert and the girl were soon sleeping, and Ruth came for Judd. She led him into the master bedroom, and there the suburban Lady Macbeth told him to screw his courage to the sticking point. He would rather have peed.

Judd screwed as best he could, and—gripping the sash weight— struck. He hit the headboard rather than Albert, who woke with the crash and began struggling with the intruder. The two men were so entangled that Ruth was afraid she'd chloroform the wrong one. Albert was getting the better of it, choking Judd with his own necktie. "Help me, Momsie! For God's sake, help me!" Judd gasped.

Momsie grabbed the sash weight from the befuddled Judd and battered Albert into eternity. To make sure he had arrived, one or both of them strangled him with the piano wire and smothered him with the chloroform-soaked bedclothes. Then they bound his wrists with a towel and his ankles with a necktie.

Ruth's umpteenth murder attempt had succeeded.

She burned her bloody nightdress and Judd's bloody shirt in the cellar furnace and, after changing, gave Judd one of Albert's new shirts. Now for their watertight alibis.

They opened drawers and scattered clothes all over the floor. Ruth hid her most valuable jewels under a mattress. They'd say the thief who killed Albert got away with the jewels. To make sure even the dumbest cop would buy their story that an immigrant was the guilty party, Judd dropped an Italian newspaper in plain view. He then tied up and gagged Ruth in the guest bedroom, but left the rope around her ankles loose enough for her to be able to walk.

Breathing heavily and weaving slightly as he walked, Judd left to catch an early morning train to Syracuse, New York; he passed a policeman who was firing his gun at bottles in the road; he got a cabdriver off to a bad start by undertipping him. A friend had booked a room in Judd's name in a Syracuse hotel. He had disarranged the bedclothes there as if Judd had slept in the bed, and had mailed a letter Judd had written to his wife so the postmark would substantiate his alibi.

Ruth waited until about eight A.M. before shuffling to her daughter's bedroom door and making noises. The girl ungagged her mom, who sent her to the neighbors. They called the cops.

When the police discovered Albert's corpse, Ruth gave a good simulation of the grieving widow. Tearfully, she told how a dark thug with an Italian accent had beaten them, tied them up, and stolen her jewelry. The evidence was plain even for a rookie detective—the dead man, the bloody sash weight and the piano-wire garrotte, the weeping widow, the messed-up rooms and scattered clothes, and what's this? Ah, an Italian newspaper!

Except that the jewelry wasn't missing. Police found it under Ruth's mattress. On the floor a detective found a tie pin that formed the initials J. G., and in her address book one of the twenty-eight men listed was a Judd Gray. He read the name aloud and noticed it made Ruth tremble slightly as if she were starting a cold. When they discovered that Albert's life insurance paid Ruth $96,000 if he was killed, they asked her to go with them to the police station.

There she gave the district attorney confused and contradictory statements, and when he showed her a piece of paper with Judd's name and address on it, she blew her alibi. "Has he confessed?" she asked. Yes, the police said, he has confessed to your husband's murder—although they hadn't even located Judd yet, let alone spoken to him.

"Poor Judd. I promised not to tell," she said. And began to tell. She admitted they had been lovers, but blamed him for the murder, which she claimed she had tried desperately to prevent. And she told the police where to find him.

Judd expressed astonishment when confronted by the police. "My word, gentlemen," he said, "when you know me better you'll see how utterly ridiculous it is for a man like me to be in the clutches of the law. I've never even been given a ticket for speeding."

When told the charge was homicide, it had to be explained to him that "homicide" meant murder. He maintained his air of innocence, saying, "I've never killed anything more than a fly."

He didn't hold out for long. On the train back from Syracuse, he told the police he had killed Albert with Ruth's help. "I absolutely refused at first to be a party to any such plan," he explained earnestly, "and with some veiled threats and hints of lovemaking, she reached the point where she got me in such a whirl that I didn't know where I was. During the past weeks since this plan was concocted I have been in a literal hell. That is the truth, because I have a very fine wife and a wonderful daughter. You may say that is strange to say that now."

Bad timing, perhaps.

In an attempt to save Ruth from the electric chair, her attorney portrayed her as the typical good woman next door, citing the Sunday School hymns she taught her daughter and the hours she spent at home making lampshades and quince jelly. He said that her husband drove love from the house by pining over a sweetheart who had died young and had even named his boat after the young woman.

Ruth took the stand to deny any part in the murder, saying Judd had threatened to reveal their illicit relations if she didn't take out the life insurance on her husband.

When the murder was described, the victim's brother collapsed and the brother's wife screamed.

Judd Gray maintained one expression throughout the trial, a dull stare magnified by his glasses—except when he told of the blazing affair that led to the killing, and then his eyes caught fire and tears streamed down his cheeks.

Listening to him, United Press reporter Sam Love was moved to mirth and compassion. "His story of his plight," wrote Love, "would have stirred laughter in an audience at a French farce and pity in the heart of a wooden Indian. At its completion—the murder done—the unsuspecting husband cold in death—foolish plans for deceiving the police accomplished—the bloodstained garments of the conspirators consumed odoriferously in the furnace—Gray told of his leave-taking from the mistress who had brought him to ruin."

Judd's attorney, Samuel Miller, pulled out all the stops. "We will present to you the most tragic story that has ever gripped the human heart," he told the court, "a story of a human triangle, of illicit love and of unnatural relations and of dishonor, that ever fell to a man to submit to a court of justice. Judd's childhood was spent in a wonderful home. A lovely mother watched over and reared him with jealous care. Then a sinister, fascinating woman came across his path. This woman, this peculiar venomous species of humanity, was abnormal; possessed of an all-consuming, all-absorbing sexual passion, animal lust, which seemingly was never satisfied."

William Millard, Judd's other impassioned attorney, went on to describe how Judd had been ensnared by Ruth's body, how she had turned him into a human mannequin or dummy to do her fiendish will.

Miller told how Judd "was dominated by a cold, heartless, calculating master mind and master will. He was a helpless mendicant of a designing, deadly, conscienceless, abnormal woman, a human serpent, a human fiend in the guise of a woman. He became inveigled and drawn into this hopeless chasm when reason was gone, and when his mind was weakened by lust and passion."

Now Millard took over and asked the jury to treat Judd "tenderly" because he was not to blame and to find him guilty only of manslaughter.

The mistake was to let Judd Gray testify. When he ended his testimony, Ruth Snyder was crying from fear. Judd had doomed her as well as himself by his frank, detailed confession. Even his attorneys were looking grim, and one was sweating profusely and mopping his brow, realizing Judd had talked himself to death.

Both were sentenced to die in Sing Sing's electric chair. Along the route, as they were driven from the court to the prison, groups of people screamed insults and threats at them. A large crowd waited outside Sing Sing with more insults and jeers.

Judd's concluding words in court were, "I tied her feet and I tied her hands. I told her it might be two months, it might be a year, it might be never before she saw me again. I left her lying on her mother's bed and I went out." It was never before he saw her again. The man of whom she had said, "I could eat you all up," and called "lover boy" and "you darn lovable little cuss," had earned a different name from her now. He was "that Judas who spells his name with two d's."

The trial ended their passionate encounter. During the eight-month wait on death row, they neither met nor wrote to each other. Though both had almost too much mail from others.

Many letters to Ruth were from sadists relishing her predicament or from moralists saying she'd got her just deserts, or the religious advising her to repent. Hundreds were from apparently intelligent and educated men proposing marriage should she escape the electric chair.

Warden Lewis Lawes gave her only letters that he thought would not upset her. They did not include the threat that "When Ruth Snyder is executed, the Heavens will heave forth in storm and I shall create it and blast the wicked from the earth," or "The executioner will never reach the prison alive. I will bomb him before he gets there." Another message came from "The Lord God Almighty," who wrote in a shaky hand and simply forbade the execution.

Judd Gray received fewer proposals but more business proposi-
tions. One correspondent wanted to buy the Bible Judd was reported to be constantly reading, offering half the profit from its sale
to charity. The warden said no, and it went to Judd's family. Another man was eager to purchase the beds and chairs the couple used
in their death-row cells. He was told that state property is not for
sale.

A barber made an offer to buy Ruth's hair that he felt the warden
couldn't refuse. He was willing to pay $100 to a prisoners' welfare
fund and $100 to Ruth's surviving relatives. When the warden
surprised him by refusing, he phoned the prison and asked for the
address of Ruth's mother. "Don't you think it would be indecent
to disturb the grief-stricken old woman with such a request?" the
warden asked. The barber thought it over and reluctantly replied,
"I guess I'll forget about it."

But even those callous money grubbers were outmatched by Ruth
Snyder herself. A convicted husband killer, she was still in lively
correspondence with the insurance company, insisting that when
she was reprieved, as she anticipated, they must cough up her
victim's $96,000.

Fantastic rumors reached the warden that, even without a reprieve, Ruth would live to claim the cash. He was told of an extraordinary plan to restore her to life after the prison doctor had declared
her dead. Rescuers, said the rumor, intended to claim her corpse
and resurrect it with injections of Adrenalin.

Even if possible, said the warden, they would have revived a
zombie, a woman without a mind, because the massive electric
current used for the execution instantly destroys brain cells. He
quoted expert opinion that she would be shocked unconscious in less
than 240ths of a second, much faster than her nervous system could
register pain. The real experts with firsthand knowledge, of course,
weren't around to dispute him.

The resurrection rumor heated up when the warden received a
lawyer's letter forbidding an autopsy on Ruth Snyder.

Ruth scoffed at the plan to revive her, though her demanding
letters to the insurance company indicated she expected to survive,
and her frequent recourse to the Bible may have reassured her that
she wouldn't be the first to be restored to life.

Her sudden conversion to Catholicism was regarded as a blatant
ploy to sway the Catholic governor of New York, Al Smith. Instead,

it made it less likely that he'd commute her sentence—if he had ever intended to do so.

Robert Elliott, the man hired to make sure she died and stayed dead, was a kind, soft-spoken son of an Irish immigrant father. As official executioner for six Eastern states, the grayhaired little electrician eventually executed some three hundred and eighty-two men and five women. His fee for executing Snyder and Gray was $150 apiece. A devout Methodist, he began his killing career by electrocuting two men at Sing Sing. The first was an immense Scandinavian who glared at Elliott as if he hoped looks could make them switch places. The other had hysterics and was strapped to a plank and carried to the electric chair screaming hideously. "He was sick all over me," Elliott recalled. "But he was a killer and it didn't bother me too much."

Ruth would be the first woman he executed. And he was nervous about it, but not nearly so much as she. As the time drew near, she had frequent fainting fits and came to screaming in terror.

The warden had decided to execute Judd first, thinking he was the weaker of the two and might give the most trouble. Now he changed his mind. Guards moved Ruth to the holding cell only twenty paces from the electric chair.

She recovered sufficiently to eat a last meal of soup, roast chicken with celery, and mashed potatoes and coffee. Judd had the same, asking a guard to make sure the coffee was really good.

After dinner Ruth fell into a coma, but a few hours later she was playing cards with women guards. Then she read the Bible.

Late on that last night of January 12, 1928, she dressed in a brown smock, cotton stockings, and a black cotton skirt. She put her feet into brown felt slippers. The barber arrived and began to clip away a patch of her dark blond hair. The patch of bare skull would make a better contact for the electrode. She asked him if he'd make what was left of her hair look attractive. She wanted to die looking her best. The matron said okay.

Before she left the cell, her right stocking was rolled down for a second electrode to be attached to the bare skin. She got neither opiates nor sedatives to ease her final moments.

At 11:01 P.M., twenty-four invited witnesses, most of them reporters, had their first glimpse of the woman they had come to watch die. She had become slim on death row and looked as if she'd just left the beauty parlor.

But her eyes were red-rimmed from weeping, and at thirty-three she appeared middle-aged. Six remorseless overhead lights revealed her anguish and bleached her already white face. She shuffled rather than walked—an ironic replay of her shuffle to her daughter's bedroom door—and she groped for assistance from the matrons walking on either side of her.

"Jesus have mercy!" she responded to the Catholic chaplain's litany, her voice subdued but high-pitched like a scared child's.

"When her eyes fell on the death instrument, she all but collapsed," the warden recalled. "Her knees buckled. Two guards reached out to steady her; then she walked the rest of the short distance mechanically, woodenly, as if in a trance."

Executioner Elliott watched anxiously out of her sight in an alcove as guards urgently strapped Ruth Snyder into the high-backed wooden chair and covered her hair with a football helmet containing the upper electrode while she continued to respond in a weak, quavering voice to the priest's litany.

The matron who had agreed to act as a shield was overcome, began to sob, and hurried out—leaving Ruth exposed to the witnesses. It was just what Thomas Howard had hoped for. He had been hired from "anything goes" Chicago by the New York *Daily News* to try to evade the no-photographs rule and snap the dying moment of the first woman to be executed in Sing Sing's electric chair. Warden Lawes had put all present on their honor not to break the rule, not realizing photographers have a higher allegiance to posterity.

As Ruth responded, "Father forgive them," Elliott the executioner moved a short copper lever and made contact. There was a buzzing drone. Ruth Snyder shot forward against the straps. At that moment Howard squeezed a rubber bulb hidden in his jacket, which triggered the shutter of a small camera strapped to his ankle. It recorded the dying woman twelve feet from him—and the photo, blurred, slightly out of focus, which gave it an added touch of horror, took up the whole front page of next day's *Daily News.*

Her flesh had turned brick-red; then slowly as the seconds ticked away, her exposed arms, right leg, and the lower part of her face became deadly white again. Spirals of pale, wispy smoke rose from her head. Some witnesses retched, others turned their heads away or closed their eyes.

Three times Elliott increased the current, held it steady, then finally shut it off.

Dr. Sweet, the prison doctor, put a stethoscope to her chest. As he listened for a heartbeat, an attendant vainly tried to screen Ruth's leg with a towel. Water dripped down her leg from the moist electrode and the burn had left a large greenish-purple blister on her calf.

The doctor's curt nod indicated she was dead. Two white-clad attendants unstrapped the body of Ruth Snyder and carried her, mouth agape and arms swinging limply, to a stretcher on wheels. The priest left, head bowed.

Among the thousand people gathered outside the prison were Ruth's mother and brother. They were the ones who had hoped for a miracle. The attorney's letter forbidding the prison doctor from making a surgical incision in Ruth's body after her execution was the last desperate move to save her.

Was their presence a confirmation that there would still be an extraordinary attempt to restore Ruth to life?

If so, they were disappointed. The macabre experiment never took place because the Attorney General had advised Warden Lawes to ignore the letter and carry out a routine autopsy.

And that's what was happening, as guards mopped up the floor and cleaned the chair.

In his holding cell Judd had just received a letter from his wife, who had visited him surreptitiously during his trial. She forgave him and so did her mother, who also signed the letter. After reading it he looked up and said, "I am ready to go. I have nothing to fear."

Three minutes after the cadaver of his mistress left the death chamber, Judd Gray entered as if walking in his sleep. His right pants leg flapped. It had been split to the knee to make way for an electrode. The mauve sock on his right leg had been rolled down and his long underwear on that same leg rolled up to the knee. He wore a white shirt and, like Ruth, brown slippers. He walked now as if he had arthritis, yet somehow he still retained an air of dignity.

He responded in a choked voice to the words of the large, gray-haired Protestant chaplain at his side.

"Blessed are the pure in heart," said the chaplain.

Judd's response was incoherent.

The guards soon had him strapped in the chair with his eyes

masked and electrodes attached. He couldn't see, but he could still hear the chaplain.

"For God so loved the world," said the Reverend Anthony Peterson as the executioner made contact.

A blue spark flashed at the leg electrode and Judd's body shot forward. Smoke rose from the leg and head electrode.

". . . that he gave his only begotten son."

Judd's throat was suddenly swollen, and what could be seen of his face flushed a deep crimson.

After two surges, Elliott shut off the current. Judd's color faded.

Dr. Sweet listened for a heartbeat, found none, and said Judd Gray was dead. The men in white wheeled him away for an autopsy.

Thirty minutes after the double execution, an eyewitness reporter, Gene Fowler, began his account:

> They led Ruth Brown Snyder from her steel cage tonight. Then the powerful guards thrust her irrevocably into the obscene, sprawling oaken arms of the ugly electric chair. The memory of the crazed woman in her last agony as she struggled against the unholy embrace of the chair is yet too harrowing to permit of calm portrayal of the law's ghastly ritual. The formal destruction of the killers of poor, stolid, unemotional Albert Snyder in his rumpled sleep was hardly less revolting than the crime itself. Both victims of the chair met their deaths trembling but bravely. . . . Their bodies, shrouded in white sheets, are in the prison morgue, a small room not fifty feet from the chair. This, then, was the end of the road, the close of their two years of stolen love.

World-famous author Thomas Hardy, acclaimed by both critics and public, also died on the day of the Snyder-Gray executions, January 12, 1928. One newspaper covered his obituary in two inches. To the pair of murderers it devoted 289 inches.

Crippen for love. Snyder and Gray for love and money. Gordon Northcott killed for kicks.

3

Gordon Northcott
Evil or Insane?

A whole army of experts . . . is ready for action to explain away every proffered cause of violence. Murder is not murder but always something else; an eruption of the unconscious, existential anxiety, natural need for aggression, senseless lust for destruction, frustrating of the infant in his crib, the hot weather, and so on.

—FREDERIC WERTHAM, M.D., the sole psychiatric consultant to the Kefauver Senate Subcommittee for the Study of Organized Crime. He directed the first psychiatric clinic in a major U.S. court in which all convicted felons were examined.

"How," the psychologist asks himself, "can an angelic little boy sucking a bottle and cuddling his blanket be transformed into a diabolical force?"

—REX JULIAN BEABER

To help juries decide if a convicted murderer's life should be spared, the California Supreme Court lets them hear expert testimony on the psychology of the killer. But only if the report is in the killer's favor and may save his life. Anything else he tells the psychologist that might send him to the gas chamber is a strict secret between murderer and psychologist, as confidential as the confessional.

So, once a week Rex Julian Beaber, an assistant professor of family medicine at the UCLA Medical School, went to death row on a mission of mercy. There, he heard tales of horror. Protected by the promise of confidentiality, murderers confessed to committing brutal crimes which had gone undetected and seemed to revel in revealing the gruesome details of their killings: the unheeded, frantic pleas of mercy from their victims; the terror and heartbreak they caused.

Even allowing for the tormented, deprived childhoods of some of these murderers—and for their physical and mental handicaps—how is it, Beaber wondered, that they become human monsters who torture, maim, and kill, while millions with similar backgrounds and deprivations do not?

He speculated that such torture-killers are simply evil. Now, to call someone evil denotes to most scientists a medieval mentality and superstitious belief in witchcraft and diabolical possession. There is, however, a modern definition of evil for our more enlightened times: a total lack of concern for the feelings of others.

How else explain Gordon Northcott?

A twenty one-year-old pervert with pale blue eyes and a pasty, fleshy face, Northcott lived with his no less twisted mother and his teenage nephew. Their home was an isolated chicken ranch in Riverside County, Southern California.

Northcott trafficked in children, taking them to his ranch and keeping them captive for the depraved pleasure of a growing list of clients, among them business tycoons from Los Angeles.

He made sure no child ever testified against him, because he or his partners killed them and discarded or buried their dismembered bodies in the nearby desert.

Murder was truly a family affair for the Northcotts. Gordon's Uncle Ephrium had beaten the rap on two murder charges, but got life in San Quentin—where he was spending his declining years— for a third. Gordon and his mother were murderers, too, but so far had escaped detection.

One victim was a ten-year-old Mexican boy. On February 1, 1928, his naked, headless body was found in a ditch near Puent in Riverside County. Northcott may have been surprised and have taken off before he had a chance to bury it, but he had no reason to worry, because no one had claimed or identified the body.

Less than three months later, two brothers named Winslow, aged eight and ten, were reported missing after attending a boys' club. Someone warned Northcott the police had been tipped off that he had kidnapped the boys and were on their way to question him.

When they arrived at his ranch, he had escaped across the border and was hiding in Canada.

After searching the grounds, the police unearthed a small, battered head. It was from the severed body of the Mexican boy.

Northcott had left two witnesses behind, his mother and nephew. The nephew, Sanford Clark, broke first—hoping to save himself by telling all. He said that Northcott had subjected the Winslow boys to sexual abuse for ten days before beating them to death. Northcott's mom, he said, made no attempt to protect or save the youngsters. On the contrary, she had been a willing partner, either watching or joining in the sex and sadism; and even killing one of the victims.

The police traced Northcott to his Canadian hideout, and he was soon extradited to the United States. He and his mother, Sarah, were charged with first-degree murder. In exchange for his life, Sanford Clark agreed to be a witness for the prosecution.

There was no problem getting Northcott to talk, but he never told the same story twice. After giving Captain William Bright of the Sheriff's Homicide Squad several conflicting accounts of what happened at the chicken ranch, he sent for Bright on New Year's Day, 1929. Apparently his New Year's resolution was to tell the whole truth.

Since the discovery of the Mexican boy, none of the other twenty children Northcott was believed to have murdered had been found.

Now he told Captain Bright he could only recall killing seventeen children, most of them boys. He did remember one little girl whom he had kidnapped by first asphyxiating her—to fill an order from a Los Angeles car dealer. He wouldn't say or couldn't recall where he had buried any of his victims. But Northcott did pinpoint times when and places where he had first met them before taking them to his ranch. This jibed with details of missing-children reports.

Meanwhile, the prosecution had found another witness. Clarence Robertson, nineteen, of Greensboro, North Carolina, an ex-soldier, admitted helping Northcott to kill four children.

While awaiting trial, Northcott pretended to have remembered where the bodies were buried. Following his directions, deputies dug for hours but unearthed nothing but chicken bones. He tried the same trick several times. Once, when they walked past his cell after another futile search, he jeered at them, "I just had to send you on another wild-goose chase before I was through."

Later that day, he called for a priest; but whatever he said remained their secret.

Two nights later, he woke in a panic to the sound of an angry mob. Two hundred and fifty men had arrived in fifty-five cars and surrounded the county jail. Northcott pleaded with the guards to protect him.

Outside, backed up by five armed men, the father of the two brothers Northcott had murdered rang the night bell of the jail. The sheriff and three deputies answered it. All the bereaved father wanted, he said, was for Northcott to tell where the boys were buried.

The sheriff led the six men into the jail waiting room, where he explained that Northcott had resisted all attempts to get that information from him. "I know we are outnumbered fifty to one," said the sheriff, "but you men can only get Northcott over our dead bodies. We are here to safeguard the prisoner. Bloodshed now would be foolish."

Winslow offered the deeds to his property to back his promise that Northcott would not be hurt. The sheriff refused the offer, and realizing he was adamant, Winslow and his friends shook hands with him and left.

The sheriff immediately called for twenty more deputies, who helped to protect Northcott throughout the night, although the thinning crowd made no attempt to break in.

At his trial Northcott dismissed his attorney and defended himself. "This whole thing is unreasonable," he told the all-male jury in a confidential, man-to-man manner. "It's impossible. To do the things they have charged me with, a person would have to be a maniac, and I believe I am sane."*

It seemed open to question. Northcott's father had died insane in a mental asylum. So Judge George Freeman ordered two psychiatrists to examine Northcott to see if he was fit for trial. They agreed with Northcott's self-diagnosis that he was sane.

"I'm fighting, fighting all alone for my life," he told the jury, like an existential hero against an unfeeling world. "Not only am I fighting for my life, but I am fighting also that I may be free, free to fight again for the little woman up in San Quentin."

The "little woman"—his mother—now had a permanent home in

---

*Serial killers Henri Landru and Theodore Bundy used the same defense. Bundy also dismissed his attorney and defended himself.

that prison after admitting to having killed nine-year-old William Collins. She escaped execution only because she was a woman and no woman had ever been executed at San Quentin.

Sounding more like Socrates than de Sade, Northcott concluded his defense by saying, "It is almost beyond human understanding that any person should do the things that he [his witness nephew] has accused me of doing. I hope you will fully consider just what the verdict will mean, no matter which way it goes. I have done the best I could. Thank you."

He couldn't have been too satisfied with his own defense. Waiting for the verdict in his cell, he began to scream hysterically. But he had calmed down when they brought him back into court.

Nervous and even paler than usual, he heard the jury verdict—guilty of the three murders with which he was charged. He listened patiently as the judge read a long, formal document that ended with the instruction that Northcott would "hang by the neck until he is dead."

Invited to respond, he maintained his restrained courtroom decorum. He thanked the judge for overlooking the mistakes he had made as his own defense attorney. And he complimented him on being "a fair and square judge."

Northcott was transferred to San Quentin's death row, where Clinton Duffy, soon to become warden, met him in November 1929. At the time Duffy was assistant to Warden Holohan.

Duffy was a compassionate man who eventually saw eighty-eight men and two women put to death. He opposed the death penalty even for Northcott, whom he called "a loathsome young pervert . . . pathological liar, sadist, degenerate . . . a cold, heartless physical and mental misfit."

One day Northcott would admit he had committed twenty murders. Next day he'd say, "You've got to get me out of this. They're making a terrible mistake. I never killed anyone."

Groaning in agony and clutching his stomach, Northcott was taken to the prison hospital. He thought he was going to die from appendicitis, and made what he believed would be a deathbed confession to Duffy. The pain was a false alarm, but the confession stuck and was kept in the prison files.

Duffy described it as "a lurid account of mass murder, sodomy, oral copulation, and torture so vivid it made my flesh creep." Duffy's wife, who probably regretted her curiosity, said it was "the most revolting account of sodomy and mass murder ever placed in the prison files," and that of all the human monsters she had known on death row, Northcott was the most monstrous.

Clinton Duffy tried to glimpse gleams of good in his most depraved charges, but to him Northcott seemed totally evil.

Duffy hoped that, with his confession, Northcott would also reveal where he'd buried the bodies; but when asked he turned away, saying, "I don't feel well. I'll tell you some other time."

A few days before Northcott's execution, two women in mourning arrived at San Quentin. One was the mother of the murdered Winslow brothers, her companion the mother of another of Northcott's victims. They wanted to give their sons Christian burials.

Duffy explained that Northcott had repeatedly sent deputies on futile searches for the bodies, but he'd give it another try. He sat on the cell bunk beside Northcott and told him he had a chance to do one nice thing before he died.

Northcott agreed to cooperate but only if he could meet the two women face-to-face. The women agreed to the meeting, and two guards escorted Northcott from death row to a prison office overlooking a garden maintained by prisoners.

He told the women he didn't know where the boys were buried; he had been lying when he said he could help to locate them. Her cheeks wet with tears, the mother of the Winslow boys pleaded with him to tell the truth. She didn't blame him for the boys' terrible fate. Nothing could bring them back to life. All she and her friend wanted was to know where they were.

Northcott took a new tack. He denied killing the boys and said he had no idea what had happened to them. "I'm very sorry, ma'am. I'd be glad to help if I could," he said.

Both women were crying when Duffy made a final appeal to Northcott: "You told me you knew where the bodies were buried."

"I tell lies," Northcott replied coolly. "And then I cover them up with more lies. I lied when I confessed and now I'm going to die for it."

The warden and Duffy and guards kept after Northcott until just before his execution. Perhaps he was being truthful when he said, "There were so many of them. How d'you expect me to know which kid was buried where?"

A deathwatch officer woke Duffy at two A.M. with the news that Northcott had revealed exactly where the bodies were buried and had drawn a detailed map. Within an hour two officials were driving from San Quentin to the Riverside ranch.

At midnight the following night, an officer phoned Duffy to say a dozen men had been digging for several hours following Northcott's directions and had found nothing. He'd fooled them again.

The mother of the Winslow boys returned to the prison just in case Northcott had a change of heart. It seemed he had. But he kept her waiting several hours, through the day and most of the night. At eleven P.M. he said he was ready to talk. He would tell her what she wanted to know, he said, but he would do it his way.

His way was to describe in detail the tortures he had inflicted on her sons. She listened because that was the price she felt she must pay to give them a decent burial. But Northcott never told her what she wanted to hear.

Two days before his execution, at about five in the afternoon, Northcott was moved to one of two holding cells with a mattress on the floor, a lidless toilet, and nothing else. The wooden cell was enclosed by slats with inch-wide openings for deathwatch officers to keep an eye on him.

Although prisoners got paper and pencil for any last messages, many chose the wooden walls to scratch, write, or draw their often filthy or four-letter-word thoughts; claims of innocence; hearts intertwined along with the names of the prisoners and their loves who were sometimes also their victims; messages to their Maker and their mothers; dirty drawings and dirty jokes; prayers and hymns.

The hangman called on Northcott and carefully weighed and measured him. In the nearby storage area, ropes had been hanging from the ceiling for at least two years with 150-pound weights attached. This got rid of any "bounce" in the rope that might cause the victim to die from slow strangulation rather than a quick broken neck. The hangman chose one most suitable for Northcott and had an assistant put it on the scaffold.

A guard handed Northcott his clothes for the execution—a white shirt, blue jeans, and slippers.

At nine A.M. on October 2, 1930, the day of Northcott's execution, he stood in his cell as if in a trance, not responding to the guards' remarks. Suddenly he fell to the floor writhing and screaming. Guards hurried into his cell. In between screams he said he'd taken poison.

The prison doctor soon diagnosed the problem as "scared to death."

Other than a stay by the governor or a successful suicide, there was only one justification for postponing the execution: if the warden thought it could not be carried out in a reasonably normal manner. Although he expected the guards might have to manhandle Northcott to get him to the gallows, Warden Holohan decided the execution was on.

When Duffy arrived at the holding cell Northcott was trembling. He plaintively asked the doctor, "Will it hurt?"

"No," the doctor replied, "I've never heard anyone complain."

His hands were shaking so much that two guards were needed to strap Northcott's wrists together. One guard put a belt around his waist. Because he said he didn't want to see anything, they blindfolded him.

Three men escorted him up the iron stairway, one on either side holding his arms and the third following and holding the belt. Northcott didn't know it, but the man gripping his left arm was the hangman.

Until Northcott was about halfway up the thirteen steps that led to the gallows, Duffy was thinking that if anyone deserved to die this one did. Then he recalled Clarence Darrow's words, "Can you look at any man and say what he deserves?"

Northcott stopped suddenly, saying, "Please don't make me walk so fast." They waited for him. He was rigid with terror. They dragged him up the rest of the steps while he screamed and moaned like the lunatic some believed him to be.

They carried him to the trap. The three officers on the platform usually moved with merciful speed, but Northcott's deadweight delayed them. As he swayed and screamed, the hangman put the rope around his neck and a guard strapped his ankles together. Even though Northcott already had a black cloth over his eyes, the hangman followed protocol and put a black cap over his head and secured it with a drawstring. It did little to muffle his cries.

The clock on the wall showed 10:06 A.M. Northcott had less than half a minute to live; but to the tense, emotionally drained witnesses listening to the animal screams of terror, it seemed much longer.

With three seconds to go Northcott shouted, "Say a prayer for me!"

The warden signaled to the hangman to go ahead. The hangman

signaled to three men in a hidden booth. The cords were cut, the trap sprung. Northcott dropped exactly five feet ten and a half inches and the rope snapped rigid. His screams stopped. His neck broke with a crunch, but he kicked and squirmed in his death agonies.

An officer under the gallows grabbed him and held him steady to prevent the rope from breaking.

The witnesses, too, showed signs of suffering. Some had fainted and been carried to an open window. Others looked anxiously at the exit, but no one was allowed to leave until the doctor had announced the time of death and twelve of the witnesses had signed the visitors' book.

They watched the doctor put his stethoscope to the chest of the still writhing body, counting the heartbeats in a monotone as an assistant made a note of the slowing rate every half minute.

Fifteen minutes after his neck was broken, Northcott's heart gave up. The witnesses were free to go. They left in a hurry. A crew of prisoners came in to clean up the mess the dying man had made. Others waited with a redwood coffin placed under the still hanging man. Two officers cut him down and lowered him into the coffin. They took off the black cap and the blindfold and removed the rope. Before being buried, he was taken to the morgue.

After that traumatic execution, Duffy and his wife were discussing Northcott. She wondered how those against capital punishment justified keeping a monster like him alive. He wondered how killing one psychopath solved a problem constantly menacing society.

"What if he'd killed Jack?" she asked. Jack was their son.

"That's why we have capital punishment," Duffy said. "There's an emotional drive to punish someone for such atrocious crimes. That's why juries find psychopaths sane and vote for the death penalty."

"He was detestably evil," she said. "He deserved to hang."

"But can you condemn him without taking into account his heredity and environment?" Duffy asked.

"Would you have spared him, had it been left to you?"

In fact, Duffy would have done so. He proposed that twisted killers like Northcott should be imprisoned in isolation and carefully studied by psychiatrists in the hope of gaining insight into the minds of such murderers in order to anticipate and prevent future murders.

It's an idea others have suggested, but no country has ever tried.

Did Northcott belong in a mental asylum or on the end of a rope? Was he warped, maladjusted, insane—or evil? As psychologist Beaber found on his San Quentin death-row visits, Northcotts exist in droves.

Such kinky, callous killers are usually, but not always, men.

There are, of course, murders and murders: those committed in a jealous rage, sexual frenzy, or surge of hatred.

And then there are the cool, conniving killers like Eva Coo.

4

Eva Coo
The Saintly Sinner

When people first heard her name they thought of a dove, or a pigeon. Wouldn't you? Eva Coo. On closer acquaintance they'd change pigeon to lovebird, because Eva was a warm, affectionate woman with a loving heart. Ask anyone who knew her.

Ask the prominent lawyers and local politicians who frequented the brothel Eva ran in The Woodbine Inn near Cooperstown, New York. Ask the derelicts, drunks, and drug addicts who went to Eva for a handout and ended up as permanent fixtures.

And a barrel of fun. Where Eva was, laughter wasn't far behind. With Eva you might say life was a movable feast. So what if she was a well-padded 170 pounds? Made it all the more entertaining when she laughed, because all that poundage went along for the ride. There was your movable feast.

Sure, she had her critics. But who hasn't? Didn't someone shoot Huey Long?

Eva earned her almost saintly reputation when Harry Wright's old mother croaked. Harry was an alcoholic, and Eva had promised his mom that when she wasn't there to take care of him, Eva would.

For all her bulk, Eva moved fast. The afternoon they buried Harry's mother, Eva told him he could move in with her.

From then on Harry was usually holding court in a rocking chair just inside the front door, like a shaky hat rack. He never refused a drink and rarely sparked a conversation. Even sober, Harry was a man of few words.

Toward evening he'd walk in a weird shuffle—he was lame—to give the local bars a break. Kids would imitate his walk, but it didn't seem to bother Harry. Live and let live was Harry's unexpressed motto.

Somehow he always made it back to Eva's place and slept himself sober on a couch in the kitchen. Didn't even take off his shoes.

Customers had no doubt when Harry was around, because he never took a bath.

"How the hell d'you put up with him?" one client asked, talking through his nose. "He's fifty-three, acts like a kid, and stinks!"

Eva laughed and promised to deodorize Harry. She bundled him into her car, drove him to a nearby lake, pushed him out, and wouldn't let him in until he'd dunked himself. That was Harry's bath; and Eva took him there whenever he got too high or customers complained.

Mind you, Eva was no pushover. When Harry acted up she'd knock him down, clout him on the head, or kick him in the ass. Harry didn't seem to mind too much. At any rate, he stayed.

Yet, despite Eva's open-door policy and her easy laughter, when she gave a good imitation of a truck idling in neutral, she intimidated—even scared—some people. Nothing they could put their finger on, but there was something about Eva—and here they might give a horizontal hand wobble—something they couldn't quite fathom.

One summer night about eleven Eva called the local police, apparently worried because Harry hadn't come back from his tour of the local taverns. The police told her to take it easy, it was still early. Maybe he was sleeping it off somewhere. Eva wasn't pacified until a state trooper promised to keep his eyes open for Harry.

He seemed to be sleeping it off, all right; in a ditch at the side of the road. But this was a sleep from which Harry would never wake. The state trooper saw Harry's head and chest had been smashed in: obviously another hit-and-run victim.

When told the news, Eva began to cry. The state trooper understood why. She'd been like a big sister to Harry.

The coroner confirmed the police report: accidental death, internal bleeding. Good-bye Harry.

And that would have been the end of that, except for a local reporter who should have been a detective. He had his doubts and scented a cover-up. Harry might have wandered when he walked, but not into the middle of the road. He went to the spot where Harry's body was found. Why, he asked himself, is there no sign of a hit-and-run accident, no broken glass, no skid marks, no blood? Who said it was an accident? An eyewitness? There hadn't been one.

He raised these questions in the Oneonta *Daily Star* and readers stirred the police into reopening the case. They began grilling Eva's contacts, customers, employees, and friends. And hit on a suspect.

One friendly acquaintance, Martha Clift, wilted under questioning and the promise that if she cooperated she'd escape with her life. Eva, she confided, had insured Harry's life and was the beneficiary. If Harry died Eva would get it all. She had tempted Martha with an offer she didn't refuse—$200 toward buying a car—if she'd help to kill Harry.

With murder in mind, the two women persuaded the unsuspecting Harry to join them in a little jaunt to steal shrubs from a deserted farm. He was a bit scared because the farm was reputed to be haunted and they were going there after dark, but Eva laughed him out of his fears.

When the trio reached the farm and got out of the car Eva left the lights on, pretending she needed them to spot the shrubs she was after. But the lights were really to make Harry a clear target. Eva waited until his back was turned, raised a mallet, and smashed his skull. He was probably dead before he hit the driveway.

To make him look like a hit-and-run victim, Martha ran the car over him. They dumped Harry's battered body in the backseat and took him for a ride—said Martha—before dropping him off in a roadside ditch.

Eva denied everything. She was very fond of Harry. Martha Clift must be crazy!

Finding her a hard nut to crack, the police changed their MO and used tactics which Edgar Allan Poe would have envied. Late one night they drove Eva back to the "haunted" farmhouse where Martha admitted they had murdered Harry. An awful surprise awaited Eva: Harry.

They'd dug him up in his coffin and brought him there. They

removed the coffin lid and challenged her as a proof of her innocence to look at the corpse of the man they believed she had murdered.

Did Eva quake and shake and scream in terror and then babble out a confession? She did not. If anything, Eva was calmer than the cops, some of whom looked none too happy.

If that didn't break her, maybe this would: "Shake hands with the corpse, Eva."

That didn't faze her either. "Hi, Harry!"

They all went back home and Harry was buried a second time. Where scare tactics failed, plodding paid off.

The sheriff investigated Martha Clift's claim about Harry's life insurance. Sure enough, Harry had left everything to Eva, including the proceeds of his life insurance. What's more, according to the policy, if Harry died before he was fifty Eva's take doubled to $3,000.

Eva had already put in for the jackpot by reporting that Harry had died aged forty-nine. That was suspicious in itself. But she gave evidence for his age by citing his birthdate engraved on his tombstone.

That was proved to be fake. The prosecution at her trial produced the stonemason she had hired to alter the chiseled birthdate from the true 1880 to the false 1885.

Witnesses at Eva's murder trial showed she was mean as well as mad about money. The undertaker told how she had browbeaten him into giving Harry a cut-price casket. The minister told how she had bullied him into giving low-price prayers for Harry's soul.

Woodbine Inn customers reading the news reports of the trial were shocked to find their Eva described as "pig woman," "cave woman," and "tiger woman," and to see photos of her looking like a bag woman or a hard-faced hag. That wasn't the almost saintly Eva they knew.

She was sentenced to death in Sing Sing's electric chair and the police kept their promise to Martha Clift, her accomplice. For helping to send Eva to the chair, Martha got only twenty years to life.

Eva arrived in the death house as if returning to her brothel. She was cheerful, almost jaunty. Judging by appearances, the two matrons in charge of her were the condemned prisoners and Eva was trying to keep their thoughts off their fates.

Close your eyes and listen to Eva's cheerful chatter and you'd swear you were back in her Woodbine Inn and she was entertaining the customers. The women guards had never had such fun with a prisoner or laughed so long.

Warden Lewis Lawes was astonished to find her so much more human than her press photos. In his eyes the "pig woman" was neat and even attractive. "She displayed none of the tigerish qualities attributed to her," he said, "but was soft, ladylike, well-spoken, and never coarse or vulgar. She constantly protested her innocence, and brooded over the treachery of friends."

After her appeal was turned down, she was subdued for a while. "I guess little Eva was never in line for a break," she said with a sigh.

The two prison matrons tried to comfort her. They had become her affectionate friends. They saw only the warm, wisecracking Eva, the woman who refused a last meal saying, "I don't want to eat. It's bad for my figure."

Like an actress preparing for a performance, she devoted her last few hours to carefully manicuring her nails and making up her face. When the prison barber arrived, she didn't ask why he was shaving her head. She knew it was to make better contact for the electric current to shoot through her body.

She stopped him for a moment to ask: "Would you just leave some hair in front?" He did.

When he had finished, a matron held up a mirror. "Thanks," Eva said. "It looks real nice."

She was due to die at eleven P.M. on June 27, 1935.

A few minutes before that time, the two matrons joined Eva to escort her on her last, short walk. One of the matrons began to cry and Eva put her arm around the woman to console her.

Eva sat in the battered walnut electric chair and looked up to see both matrons crying. She patted the hand of one of them and said to both, "You've been good to me. Thanks, darlings." Her voice was steady, but just above a whisper.

There was no more time for good-byes. The guards strapped Eva tightly in the chair to make sure she couldn't get out or move enough to break contact with the electrodes.

Elliott the executioner checked the mask over her face and that both head and leg electrodes were in place. He walked to the instrument panel behind the chair and at a nod from the warden threw the switch.

Eva jerked toward the witnesses as though in a violent car crash. Instead of the noise of shattering glass and squealing tires, there was the sputtering drone of the electricity and the smell of burning flesh. Her hands reddened, then suddenly drained of blood. The veins on her neck seemed about to burst.

After a minute, Elliott reduced the current from 2,000 to 1,500 volts, and a wisp of gray smoke, fainter than the smoke from a cigarette, rose from the electrode on Eva's head.

Elliott switched off, and Eva slumped back as if giving up a frantic effort to force her way out of the chair.

He again threw the switch. Now Eva's movements were an awful mockery of the laughing lady in her days at The Woodbine Inn, when her body had shaken not in its death throes but in helpless merriment.

It took seven minutes to kill Eva Coo.

The woman who murdered and killed for love of money died broke and so was buried in a pauper's grave.

Eva Coo "fried," as some bluntly called it. Frying was the choice of the East Coast crowd. But in California, condemned killers were put to sleep, as Warden Duffy put it; just a few whiffs of gas and dreamless sleep followed. The Big Sleep.

5

Leandress Riley, Richard Cooper, Robert Pierce, Smith Jordan, and Oscar Brust
The Big Sleep at San Quentin

Switching from rope to gas was considered a humane move, but there was a macabre catch to it. By merely breathing, the prisoner actively cooperated in his own execution. In a sense it was enforced suicide. San Quentin's warden James Holohan decided to make the switch to lethal gas. Unlike Clinton Duffy, Holohan was for capital punishment but thought hanging too close to torture. Magnanimously anxious to ease the condemned prisoners' last moments, despite his recent serious wounding by inmates in a prison break, he rejected the electric chair as no better than the rope. In fact, he thought the rigmarole of preparing a prisoner for electrocution—the shaved head, the split pants—was an added sadistic ordeal.

It was a downer, too, for surviving prisoners who knew exactly when the man died; because when the executioner threw the switch all the prison lights dimmed.

So Holohan brought the gas chamber to San Quentin, though it was first used in December 1938 when his successor, Court Smith, was warden.

It had eight sides and five windows of thick glass, not unlike a sinister claustrophobic lighthouse, or as one witness said, "an ugly green wart."

Among the first to use it were Leandress Riley and Richard Cooper.

Before he left to become a politician, Holohan assured the men lined up to die that gas would be quick and painless. "One breath and you're unconscious," he told them.

The doomed men discussed the prospect frequently. How the hell did the warden know? Let him try it. THEN he could tell them. Ha,ha,ha!

He was right for Richard Cooper; wrong for Leandress Riley.

None went to death with more grace under pressure than Cooper.

None fought more fiercely and desperately to stay alive than Riley.

Riley, in his early twenties, had killed during an armed robbery. An hour before he was to be gassed, a guard sent an urgent message: "Riley's gone crazy. He spent the night spitting in his toilet and flushing it. Now he's shrieking his head off."

The prison pacifier hurried through the rain to Riley's holding cell on death row, passing guards griping about the downpour spoiling their golf that afternoon, and found Riley squatting on his rolled-up mattress and snarling like a wild dog.

Raising his voice as if giving a sermon to a noisy congregation, the chaplain tried to tranquilize Riley with the word of God. It didn't work. He silenced the chaplain with a curt gesture that meant "shut up!" and at sight of guards come to prepare him for the gas chamber shrieked.

Clinging to the bars, he fought them off by kicking. Fortunately for them, he was barefoot. Eventually they forced him from the bars and held him down while the doctor strapped the end of a stethoscope over his heart. That done, they had to dress him in a new white shirt and blue pants required for every execution. And all the time he screamed and howled and kept fighting.

Witnesses already seated outside the gas chamber heard Riley long before he arrived. This was better than hanging?

The nearly exhausted guards had bound him hand and foot and carried him to the gas chamber. They had to free his wrists and ankles to strap him in the chair. The bigger of the two guards, a heavyweight, slammed Riley into the chair while the other strapped him in fast. They hurried out, quickly closed the metal door, and began to turn the wheel that sealed the chamber airtight.

Some men will put on weight on death row and jest about being fattened for the kill, but Riley had stayed as trim and wiry as when he arrived. That's why he was able to do the unthinkable.

As the warden was about to give the signal to drop the cyanide tablets into the sulphuric acid under Riley's chair, he began to escape.

The witnesses saw him slip his arms free from the leather straps, and then his legs, and get out of the chair, race to the door, and beat on it, screaming to be let out.

What was the warden to do? Gas a man as he wildly roamed the gas chamber crying for help?

He sent the two guards back in.

Perhaps for one bright, demented moment, Riley thought he'd been reprieved. But he was soon disillusioned. Another uneven, furious fight, and the guards strapped him down again, really tight this time. The guards backed out even faster than before and locked Riley in.

Swifter than any stage escape-artist, Riley freed his right hand and used it to unstrap his left. Both hands were free.

The warden gave the signal and the cyanide pellets plopped into the acid. Almost invisible poison gas, hydrocyanic acid, which smelled like rotten eggs, began to rise from under the chair.*

Riley had opened the strap over his chest and was working on the waist strap when the gas reached his lungs. He slammed both hands over his face as if that would save him, but a few moments later his hands fell into his lap.

In one last attempt to prolong his life, he flung back his head and

---

*Some described the lethal gas as having a sickly sweet smell like peach blossom.

lifted his chin. And that was how the guards found him when the gas had been cleared two hours later. Riley's eyes were wide open, and he seemed to be staring at the ceiling as if looking for help from above.

Byron Eshelman, the Protestant chaplain who arrived at San Quentin a few years later, sympathized with prisoners who died fighting and wondered why guards expected them to make things easy by cooperating in their own killing. Although he was especially moved by one prisoner, Richard Cooper, who did just that.

Cooper was to die in the gas chamber in sixty-five minutes for strangling two women in a skid row hotel during a weekend drinking spree he could only dimly remember. He lay facedown on his mattress, shielding his eyes from the bright light overhead. A nearby radio broadcast pop music and local news flashes.

During the 322 days and nights he had been awaiting death, he and Chaplain Eshelman had exchanged only a few words. Now was their last chance to talk.

Eshelman arrived in a light rain squall, skirted the gas chamber —the ultimate in therapy, as some cynic or realist called it—and sat on a stool outside Cooper's holding cell.

Cooper told the chaplain he hadn't sent for him. That wasn't exactly a dismissal. The chaplain waited.

"How are you this morning?" Cooper asked.

"All right," Eshelman replied. "Did you get any sleep last night?"

Cooper said he didn't. He rolled over on his bunk and faced the chaplain and said he intended to take a nap about ten o'clock. He smiled, adding, "A good long one." Ten was to be the time of his execution.

The chaplain didn't know how to handle that. He just smiled back.

"Did you know I'm going to college this afternoon?" Cooper asked.

The chaplain frowned. Had the prisoner flipped?

Cooper explained. He realized the only way he'd ever get to college was to donate his body to medical science, which he had done. "Tomorrow morning," he said with an air of triumph, "I may be staring up at the college students from a table in some classroom."

Eshelman recalled a young man who had talked the warden

into bending the rules and bringing him a small bottle of whiskey just before he entered the death chamber. At the last moment, seeing the stricken face of the warden walking at his side, the prisoner handed the drink to him with a gallant, "You need this more than I do."

Cooper seemed to be of the same breed. But the chaplain got whimsy instead of whiskey.

They listened to a newscaster announce an accident expected to delay traffic until about 10:30 A.M. The two men exchanged wry glances. By the time traffic had cleared, Cooper would be dead.

In an extraordinary attempt to look on the bright side, Cooper said he was glad he was helping several families earn extra cash. The lieutenant in charge of the execution would receive a bonus of $150, the executioner's fee was $125, and the two guards would split $100.

He told the chaplain he was sorry a guard he liked and had requested for his deathwatch hadn't turned up, because the death duty would have earned the man an extra $75.

Eshelman appreciated Cooper's tact in not mentioning that the chaplain was paid $50 per killing. But only if the prisoner had asked to see him. Cooper hadn't requested Eshelman, so on this occasion no fee was involved.

A guard lit a cigarette and handed it to Cooper. With twenty minutes to go, he'd have plenty of time to smoke it. "Coffee?" the guard asked. Cooper nodded and took the paper cup of black coffee. Eshelman got coffee too, but in a china cup. There was no danger the chaplain would break it to use as a weapon.

"Wish this was whiskey," Cooper said. "I don't need it," he reassured the others, "but I'd just like it."

In the good old days, some prisoners had been given several shots of whiskey to tranquilize them on the way to the gas chamber.

Cooper complained of acid stomach, blaming the canned orange juice he drank for breakfast, but he kept sipping his black coffee.

Dr. Schmidt, the prison's chief psychiatrist, entered the holding area. As he approached Cooper's cell, guards unrolled a green carpet to cover the ten feet of concrete from cell to death chamber. It was a pathetic concession to the doomed man to prevent him from getting cold feet as he walked those few final steps.

"Richard Cooper?" the psychiatrist asked quietly.

"I think I've heard that name before," Cooper replied.

They had spoken together before briefly and casually, but now the psychiatrist wanted to ask Cooper a painfully hypothetical question. "Would you have done anything different if you had your life to live over again?"

"Lots," Cooper said. But who's going to give him the chance? "Life is like a horse race," he said. "If you knew in advance which horse would win, you'd know which to bet on."

Warden Dickson arrived with the usual press request for the prisoner's last words. There weren't going to be any.

Then Cooper made things easy for everyone, getting into the new clothes he was to die in, white shirt, blue pants, and standing still for the doctor to strap on the stethoscope. He accepted a final cigarette. The warden shook his hand in farewell, surprised to find it cool and dry.

The chaplain said he was glad they'd had the chance to know each other better, and Cooper thanked him.

It was time to leave. But he wasn't ready to go. Despite Cooper's unusual self-control, the orange juice and black coffee were not subject to his will. He hurried to the toilet as an officer near the gas chamber gave urgent signals that the ceremony must start at once.

The guard near the toilet signaled back with two open upraised hands. Nature was stealing a few extra seconds for Cooper.

Hands in his pockets, Cooper strolled from the toilet onto the green carpet, guards at his heels. He turned a corner after a couple of yards and saw for the first time the open door to the gas chamber. He passed a guard hovering near a phone in case of a last-moment stay of execution.

Another guard politely warned him to watch his step as he entered the gas chamber and sat in the nearest chair. There are two chairs, and sometimes two men are gassed together. But Cooper was to travel alone.

Twenty-two witnesses watched him through the glass windows, prevented from pressing their faces to the glass by a handrail with a sign: Keep Outside Railing at All Times. They spoke in subdued whispers like people at a funeral service.

Cooper said the chest strap was too tight, and a guard nodded and loosened it while another attached rubber tubing to the heartbeat recorder on Cooper's chest. The doctor listened in at the other end, safely outside the gas chamber.

He had already been given the tip to take a deep breath at his first whiff of bad eggs or peach blossom; but just in case, a guard advised him to do it. "It'll make it easier for you." Someone else had told him to count to ten after hearing the pellets plop in the acid and then to inhale.

Witnesses thought he responded to the guard's words with a slight smile. When and how to breathe for a quick and painless end was a subject of intense concern to death-row prisoners and a constant subject of conversation. Clinton Duffy said it was just like going to sleep, and some wag called it The Big Sleep, which stuck.

The guards worked as efficiently as a champion boxer's seconds. One patted him on the shoulder and, like a fight fan, wished him luck. He nodded thanks.

At the far side of the gas chamber, the executioner, the warden, and Dr. Gross—the prison's chief medical officer—were watching Cooper. They had fixed a Venetian blind so they could see him without being seen. At the left of the chamber door, Dr. Schmidt had clamped the stethoscope headset to his ears, monitoring Cooper's heartbeats.

Cooper looked straight ahead and level, as if in a car's passenger seat and going for a ride.

The phone didn't ring. There was no reprieve. The cyanide eggs dropped into the acid, and their splash and his own breathing were the last sounds Cooper heard.

The chaplain prayed: "Oh God, receive this thy son Richard Cooper, our brother in the human family, whom thou dost love as dearly as thou dost love any of us."

As his body fought the poison rising from beneath him and the adrenaline raced to meet this final challenge, the doctor at the stethoscope heard the heartbeats accelerate wildly, like a racehorse in sight of the finishing post.

Cooper closed his eyes. His heartbeats began to slow. His mouth twisted like a stroke victim's and stayed that way. He drooled and sagged onto the straps. And was still. And didn't move again.

The doctor noted on his clipboard notepad the time Cooper's heart had stopped.

It had taken eight and a half minutes to kill him. Witnesses assured each other that he was unconscious long before that. Two of them left before the end, murmuring they needed air.

The chaplain was among the last witnesses to leave, after signing the visitors' register. The rain had cleared. There was a big patch of blue. Seagulls wheeled and cried in the bright sunshine, gliding in the light breeze coming in from San Francisco Bay.

Cooper's body was left in the sealed chamber for thirty minutes. An officer pumped out the gas and flushed out the wells under the chair with water. He sprayed Cooper's body with liquid ammonia to get rid of any lingering gas.

Cooper was ready for college.

Chaplain Eshelman broke down and cried after Caryl Chessman was executed—not for murder but for rape and kidnapping. Chessman died smiling until the gas got him.

The chaplain often fought back tears, especially when the condemned men had become his friends.

He was moved by almost all of them, those who died bravely as well as those who died fighting or terrified.

Robert Pierce died a fighter, and Smith Jordan "died like a man," as they used to say.

They were both twenty-four when Pierce and Jordan killed a cabbie. The murder netted them seven dollars, a cheap watch, and a death sentence apiece.

Pierce, a bitter bruiser, threatened to give the guards hell when they took him downstairs to the gas chamber. The day before his execution he gave a preview of what to expect. He kicked the toilet loose from the wall. For that he spent the night in an isolation cell.

Next morning they transferred him back to the holding cell to prepare him for the gas chamber. Pierce asked to see the Catholic chaplain, Father Edward Dingberg. Dingberg was surprised to find Pierce, who had shown little interest in religion, on his knees as if in prayer. He wasn't praying. He suddenly lowered his hands and gave a triumphant grin. He had cut his throat. He held the weapon in his hand, a piece of glass he'd smuggled in to beat the gas chamber.

The chaplain yelled for help and guards, and the doctor came running. Pierce, squat and strong, put up a ferocious fight, using his feet, knees, fists, elbows, nails, and teeth.

They'd promised Jordan that he'd die first because he'd given the guards no trouble. Now he was told he and Pierce were to die together. But they'd have to hurry to get Pierce to the gas chamber alive, before he bled to death.

It took four guards to overpower Pierce, drag him from the cell, and carry him, blood spraying from his wound, to the gas chamber.

He was screaming, "I'm innocent! Don't let me go like this!" as guards strapped him in the seat.

While he continued to cry and scream and curse and splatter guards with his blood, several witnesses hurried out looking nauseated.

Suddenly Pierce stopped screaming and gasped, "All right, Lord, if you want me to go I won't curse you."

But when Jordan entered the chamber, he began to scream and curse again—cursing all the men in sight as well as God. He twisted his head to show Jordan the bleeding four-inch gash that had turned his white shirt red.

Jordan calmly shook hands with the warden, sat in the other chair, and was quickly readied. His last words were, "It's okay." Seconds after the cyanide pellets began their work, he took a few deep breaths and fell forward, never to move again.

Pierce had stopped screaming to hold his breath. But he couldn't resist opening his mouth to give a last yell of protest. Instead, he began to choke, strain against the straps, and go into convulsions.

Listening outside on twin stethoscopes, doctors heard both men's hearts stop at the same moment—exactly 10:15.

Pierce didn't beat the gas chamber.

But, a year later, a guard looked into Oscar Brust's cell. Brust, a mailman, had killed his wife and stepson. The night before his execution, he seemed to be sleeping peacefully, the blanket pulled up to his chin.

Just in case, the guard unlocked the cell door and went inside. The prisoner seemed not to be breathing. The guard lowered the blanket. Brust had cut his throat, like Pierce, with a piece of glass. He'd been dead about half an hour.

Those prisoners that death row doesn't drive crazy or to suicide sometimes endear themselves to deathwatch guards who try to make the killers' hours less of an ordeal. Crippen's guards liked the nondescript little doctor; Eva Coo's treated her like a favorite sister and were heartbroken when she went to the chair.

Even when killers on death row arouse no affection, the prison staff will go to extraordinary trouble to fulfill their last requests.

Take, for example, Farrington Graham Hill.

6

Farrington Graham Hill
The Last Waltz

To the others on death row, guards as well as prisoners, Farrington Graham Hill was a surly, friendless son of a bitch. He responded to their remarks with grunts or not at all, and filled his cell with cigarette smoke as if to keep everyone at bay or asphyxiate himself before it was his time to go.

He was to die at thirty-one for the holdup killing of a hotel clerk.

Warden Duffy asked him if he had any last requests. Nothing. He wanted nothing.

As Hill was taken along death row toward the holding cell near the gas chamber, other condemned men called out or beat on their bars a last salute.

Hill ignored them. He was a loner, all right. He wanted nothing from anyone.

Even so, deathwatch guards thought to give him a lift by playing phonograph records just outside his cell. This time he responded by shouting, "Shut the damn thing off!"

"Does Hill want anything?" Duffy asked on a return visit.

"Doesn't even want music," a guard said. "At least, nothing we've got."

"He doesn't give a shit about anything," another guard said. "Doesn't even want to know if the governor had given him a reprieve."

Duffy guessed that the guards wouldn't have minded some music to relieve the gloomy silence of their deathwatch. They'd obviously get no conversation out of Hill.

The warden walked to Hill's cell where he was lying on his mattress, eyes closed. "Anything I can do for you?"

Hill opened his eyes. "You got me here. Now get it over."

"You don't like music?"

"Not what they've got."

"What do you like?"

"Something about Vienna."

" 'Tales from the Vienna Woods'?"

"Yeah, I think that's it."

"I'll try to get it for you."

The warden went to the prison library and flipped through all the records there. No Strauss. He phoned several record stores and was surprised when none replied until he noticed the time, nearly eleven P.M. Everything was closed.

His wife was already asleep but he knew she'd understand. He woke her, explained it was the first and only request Hill had ever made. She began phoning friends. "Sorry to wake you, dear, but . . ."

She continued to call friends from her home, while Duffy went to his office and phoned every guard and prison official who had a phonograph. None had the record Hill wanted.

It was after midnight when Duffy thought of one last possibility. With the night watch officer, he went to John Hendricks' cell and woke him. Hendricks, a murderer serving a life term, led the prison orchestra.

These prisoner musicians were known throughout the United States: their musical show, "San Quentin on the Air," with its amusing theme song "Time on My Hands," was broadcast nation-wide.*

Duffy explained what he wanted. Hendricks was pessimistic but willing to try.

The other orchestra members were awakened and hustled, bewildered, yawning, and bellyaching, to the mess hall.

Hendricks said, "There's a guy checking out in the morning and he wants to hear 'Tales from the Vienna Woods.' Who's played it before?"

No one had.

"We can't play it without the score," someone objected, and everyone seemed to agree.

"Sure we can. I'll be the score," Hendricks said.

---

*When a new warden took over he disbanded the orchestra for fear prisoners might use guitar strings as weapons.

And he soon revealed himself as deserving his reputation as a musical wizard.

He whistled the music over and over for each instrument, even telling the drummer what to do. This man who could compose, orchestrate, conduct, and play several instruments gave a one-man performance of the Strauss waltz, again and again and again.

Then he rehearsed the orchestra over and over.

Two hours later he decided they had peaked. Guards brought in the machine the orchestra used for their broadcasts and cut a record.

Duffy thanked them with coffee and sandwiches and his say-so that they could sleep in that morning for as long as they liked.

A fog had been deepening, coming in from the ocean. The prison buildings looked like massive ships at sea.

Carrying the record through the fog-shrouded prison yard, Duffy wondered if all that effort had been wasted. Perhaps Hill was asleep and would only wake when it was time to execute him.

But Hill was awake and still creating his own smoke screen, lying on his bunk and staring at the ceiling.

"I've got what you wanted, son."

Hill stood up quickly, and for the first time Duffy saw him smile. "I nearly gave up," Hill said. "Thanks a million."

Duffy explained how he got the record as a guard started to play the spirited waltz.

The warden, the guards, and the prisoner listened to it all the way through. It sounded great.

Hill had one more request. Could they keep playing the music all through the night? Request granted.

It was still playing when the warden returned to supervise Hill's execution. The music seemed to have transformed him. The killer who had sneered at religion was kneeling in prayer before the chaplain. And he greeted Duffy with a friendly, "Hello, Warden!"

A guard started the record again, and Hill explained why he'd wanted to hear it. He had just pulled a holdup, he said, and was running from the police. He stopped to hide in bushes near the bandstand in Golden Gate Park. The conductor had begun to announce the next piece. Hill caught the word *Vienna,* but then tuned out to focus on an approaching police car siren. So he missed the full title. He stayed long enough to hear some of the waltz and liked the little he heard. He took off when the police were too close for comfort. But wondered ever since how the music ended.

Duffy agreed to Hill's request—to have the music play even when he was shut in the gas chamber. He realized he might not hear it, but it would make him feel good to know it was playing.

Hill said he didn't know where he was going after his death, but if it was somewhere where you could still remember your past life, then he'd never forget what the warden and orchestra had done for him.

"Thank them for me," he said. "Tell them the last thing I did was pray for them. And that was the first time I ever talked to God."

As they walked together to the gas chamber, Hill mentioned that his brother was also in prison. "Would you send him a Bible and tell him it came from me?"

Duffy agreed to this final request and gave his usual painless-death advice. "Take deep breaths when you see the fumes reach your waist."

Hill nodded, said, "So long," and stepped over the lip of the gas chamber. He looked as relaxed as a man in a barber chair as he was strapped in, smiling to show he could still hear the music.

The officers backed out and one shut the airtight and soundproof steel door.

When a guard moved to stop the music, Duffy held up his hand in a "Let it play on" motion, even though he knew Hill couldn't hear it. Seeing him through the observation window as he took his first breath of the gas, Duffy wanted to keep his word to the dying man.

Although Hill soon appeared to be unconscious, he moved his head slightly to and fro. With a little imagination you might think he was keeping time with the lively music.

It was still playing when the prison doctor signaled to Warden Duffy that the gas had done its work.

A British Royal Commission on Capital Punishment gave a second-by-second account of execution with lethal gas in the United States.

Guards enter prisoner's cell	5.56 A.M.
Prisoner enters gas chamber	5.58
Strapped in chair	5.59:30
Door closed	6.01:30
Gas strikes face	6.02:30

Apparently unconscious	6.02:35
Certainly unconscious	6.03
Respiration stopped	6.03
Heart stopped beating	6.04
Suction fan started	6.10
Body removed	6.40

That less-than-two-minute death occurred in Nevada.

"When this method was first employed, medical opinion was not unanimous about it," the 1949–1953 Commission reported.

"There were some who thought that gas had a suffocating effect which would cause acute distress, if not actual pain, before the prisoner became unconscious. It seems to be now generally agreed that unconsciousness ensues very rapidly."

The official report gives some idea of what Farrington Graham Hill experienced, except it left out the music.

His last hours transformed Hill. Death row drives some men mad, if they're not already crazy. Do we really send madmen to death row—and execute them? It happens. Albert Fish for one; Billy Cook, another; and Morris Mason a third, to name a few.

7

Albert Fish, Billy Cook, Morris Mason Executing Madmen

Strolling hand in hand with a boy or girl, Albert Fish seemed the epitome of an amiable old man taking his grandchild for a treat. He made over a hundred such little trips, but with a different child each time, all strangers he had lured from their homes. At least fifteen children never returned, because Fish killed, dismembered, and ate them. About a hundred others escaped with their lives, but usually only after he had sexually molested or tortured them.

Fish's perversions—and in time he practiced every one known to man—began early. Sent to an orphanage when he was five, he developed the urge to hurt himself after a woman teacher there often beat him on his bare behind.

At fifteen he left the institution to start his lifelong career as a housepainter-handyman, though he spent more time in prison—for sexually molesting children and for petty thefts—than at his work.

He married at twenty-eight, to a nineteen-year-old, and they had six children. After twenty years of marriage his wife ran off with a lodger, and in the following years Fish lived with several women.

Apparently these common-law wives couldn't satisfy his sexual needs. After a few spells in prison for sending obscene letters to women, he restricted such communications to women of like mind who advertised in "Lonely Hearts" columns. To pay for the services of those who replied and were willing to join him in masochistic orgies, he stole. That got him more time behind bars.

He came out to hunt children, taking them to unoccupied buildings where, if questioned, he could say he was a housepainter looking over a potential job. One victim was ten-year-old Grace Budd. Fish told her they were off to a party. Instead, he took her to an empty house in Greenburgh, New York, and strangled her. He cut her up, cooked pieces of her body with carrots and onions, and ate them.

Police searched for but naturally didn't find the missing girl. Fish had reduced her to bones buried in a backyard.

Two years later psychiatrists had two chances to prevent Fish from murdering more children. He was twice confined in a mental hospital for observation. Although the first time a psychiatrist noted that "he showed signs of mental disturbance," he thought Fish harmless and let him go. The second time, the psychiatrist found a whip in Fish's room and correctly assumed he was dealing with a sadist—among other things—but saw no reason to hold him.

So Fish continued to rape, torture, and eat children.

In 1934, six years after he'd killed Grace Budd, Fish wrote to her mother. A fatal masochistic urge trapped him into confessing his guilt.

He wrote:

> Some years ago a friend of mine, Captain John Davis, shipped from California to Hong Kong, China, where at that time there was a great famine. It was dangerous

for a child under 12 to be on the streets, as the custom was for them to be seized, cut up, and their meat sold for food. On his return to New York, my friend seized two boys, one six and the other eleven, killed, cooked, and ate them. So it was that I came to your house on June 3, 1928, and under the pretense of taking your daughter Grace to a party at my sister's, I took her to Westchester County, to an empty house up there, and I choked her to death. I did not have sex with her. She died a virgin.

Mrs. Budd called a New York City detective assigned to the case, who found Fish in a Manhattan apartment. At police headquarters Fish willingly gave a detailed description of how he murdered Grace Budd, and led the police to the girl's bones. In all he made six statements, each more detailed than the last; yet he expressed regret for what he had done, saying, "I would have done anything to bring her back to life."

The defense recruited Frederic Wertham, one of the leading psychiatrists in the United States. Wertham's first impression of the sixty-two-year-old cannibal was "of a meek and innocuous little old man; gentle and benevolent, friendly and polite. If you wanted someone to entrust your children to, he would be the one you would choose."

With the time available to him, Wertham made an in-depth study of Fish, tested him, interviewed him and people who knew him.

At Fish's trial Wertham told the court that among other mental illnesses Fish suffered from religious insanity which manifested itself as visions of Christ, his angels, and of hell. Fish, he said, believed himself to be a very holy man who had to sacrifice children to purge himself "of iniquities."

"He has told me," Wertham testified, "that he feels driven to torment and kill children. Sometimes he would gag them, tie them up, and beat them, though he preferred not to gag them, as he liked to hear their cries. In this case his original intentions were to take Grace's brother and castrate him—he claims he is ordered by God to castrate small boys—but Edward Budd was too large. Instead, he took Grace. He explained that he had to sacrifice her to prevent her future outrage in the adult world. He felt that this was the only way she could be saved. That is why he killed her."

To indulge his masochism, Fish pushed alcohol-soaked cotton up his rectum and set it alight. To satisfy his sadism, he did the same thing to his child victims. He also drove needles deep into his own flesh near his scrotum. Wertham said that X rays had revealed twenty-seven needles under Fish's skin, but because he didn't complain there had been no attempt to remove them.

Wertham damned the psychiatrist who had twice diagnosed Fish as harmless but was not available to testify in court to his patient's abnormalities.

"Each time, the examination was most perfunctory," Wertham charged, "the observations almost nil, the report cursory and wrong."

Because of the deadly mistake of this psychiatrist, Wertham accused the hospital authorities of covering up and deliberately keeping the psychiatrist who knew the truth out of the city "so that he could not be subpoenaed and forced to testify."

Wertham was emphatic that if anyone was insane Fish was, that he was a psychotic with delusions who practiced every possible type of perversion, among them eating human feces and cannibalism.

Four psychiatrists testified for the prosecution. They all admitted that Fish practiced the multiple perversions described by Wertham. None agreed with him that this indicated Fish was legally insane.

These perversions were practiced by many people, said the chief psychiatrist for New York City, who appeared for the prosecution. Even the eating of human excrement, he went on, was an appetite shared by some prominent citizens.

Another of the psychiatrists for the prosecution backed his chief up, saying, "A quarter of the population walking the streets are psychopaths."

Fish sat impassively throughout the proceedings, his most striking reaction a slight smile, his most dramatic gesture, absentmindedly fondling his faint mustache.

Reporters at the trial, who had seen more than their fair share of perverts and psychopaths, took a poll among themselves and decided Dr. Wertham was right, and that Fish would be found insane.

They were wrong.

The jury verdict was first-degree murder, and the judge sentenced the lunatic to death.

Albert Fish smiled vaguely and was taken to Sing Sing. He arrived in his death-row cell clutching a Bible.

He admitted he was looking forward to his execution with mounting excitement.

The "very holy man"—his self-description—was allowed to leave his cell to attend church. During the service, Fish exposed himself.

At his appeal hearing the chief judge conceded Fish was undoubtedly crazy, but not legally insane; that is, he knew what he had done was wrong.

Fish's attorney appealed to the governor for clemency, suggesting he change the sentence from death to life imprisonment.

At that hearing, psychiatrist Wertham appeared again and said, "This man is not only incurable and unreformable, but unpunishable. In his own distorted mind he is looking forward to the electric chair as the final experience of supreme pain. To execute a sick man is like burning witches.

"I am not appealing to you as a politician, a lawyer, or anything else—I am appealing to you as a man."

The governor, Herbert Lehman, decided Fish should die.

Shortly before his execution Fish had a lamb chop for lunch. He hid part of the bone and sharpened it on the stone floor of his cell, then used the bone to make a deep cross-shaped gash on his abdomen.

He survived what guards called a last-minute suicide attempt.

Witnesses for his execution saw a stooped, gray-haired old man, looking twenty years older than his sixty-six years, hobbling to the electric chair. But he was grinning as if about to go on a thrilling ride at Coney Island. He behaved as if eagerly anticipating his last masochistic experience, and this time one that was quite legal.

A news reporter began his account of the execution: "Albert Fish, cannibal extraordinary, has gone the way of all flesh."

Psychiatrist Wertham was convinced the state had electrocuted a madman.

He was killed, Wertham believed, "because the public was aroused over the murders, and the authorities needed to have him declared normal. It is only against this social background that this miscarriage of justice is understandable. I discussed this case with several members of the jury. What prompted their decision was their—not unjustified—fear that Fish might be released again to commit further crimes."

Over the years, Wertham discussed Fish with many other psychiatrists, with attorneys and judges. Without exception, they all agreed that Fish was legally insane.

In executing him, Wertham thought a great chance was lost in finding out how a man so severely mentally diseased, often in prison and twice in psychiatric hospitals, could persist undetected in his awful practices for decades.

"Killing him was considered the final solution," Wertham concluded. "What should have been done was to use this case for an overhauling of the haphazard procedures which are still costing the lives of children."

Albert Fish wasn't the first madman to be executed and won't be the last, as long as psychiatrists with their "he is mad" and "he isn't mad" cancel one another out.

Billy Cook hitchhiked around the country after World War II, killing as he went. A federal judge agreed with the defense that Cook was incurably insane and sentenced him to three hundred years in Alcatraz.

However, he was also tried for another murder by the state of California, and found guilty. This judge thought Cook was sane and sentenced him to Sing Sing's gas chamber.

When the chaplain asked for a last message, Cook said, "I hate everybody's guts."

On the way to his execution he slammed his elbow in the prison doctor's stomach, shook his fist at the witnesses, and died snarling.

An undertaker took his body, dressed it in a blue suit, and put it on display, using a loudspeaker to encourage the crowds to "Step right up!"

Thousands responded, many with children, to see what a murderer looked like after he'd been gassed.

A minister got into the act, agreeing to officiate at a massive funeral, and the undertaker assured everyone they'd get another chance to gawp at the corpse at the graveside.

Cook's relatives stopped the circus and buried him in a small Kansas cemetery.

Can an "incurably insane" man in one court become sane in another? Don't the court decisions themselves seem less than sane?

The state of Virginia had three times diagnosed Morris Mason as a paranoid schizophrenic. Mason was a thirty-two-year-old black man with an IQ of 66.

He pleaded with the state to take him back into custody. The state declined.

After which Mason raped and murdered an elderly woman, nailing her hand to a chair and setting fire to her house.

The state that had ignored the cries for help from a paranoid schizophrenic executed him in June 1985.

And what if a prisoner goes mad on death row? Should he still be executed? And who is to decide if he is insane or cleverly simulating insanity?

Alvin Bernard Ford has been on Florida's death row for eleven years awaiting death for killing a policeman. Ford had worked as a prison guard while studying criminology at a nearby junior college. He began using drugs, and in the summer of 1974 with several friends headed for Fort Lauderdale to buy cocaine. En route they robbed a Red Lobster restaurant, but were interrupted by Policeman Walter Ilyankoff. Ford shot him three times, firing the last shot in the head—execution style, said the prosecution. Ford denied it, saying he shot only when the officer went for his gun.

Two psychiatrists were asked by his attorney to examine Ford after he began to behave irrationally in 1981, claiming he could communicate with the news media by telepathy. He said that he was Pope Paul III, and that the Ku Klux Klan had seized his relatives and were torturing them near his cell. Eventually, he said he had joined the KKK, freed their hostages, and appointed new judges to the Florida Supreme Court. That court, he said, had overturned his sentence and so he was at liberty to leave death row.

Both psychiatrists diagnosed Ford as a paranoid schizophrenic, and one said that consequently he should not be executed. Psychiatrist Dr. Jamal Amin recommended psychotropic medication, but he was not given it and his mental condition deteriorated until he was at times incoherent.

Florida's Governor Graham appointed three additional psychiatrists to examine Ford. They went as a group and spent about half an hour with him, discussed his condition with prison and medical staff, and read his prison records. Ford spoke to them sometimes in what appeared to be a code.

When one psychiatrist asked: "Are you aware that they can electrocute you?" Ford answered, "Nine one, C one, hot one, die one . . . die one, gone one."

Asked, "What happens when you die?" he said, "Hell one, Heaven one . . . If I die, no more fat cats, no more homicide, no more racism in heaven with God."

Two of the state-appointed psychiatrists concluded Ford was psychotic, although one of them noted that his "gibberish talk and bizarre behavior started after all his appeals failed." The third psychiatrist thought Ford was faking insanity, that although his mental disorder was severe, it was "contrived and recently learned." All three believed he was sane enough to be electrocuted.

After reading their reports, the governor issued Ford's death warrant.

Ford had been on death row eight years when his attorneys hired psychiatrist Harold Kaufman to do a careful analysis of his mental state. Kaufman interviewed Ford on November 3, 1983, and recorded his responses: "The guard stands outside my cell and reads my mind. Then he puts it on tape and sends it to the Reagans and CBS. . . . I know there is some sort of death penalty, but I am free to go whenever I want to because it would be illegal and the executioner would be executed. . . . CBS is trying to do a movie about the case. . . . I know the KKK and news reporters all disrupting me and CBS knows it. Just call the CBS Crime Watch. . . . There are all kinds of people in pipe alley [an area near Ford's cell] bothering me. Sinatra, Hugh Hefner, people from the dog show, Richard Burr, my sisters and brother trying to sign the death warrants so they don't keep bothering me. . . . I never see them. I only hear them especially at night."

Dr. Kaufman commented: "Note that Mr. Ford denies *seeing* these people in his delusions. This suggests that he is honestly reporting what his mental processes are."

Here are more of Ford's remarks which Kaufman recorded: "I won't be executed because of no crime . . . maybe because I'm a smartass . . . my family's back there [in pipe alley] . . . you can't evaluate me . . . I did a study in the army . . . a lot of masturbation . . . I lost a lot of money on the stock market. They're back there investigating my case. Then this guy motions with his finger like when I pulled the trigger. Come on back, you'll see what they're up to—Reagan's back there, too. Me and Gail bought the prison and I have to sell it back. State and federal prisons. We changed all the other countries because we've got a pretty good group back there. I'm completely harmless. That's how Jimmy Hoffa got it. My case is gonna save me."

Dr. Kaufman concluded that, "Because of his psychiatric illness, while he does understand the nature of the death penalty, he lacks the mental capacity to understand the reasons why it is being imposed on him. His ability to reason is occluded, disorganized, and confused when thinking about his possible execution. He can make no connections between the homicide he committed and the death penalty. Even when I pointed this connection out to him, he laughed derisively at me. He sincerely believes that he is not going to be executed because he owns the prisons, could send mind waves to the governor and control him; President Reagan's interference in the execution process, etc."

Kaufman saw Ford again six months later and reported his mental condition had seriously deteriorated "so that he now has at best minimal contact with the external world."

Eighteen months after that, in between bouts of wild, uncontrollable laughter, Ford told a Washington *Post* reporter that to make sure his family was safe he'd send them on spaceships to another planet, and he volunteered to stay in the Florida State Prison to make changes there. "I'm going to decide who gets killed," he said. However, he said he expected to leave prison soon to solve world problems, including leprosy.

Denied the right to rebut the opinions of the state-appointed psychiatrists with their own opposing medical testimony, Ford's attorneys made unsuccessful appeals in three state and two federal courts.

In 1986, the U.S. Supreme Court considered the arguments of Ford's public defenders, Craig Barnard and Richard Burr III, who asked:

> **1.** Does the Eighth Amendment's ban on "cruel and unusual punishments" or the Fourteenth Amendment's requirement of "due process of law" prohibit states from executing prisoners who become insane?

> **2.** Must the thirty-seven states with capital punishment laws give the defense an opportunity to challenge state psychiatrists and present expert testimony of its own in court?

The reluctance to execute the insane is based on humane and rational grounds. The condemned prisoner should be sane enough to make his peace with his god if he has one, and to cooperate in final legal appeals for clemency. It is also argued that because the death penalty is meant to punish, the prisoner should be rational enough to realize he or she is being punished.*

Or as defender Barnard puts it, "It is contrary to our sense of decency, and our society is better than that."

Barnard points out that "Dr. Ivory's crucial inferential finding, that Mr. Ford was feigning psychosis because his cell was far better organized than his thought processes seemed to be, has no basis in the medical literature."

What's more, says Barnard, "Dr. Ivory did not look at any of the past history of Ford or any of the past correspondence. His thirty-minute interview with Ford in a crowded courtroom and with the two other psychiatrists was below the limited standards of competency for the medical profession; an inadequate way of doing psychiatric interviews.

"The real point of the case is, Shouldn't we have this decided in a situation where we can bring all these opinions and have it decided by a neutral magistrate? He would have a chance to examine these doctors and to examine our doctors. And we would then come to some resolution of what is true."

There is no move to free Ford. It's a matter of whether he should be granted clemency and his life spared.

The U.S. Supreme Court ruled in June 1986 by a 5–4 vote that it is unconstitutionally cruel to execute an insane killer. It also ruled by a 7–2 vote that defense lawyers are entitled to cross-examine state psychiatrists and present evidence to determine if a condemned inmate is insane.

Florida's Governor Graham complained: "The court has created another hoop we have to jump through."

Psychiatrist Frederic Wertham has stressed the danger of setting free murderers after they have been diagnosed as insane. He cited the case of Martin Lavin, a professional killer with twenty arrests for major crimes. Lavin conned judge, jury, and psychiatrists into believing he was crazy after he had committed a cold-blooded murder. Instead of the electric chair he went to an institution for the criminally insane. He was released a year later as cured, and soon after fought a gun duel with a New York policeman. The policeman

---

*Did sixty-six-year-old Anthony Antone realize he was being punished? He went to the Florida electric chair on January 26, 1984, saying his spirit would ooze out through his pineal gland, rise through seven layers of the universe, and take up residence in the eighth, from where he would rule the universe.

fell wounded. Lavin walked up to him and killed him with two bullets in the back.

Is it easy for prisoners to emulate Lavin and simulate madness long enough to escape execution? Psychiatrist Wertham said that frequently a prisoner who had been under psychiatric observation would tell another how to behave in order to be sent to the psychiatric ward and how to act crazy when he gets there, instructing him how to answer questions and how to interpret Rorschach inkblots to appear mad.

In Wertham's experience it was not uncommon for a prisoner to simulate insanity to escape punishment. And he said that those psychiatrists who had dealt with many criminals but denied ever having encountered a successful faker had obviously been fooled.

A study at Washington's St. Elizabeth Hospital concluded that more than 100 criminals who were judged not guilty by reason of insanity were sane all right, and "highly clever, manipulative individuals."

Was George Fitzsimmons faking it? He murdered his parents in New York and took the not-guilty-by-reason-of-insanity trip to a mental institution. He told psychiatrists there that he wanted to live with his aunt and his uncle, whom he "loved like his own father." That alone should have given them pause, but the psychiatrists freed him. Soon afterwards he fatally stabbed his aunt and uncle. Investigators belatedly discovered that Fitzsimmons had named himself as beneficiary of his four victims' life insurance.

And what of "Son of Sam" David Berkowitz? He murdered six people and wounded seven. He said the devil, talking to him through a dog, had ordered the killings. Berkowitz later admitted in a newspaper interview that he had pretended to be crazy. "There were no real demons, no talking dogs, no satanic henchmen," he said. "I made it all up via my wild imagination so as to find some form of justification for my criminal acts against society."

We do execute the insane from time to time, especially for atrocious crimes. We have stopped executing children. The reluctance to send a woman to the California gas chamber saved Gordon Northcott's mother from execution for her part in the sex-torture killings of children in the late 1920s.

But in 1941, on the eve of World War II, the state of California overcame its reluctance, when it found that the vicious leader of a gang of killers was a woman—Juanita Spinelli.

8

Juanita Spinelli and Louise Peete
Executing Women

Al Capone a ruthless gang leader? Sure. But, Juanita Spinelli? You must be kidding. And her nickname "Duchess" was a laugh, unless your idea of a duchess was a scrawny little woman with thick legs, thin lips, sharp features and matching tongue.

But Mrs. Spinelli, shortly to become a grandmother, belied her broken-down bag-woman looks. "She was," said San Quentin's Warden Duffy, "the coldest, hardest character, male or female, I have ever known."

After her mob killed and robbed the owner of a barbecue stand, they holed up in a Sacramento hotel.

Spinelli suspected one of them, nineteen-year-old Robert Sherrard, of running off at the mouth. He was knocking back whiskey as if it were Coca-Cola, raising his voice and talking incautiously.

Afraid he'd incriminate them in the murder, Spinelli handed him his next whiskey on the house. She'd doctored it with knockout drops.

As soon as he was unconscious, she ordered the rest of her gang to take him for a last ride. It was dark when they set out on Spinelli's orders. They drove the drugged teenager to the Sacramento River and dumped him in, making sure he didn't float.

Spinelli had recruited her four gang members unwisely. One had already talked himself to death. Now, a second—Albert Ives—also talked too much . . . and was to become the death of her. He squealed on the Duchess.

She, and the man she lived with, Mike Simeone, and Gordon Hawkins, were found guilty of Sherrard's murder and sentenced to death by lethal gas.

Spinelli was driven to the Tehachapi Women's Prison, the two men to San Quentin.

Psychiatrists agreed that Albert Ives was insane, and he was committed for life to Mendocino State Hospital.

When it was time to kill Spinelli, San Quentin prison officials drove the seven hundred miles round-trip to get her.

Her first words to the warden were, "I'm innocent. They're making a terrible mistake."

He had no doubt of her guilt, but because no woman had been executed at San Quentin, he expected her to be reprieved at any moment.

The warden offered to convey a message to her daughter. She wasn't interested. But she had a message for her common-law husband: "Tell that son-of-a-bitch Simeone to tell the truth. He's the only one can get me out of this."

Simeone showed no enthusiasm for saving her life but other prisoners did. One of them brought Warden Duffy a petition to the governor signed by about thirty prisoners.

California, it stated, had the proud record of never executing a woman. Now it intended to do so. The very thought was repulsive, and if carried out would degrade the state in the eyes of the whole world. To commit the crime of which Juanita Spinelli had been found guilty, she must have been insane. If that didn't justify saving her from the gas chamber, wouldn't the governor take into account that she was the mother of three and a grandmother?

And if the governor could find it in his heart to free her, any one of the undersigned offered to serve out her commuted sentence, after their own terms had ended. There was a slight catch to this provision. What the warden knew, but the governor did not, was that most of the signers of the petition were lifers. It would be unlikely they would have much if any freedom to offer. Nevertheless, it was a generous thought.

Just in case none of these comments or proposals stirred the governor to stop the execution, they were willing to go to the gas chamber in her place. The governor had only to give the word and they would draw straws for the privilege of sustaining California's proud record.

It was midnight, a few hours before Spinelli was to be executed. The warden couldn't sleep. He too was repulsed at the idea of executing a woman, even an evil hag like Spinelli who was "horrible to look at and impossible to like."

His phone rang. Governor Olson on the line. He was giving Spinelli a thirty-day reprieve to study new evidence he'd received.

Duffy dressed and went to tell her.

"Thank God!" she gasped. "God listened to my prayers. I hope He'll save me. Perhaps Mike will tell the truth now." She was on her knees as if praying to get Mike Simeone to change his story.

After the thirty days were up, the governor gave them a further thirty-day reprieve and after that again delayed their executions.

Abolitionists were pressuring him to commute her sentence, especially the Men's League of Mercy.

Death penalty diehards denounced the governor for dithering, charging that if Spinelli were a man she already would have been gassed. It was, they said, blatant sex discrimination, or words to that effect.

Governor Olson made up his mind to make up his mind after meeting Mrs. Spinelli. He met her and decided to kill her as well as the two men.

On November 20, 1941, the day before the death date, she held a press conference in the warden's office. If any of the reporters had expected a last-minute confession or tears, they were immediately disillusioned. She was innocent, she snapped at them. Who was to blame for getting her into this terrible predicament? They were. Their lies and headlines were sending her to her death. When she began to curse the reporters, the warden called off the conference and took Spinelli back to the holding cell. She had apparently not read *How to Win Friends and Influence People*.

Her mood had mellowed slightly when Duffy saw her later. She asked him if when she went into the death chamber she could have photos of her three children and newly born grandchild taped over her heart. He said he'd tell the doctor to do it. When he asked her if there was anything else he could do for her, she replied, sharply, "Nothing!" and turned her back on him.

She was asleep when he again looked in on her later that night.

When Duffy returned to his office, a San Francisco *Examiner* reporter was waiting to see him. The newsman had a hot inside tip that the prisoners were so aroused over the imminent execution of a woman that they were going to riot.

On the contrary, the warden said. Since the petition, there had been no organized move by the prisoners to save her. His recent rounds of the prison had satisfied him that there would be no riot, not even a hunger strike.

He was right. She was on her own now.

Next morning, after briefly talking with reporters crowded in his office, Duffy left to supervise Spinelli's execution.

She told him she was glad he hadn't wakened her on his previous visit, because it allowed her to get some sleep. He promised to deliver letters she had written, and then hesitated, unable to find any words of comfort for this malevolent woman who had endeared herself to no one.

"It's all right," she said as if reading his thoughts. "You don't have to worry about me. I'm ready to go."

Two matrons joined them to help dress her for her execution, and the doctor taped family photos over her heart alongside the stethoscope. Duffy left briefly to see how things were going elsewhere.

Nearly a hundred people surrounded the gas chamber, more than three times the usual witnesses. The wish to see history made? Or the urge to see a nasty old woman put to death? Perhaps some of both.

The eight-sided apple-green gas chamber is not a thing of beauty even to a disinterested observer. Duffy thought it looked like a medieval torture chamber.

The anonymous executioner had everything ready; the pound bag of cyanide pellets had been hooked under the chair. He'd mixed three pints of sulphuric acid in six pints of water in a lead container below the pellets. When pellets met acid, the resulting poison gas proved infallibly deadly.

Because the governor had dithered three times, Spinelli and the other two gang members were still expecting another reprieve.

Duffy also anticipated a reprieve, or even a commutation, for Spinelli. San Quentin had never executed a woman, he kept reminding himself. Why should she be the first? So he hovered near the phone as much as possible, waiting for a fourth call from the governor.

Before handing Spinelli a new set of clothes to die in, the matrons conducted a body search, probing every orifice on the lookout for a pill, a hairpin, a piece of broken glass, a nail—anything she might use to open an artery and bleed to death and so cheat the state of its rights. They found nothing.

The warden rejoined them as the matrons were strapping Spinelli's wrists together. Duffy got the word that it was time to go, and the small death party set off.

And then the phone rang.

It rang only once; then Duffy grabbed it. "Hold the execution!" said Phil Gibson, Chief Justice of the California Supreme Court. He'd just received a writ from Spinelli's attorney protesting the execution. As soon as he read it, he'd call Duffy back with a Stop or Go decision.

The matrons took Spinelli back to her cell. The witnesses slowly filed out of the death chamber, relieved or disappointed. Duffy waited close to the phone. It rang again in ten minutes, Gibson on the line. Writ denied. Spinelli must die.

"I expected it," she said. "Why did they bother? Now we have to go through the whole thing again." She spoke with weary bitterness. It was remarkable that she was able to speak coherently.

As they approached the death chamber a second time, Duffy noticed none of the witnesses had returned.

He apologized to Mrs. Spinelli, saying he had to get them back in place—that was the law. He told her that meanwhile she could wait in her cell.

She chose to stay put, standing just outside the gas chamber while Duffy sent a guard to round up the scattered witnesses.

Then followed the remarkable spectacle of the warden and condemned grandmother chatting together, like friendly acquaintances at the supermarket, as the chaplain nearby murmured prayers.

"I believe the sun's come out," she said.

"Yes it has," Duffy replied. "It's a beautiful sunny day."

She seemed pleased that she had a good day to die. He agreed with her that it was often damp and foggy at San Quentin.

She glanced at the death chair and asked him what it would be like. He had a comforting answer ready, which he believed: "It's like going to sleep." He advised her, as he had many others, to sit far back in the chair to be in the thick of the fumes. He suggested that she should wait until she heard the cyanide pellets drop into the liquid, to say a brief prayer, and then look at him. He would be on her left looking through the window. "The moment I nod, take a few deep breaths. That way it will be easier."

She asked how long it would take. Just a few seconds, he reassured her. The chaplain agreed.

At about ten A.M., when the witnesses were back in place, Duffy, still listening out for a ringing phone, gave orders to begin.

"Keep your chin up," he said to Spinelli.

"Okay," she replied, and stepped into the gas chamber.

Alone in the sealed chamber, she bent her head briefly, apparently taking the warden's advice to pray. She raised her head and looked at him. He was staring at the spot under her seat. He saw the cyanide tablets drop into the acid mixture and the faint, almost invisible, fumes begin to rise.

When the gas reached the taped photos and stethoscope on her chest, he met her eyes and nodded.

She took a deep breath that lifted her chin. She started to tremble, then shook violently.

Duffy glanced anxiously from Spinelli to the doctor listening through the stethoscope. Minutes passed, and Spinelli's heart still beat frantically. Five minutes went by, six, seven, eight. Still the doctor listened.

It was 10 minutes 14½ seconds before the doctor looked at the warden. Spinelli's heart had finally stopped.

The startling, eerie noise that followed was not her soul taking wing, but the suction fan clearing the poison gas from the chamber before attendants went in to remove her body. A few days later Simeone and Hawkins were gassed.

If the Duchess was a lesson in not judging by appearances, Louise Peete was the clincher. Even the softhearted Warden Duffy thought the first woman to die in California's gas chamber was repulsive. But he would never have guessed, to look at her, that she was a gang leader. That had been a big surprise.

Louise Peete, the second woman to be executed in San Quentin, was a shock he never got over.

She was a devastating charmer. Devastating, that is, to almost everyone who got close to her. And plenty did. First impression was bright eyes, an earnest, innocent look, and pure complexion. Next, an outgoing, guileless manner and soft, musical voice. Pleasingly plump, people called her. A beautiful woman, said others, and sweet as candy. She was all that; and like candy should have been labeled: This may be dangerous to your health.

Louise Peete breezed in and out of people's lives leaving a trail of corpses behind her.

She buried three husbands. Suicides all. Or so read their death certificates. But she was never alone for long. After three stints as a widow, she shared her house with a woman companion who died suddenly and unexpectedly of a mysterious illness. A sympathetic hotel clerk who befriended Louise in her grief killed himself, like her three husbands.

Despite her deadly record, men couldn't keep away from her. One in particular, in Dallas, Texas, wanted to help her forget her tragic past. He was found dead, a bullet in his brain.

By now the police were a mite suspicious. Louise was questioned, but instead of her breaking down, her interrogators did. She was so adorable. How could she possibly have done it? So, for the umpteenth time, lovely Louise got away with murder.

She probably saved the lives of several smitten Dallas cops by moving to Los Angeles. City of Angels seemed just the place for the angelic Louise. And there she hoped to make another coup.

Louise read newspapers the way others read bank statements: with money in mind.

She spotted her prey in a newspaper column. He was Jacob Denton, a wealthy mining executive. According to the news story, he was moving East for a spell. Louise called on him and asked if he might rent his home while he was away. He hadn't thought of it, but was already quite taken by her. She had fallen in love with it at first sight, she told him in her cultured, softly modulated voice. Would he consider renting it to her?

She was such a delightful change from the hard-bitten, corncrake-voiced floozies he'd encountered that he even let her move in before he moved out. He never moved out.

Puzzled by Jacob's apparent disappearance, friends and relatives persuaded the police to search his home. They found him buried in the basement. He had been shot to death. This time Louise was charged with murder.

"How could you possibly suspect me?" Louise asked the DA, who began to waver.

She called in a witness who swore that soon after Jacob Denton's death—the time pinpointed by the coroner—Louise had been arranging flowers, as happy as a lark, dancing around the room and singing in her sweet voice.

"How could I possibly have danced and sung after committing such a terrible, terrible crime?" she asked the DA, direct as a child. She smiled as if forgiving his mistake, and added, "How could I possibly have lived in the house for four months if I knew there was a corpse in the basement?" She gave a little shudder which the DA found quite charming.

Only a monster could have done such a thing, Louise implied, and anyone could see she was utterly adorable.

However, since her hasty flight from Texas, the police there had continued investigating. They computed that Louise had at least six corpses to her credit. They sent this information to the Los Angeles DA and he went ahead and prosecuted.

She was found responsible for Denton's death, despite her singing-and-dancing-routine alibi, and sent to prison, at first in the new cell block for women at San Quentin. When there was room for her in the prison for women at Tehachapi, some three hundred miles away, she was transferred.

Louise wept softly much of the way, telling the guards escorting her that she'd miss her "little gray home in the West." What an adorable way to think of San Quentin.

Although, she had a point. In comparison, Tehachapi was a hellhole. With no men around, the women cons freaked out, had hysterical crying jags, fell in dead faints, fought each other like fury, and filled up the hospital medical records with their psychosomatic symptoms. Lesbian lovers had maniacal fits of jealousy, sex-starved heterosexuals turned, in frenzied frustrations, on the prison staff. Even the toughest women guards at times had a good cry. It was just too much.

Until Louise arrived. How she stood out among those other brazen bitches. She was a real darling. Rarely complained, never gave any trouble. It was a pleasure to talk with her. Such a sweet thing! There must have been some mistake. Louise Peete didn't belong in prison.

She didn't for long. Louise was released on parole with a near-perfect record in 1939.

Five years later, a Margaret Logan of Pacific Palisades was shot to death.

A close friend immediately named the murderer—Margaret's husband. The friend was charming and convincing until the police took her name and found she had a record. The name? Louise Peete.

Of course the police suspected that Louise might have been, well, stretching the truth. But they had no positive evidence against her, and despite her past she was so persuasive that suspicion began to teeter away from her to him.

The suspected widower went mad under the strain and was committed to a mental asylum, where he died.

Meanwhile, Louise, with the chutzpah of a Barbary Coast pirate and the easy charm of a society social director, had moved into the Logans' house as if it were hers.

Within a few months she had attracted a loyal circle of doting friends.

They were incredulous when she was arrested for Margaret Logan's murder, found guilty, and sentenced to death.

Awaiting execution, she revealed her carefully hidden nature. Women guards found her to be the coldest human being they had ever known and that she only turned on her formerly irresistible charm when she wanted something. Even those guards who had approved her parole and said then that Louise Peete didn't belong in prison now agreed that she should have been locked up forever.

Arriving at San Quentin for her execution after the long journey from the women's prison, she complained that guards had humiliated her by keeping her in handcuffs. The warden apologized. In her sixties, Louise had retained her flawless complexion, and to the warden's wife looked like "a comparatively young and incomparably amiable housewife."

Capital crime was obviously good for Louise Peete's complexion.

The evening before her death, a tiny woman in bright yellow—who seemed to be imitating a canary—pleaded with the warden's wife to let her stay close to Louise in her last hours. Mrs. Duffy put her up in her home at the prison and they talked until late into the night.

The visitor admitted that even after Louise's arrest for murder she had still wanted to make her a partner in a successful business.

"She's the finest woman I've ever known and I'm sure she's innocent," said the gullible little birdlike widow as she alternately sipped coffee and prayed for her friend.

There were no delays or reprieves for Louise Peete, and she was smiling until the last moment when the gas hit her. Charming to the end.

"I've never seen anything like it," said the warden afterwards. "She must have had ice water in her veins."

When the autopsy was completed, the diminutive widow claimed the body. A week later she wrote to the warden, "Today I stood by the little grave and bid her good-bye. I know she is safe with Jesus, and in that morning when Jesus comes she will be safe there with us."

She was lucky she hadn't beaten Louise to the cemetery.

California had converted to gas when Juanita Spinelli and Louise Peete, in that order, were first and second to be executed by that state. Britain stuck with the hangman, as did some American states. The French seemed more comfortable with the guillotine.

9

Henri Désiré Landru and Marcel Petiot Crime and Punishment French Style

During the Middle Ages in France, convicted aristocrats were beheaded with an ax or sword. Peasants were hanged. Centuries later a doctor, Joseph Guillotine, suggested beheading everyone, the nobles and hoi polloi, alike. His timing was good. It was 1789 and the start of the French Revolution, when equality was the name of the game.

His reasoning was hard to refute. What was fit for a king was surely fine for a commoner. *Égalité* won the day. But instead of still using a sword or ax, the French government approved Guillotine's further idea of a decapitating machine.

A prototype was built, and needed to be tested. Lacking volunteers, the builders asked a hospital to hand over a few dead patients. The machine worked like a charm.

The public dubbed it *guillotine* after the physician who had proposed it.* The name stuck and became official.

If anything, executions became an even more popular form of mass entertainment.

But there was a furious debate in 1795, in which opponents of the guillotine said it did not kill quickly. They cited the case of Char-

---

*Curious, isn't it, that a dentist should promote electrocution and a doctor decapitation?

lotte Corday. While the revolutionary leader Jean-Paul Marat sat in a bath to ease the pain of a skin disease, she had stabbed him to death with a kitchen knife. Her attorney's plea of insanity failed to save her.

When she was decapitated, the executioner demonstrated his patriotism by grabbing her head by the hair, lifting it, and hitting it with his fist. Witnesses swore they saw her head blush. And that started the fierce controversy.

It lost steam when someone suggested that her red face was probably a reflection of the sunset that evening and not evidence that a disembodied head can have feelings, or that Charlotte Corday had died a lingering death.

A physician, Dr. Beaurieux, was not convinced, and got permission to put a macabre experiment to the test. He attended the execution of bandit Henri Languille. The moment the bandit's head dropped into the waiting basket, the doctor picked it up, stared at it face-to-face, and repeatedly shouted the dead man's name. Slowly the eyelids opened and the bandit's eyes stared back at him, and then closed—said the doctor.

He repeated the experiment with two other freshly guillotined heads and claimed that the eyes of both opened for a while, and the last head was consciously alive for thirty seconds.

His astonishing report was published in the respected newspaper *Le Matin,* but fellow doctors throughout France ridiculed him, asserting that muscular spasms following death had given Beaurieux the false impression of conscious life.

The British acknowledged the guillotine was quick, certain, and foolproof, but found the mutilation too shocking to follow the French. It was never seriously considered in the U.S., not even in Louisiana, the state most under French influence.

For almost two centuries the French used nothing but the guillotine to execute their murderers. Intrigued by the antics of one Frenchman who lost his head that way, Orson Welles urged Charlie Chaplin to dramatize his life and death. Chaplin did. He wrote, directed, and starred in a movie satirizing the life of the mass murderer, entitled *Monsieur Verdoux.*

In his autobiography Chaplin characterized Verdoux as "a paradox of virtue and vice; a man who, as he trims his rose bushes, avoids stepping on a caterpillar, while at the end of the garden one of his victims is being consumed by an incinerator."

The fictional Verdoux was based on the life of Henri Désiré Landru, who also epitomized that curious cliche, the heartless killer who loves his pet canary.

Selling and buying used furniture in Paris during World War I, Landru seized the opportunity to extend his business to killing for profit.

Many married men and eligible bachelors were fighting at the front, and Paris was a city of sex-starved spinsters and wistful widows, all ripe for plucking.

Landru, with a wife and four children, advertised in lonely-hearts newspaper columns, posing as a warm-hearted widower wanting a wife. While his loving family thought he was moving furniture, this middle-aged, undersized, bald, bearded Frenchman was captivating hundreds of women. He used a compelling approach: passion for them and presents for their moms.

Courting dozens of women at the same time, he risked giving the game away by using the wrong name—especially in the heat of passion—or making other *faux pas* such as confusing Monique's craze for candy with Simone's for savories.

Landru avoided this by updating an elaborate card index file with detailed physical descriptions of his victims, notes on their fancies and foibles, birth dates, pet names, prejudices, and peculiarities.

His technique was to be a perfect gentleman on the first date. On the second or third, he seduced them. If they resisted, he promised to marry them. That usually did the trick. If it didn't he brought the Almighty into the act. Landru told them, truthfully, that he had been an altar boy. He spoke of God as if they were good pals. If the woman still resisted, he suggested they should pray together for guidance. Landru would close his eyes, raise his head, count to ten or twenty—depending on the anticipated resistance—and then open his eyes and with a gentle smile announce that God had given them the go-ahead.

God and Landru were usually a winning combination.

Once, on meeting stiff opposition, Landru led his quarry to church and invited her to join him on his knees. They were to ask God to say yes or no to their sexual union. God again said okay, according to Landru, and the woman apparently took his word for it.

Despite all his precautions, there was always the danger that one woman would catch him out on the town, or on his knees, with another. So he constantly assumed new names and varied the scenes of his seductions.

Working with almost superhuman industry and energy, in a few years he seduced and robbed close to three hundred women. He bilked them of their life savings, their furniture, and jewelry before running out on them.

About ten of the duped women tracked him down and threatened to expose him. It was a terrible misunderstanding, he said. But they couldn't possibly discuss it in public. If they'd just come with him, he'd explain everything and give them all the money he owed them.

Landru, it seemed, could talk a woman into anything. They all went with him to a building he owned on the outskirts of Paris in which he stored the mostly stolen furniture. One even brought her son with her.

He strangled his ten critics and the boy, cut them into small pieces and burned them in a stove, and resumed business as usual.

Until the sister of one "missing" woman recognized Landru in the street, tailed him home, and called the gendarmes.

When arrested, Landru was courting Fernande Segret, an attractive twenty-nine-year-old who had broken off her engagement to a soldier fighting in the trenches in favor of this middle-aged mass murderer.

She refused to testify against him. Even when told she was wearing a well-worn engagement ring Landru had used on many previous victims—some now in ashes—she stuck by him. "He was such a good and gentle man," she told reporters. "And such a passionate lover. I still love him and I would have married him. And he was so thoughtful. He always used to bring my mother flowers."

At his trial, neighbors told of the dense clouds of sickening smoke that billowed from Landru's chimney. Detectives nailed him with their discovery of a cupboard stocked with bottles of tissue-destroying chemicals, as well as hundreds of fragments of human bones among the ashes of his stove, together with partly melted corset stays and buttons.

Landru kept a cool, at times flippant, manner in court. A psychiatrist described him as remarkably intelligent, and a charming talker with a pleasing manner. How did the psychiatrist explain his incredible success with women? He may have hypnotized them, suggested the psychiatrist, especially those who were inclined to be hysterical.

Was Landru sane? Perfectly sane, replied the psychiatrist.

The psychiatrist, Landru said, had just proved his innocence. He had been judged sane, and only a lunatic could have committed the crimes of which he was accused.

It didn't work. Landru was sentenced to death.

His wife and four children tried to visit him in prison, but he refused to see them. They had known him only as a loving husband and father, they said, and were completely unaware of his crimes until the day of his arrest.

He had not lost his attraction for women. Every day he received over a hundred letters from them with gifts of cakes and candies. Many offered themselves should he escape the guillotine. They were all to be disappointed.

It was still dark when the executioner and his assistants arrived in the prison courtyard in a horse-drawn wagon. The executioner was dressed to kill in a long white cotton jacket, like a butcher's, and spotless white gloves. The three men unloaded the guillotine that came in pieces and put it together.

Inside, the prison guards had woken Landru, and one of them strapped his wrists behind his back. Landru's attorney murmured "Courage."

"Thanks," he replied. "I've always had that."

Two baskets had been taken from the wagon. Both contained bran to soak up Landru's blood. An assistant put the smaller wicker basket at the spot where Landru's head would fall. The other positioned a coffin-size basket to hold Landru's headless body.

About a hundred people had gathered in the cobblestoned courtyard, many of them women. At the first hint of the morning sun, guards opened the wooden prison doors.

Landru appeared with his escort. He was barefoot, and the collar and neck of his shirt had been removed as if they would prove an obstacle to the guillotine. He seemed reluctant or unable to move. He took a few steps and then stopped. Guards supported Landru, then dragged him forward. His face was unusually pale.

But when he first saw the waiting guillotine, he flushed a vivid red.

In one swift movement, the guards rushed him to an upright board of the guillotine which collapsed under his weight, holding him in a horizontal position.

Immediately a heavy wooden block with a semicircle cut out of it dropped over his neck, pinning him down.

The executioner pulled a lever with his white-gloved hand, the guillotine blade fell noisily, and Landru's head dropped neatly into the smaller basket.

His body was another story. The assistants rolled it into the large basket, but either there was too much blood or not enough bran. Blood continued to spurt and soak the assistants.

Dr. Guillotine would have approved the speed. Twenty-six seconds after Landru first tottered into the prison courtyard, he was unquestionably dead.

Had the French executed a madman? There was insanity in his family: his father had gone mad and killed himself. Even today's psychiatrists argue over who is insane and question the simple legal definition of insanity—the inability to know right from wrong.

Henri Désiré Landru was not the first or last cornered criminal to claim that only a lunatic could have committed the atrocious crimes of which he was accused. But he never went the next step and confessed to the "insane" crimes. When the prosecutor had asked him tough questions, he took the French equivalent of the Fifth Amendment.

The public was welcome to executions, and despite the early hour —soon after dawn—they were always well attended.

. . . Until 1939, just before the outbreak of World War II, when mass murderer Eugen Weidmann was executed. He had a large head that got stuck in the guillotine, and assistants pulled hard at his ear and hair to clamp him in properly. The spectators behaved like vacationers at a carnival. As Weidmann's severed head fell, they rushed the police barricades and broke through, and several women in search of mementoes soaked handkerchiefs in pools of the dead man's blood. After that ghoulish rush for blood, the public was banned from future executions.

As World War II surpassed World War I in atrocities, so Dr. Marcel Petiot, another outrageous Parisian, matched the sickly spirit of the times.

Had they voted for the kindest man in town, Petiot would have won hands down. As doctor in a small town near Paris, whatever the weather, however late the hour, if a child was sick Petiot would be at the bedside. He never refused a patient, even those who couldn't pay. And there was no disease he seemed unable to cure.

"Ministering angel" were perhaps the mildest words the locals used to describe this physician with the dark, arresting eyes and gentle hands. Many women adored him as a godlike character.

Yet Petiot was also a pitiless mass murderer, believed to have watched through a peephole as his poisoned victims slowly died in agony.

Like Landru, he too found wartime Paris a rich hunting ground.

Dr. Petiot was charged with luring twenty-seven frightened, trusting people to their deaths during the Nazi occupation of Paris in World War II; by falsely promising to help them escape to safety.

He claimed to lead a resistance group running an escape organization for a cut-price fee. He advised them to bring money, clothes, and jewelry to finance their new lives abroad. Under the pretense of giving inoculations he said were needed for foreign travel, Petiot poisoned them.

Exactly how he killed is still a mystery, but *why* is not. His victims left behind property worth $4 million.

After storing their corpses in his cellar, he carved them up with professional skill and either dumped them at night in the nearby Seine or burned them in a stove.

The stench of burning corpses brought Petiot to trial. A neighbor called firemen, who broke into the building and soon emerged, gagging and horrified at the sight of piled bodies, their hair and eyebrows shaved off, awaiting cremation. Even more horrible was a severed female hand dangling from the stove door.

The firemen called the police, who searched the whole building and concluded the crematorium's owner was a collector of erotica. Besides large amounts of morphine, he had a bottle of alcohol containing male and female genitalia, believed stolen from his medical school, and, perhaps as a change from carving up corpses, a hand-carved wood statue he had carved of the devil with an outsize penis.

Petiot arrived on a bicycle soon after the police and took them into his confidence. He said the corpses were those of Germans and collaborators: It had been his duty, as a Resistance leader, to eliminate them. And he took them in. The patriotic police believed him and told him to beat it.

But the awful smoke signals from Petiot's cellar had already reached the Gestapo, and the order went out to arrest Dr. Petiot as a homicidal lunatic. They seemed to know their man.

The Gestapo caught him and tried to force Petiot to reveal the details of his escape organization. They, like his victims, believed it existed.

He could hardly tell the same story he told the police, that it was a front to kill Germans and traitors—or the truth, that it was a ruse to commit wholesale murder for profit. So he kept his mouth shut except to scream or curse them as they tortured him for several days.

A genuine Resistance leader shared a cell with Petiot and was astonished and inspired by his courage and endurance. The Gestapo held him underwater, nearly drowning and then reviving him again and again. They filed his teeth until metal hit nerve. They crushed his skull in iron bands and suspended him by his jaw.

He screamed and groaned, but he didn't talk.

When they returned him to his cell, he shouted out his loathing and scorn for his Nazi jailers within their hearing, saying he didn't give a shit what they did with him because he had terminal cancer, which wasn't true.

Why they released him instead of sending him to their own ovens is still puzzling, and no one has yet probed those Gestapo records. Maybe he told his interrogators that his victims were mostly Jews and that consequently they should thank him for doing their work for them. Or, more likely, having failed to torture the nonexistent escape route out of him, they let him go, intending to tail him until he gave the route away.

A French criminal trial starts with a biography of the accused. The jury, after all, has his life in their hands. An insight into his background helps them to think of a person rather than a cipher when the evidence starts to be presented. So the judge began with this pocket history:

Marcel Petiot's schoolteachers thought he was extremely intelligent but weird. He tortured birds and small animals, including a kitten. At eleven he stole a revolver, and to liven up a boring lesson fired it at the ceiling.

During recess, he threw knives with professional accuracy around the shaky edges of a fellow student. He had occasional convulsions, walked in his sleep, and wet his bed until he was twelve.

He was kicked out of three schools.

At seventeen, he was charged with stealing letters from mailboxes by using a stick dipped in glue. A psychiatrist said he was abnormal and the charge was dropped.

To escape further fighting after being lightly gassed in World War I, he faked a nervous breakdown and shot himself in the foot.

A psychiatrist recommended sending him to a mental hospital. But Petiot now planned to become a doctor and somehow got sent to the mental hospital as a student intern, rather than as a patient. Perhaps his sponsors believed it takes one to know one. It may even have been a genuine mistake, because the French word for intern and patient is *interne,* and one is only distinguished from the other by an accent over the final *e.* Someone may have accidentally dropped or deliberately erased the accent, converting him immediately from patient to doctor.

After graduation, he started a family practice in a small town, where he earned a saintly reputation as a medical wonder-worker who could cure anything, was compassionate, and always available.

His only critics were the other two doctors in town who had lost most of their patients to him. But even they conceded he treated the poor for free. What nobody knew then was that the sly dog had secretly signed up paying and non-paying patients in a state medical scheme, so he was reimbursed for all his work by whopping government checks.

The idolized doctor hired a beautiful young housekeeper. Soon after it became evident she was pregnant, she disappeared. Petiot was seen loading a large trunk into his car, and a day or two later a similar trunk was found floating in a nearby river and pulled ashore. In it was a headless female corpse. Police were unable to identify the body and never found the head. Another woman who quarreled with Petiot and threatened to sue him also disappeared.

With the exception of his two rival doctors, Petiot could say he hadn't an enemy in the world. He was so popular that he decided to run for mayor on a risky platform: coming clean. He admitted to one big fault, he said, and that was loving people too much. Then he confessed to having pretended to be mad in World War I to get a discharge and a big pension.

Despite that admission, he won a landslide election. His record as mayor was spotty at best, but he never lost his patients' loyalty.

Married, and bored with small-town challenges, he moved to Paris, where he signed up literally thousands by confidently claiming he could cure almost everything. He spoke proudly of having invented a perpetual-motion machine and finding a cure for constipation, though apparently the two were not connected.

When he was arrested for stealing a book from a store, he went berserk and a judge sent him to a mental hospital for observation. All three psychiatrists who examined Petiot believed him to be an unscrupulous and totally immoral man who had feigned insanity both to get out of the army with a pension and to escape the shoplifting charge. They wrote a warning to future judges who might encounter Petiot not to be taken in by his acting the madman in order to commit crimes without punishment.

This account of Petiot's life brought the jury up to World War II, during which he had committed the crimes for which he now stood in the dock.

By turns charming and chilling, Petiot told the packed courtroom that he hoped to entertain them. His defense was to admit killing sixty-three people, many more than the twenty-seven of which he was accused, but to say he had done so as a Resistance leader ridding the state of traitors, collaborators, black market operators, prostitutes, and Nazi soldiers. For this he had expected to be treated as a national hero.

He paused in his testimony to call one witness a "punk" and to glare at another.

Michel Cadoret de l'Einguen, a witness for the prosecution, said he and his family survived the war only by declining Petiot's offer to help them escape.

He explained: "Petiot told us we would have to spend three days hidden in a house before leaving and would be given false identity papers. I was suspicious of the arrangements. He told us we would need to be vaccinated to get to Argentina and that 'These injections will render you invisible to the eyes of the world.' "

Petiot suddenly stood up and assumed a melodramatic, mocking stance and tone, saying, "Now I see it all. The crazy doctor with the syringe. It was a dark and stormy night. The wind howled under the roof and rattled the windows of the old, oak-paneled library."

He was living up to his hopes of entertaining the spectators.

Speaking of his first victim, Jo le Boxeur, as he was known, Petiot remarked, "He was easy to spot as a collaborator. He had a head like a pimp—you know, like a police inspector." Laughter in court.

Asked how he had killed, he replied, "None of your damn business!" It is still not known whether he gassed, poisoned, or used lethal injections.

When the prosecutor suggested that he kept huge stocks of morphine for murder, he said it was for painless childbirths.

A fellow physician characterized Petiot as either a genius or a lunatic. Dr. Genil-Perrin, one of the three psychiatrists who had examined him in 1937 after the shoplifting incident, made sure Petiot would not get away with murder by again feigning insanity, saying, "Although he has a stunted moral development, he is entirely responsible for his actions. I found him remarkably intelligent and endowed with a great gift for repartee."

The courtroom rocked with laughter, having already enjoyed many samples of Petiot's sardonic responses.

Dr. Gouriou, another prosecution psychiatrist, called Petiot "perverse, amoral, and deceitful. Throughout his life he has at times claimed to be insane when it suited him. Although I don't think he is a monster, he has acquired a taste for evil."

In rebuttal, Floriot, the defense attorney emphasized that Petiot's patients considered him brilliant and utterly devoted to their well-being.

"I have treated other doctors," Gouriou replied, "whose mental illness was manifest through the same exaggerated devotion to patients."

"How about Dr. Petiot's sister?" Floriot asked.

Gouriou admitted he had briefly examined her and found her normal.

"But he doesn't have a sister," the defense attorney said; and the embarrassed psychiatrist left in a hurry to loud, derisive laughter, including Petiot's.

Although his World War II cellmate testified to Petiot's anti-Nazi stance, and courage under Gestapo torture, other leading members of the Resistance said he was not known to them as a member of any clandestine group fighting the Germans; that his knowledge of the Resistance was scanty and inaccurate; and the little that was accurate could have been learned in his conversation with his fellow prisoner.

He was found guilty of murderering twenty-six people, most of them Jews desperate to escape from the Nazis. Sentenced to the guillotine, he strode from the court shouting—to whom was unclear—"I must be avenged!"

In his cell the deadly doctor wrote poetry and a manuscript entitled *Beating the Odds,* a curious hodgepodge of how not to lose your shirt gambling; an allegorical prose version of Milton's *Paradise Lost;* and parting shots at the psychiatrists who had the effrontery to call him sane.

"Since these gentlemen refused to be examined and have *their* sanity judged, I do not have the least confidence in them," he wrote.

A guard confiscated a vial of sedative he found in a seam of Petiot's pants, though it wasn't enough to kill him.

Petiot was particularly curious to know how long he had to live. Executions took place soon after dawn. French law forbade telling a condemned prisoner the date until six P.M. on the eve of the execution. However, Floriot promised to flout the law and inform Petiot the moment he knew. But in the early afternoon when Floriot did learn the date, he was occupied in court. He told his assistant, Paul Cousins, to go in his place and tell Petiot he was to die next morning.

Cousins was reluctant to give Petiot the grim news, and circled the prison for two hours until he got up the nerve to enter. Even then, it was Petiot who broached the subject. Cousins replied evasively that it could be tomorrow morning.

Noticing the attorney was trembling, Petiot patted him on the shoulder, saying, "Don't let it affect you so much. Let's change the subject."

In fact, the execution was delayed a day to give the executioner time to repair the guillotine, which had been damaged by an Allied bombing raid.

At about two A.M. on May 25, 1946, hundreds of police appeared and barricaded the streets leading to the prison, then stayed to form a human barricade to keep the public out.

An hour and a half later, the executioner, Henri Desfourneaux, arrived in the traditional horse-drawn cart with the repaired guillotine and three assistants. They were let through the barricade and stopped in the prison courtyard. By the light of street lamps, the beheading party put the fifteen-foot-high guillotine together. Finally, Desfourneaux, a big man with small features, took the triangular blade from a leather sheath and mounted it under a weight. The weight made sure it needed to fall only once to do the job. Desfourneaux normally worked in a factory, but came from a long line of part-time executioners.

Petiot's last dawn arrived about 4:30, but he was still asleep. When the sun had dimmed streetlights, four carloads of police officers and court officials were directed through the barricades to the prison. The judge at his trial, with the defense and prosecution attorneys, went to Petiot's cell, surprised to see that despite the chains around his wrists and ankles and his imminent execution, he was still sleeping.

When Petiot woke, the prosecutor greeted him with the customary, "Have courage, Petiot. It is time to go."

"Fuck you!" Petiot replied or, rather, the French equivalent.

Guards removed his chains and he changed from black prison garb into a gray business suit he had worn during the trial. He wrote letters to his wife and son, which his attorney promised would reach them.

Unnerved by the occasion, both judge and prosecuting attorney were on the verge of collapse. Petiot jokingly offered, as a doctor, to give them tranquilizing injections, which they declined with weak smiles. But his spirited attitude eased the tension.

It was time to leave. Instead of the expected bitter wisecrack, he said, "Gentlemen, I am at your disposal."

He said no thanks to the traditional glass of rum, but accepted a last cigarette and nodded to the hovering chaplain who offered to hear his confession.

"I'm not religious and my conscience is clean," Petiot said. When the chaplain looked disappointed, Petiot added, "I'd be pleased to talk with you man-to-man."

That gave the chaplain the opportunity to give Petiot a message from his wife. "She wants you to hear Mass," he said.

"If it will help my wife, go ahead."

Mass over, Petiot and the others walked down the length of the cells while other prisoners beat a sympathetic tattoo.

After Petiot had signed the prison clerk's register with a flourish, a guard tied Petiot's wrists behind his back and the barber cut off his shirt collar and shaved his neck.

In the prison courtyard, chief coroner Dr. Albert Paul watched the prison doors open and Dr. Petiot emerge, flanked by two executioner's assistants. Paul had witnessed hundreds of executions, but not one of the doomed prisoners had walked to his death with the insouciance of Petiot.

He recalled: "For the first time ever I saw a man leave death row, if not dancing for joy, showing perfect calm. Most people about to be executed try to be courageous, but one senses it is forced courage. Petiot moved with ease, as though he were walking into his own office for a routine appointment."

Though he smiled disdainfully at his bulky executioner, Petiot's last thought seemed to be to protect the sensibilities of onlookers. He had reverted to the role of caring doctor when he said, "Gentlemen, I advise you not to look. It will not be a pretty sight."

He knew what he was talking about.

The executioner was certainly less calm than Petiot. He was long out of practice, his last execution having been seven years previously, in the summer of 1939. Then the prisoner had to be forced into the guillotine and afterwards women had rushed for bloody keepsakes. Now that the public had been forbidden, at least that was unlikely to recur.

He bound Petiot's feet together, just in case he thought of making a break for it, and strapped him to a board on the base of the guillotine which tilted to the horizontal. Seconds later, the blade fell and severed Petiot's head, which landed in the small waiting basket.

A cameraman was standing by. He had been denied permission to record the execution. So he waited until Petiot's head and body had been removed and the beheading party began to dismantle the scene, and then he took a photo.

Ironically, he got away with a memento of Petiot's blood. His photo shows small pools of it on the pavement near the guillotine.

Landru and Petiot had a lot in common. They were French, married with offspring, preyed on the desperate and gullible, had singular powers of persuasion—especially over women—operated under the cover of wartime, cremated their victims, and were driven by the same insatiable greed.

But they did not corner the market. Across the Atlantic, while Petiot was on trial, another callous con man was rivaling their murder-for-profit exploits: sometimes using a French accent to snare women.

He, however, worked with a female partner—and together they earned a reputation as America's most hated murderers. Cynics said they gave murder a bad name.

10

Raymond Fernandez and Martha Beck
America's Most Hated Murderers

Raymond Fernandez had three ways to win a woman. First, he'd stick out his thick lower lip and do a fair imitation of screen lover Charles Boyer: "Come wizz me to zee Casbah." If that didn't turn them on, he gave them a you're-a-sandwich-and-I'm-hungry look. His backup technique to make them say yes was using an elementary knowledge of hypnosis and the black arts. At least it aroused their curiosity and at times weakened their resistance.

But he wanted volume. He'd deserted his wife and children in Spain to make a killing in America, and his pickings were slim. He needed a steady supply of suckers. So he emulated Landru and answered women who advertised for mates in Lonely-Hearts columns.

He met his match in one of them, Martha Beck. She had introduced herself as "witty, vivacious and oozing personality." Oozing was accurate. A woman acquaintance said with cruel candor: "The first thing you noticed about Martha was her soft, blubbery, quivering fat."

She hadn't prepared Fernandez for her bulk. At almost six feet in high-heeled shoes, she towered over him, and at 240 pounds outweighed him by eighty. She was looking for love and marriage, she told him, and had been head nurse in a home for crippled children in Pensacola, Florida. She didn't tell him she had also worked in a mortuary, and that after three failed marriages her two children had been taken away from her because she was an unfit mother.

Had she told him of her mortuary experience, he probably would have realized right away that they were made for each other.

He sensed that this was more woman than he could handle, but she smothered his instinct for self-preservation with her almost frenzied passion.

His usual MO was love 'em, clean 'em out, and leave 'em. But Martha had very little of value except her obvious passion to please. And Fernandez at first was flattered by his ability to set her aquiver without even reverting to a French accent.

Eventually he confided his line of work, and she eagerly offered to join him. Working as a team, they planned a Lonely-Heart-of-the-Month-Club: their goal, to rob at least one woman who advertised in such columns every month.

Her role was to plug her "brother" as a man with a gift for turning small investments into huge profits. "Wouldn't you like Raymond to turn your little nest egg into a fortune?"

It worked. If a woman resisted both Beck's sales talk and Fernandez' love lyrics, stubbornly insisting on marriage before any cash transaction, he married her—bigamously, of course. Then he got the money and he and Martha disappeared.

They might still be at it, except that Beck had not given up her lust for a lover; and Fernandez was the one she wanted even if it jeopardized their business.

Things came to a hysterical head when Fernandez put up a weak pretense that he had to go on a honeymoon with his bigamous bride, otherwise they'd never get her money. Pleasure before business was not part of their deal. Beck only calmed down when he agreed she could join them on the honeymoon.

There, she accused him of enjoying himself by behaving too much like a real bridegroom. He told her in urgent whispers he was only acting, but he had to convince his bride it was real.

Beck didn't buy it. She threw a fit and the honeymoon became more like a divorce court.

The man who preyed on women soon had sharp twinges of concern that a woman was trapping him. But by this time he needed Martha Beck, and she would have been as difficult to lose as a magnetic mine.

A Chicago widow, Myrtle Young, invited Fernandez to join her for a get-acquainted visit. Beck invited herself as chaperone. She followed the couple around all day, and at night shared the widow's bed to make sure Fernandez didn't.

Mrs. Young did not survive their visit: they gave her a fatal overdose of barbiturates—to calm her after the jealous arguments with Martha—and left with her car and $4,000.

With the loot they rented a house in Long Island, where Beck asked another lonely widow, Janet Fay, to spend a few days with her and her "brother." Mrs. Fay fell heavily for Fernandez and handed over $6,000 for him to multiply.

Beck began to quiver, scenting a budding romance, and while Fernandez was splashing on after-shave in the bathroom she gave Mrs. Fay a nasty piece of her mind. Aroused, Mrs. Fay responded in kind. Beck ended the fight abruptly by grabbing a hammer and knocking Fay unconscious.

Fernandez rushed from the bathroom screaming, "We had her money! There was no need for this!"

Still, he was a practical man, and to make sure Mrs. Fay didn't complain about being robbed and roughed up, he strangled her with a scarf. The couple then carried the corpse down to the cellar and buried it.

The month of that murder, another widow, Delphine Dowling, welcomed the pair to her Grand Rapids, Michigan, home. At twenty-eight, Dowling was distinctly more attractive than the usual Lonely-Heart, and had a two-year-old daughter.

It looked as if Fernandez would have to "marry" this woman to get her money. As the prospect seemed to please him, Beck, on full alert, doggedly tailed them.

They stayed out of sight long enough for Beck to suspect that Fernandez had at least once escaped her surveillance and made the widow pregnant. Dowling confided in her that she might well be right, and Beck talked her rival into taking a drug to cause an abortion. Instead, Beck gave her an overdose of sleeping pills.

As Mrs. Dowling struggled to stay awake, Fernandez shot her. Following their usual practice, they buried the body in the basement.

To pacify the baby girl who cried for her mother, they bought her a pet dog. But she kept crying. Beck feared the noise might alert the neighbors, so she drowned the child in a basement washtub and buried her next to her mother. Then she and Fernandez went to see a movie.

Neighbors thought the Dowling house was strangely quiet and called the police. Detectives searched the place and noticed a layer of still wet cement in the basement. They dug and found the corpses.

Outside the Bronx Supreme Court, what looked like the sale of the season was a large crowd of women pushing and screaming to get opening-performance seats at the Fernandez-Beck murder trial. A riot squad was called to disperse the women, but seventy out of several hundred got in.

The couple pleaded innocent, claiming that at the time of their crimes they were insane and so not responsible for their actions.

Fernandez confessed to only three murders but was believed to have killed at least seventeen women. He had, for example, gone on a "honeymoon" to Spain with a Mrs. Jane Thompson. He returned alone, saying she had died in a train crash.

"What train and where?" he was asked.

"I mean, she died of a heart attack," he replied. In fact, an overdose of digitalis had killed her.

Psychiatrists, said the defense attorney, would testify that the accused became so sexually involved with each other it was impossible for them to behave normally; that Martha Beck had made six suicide attempts after disappointed love affairs and had often contemplated killing herself at the thought of losing Fernandez. In other words, love made them do it.

When the fat, former nurse appeared in court, she appeared to confirm the defense attorney's assertion by breaking away from her guard to smother Fernandez with heavy kisses, smearing his cheeks and bald head with lipstick.

Defense psychiatrists pictured her as a victim; constantly ridiculed for her obesity due to a glandular defect; hired last of her nursing class although she got the top marks; and with a pathetic eagerness to please.

When she finally landed a job, it was a gruesome one of preparing female corpses for burial. She became pregnant by one of her lovers, a bus driver. Rather than marry her as she demanded, to her humiliation he attempted suicide and then left town. She married another bus driver, who also made her pregnant. Their life together was so miserable that she divorced him before the birth of the second baby. A few years later, Raymond Fernandez came into her life.

Fernandez, born in Hawaii, had fought for the Franco side during the Spanish Civil War, from which he returned with tales of mutilation and rape which he told with zest. He worked for British Intelligence during World War II and claimed to have suffered a blow on the head in 1945 that caused a personality change. There was evidence of scar tissue on his brain.

Dr. Richard Hoffman, chief defense psychiatrist, believed Martha Beck was a victim of physical and psychopathic abnormalities that made her a slave of Fernandez. He testified that she was "a pathological liar" and victim, rather than executioner of "a compulsive and obsessive act."

Psychiatrist Frederic Wertham disagreed. He examined the guilty pair and initially speculated that she might have fallen under Fernandez' hypnotic-like spell.

As Wertham sat with Martha Beck in the Women's Detention Center in Manhattan, he asked her to tell him about the drowning of the little child "in a bathtub." She surprised him by laughing. "It wasn't a bathtub," she corrected him. "It was a washtub in the basement."

She gave two reasons for killing the child: its crying might have drawn attention to the house with the mother's corpse in the basement, and the girl might have been able to identify Beck, at least to the extent of telling investigators that a woman had been in the house.

Beck's hearty, carefree laugh, showing no sign of remorse—and her explanations for the murder—convinced Wertham that she had not been under Fernandez' "spell."

During a conversation with this writer Dr. Wertham said he thought their motives for the cold-blooded killings were "excessive greed."

He ridiculed the suggestion that they had a compulsion to kill or were mentally ill. "What compulsion is there to kill a two-year-old girl?" he asked rhetorically. "What compulsion is there to cover up their tracks after the murders?"

The only abnormality in the couple, he conceded, was abnormal greed. Despite many hours of questioning them, he found no evidence that they were pathological cases.

Fernandez put all the blame on Beck. "I'm a gentleman," he insisted. "I wouldn't hurt nobody. But that woman, she's evil. She ought to die."

The jury agreed with him. They were both found guilty and sentenced to death.

In his death cell, Fernandez switched from calling Beck "that fat bitch" and complaining of her bad breath to declaring his undying love for her. He told a fellow prisoner that he had bigamously married at least fifty-five of the women he duped; that Beck was madly in love with him and insanely jealous; and when she lost her violent temper, would beat the hell out of him.

He explained that Beck killed Janet Fay to prevent him from consummating their "marriage," and had then drowned the little girl out of spite, because she suspected he had liked the girl's mother.

"What does it matter who is to blame?" Beck told the press. "My story is a love story, but only those tortured with love can understand what I mean. I was pictured as a fat, unfeeling woman. True, I am fat, that I cannot deny, but if that is a crime, how many of my sex are guilty? I am not stupid, moronic, or unfeeling. The prison and the death house have only strengthened my feeling for Raymond, and in the history of the world, how many crimes have been attributed to love?"

She brooded on the newspaper headlines that characterized her as the "Obese Ogress" and "Overweight Juliet," questioning whether she had been tried for murder or, as the reports seemed to imply, for being too fat.

When their last appeals failed and they faced the chair for sure, Fernandez admitted his guilt. "I've done terrible things," he said, "but I'm not afraid of the chair. I guess that's the way I ought to die."

Beck broke down and sobbed, "I'm afraid of the electric chair."

Fernandez scoffed at reports that he used black magic to seduce hundreds of women—explaining, though, that he did have the ability to make a woman obey him simply by concentrating. He called it "hypnosis at a distance." But he attributed most of his success because "I'm a gentle person and I pay them little attentions they all look for in a man. They figure I'm the sweet and lovable kind. In back of everything, that's what I am."

They continued their love-hate affair in prison, waving and smiling at each other across the exercise yard. Some male prisoners, listening to Fernandez' lurid confessions, thought of Martha Beck as a frustrated beast. They soon found he too was far from phlegmatic. After he had boasted of their bizarre and steamy sex life, fellow cons spread a rumor that Beck was having sex with someone in the women's wing of the prison. When Fernandez heard it, he simulated an erupting volcano.

His vanity was fed by the mail he received from women hoping he'd escape the chair and add them to his list of conquests.

She too enjoyed a steady arrival of letters heavy on obscene suggestions, but there were also marriage proposals—contingent, of course, on her survival. Some of the crudest proposals may have been triggered by the writers' learning of court testimony that she had indulged in sex practices "that might be considered unusual in some sections of the country, but not in others such as Greenwich Village."*

Assuming Fernandez to be the weaker of the two, the warden decided to execute him first to get it over with. He promised the Catholic chaplain Father Thomas Donovan "to die like a man" and ate a last meal of onion omelet followed by almond ice cream and coffee.

Two hours before Fernandez was to die, Beck wrote a poem and sent it to him. He scribbled a reply, "I would like to shout my love for you to the world."

After reading his note, Beck beamed and embraced the matron, saying, "Now I know he loves me I can go to my death bursting with joy!"

Walking into the execution chamber, the man who had once boasted of hypnotic powers avoided the eyes of witnesses. He sat in the chair and plucked at his pants as if to preserve the crease.

The first jolt of two thousand volts probably killed him, but the executioner followed the routine by sending three more blasts through his body. Each time, lights dimmed and flickered in the prison corridors.

Beck waited in her holding cell after a last meal of southern-fried chicken. A matron told her it was time to go. "Then what the hell are we waiting for?" she replied impatiently, but managed a smile. She had not lost her bouncy, almost jaunty walk.

Dressed in a blue-gray housedress, she sat on the edge of the chair twelve minutes after Fernandez' body had been wheeled out. The thirteenth woman to be executed by the State of New York endured a few embarrassing moments as she struggled to squeeze her huge body fully into the electric chair.

Just before a guard put a mask over her face, either a nerve twitched in her cheek or she tried a farewell smile to the two matrons nearby.

Unlike Fernandez, it took four shocks before Beck showed no

*The view of state psychiatrist Dr. James McCartney.

signs of life and Dr. Howard Kipp, Sing Sing's chief surgeon, officially pronounced her dead.

Truman Capote knew Martha Beck in her young days. When they were children, they ran away from home together and stayed overnight at a hotel run by her uncle in Evergreen, Alabama.

"After that her family took her away," Capote told me. "I didn't even realize it was the same person until years later all my relatives in that town said, 'Oh, Martha Beck's the girl who was here that summer. She's the one you ran away with.'"

I told Capote that psychiatrist Frederick Wertham believed Martha Beck's motive for murder was greed.

"Yes," said Capote. "Sexual greed on her part, and financial greed on the man's part."

Although Capote went on to remark that he never had any particular interest in crime, he spent several years in close and frequent contact with two condemned murderers gathering material for his book *In Cold Blood*.

It is an account of the crimes and punishment of Perry Smith and Richard Hickock.

11

Perry Smith and Richard Hickock
The *In Cold Blood* Killers

Richard Hickock wasn't your all-American boy, but he might have qualified for runner-up. He was polite and outgoing, and he smiled a lot. He had been the popular star of his high school basketball team, making up for his slight build and lack of height with dash and determination. His face was oddly unsymmetrical, his left eye being smaller than his right.

There was a dark side to him. When he drove a car he was on the lookout for stray dogs, not to help, but to hurt. Because he used his car as a weapon to kill or injure them.

He went from bouncing balls to bouncing checks, and finally landed in jail. There he met Perry Smith.

Smith was also in jail for petty crimes. He was a short, swarthy, almost stunted man with sleepy eyes and a censorious, prudish manner. He hated it when Hickock talked about what he intended to do to women when he got out.

A brutal father and alcoholic mother had abandoned Smith to the various cruelties of nuns and Salvation Army workers in Children's Homes.

For wetting his mattress, one woman had yanked him out of bed by his hair and dunked him in a tub of ice-cold water, almost drowning him. When he again wet his bed, another woman put a stinging ointment on his penis and laughed when he yelled in pain.

Although minor crimes had landed both men in the same Kansas prison, they planned to team up and join the major criminal leagues when they were let out. Their aim was to hitchhike as a team across America, thumbing rides only from prosperous-looking dudes in expensive cars. Then they'd rob and kill them.

With enough loot to support their junk-food tastes, they'd hotfoot it across the Mexican border. There, they'd search for buried treasure, like Humphrey Bogart in *The Treasure of Sierra Madre.* Only they wouldn't be suckers and blow it.

Then a fellow con said he'd once worked for a prosperous Kansas farmer named Clutter, who kept $10,000 in a safe in his isolated farmhouse. Here was a sitting duck. The hitchhiking plan could wait.

Freed from prison, and soon equipped with a knife, shotgun, ammunition, and a length of nylon rope, the pair drove through the night to the home of the Clutter family.

Hickock wasn't only in it for the money. He hoped to rape the farmer's teenage daughter.

Smith took an immediate liking to William Clutter, the head of the family; a quiet-spoken, straightforward man. He tried to talk Clutter into leading him to the safe with the small fortune inside— but Clutter said there was no such safe.

The two men decided to look for themselves. After ripping out the phones, they bound Clutter to a chair and gagged him. They trussed up the fifteen-year-old son, Kenyon, near his father. Next they went for the women—first Clutter's ailing wife, Bonnie, who was in bed, and finally his sixteen-year-old daughter, Nancy. She was the only one they didn't gag.

A frantic search of the house revealed Clutter had been telling the truth: there was no safe, no hidden fortune. They took what they could find, a few dollars from a drawer, a few more from a billfold, in all about $40.

They had agreed to leave no witnesses to their crime, so, still thinking what a pleasant guy he was, Smith cut the farmer's throat. As Clutter struggled in terror and agony, Smith shot him in the head. Next, he fatally shot the son.

The stunted little killer was disgusted with people who could not control their sexual urges. He felt good about talking Hickock out of raping Nancy. He felt good about it as she begged him to spare her life, and as he shot her dead. Then he went to kill her mother.

Despite their disappointing haul, the ex-cons laughed as they drove away. "It was like picking off targets in a shooting gallery," Smith said later.

Reading a newspaper report about the brutal Clutter murders, Truman Capote thought he might write a book about it, sticking to facts but shaping them in fictional form. He arrived at the small Kansas town of Holcomb in time for the Clutters' funeral.

The convict who had misled Hickock about the Clutter fortune heard a radio report offering $1,000 for information that would convict the murderers. His information made Hickock a suspect.

Even so, the pair might have escaped, except that they stole a Chevrolet and were picked up in Las Vegas for driving a hot car. Their fingerprints were on file. And the soles of their shoes matched the shoe marks left in their victims' blood. They were sent to Garden City, Kansas, for questioning.

After the police, Capote was one of the first to see the killers and to persuade them to talk with him.

Hickock spent much of his waking hours whistling—"You Must Have Been a Beautiful Baby" was one favorite—reading sports journals, paperback thrillers, and secretly shaping parts of an old toilet brush into a lethal weapon. He hoped to use it on one of his jailers in an escape bid. But the sheriff found it under Hickock's mattress. Hickock entertained the other prisoners with talk of his sexual prowess, with dirty jokes, and badinage. One con interrupted the entertainment by hissing "Killer!" as he walked past Hickock's cell and then dousing him with a bucketful of dirty water.

When the undersheriff's wife asked Smith if he'd like to see a priest, Smith said: "Priests and nuns have had their chance with me. I'm still wearing the scars to prove it."

Smith wrote to an old army buddy, Donald Cullivan—who had initiated the correspondence—that he knew his crime was unforgivable and that he expected to pay for it.

Cullivan got to have dinner with Smith in his cell, and then Smith said that people had hurt him all his life and maybe the Clutters— who never hurt him—were the ones who had to pay for it.

The two accused men sat through their trial chewing gum, and often looked bored. Psychiatrist Mitchell Jones believed Smith showed signs of severe mental illness and that through a brutalized childhood he had grown up "without direction, without love, and without . . . any fixed sense of moral values." Jones thought Smith was very nearly a paranoid schizophrenic. The psychiatrist also considered Hickock to have a severe character disorder and suspected brain damage.

But under Kansas State law, all Dr. Jones was able to say in court —through yes or no answers—was that both men knew right from wrong when they committed their crime.

Prosecutor Duane West told the all-male jury of the "strange, ferocious murders in which four of your fellow citizens were slaughtered like hogs in a pen, not out of vengeance or hatred, but for money. . . . And how cheaply their lives were bought, for forty dollars! Ten dollars a life."

Cullivan told me: "I talked quite a bit to Perry in the courtroom. Their security conditions were perhaps much less sophisticated than they seem to be these days, so I was able to sit right beside him during many of the court sessions. And he'd whisper some remark to me during the proceedings. So we had a chance to chat almost every day. We had quite a few chats about Truman Capote. I think Perry was fascinated by Truman, the difference between Truman's mannerisms and way of speaking versus a tremendous facility for getting to know you. Perry had quite a few comments about Truman. Some nice. Some not so nice.

"Some of the comments were about the book Truman had given Perry, *Breakfast at Tiffany's,* and he had written a comment in the flyleaf of it. On the inside cover it says: 'For Perry from Truman who wishes you well. March 1960.'

"And Perry had the feeling that that was a very cold sort of thing to write. He was a very effusive person himself in many respects. It wasn't the sort of thing he would have written. He expected more. I remember mentioning this to Truman later on, and I think it bothered Truman a little bit that Perry would interpret it this way. He thought it was a very natural sort of greeting. I remember passing Truman's comments back to Perry. And so, following these remarks, Perry then wrote, on the opposite cover, a little note of his own. It's dated Garden City, Kansas, March 28, 1960, and it's liberally sprinkled with quotation marks.

"It starts off 'Capote, you little bastard! I know you went south with the rest of my maps and books from Mexico. I really don't care, though. In fact I'm kinda glad you're the one that got 'em. You're a fool for paying what you did for them. You'd of been better off if you'd of left them there as I first wished. I hope my surprised expression "Is that all?" '—and this refers to the comment of Truman on the flyleaf—'reminds you of me. I wanted to call you a name at the time. I was getting angered. It's not too late yet—"You little Piss Pot!" Best of luck and wishes. Your friend Perry.' "

I asked Cullivan what Smith meant about Capote's having "got away with the maps."

"Perry was an incurable romantic and carried maps around with him. Every time there was any article on buried treasure or sunken galleons off the Mexican coast—these were things that reached Perry in a very large sense. So he collected such articles, picked up maps to give him guidance on how to go searching for treasure. In Capote's book *In Cold Blood,* he tells how one time Perry and Dick spent some time in Mexico—this is why Perry wanted to go there, to find this treasure. So the maps and books he's referring to, he carried around with him in a fairly substantial footlocker. Near the end, after they had to sell the car and were traveling light, he wrapped all the stuff up and stored it somewhere. He gave Truman enough information to find out where it was. And Truman went down and got it out of hock, so to speak."

What made you try to help Perry?
Cullivan: At that time, I was three years out of graduate school, struggling along. Here I am taking my vacation time, spending money out of my own pocket because the defense had no money at all. So, considering all the normal needs when you have small children . . . perhaps I was a better Christian in those days than I am now—unfortunately. [He laughs] I look

back at it as something, that at the time and in the particular framework I was in, my religious and social experience, and moral feelings about life, it was something I felt I had to do.

Did you feel that Perry had saved his soul?

Cullivan: This became less important to me after I got to know him. I felt that it was really not so much my business anymore, if it ever was. After I got to see him, I felt that perhaps I was doing more good for myself than I was for him. God knows if it was any help to Perry. My testimony was of little use in helping him. And he was not interested at all in saving his soul. He made it very clear that any of my comments on religion were not within his framework of thinking. Once he made this clear, I never again brought the subject up.

So you agree with Capote that Smith did all the killings? Some believe that Hickock killed two of the Clutters.

Cullivan: Perry told me that he killed all of them. I have no doubt he killed them, because he told it to me over a long period and had no reason to tell me.

Prosecutor Duane West had his doubts about Smith killing all four, because, as he explained to me:

"They made the mistake the first night of putting Smith and Hickock in the same cell block, so they hollered back and forth to each other and decided what to say about the killings. The only thing we went on was what Hickock first said."

I asked Cullivan if he thought Perry Smith's childhood and the battering he got from life were largely responsible for the almost conscienceless human being he became.

"From my own personal experience with him and discussions with him, it seemed as though he did have the feeling that he had had a raw deal in life and that his family background was such that he felt these were mitigating circumstances and since life had treated him badly, then life couldn't really complain if he kind of turned and snarled at it."

Prosecutor West told the court how Perry Smith had more than snarled. He spoke of Kenyon Clutter, a boy with his whole life before him, being tied helplessly in sight of his father's dying struggles, of Nancy hearing the fatal shots and knowing she was next, of begging for her life. "What agony! What unspeakable torture." And then, said West to the hushed court, there remains the ailing mother, bound and gagged and "having to listen as her husband, her beloved children died one by one . . . listen, until at last the killers, these defendants before you, entered her room, focused a flashlight in her eyes, and let the blast of a shotgun end the existence of an entire household. . . .

"So, gentleman," concluded the prosecutor to the jury, "what are you going to do? Give them the minimum? Send them back to the penitentiary and take the chance of their escaping or being paroled?

"The next time they go slaughtering, it may be *your* family. I say to you, some of our enormous crimes only happen because once upon a time a pack of chickenhearted jurors refused to do their duty."

The jury did its duty in forty minutes, finding the two men guilty of first-degree murder, for which the sentence was death.

Hickock said he wasn't against capital punishment: "Revenge is all it is, but what's wrong with revenge? It's very important. If I was kin to the Clutters, I couldn't rest in peace till the ones responsible had taken that ride on the Big Swing. I believe in hanging, just as long as I'm not the one being hanged."

On their arrival at Kansas State Penitentiary for Men in Lansing, both men were taken to death row, on the second story of the two-story prison. After climbing a circular staircase, they stripped and took showers. They were given close-cropped haircuts and handed denim uniforms and slippers.

They were locked in two of the seven-by-ten-feet cells always lit by an overhead light bulb. Each had a cot, toilet, and washbasin. Through the narrow, barred window covered by wire mesh, they could glimpse the dirt lot where other cons played baseball and, beyond, a door in a wall that led to the storage room that also held the gallows. It was known as the warehouse.

Their bunks were sweat-soaked; their cells, bug-infested hot-houses in summer and refrigerators in winter. Fellow inmates in cells below kept them awake at night—if the heat and bugs didn't —with screams and curses.

Meanwhile, their crime and punishment was being recorded by Capote, motivated by curiosity, empathy for outcasts, and the urge to write a unique book. Year after year, he stayed near them, often their only visitor.

Smith spent much of his time on death row painting portraits of himself and of inmates' kids. They loaned him photos of the youngsters and he used them as his models. He was quite talented.

But as the years dragged on, he couldn't take it anymore and went on a hunger strike. The warden had him force-fed with a tube through his nose. Even so, he dropped fifty pounds, until he was 115 pounds and in danger of dying.

Eventually, he was persuaded to accept a diet of orange juice and eggnog. This kept him alive for a date with the hangman.

I asked Capote if they had lied to him, or tried to mislead him, in the early stages of his contact with them.

> *Capote:* I suppose so, inasmuch as Perry Smith had always told me that Dick killed the two women. I mean, that's what he told me earlier on. Then, later, he told me the truth that he'd killed the whole family.
>
> Why did they cooperate with you?
>
> *Capote:* Loneliness. There they were, the first year I knew them—and I knew them almost six years—in this little town in Kansas. Nobody talked to them. Nobody would do anything for them. Nobody had heard of them. Nobody had even heard of their case. You know, there was nothing. I was this person who was there doing this thing and I was very attentive to them. I was drawing them out: out of boredom and loneliness, if nothing else. Who else was paying any attention to them? They were very grateful to me, although they were both very suspicious about what I was doing.
>
> Weren't psychiatrists showing any interest?
>
> *Capote:* There was only one psychiatrist, and I don't think he was interested in them until he found out that I was. And he only saw them once.
>
> You say they were suspicious of why you were doing it. Did you ever tell them why?
>
> *Capote:* Certainly. I told them the truth from the very beginning. But they couldn't understand. I mean, they didn't understand what I was doing. Well, why should they? None of my friends did, either. Nobody

could understand what it was I was doing. They couldn't understand what the end result of it was going to be. I was very, very friendly with them. In fact I was the only friend they had in the world.

How did you interview them?

Capote: I didn't interview them in any real sense of the word: It was just talking.

How did you persuade the townspeople to talk about such a tragic and depressing subject?

Capote: It wasn't a matter of my just going in there bang, bang, bang, like some ordinary reporter. I went to that town [Holcomb] and I moved into the town. I began to cultivate people, and on a very friendly basis, they'd introduce me to another person, who introduced me to another person. When I first lived there the case had only just happened. It was a couple of months before it was solved. Nobody had ever heard of Perry and Dick. I didn't know whether I'd have a book or not. I was experimenting with the whole thing. So I just cultivated people and by the time the case broke, I was on such friendly terms with Alvin Dewey, the detective in charge of the case, that I was the first person he told.

You did this very deliberately?

Capote: Of course. I don't ordinarily go to Sunday School, I can tell you that. That was the first time I ever went to Sunday School classes.

Did you enjoy it?

Capote: [laughs] Not much. I came to respect all those people, though.

Initially, to get them to talk, you gave Smith and Hickock $50 each. After they'd accepted the money, what was the gist of your talk to get them to agree to be interviewed or to talk with you?

Capote: It was very brief, because they had their lawyers in the room and were terribly uptight. They'd only just been caught. This was maybe the day after they were returned to Garden City. They wanted $50. They wouldn't speak to any other reporter and I think that the only reason that the lawyers were able to arrange it was the money. If it hadn't been for that, I would never have been able to have spoken, so the whole thing would never have started. I just wanted to establish contact with them on which I could build. From that point on I supplied them with magazines and writing paper and all the little things that nobody else would think of doing, and they became very dependent on me, you see.

Could you ever feel warmly toward Hickock, knowing that he delighted in killing dogs by hitting them with his car?

Capote: It isn't a question of feeling warmly, but when you get to know somebody as well as I got to know those two boys—I knew them better than they knew themselves—feelings don't enter, of like or dislike. It's some kind of extraordinary condition of knowledge takes place. I found the killing of dogs appalling and repulsive, of course. But there it is, it was part of his insensitivity and indifference to life in general.

Mrs. Meier is reported to have denied your account in *In Cold Blood* that she said she had seen worse men than Perry Smith; denied that she ever heard him cry; denied that he ever held her hand and said, "I'm embraced by shame." And although you say that Perry Smith killed all four victims, Duane West, the prosecuting attorney, and chief detective Alvin Dewey still believe that Dick Hickock killed the two women. Is this just a difference of opinion?

Capote: What I wrote in the book was true. It is absolutely accurate. Mrs. Meier, wife of the undersheriff at the jail, turned against me. And Duane West is one of my bitterest enemies. [In a 1984 interview with UPI, West called Capote's *In Cold Blood* "A bunch of garbage as far as I'm concerned."] And they were sort of working tooth and nail. As for Alvin Dewey, I don't know why he believed that. He always has, and I don't know why he does because it's absolutely untrue. And Mrs. Meier is just not telling the truth.

When their last appeal failed, someone suggested the two men should draw straws to see who was to die first. Smith objected.

"Let's go in alphabetical order," he said. In fact, that's the way it was arranged.

Hickock sent Capote a postcard saying he was quitting smoking because it was bad for his health.

Just before he was executed, Smith gave Capote a hundred-page farewell letter. I asked Capote what Smith had written.

> *Capote:* It was about . . . it was about . . . Oh my God, I really shouldn't go into this. It just upsets me so much anyway. [He sighed.] All the time they had been in prison, all those years, they were only allowed to have a certain amount of money. And I always gave them each whatever it was they were allowed to have. Anyway, the thing was, that in the letter there was a check for the money. Perry had never spent a penny of it and he was, you know, giving it back to me. I don't know why, but that upset me more than any other thing. It just tore me up. Because, I mean . . . oh God . . . it was touching, as though that all along . . . I can't go on with it. . . .

Capote vomited and cried for days before the execution date. The two condemned men remained calm. They settled for the same last dinner of shrimp, French fries, garlic bread, ice cream, and strawberries with whipped cream. Smith left most of his.

It was raining hard, soon after midnight on April 14, 1965, when six guards entered Hickock's cell and told him this was it. One handcuffed his wrists, another pinioned his arms to his sides with a leather harness. He was helpless now, just like his victims. Then the group clattered down the circular iron stairs to the ground floor.

Joined by the chaplain intoning prayers, the group crossed the dirt lot, through the rusty-hinged door in the wall, and into the "warehouse"—so named because of the piles of metal stored there for license plates and the litter of baseball equipment.

Hickock glanced at the waiting witnesses, Capote among them, and then at the thirteen wooden steps leading to the platform where two stark gallows waited. Beside them stood the cadaverous hangman, incongruously wearing a cowboy hat, as if en route to a rodeo.

The chaplain raised his voice to be heard above the pounding rain

—like drumbeats on the roof—and then gave way to the warden. He read aloud the order giving official blessing to kill Hickock.

In a brief last statement, Hickock said, "I hold no hard feelings. You people are sending me to a better world than this ever was." He suited the action to the word by shaking hands with two detectives and two prosecuting attorneys, saying each time, "Nice to see you," and smiling as if he meant it.

The hangman coughed, perhaps impatiently, but hadn't long to wait to earn his $600.

The warden asked, in a lowered voice, if there were any relatives of the Clutter family among the witnesses and was told there weren't.

Hickock climbed the thirteen steps, and the hangman fitted the noose around his neck, then covered his eyes with a black mask while the chaplain said, "Blessed is the name of the Lord."

Rain beating on the roof emphasized the few seconds of silence that followed.

Then the chaplain said, "May the Lord have mercy on your soul."

The warden opened the trapdoor and Hickock dropped.

To one reporter it seemed just like jumping off a diving board— but with a rope around your neck. He thought Hickock felt nothing.

Another reporter heard Hickock gasping for breath.

Capote, too, was gasping for breath as he watched.

It was twenty minutes before the doctor made his ritual report, "I pronounce this man dead."

A hearse carried the corpse off, and then Perry Smith appeared, chewing gum vigorously and appearing jaunty and playful. He grinned, and once winked at Alvin Dewey, the Kansas Bureau of Investigation detective who got him to confess.

Capote had already said good-bye to Smith, who kissed him on the cheek with an "Adios, amigo." Smith had warned Capote that if he lied about him he'd come back from the grave and kill him.

The warden then gave Smith a chance to make a last statement, and he said: "I think it's a hell of a thing to take a life in this manner. I don't believe in capital punishment, morally or legally. Maybe I have something to contribute. It would be meaningless to apologize for what I did. Even inappropriate. But I do apologize."

His last whispered words were to Capote: "I love you and I always have." Then he spat his gum into the chaplain's waiting hand and walked toward the hangman.

Smith, too, struggled at the end of the rope for about the same length of time as Hickock. Smith was officially dead at 1:19 A.M. It was still raining.

Capote vomited and cried for days, as he had done before the executions.

Sustained by drugs and alcohol, he spent nearly three years writing *In Cold Blood*, which was first published in the *New Yorker*. It was also made into a film.

Perry Smith, the brutal little killer, had told Capote that his unfulfilled dream was to create one work of art. His cooperation with Capote was what many critics called a classic—a work of art Smith wouldn't live to see.

Capote told me that the only thing that made him cry except for those executions was "anything to do with cruelty to animals. Or cruelty in any event. Deliberate cruelty is the only thing I can't forgive."

I asked him what scared him and he replied:

"I don't think I used to be scared of anything that I automatically saw, but after doing all the research for *In Cold Blood* (the two killers planned to hitchhike and kill their benefactors) and all the murderers that I interviewed, hundreds of them (later for a TV film about capital punishment), the very sight of a hitchhiker gives me a shiver.

"I've driven back and forth across the country several times, and the idea of running out of gas in one of those lonely Midwestern places creates a tremendous sense of anxiety in me. And I have a real, true dread of being on some isolated road, depending on the kindness of strangers." He chuckled and added, "As Blanche Dubois would say."

In 1984, a quarter of a century after the *In Cold Blood* murders, Duane West, the man who prosecuted the killers, was reported to have said: "Those two guys were scum and they needed to be executed. I would have gone up and pulled the lever on those guys." [See attorney Alan Dershowitz's comment on this and Duane West's response in the final section of the book.]

Harrison Smith, Hickock's defense attorney, said, "The best we defense attorneys could hope for was life in prison, as opposed to the end of the rope. But I'd say the executions were warranted in this particular case if they ever are warranted."

Truman Capote himself died on August 25, 1984, of liver disease and other complications.

While Hickock and Smith were in prison waiting to be hanged, they had kidded around with a bright young intellectual, Lee Andrews. He seemed to have had everything going for him until the day he calmly massacred his family.

12

Lee Andrews and
Harrison Crouse
The Brain and the Survivor

Everyone in his small Kansas community expected great things of Lee Andrews: a dazzling future. Watch out, Einstein, here comes Andrews! If you saw a big fellow with his head in a hardcover book, chances were that was Lee. And it paid off. He graduated from high school with one of the highest scores ever on the National Merit Exams. His IQ, it was said, hovered near the genius mark.

But with it all he was a sweet guy. Sure, he loved to hunt squirrels with his repeater rifle—he was only human—but otherwise he wouldn't take advantage of a punch-drunk fly.

And *so* sensitive. Mention a gory traffic accident or someone's personal internal-plumbing problem, and he'd change color, tremble like an aspen, and turn away. Or ask you to change the subject.

Lee never raised his voice in anger or his fists in earnest. He didn't smoke, drink, or take the Lord's name in vain.

Until he went to the University of Kansas, this paragon regularly attended the Grandview Baptist Church with his proud parents and pretty sister, Jenny, two years his senior. The minister, the Reverend V. C. Dameron, was his dad's best friend. They had been born and raised on adjoining farms. And Dameron knew the Andrews as a loving, caring, Christian family.

But after the eighteen-year-old sophomore studied zoology and biology at college, he began to sour on religion. Darwin convinced him that the Bible wasn't all it was cracked up to be. All those "begots" divinely inspired? Come off it! The Rev. Mr. Dameron could talk about the soul as if it were sitting in one of the pews, but let him try to demonstrate the soul in the zoology lab!

Competition, of course, was tougher at the university than at high school; still, Lee was an honor student and holding his own, especially in conservation and comparative anatomy.

Fellow students knew him as even-tempered and quiet, except when he let rip with the bassoon in the college band. He was something of a loner, but that was put down to his bulk. As a compulsive eater, Lee accumulated 260 pounds. Even at six foot plus that was pretty hefty.

He also had a secret he shared with nobody. Inside the fat, bespectacled, sensitive student with the rare IQ was a sleek psychopath with a fantasy high life of flashy cars and silk suits. And murder on his mind.

Burglars had twice broken into the Andrews home, and they gave Lee hope and a blueprint. He would emulate them and realize his get-rich-quick daydreams. But he was more ambitious than those two-bit housebreakers. He planned to steal the lot—the home, the $1,800 in his parents' joint bank account, and the 250 acres of farmland worth close to $50,000.

Of course, it would mean killing his parents and his sister. But everything had a price.

It was probably during sociology classes, the one course he was failing, when he speculated on the smartest way to get rid of his family.

At first he toyed with the idea of setting the home on fire while his parents and sister were sleeping. With the insurance on the house, he'd soon have ready cash. But there were too many uncertainties. Someone might survive. The insurance investigators might cotton on. He wanted a foolproof method.

Arsenic was briefly considered and rejected. The poison purchase would be too easily traced to him.

Finally, he decided to shoot them all with his repeater rifle, a cherished gift his parents had given him for Christmas. Scores of limp squirrels confirmed his prowess as a sharpshooter. Compared to the rodents, his family would be sitting ducks.

He decided to act during the Thanksgiving break of 1958. The whole family was at home. That afternoon, he'd helped his dad crack open walnuts for an after-dinner treat.

It began to snow. Glancing out of the window, Lee noticed the baker cautiously driving up to deliver bread for the weekend. That's when Lee made his first surprising mistake. He went out and waylaid the baker before he reached the house, saying they didn't need any bread for the weekend. Only he knew why. There'd be only one mouth left to feed—his. Here he was providing his future prosecutor with a witness to his premeditated murders.

Thanksgiving dinner on Friday, November 28, was his chance. Everyone was seated at the table. Now he simply needed an excuse to leave the table for a moment and return with his gun. But the food was too tempting. He'd wait until after dinner.

He watched his mother finish washing and drying the dishes and then join the others in the living room. He had them in a bunch once again. Lee went into his bedroom and loaded his .22 automatic rifle. As a backup, he loaded his German Luger revolver. It would be stupid to run out of ammo.

To mislead the cops, he opened a window, pushed out the screen, and pulled open wide his dresser drawers.

When Lee came out of his bedroom holding his rifle, and with the revolver stuffed in his belt, the trio all had their backs to him. Mom was adjusting the TV controls, his sister was watching her, and his dad was lost in the paper.

He fired first at his mother. Four bullets slammed her to the floor, one smashing into the center of her heart, killing her instantly.

As his startled sister turned to face him, he swung the rifle and aimed at her head. He fired three bullets; the fatal one struck the middle of her forehead, destroying her brain.

Perhaps two, three seconds had passed. Enough for his father to try to escape. He was on his feet when Lee fired again and again. But he wouldn't die. He staggered toward the kitchen and reached the door to the outside. Lee followed and squeezed the trigger. His father fell dead. A bullet under his left eye severed his brain stem. Just to make sure, Lee kept pumping bullets into the corpse. Seventeen in all.

Now to hide the evidence and fix his alibi.

Dressed in a parka, he drove his dad's new Chevrolet over slippery snow-smothered roads to the Kaw River. No one was around —he made sure of that—when he threw the murder weapons into the river. They sank in the mud; about a foot of it.

Lee drove on to the campus house in Lawrence, where he told his landlady he'd come to collect his typewriter to complete a weekend

English assignment. He needed her to back his alibi that at the time of the murders he'd been on the snowbound road. So he told her it had taken him twice as long to make the journey from home to campus as it had in fact.

He also spoke briefly with a student who roomed across the hall, mentioning the rotten weather.

To provide more alibi witnesses, he went to see the movie *Mardi Gras* at the Granada Theater, lingering in the foyer over the popcorn dispenser. He enjoyed the movie so much that he almost forgot his reason for being there.

Homeward bound, he stopped to buy gas, making sure the attendant noticed him. Another good witness to support his story that he was elsewhere during the slaughter.

He reached home shortly before one in the morning, dialed the telephone operator, and asked her to call the sheriff.

The police were remarkably quick. About ten minutes later two police cars with four policemen arrived, surprised to see all the house lights ablaze and Lee calmly sitting on a glider in the enclosed sunporch.

He was stroking the family's pet peke when Lieutenant Athey approached and asked, "What's the trouble?"

Lee pointed toward the door to the kitchen as if it were some minor problem.

Although the door was unlocked, the lieutenant couldn't open it. There seemed to be a heavy weight of some sort against the door. He called a patrolman to give him a hand. The two of them forced the door open and found that the obstacle was Lee's dead father. The trail of his blood led to the other two corpses.

After the shock of discovery so soon after Thanksgiving—which seemed to emphasize the horror—the police turned their attention on Lee.

He told them he suspected burglars had killed his family while he was away in Lawrence, picking up his typewriter, going to the movies—Yes, he remembered the name, *Mardi Gras,* and it was very entertaining—and even stopping to buy gas. Yes, he had the receipt.

Just a minute, Officer. He went into his bedroom and called them in after him. He pointed out the open window and pushed-out screen and all his dresser drawers wide open.

What puzzled, even astonished, the police was his manner. Not the slightest sign of grief. Lee seemed completely unaffected by the killings. Instead of being distraught, in shock, or in hysterics, he spoke with less emotion than many a citizen who's just been given a parking ticket.

"He was the most unconcerned murderer I ever met," said the lieutenant.

And his alibi was too plausible and elaborate to be true.

Furthermore, his attempt to make them think burglars had done it was ludicrous. He'd pulled open all the drawers but otherwise hadn't disturbed a thing. The papers and clothes were all neatly in place. Burglars, especially killers, are not tidy people.

He was quite surprised when told he was a suspect. He loved his family. He had never hurt anyone in his life. He knew nothing about the murders.

His only sign of emotion was during the fifteen-mile drive to the county jail, when the police told Lee that they intended to take his fingerprints and give him a lie-detector test. Then he choked up and shed a few tears; but obviously for himself, not for his family.

Lee was dry-eyed an hour later when, at his request, the Reverend V. C. Dameron arrived at the jail.

Told the news, Dameron was stunned and incredulous. Lee's dad was his best friend. The whole family had been devoted members of his church. How could Lee have killed people who admired and cherished him? It was the most baffling and heartbreaking experience of Dameron's life. If Lee really was guilty, then he must have gone berserk. No one in his right mind could have done it.

In the land of tornados, drought, and dustbowls, surprises are as expected as spectacular sunsets, but nothing—not even his religious training—had prepared the Reverend V.C. Dameron for this tragedy.

And even if Lee were innocent, his don't-give-a-damn attitude was so at odds with his Christian upbringing; it was even inhuman.

The police had failed to get Lee to confess or even to take a lie-detector test. As a close family friend and Lee's religious advisor, Dameron thought he might penetrate his air of callous indifference. He started a stilted conversation with Lee about college courses and Thanksgiving dinner and got only conventional replies.

Lee didn't admit it then, but he had not anticipated being a suspect. The police weren't as dumb as he had hoped and expected they'd be. He also found it difficult to explain to the minister why, if he was innocent, he balked at taking a lie-detector test.

Finally, Dameron broke his resistance by saying, "You want to help find who did this, don't you? You want to take a lie-detector test so these officers can look for the right person?"

Much of what the pair said is privileged information. Dameron's wife told me that he didn't even confide in her. But even before the lie-detector test, Lee said something that persuaded the pastor that he was the killer.

"Do you believe you can get away with this?" Dameron asked, trying not to sound outraged.

"Why not?" Lee replied. "Other prisoners have beaten the lie-detector, and I can too."

Not sure he'd heard a confession, Dameron said, "You didn't do it, did you?"

"Yes, I did." His tone was casual, matter-of-fact.

"Now you've confessed, don't you feel better?" Dameron asked.

"Frankly, no."

"Why did you commit the murders?"

Lee shrugged. "I don't know."

"Do you feel any remorse?"

"I don't feel anything—period."

Repeating his confession to detectives, he admitted money was his murder motive.

Asked by a reporter if his parents had ever denied him anything he wanted, he replied, "It wasn't a case that they wouldn't give me what I wanted. It was a case they couldn't. I would like to have had a sports car and I would like to have had a million dollars."

Despite his confession, Lee Andrews still expected to escape punishment. He made clear his new tactic when someone mentioned a psychiatric exam. He said he could fool the psychiatrists by claiming temporary insanity. With this in mind he needed to show the crime had not been premeditated. So he changed his tune: now he had killed them on the spur of the moment.

The following Tuesday, some five hundred people went to the funeral service for the murder victims, spilling over into two other chapels, into waiting rooms, and crushing into the lobby. Lee Andrews was not among them. He didn't want to go. Men and women wept as Dameron eulogized the Andrews family. "I am sure that come what may," he said, "there will be no thought of hatred or animosity in their hearts."

He spoke of their love of God, devotion to one another, and good works among the community, but not of how they died.

Though the pastor didn't mention the murder, it was never off his mind. How could a brilliant young man, a churchgoer until recently, his best buddy's only son, become a cold-blooded, remorseless killer? At first he assumed Lee had gone berserk. But berserk implies a sudden frenzy. Lee's crime had obviously been carefully thought out and executed, down to the moment he sat on the porch petting his dog. Dameron was baffled. He just didn't have an answer.

Even though it wasn't necessary to recover the murder weapons for a conviction, the police began to search for them. Lee admitted he'd thrown the guns into the river. They took him there in handcuffs, and he watched divers spend a fruitless afternoon looking through the mud. Asked what he thought of their efforts, he scoffed. "Ridiculous!" Part of the rifle was later recovered.

Awaiting trial, he was kept isolated from other prisoners and wasn't even allowed to join them in the recreation room. His exercise was a short walk twice a week to take a shower.

But over several months in the summer and fall of 1959, he had his chance to fool the psychiatrists. Then he left prison to travel to the Menninger Clinic at Topeka.

Psychiatrist Joseph Satten gave Lee Andrews hours of tests and spoke with him for many more hours. He concluded that Lee had a superiority complex, believing himself a superman to whom rules —obeyed only by fools—did not apply.

He lived in a world, according to Dr. Satten, in which only he mattered or even existed. In a word, a solipsist. Other people were no more important or meaningful to Lee Andrews than small animals.

In Andrews' one-man world he felt he had the right to satisfy all his urges, even to kill others. They, on the other hand, had no right to harm him.

The psychiatrist gathered that Lee resented his fourty-one-year-old mother for imposing what he felt were restrictions on him. He thought it would be pleasant if the restrictions weren't there, and reasoned that the only way for that to happen would be to get rid of her and the rest of the family.

He thought he was committing the perfect crime. The murders themselves meant no more to him than if he'd shot three squirrels.

At his trial Lee pleaded not guilty by reason of insanity.

A deliveryman recalled that to make a petty saving Lee had declined the usual weekend delivery of bread to the family on the afternoon of the murders; indicating his crimes had been premeditated.

Dr. Satten, the Menninger psychiatrist, testified that in his opinion Lee planned to murder his family and made attempts to avoid detection by establishing an alibi. Lee had been tripped up by his superiority complex. His "perfect crime" had been exposed by what Lee reluctantly admitted was "an error in judgment in not knowing enough about police matters."

Nevertheless, Dr. Satten diagnosed Lee as mentally ill; suffering from "simple schizophrenia"—an illness in which the person's thinking and emotions or feelings are separated. It was called "simple," the psychiatrist explained, because no hallucinations or delusions occurred.

Robert Bingham, the prosecutor, asked, "Didn't he tell you he wanted you to say he was insane?"

The psychiatrist replied that Lee told him that he wanted him to and that he didn't want him to: an answer that surely puzzled the judge and the all-male jury.

Although the psychiatrist conceded that Lee probably knew murder was a crime and knew the penalty for it, before and after the killings, Dr. Satten was not sure Lee had this knowledge during the moments he was pulling the trigger. This could have saved Lee from execution, because it implied he *may* have been insane at the time of the slaughter.

But three other psychiatrists appointed by Judge Willard Benson disagreed with Dr. Satten, although they had talked with Lee for a much shorter time, two hours in all. One, Dr. Richard Schneider, "felt that he [Lee] was able to distinguish right from wrong and adhere to the right on the day of the murders," as well as to understand the nature and quality of his acts.

"I got the impression," Dr. Schneider added, "that Andrews wanted to impress us as a very unusual person."

Defense attorney Buford Braly maintained that the state had not proved Lee Andrews sane when he killed.

"They want you," he told the jury, "to rid yourselves of this young man because they think that's the best way to get rid of him. If you believe this lad is evil, and was in possession of all his mental faculties when he shot his family, then hang him."

After ten days of talking it over, the jury took the defense attorney's advice. Lee Andrews was to be hanged.

Not by a flicker did Lee betray any emotion.

Judge Miller explained why simple schizophrenia wouldn't save Lee from the gallows.

He said, "The law recognizes no form of insanity, although the faculties may be disordered or deranged, which will furnish one immunity from punishment for an act declared to be criminal, so long as the person committing the acts has the capacity to know what he was doing and the power to know that this act was wrong."

Lee may well have been mad, but not mad enough to save his life.

What is strange is that no one before the incident suspected that there was *anything* wrong with him. Until then he was a regular guy, a bit pompous, a bit prudish, and a know-it-all; but that could apply to half the fellows at college.

Soon after the sentence of death, a reporter found Lee lying on his cell bunk. He was barefoot, cool and unconcerned, eating a chocolate sucker while reading *Field and Stream*.

He asked for Lee's reaction to the verdict.

"I didn't know what to expect."

"Did it shake you up?"

"Nope. After all, it's on the books. It's the law. It was in the court's instructions." He could have been a young attorney discussing a minor tort.

Moved to a death cell at Lansing, Lee Andrews became much more sociable than he had been at college, discussing philosophy and trading quips with other condemned men. His superior attitude and compulsion to mend their split infinitives, mixed metaphors, and double negatives got him soaked with the occasional bucket of slops. And it was hard, without a dictionary, to persuade anyone that his use of "oxymoron" was not a personal insult.

But he made up for it with his quick, sardonic wit and fanciful plans. Once free, he said, he intended to hire himself out as a hit man at $1,000 a corpse; in no time at all he'd get his million dollars.

When he felt he was losing status, he wrote a few stanzas of poetry and that put him on top again. No one ever guessed it was all cribbed from minor masters.

As his appeals failed and death approached, anyone who expected him to break down was surprised. He never lost his cool. He laughed at fellow inmates who believed in heaven and were terrified of hell. Superstition, he said. As for his immortal soul, he was sure there was no such thing and that when he died Lee Andrews would convert to dust and nothing more.

The compulsive eater couldn't satisfy his appetite on death-row rations, so he fed his fantasies by cutting out photos of food from magazines and stuck them in a scrapbook. That was his food for thought.

The compulsive eater had become a compulsive bookworm, often straining his weak eyes all through the night by the light of the bare bulb that was always lit, devouring twenty-odd books a week. When he exhausted the prison's stock, the chaplain sent out for more from the public library.

A week before his execution, an aunt and uncle came to visit. He maintained his stoic, unfeeling front, chatting about everything except the crimes and coming punishment.

He greeted the news that Governor John Anderson had denied him a last-minute stay of execution with a shrug.

On his last afternoon, at five, he began to demolish his final meal of two fried chickens, French fries, lettuce, and Coca-Cola, followed by strawberries and vanilla ice cream.

Four years of prison had slimmed him down by eighty pounds, so that with his over-six-foot frame, at 180 pounds he looked gaunt.

He spent the little time left—he was due to hang at midnight—talking with James Post, the Protestant chaplain.

It was a bone-chilling starlit night, on November 30, 1962, when they led twenty-two-year-old Lee Andrews from his cell and around the prison ball diamond to the old execution chamber.

He wore only a striped prison shirt and dark blue pants, so if he shivered it was probably from the cold. His wrists were crossed and tied in front of him. Hardly necessary. He had been a model prisoner; given no trouble. His escape attempts had all been hypothetical.

Four guards walked with him, and the chaplain, who instead of chatting was saying prayers Lee no longer had any time for. He remained aloof, showing no signs of fear at what awaited him.

He entered the brightly lit execution chamber. A large, unheated storeroom with high, rough limestone walls, it offered no refuge from the cold night air. Now he saw why they called it the warehouse: spare beds, lumber, and equipment were scattered all over the place.

At first sight of the gallows and the ten prison guards and ten visitors already there to see him die, he stopped, but just for a moment; then he resumed his walk toward them.

When he reached the foot of the gallows, the warden read the

Supreme Court Warrant to execute Lee and asked if he had anything to say.

He smiled slightly and replied, "No, I don't believe so," like a man declining a second cup of coffee.

Then he calmly climbed the thirteen steps to the platform. The chaplain removed Lee's dark-rimmed spectacles. In the distance, outside the prison walls, a dog began to bark incessantly.

The hangman put a black mask over Lee's eyes and a noose around his neck.

The chaplain said, "May the Lord have mercy on your soul." And the hangman sprang the trap.

There were two quick thuds: the trap opening and Lee's neck snapping.

But he wasn't dead and witnesses heard him gasping for breath.

He took longer than expected to die.

Several times the doctor put his stethoscope to Lee's heart and found it still beating.

The doctor began to show signs of suffering along with the dying man. Prisoners saw him emerge from the warehouse more than once to take gulps of the chilly air. Maybe the cold made his eyes glisten, but some thought the doctor was crying.

Not until nineteen minutes after Lee Andrews fell through the trap was it certain that he and his lunatic daydreams of becoming a wealthy hit man were dead.

Should he have been executed?

Under the Durham Rule used in some states, he might have been spared death and have been locked away for life in a hospital for the criminally insane. Durham states that a person is not criminally responsible for a crime that is a product of a mental disease. Lee Andrews seems clearly to fit in that category. But Kansas follows the more rigorous M'Naghten Rule which says that no matter what his mental capacity or mental illness, if he knew the difference between right and wrong at the time of the crime he is guilty and must pay the penalty.

Truman Capote, in discussing with me murderers he had known —as well as Smith and Hickock, he interviewed sixteen convicted murderers in three states—believed Lee Andrews could have escaped the hangman if the jury had given more consideration to the diagnosis of the Menninger Clinic psychiatrist.

Capote also thought that by persuading him to confess, Andrews' minister, Dameron, had helped to send him to the gallows.

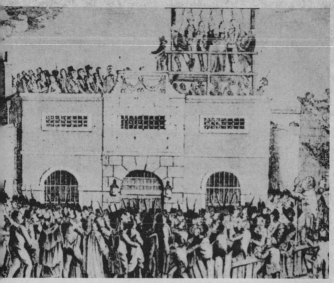

Seven at a time. Eager crowds watch multiple hangings in 18th century England. *(Author's collection)*

An artist's impression of America's first legal electrocution. Horrified witnesses see William Kemmler roasted alive rather than shocked to death at Auburn State Prison in 1890. *(Author's collection)*

One of the early victims of the electric chair in Ohio State Penitentiary. *(The American Prison Book: American Correctional Association)*

The executioner's assistants dismantle the guillotine after it had decapitated Dr. Marcel Petiot in Paris, France, on May 25, 1946. Small pools of his blood are still visible on the ground. *(Wide World)*

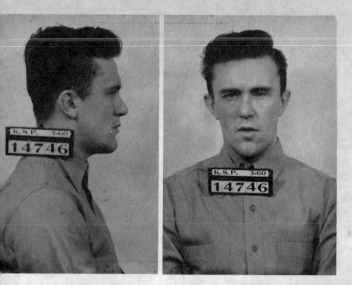

The *In Cold Blood* killers, Richard Hickock (above) and Perry Smith.
(Kansas Department of Corrections)

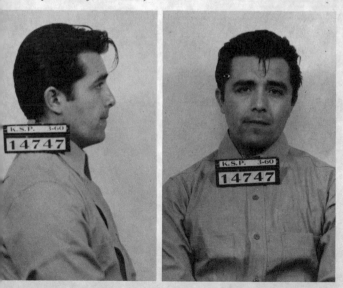

Dr. Hawley Crippen on trial for murder at the Old Bailey, London. *(Author's collection)*

Crippen's murdered wife, Belle, dreamed of fame and got it posthumously. *(Author's collection)*

Crippen's mistress, Ethel LeNeve, shows what she looked like in male attire. *(Author's collection)*

Bruno Richard Hauptmann, suspected of kidnapping the Lindbergh baby, in a police lineup in New York City, September 21, 1934. *(AP/Wide World)*

Sentenced to die in San Quentin's gas chamber, Barbara Graham is allowed a brief reunion with her 18-month-old son, Tommy. *(AP/Wide World)*

Newsmen view the chair, surrounded with sandbags, where Gary Gilmore sat when he was executed by firing squad at the Utah State Prison in 1977. *(AP/Wide World)*

Henri Desire Landru who was irresistible to scores of women in World War I Paris, with photographs of eight of the ten women he strangled. Charlie Chaplin wrote, directed and starred in a satirical film about him called *Monsieur Verdoux*. *(Author's collection)*

The many guises of Theodore R. Bundy, a former law student who is thought to have killed at least thirty women. *(AP/Wide World)*

A pro–capital punishment demonstrator smiles and waves as she drives by Florida's "death row" following the hearse containing the body of Ernest John Dobbert, Jr., who was executed in the electric chair in Florida State Prison in 1984. *(AP/Wide World)*

As they wait for the official word that child-killer Ernest John Dobbert, Jr., was dead, death penalty protesters pray outside Florida State Prison in 1984. *(AP/Wide World)*

Three years after Andrews was hanged, eighteen-year-old Harrison Crouse committed an identical crime—fatally shooting his parents and sister in their Wilmette, Illinois, home. Crouse admitted his guilt. But he wasn't executed. Instead, he was found mentally incompetent and was hospitalized.

After seven years Crouse was released as cured. He became a newspaper reporter, and in ten years rose to be president of a group of suburban newspapers. When a rival newspaper made his past public, Crouse—who had changed his name to Cochrane when he married in 1975—published his own account next day.

He said of the crime that it "wasn't something that happened—boom!—when I was eighteen. It was something that was going on from the time I was a child."

Cochrane explained that at eighteen he felt completely shut off emotionally. After the killings, doctors at Illinois state hospital had worked for years to restore his capacity to experience emotion.

"They gave me back my ability to feel love and hate and guilt and remorse," said Cochrane, who added that he is not uncomfortable discussing his past if others aren't.

Couldn't Lee Andrews have had a similar treatment and future?

13

Edward Eckwerth
No Mourners

Where do murderers come from? Lee Andrews and Harrison Crouse appeared to be products of comfortable, conventional homes where voices were rarely raised except in laughter. Yet both lived in a world we inhabit only in our dreams.

Not Edward Eckwerth. He lived in our world, all right. But in his, the laughter was fueled by alcohol and voices raucous and threatening. You might say he was programmed to kill from childhood.

Consider him at eight. He was hungry. His mother had been too drunk to think of feeding him. She sprawled on her bed making nauseating noises, and each time he approached to ask for food, cursed him. So he opened the refrigerator and helped himself.

She caught him at it and had convulsions. Grabbing him by the hair and dragging him whimpering to the gas stove, she lit a ring and held the boy's hand in the flames.

If anyone heard his screams, nobody came to his rescue.

That was only one of the frequent punishments the scrawny, half-starved boy endured at his mother's hands. There was no one around to defend him. His father had walked out long ago.

Men who called usually came and left in the dark. They shut themselves in his mother's bedroom, and when they left sometimes gave him a nickel and a pat on the head. Mostly, they were just strange voices in his mom's room.

His mother continued to neglect and mistreat him. Eventually, his cries bothered the neighbors, who called the police. They found the home a shambles, Edward's mother in a drunken stupor, and a scared, scarred, and undernourished boy.

He was taken from his mother, and for his own good—so they said—sent to the Children's Village in Dobbs Ferry, New York. He lived there for six years, until he was fifteen and considered tough enough to fend for himself.

Out in the world he looked for revenge.

One lesson he had learned from his mother was how to hate. The teachers at the Children's Village hadn't taught him to overcome his rage, but how to keep it hidden.

He shuddered at the memory of his mother, but she had moved without leaving a forwarding address, so he couldn't repay her for her many cruelties. And he was still too small and timid to take it out on others. Yet.

Eckwerth began to hit back by stealing small change, then cars. He was caught with one and sent to Elmira Reformatory. He didn't reform; he was just biding his time, waiting to get out and hit out again.

He tried marriage. He'd seen a lot of family comedies on TV. It seemed to work for a lot of people. It was 1953 and he was twenty-five when he tied the knot. Two years later he was father of a daughter and a respectable businessman, a coffee salesman with all of Yonkers as his territory.

One day when sales were slow, he sighted a woman alone on the sidewalk. She was walking slowly on crutches, her handbag hung awkwardly over her shoulder. Her broken leg was in a cast.

Her screams didn't bother him when he attacked her—he'd heard worse—and tore the handbag from her shoulder. He left her lying on the sidewalk crying in pain and fear and frustration.

But she remembered how he looked. Nice-looking guy, not very big; brown eyes. With his record he was one of the possibles brought in for a lineup and his victim picked him out—for sure.

A judge sentenced him to five-to-eight years in prison. But suddenly, a clergyman stood up in court and waved his hand. Could he say a few words? The judge told him to go ahead.

The clergyman told of Eckwerth's treatment as a boy, brutalized and half-starved by his mother; how in his youth he had known almost nothing but pain. It was a moving account that could have come unedited from a Charles Dickens novel. The courtroom spectators and officials who before had expressed by their looks nothing but contempt for Eckwerth now veered to pity, compassion.

So did the judge. Deeply impressed by the clergyman's pleas to give this slight young man with bulging eyes one more chance, the judge relented. He canceled the prison sentence and set Eckwerth free on probation.

Eckwerth was lucky to find his job was still open. He returned to work as a coffee salesman.

One customer on his route was twenty-four-year-old Rosemary Spezzo. A frail, diabetic parochial schoolteacher, she always had a few cheerful words for Eckwerth. They became friendly acquaintances; almost friends.

One warm evening when they stood outside her home talking for a while, he offered to take her for a ride and she accepted.

He drove to a wood north of Yonkers where they had sex. She was never able to say whether it was with her consent, because he battered her with a flashlight and a rock until he was sure she would never identify him.

After stealing her money, he went home to his wife and child.

He spent the night at home and next day set off for California, using the dead woman's money for gas and motel rooms.

On the way he picked up a young woman hitchhiker. Like Rosemary Spezzo she was a schoolteacher, and she too was impressed by Eckwerth's easy, friendly manner.

Witnesses confirmed that Eckwerth had delivered coffee to Rosemary Spezzo only a few hours before her murder. Police arrested him before he could harm the woman hitchhiker.

This time there was no clergyman to plead for him. So Eckwerth did it for himself. In a calm, soft voice, he told of his wretched childhood. It didn't work a second time. Neither judge nor jury was moved by his appeal for mercy.

His next stop was Sing Sing, to await death. It was a lonely wait. He was on death row for twenty-seven months, and his only visitors were his attorneys who delayed his execution six times. During that more than two years, no one else—neither wife, nor child, nor relative, nor friend—called to see him.

Two days before he was slated to die, his attorney asked Governor Rockefeller to commute the death sentence to life in prison, saying, "No public benefit would be served by putting the man to death."

The district attorney pointed out Eckwerth's long criminal record, the chances he had been given, the canceled prison sentence after he'd assaulted a woman on crutches. There was nothing in Eckwerth's background, he said, to justify clemency.

U.S. Supreme Court Justice Harlan granted a stay of execution for Eckwerth's attorney and the DA to argue further before Rockefeller.

He listened, and agreed with the DA that Eckwerth had been given all the chances he was going to get.

His execution date was rescheduled to May 23, 1959. The arguments had gained him an extra six weeks of life on death row.

An hour before midnight, a guard opened the oak door leading to the room with the electric chair. A Catholic priest walked ahead of Eckwerth, who wore a white shirt and neatly pressed, well-fitting gray denims. His footsteps were muffled by felt-soled slippers. He took short steps as if playing for time, perhaps still hoping for a stay of execution.

To a *New York Times* reporter there, Eckwerth looked "like a young boy following his priest to the altar."

The two-toned green death chamber was as brightly lit as a movie set, with six 200-watt lights. A dozen attentive witnesses waited in wooden churchlike pews; several seemed as nervous as the man about to die.

He barely glanced at the cast of characters facing him as he entered the room: guards, the warden, the executioner, and the prison doctor.

Now he was only a few feet from the electric chair and he looked scared. He seemed on the verge of tears. When he reached the chair he closed his eyes for a moment and took a deep breath.

He sat quickly, took another full breath, closed his eyes again. While his eyes were shut, he crossed his heart and murmured something—probably a prayer—though no one heard him.

He opened his eyes on the last people he would ever see—the twelve witnesses.

In a minute or two the well-rehearsed guards had everything ready.

When the phone didn't ring to announce a reprieve, the warden signaled to the executioner to kill Eckwerth.

As the two thousand volts hit him, Eckwerth strained forward and clenched his fists as if making a superhuman effort to break his bonds.

After it was clear the executioner had finished his work, the priest anointed the body, then walked out.

The doctor had pronounced Eckwerth dead at four minutes past eleven.

As witnesses were leaving, the guards began to unstrap the corpse.

Attendants waited nearby with a white stretcher to wheel the dead man, after a brief autopsy, to his grave.

There were no mourners.

14

Gary Gilmore
The Firing Squad on Request

Society is afloat in a sea of corruption, so say we all, but there is also the instinct to flush it out. So occasionally, as part of that impulse, we look for a scapegoat. We have a profound need to find a

> murderer we can execute. His deed may be less
> horrible than the crime of the man next to him on
> Death Row, but by the particular local
> circumstances of the law, he is the man we have
> chosen to execute.
>
> —NORMAN MAILER

Nobody was executed in the U.S. for ten years, between 1967 and the first two weeks of 1977, because the conscience-stricken Supreme Court stopped capital punishment after considering the *Furman* v. *Georgia* case—a possibly accidental killing—and evidence that proportionally more blacks than whites were executed.

When executions started again, it seemed appropriate that the first should not only be a white man but a man who was asking to be killed.

"He's gotta be crazy to want to do this," said a baffled fellow death-row inmate. "We spend years here trying to stay alive so we can get out, and he wants to be executed."

He was Gary Gilmore. In Utah he had the choice of a firing squad or the hangman. He asked to be shot.

Gilmore, born in the year of Pearl Harbor, grew up while Americans fought to save democracy and missed out on that war, Korea, and Vietnam. But he was no peacenik. Almost every step he took from boyhood he made a battleground strewn with smashed bones and bleeding bodies and, ultimately, three corpses—one of them his own.

As a sad-eyed youngster in Portland, Oregon, he hated his boozy, restless, ex–construction worker father, loved his mother, and doted on his younger brother. He lived on a diet of ice cream and Abbott and Costello movies, keeping trim by swimming at the Elks pool.

With his exceptional gift for drawing and painting and sharp way with words, he might have been another Norman Mailer in the making. But young Gilmore's American dream was not of literary fame. He was drawn to danger.

He woke one night from a nightmare of being beheaded, a dream he never forgot, and believed this decapitation may have been his fate in a previous incarnation.

In this life, he again risked the same fate by lingering last on the railroad tracks ahead of incoming trains.

His ambition was to be a gangster. At twelve he had already served his apprenticeship by stealing a few cars and burglarizing some fifty homes on his paper route. He was looking for guns in these houses, hoping to earn a place in a local gang by selling them firearms. But he didn't make it. At fourteen he was arrested for auto theft and sent to a reformatory in Woodburn, Oregon.

Eighteen months in that institution proved good training for a would-be gangster. He came out worse than he went in and wasted most of the rest of his short life behind bars, usually for violent crimes, once for statutory rape and once for shooting and wounding a friend.

In 1963, at twenty-two, he got fifteen years for robbery with violence, despite his plea of insanity and a futile suicide attempt by slashing his wrist with a broken light bulb.

He continued his violence in prison, leading a riot at Oregon State Penitentiary and permanently paralyzing a fellow inmate by smashing his skull with a hammer—for which, together with other infractions, he spent nine years in solitary, and the rest of his sentence at Marion, Illinois.

Warden Hoyt Cupp called Gilmore "a sick chicken" and the prison psychiatrist agreed, though in his lingo the prisoner was "a classic sociopath," that is, heartless, pitiless, without conscience, and concerned only with satisfying his immediate needs.

Out of prison on parole, thanks to the concern of a woman cousin, the sick chicken was a duck out of water, rarely able to suppress his rage or stifle his fears. Wine, painkillers, and six-packs of beer helped to fuel his furies.

While working as a shoe repairer with his Uncle Vern Damico, Gilmore met Nicole Barrett. She had three failed marriages behind her and was supporting her two children on welfare and food stamps. Despite her own burdens, she was a sucker for losers.

They had a brief, passionate relationship, until his drunken rage and fists scared her into hiding with her children.

He went looking for her, and found only her young sister, April, at the family home. April was recuperating from a two-year stay in a mental hospital with a severe mental illness. Gilmore persuaded her to join him in his car to continue his search for Nicole.

He drove to a gas station. While April waited in the car, Gilmore went inside carrying a stolen .22 pistol.

The gas station attendant, David Jensen, was a twenty-four-year-old law student with a wife and infant daughter.

With Gilmore's gun pointed at him, he handed over about $150 and then followed instructions to go into the toilet and kneel.

Gilmore killed him there with two bullets in his head.

He drove the terrorized April to a motel and tried to bed her. When she resisted, he slapped her around. She escaped and reached home early in the morning, crying hysterically to her mother, "I almost got my head blown off!"

Gilmore continued his hunt for Nicole. By next nightfall he still hadn't found her when he parked his car at a service station and walked two blocks to the Provo Motel.

The clerk on duty, Bennie Bushnell, twenty-five, was working nights to earn enough to go back to college. He was also married and had a young child.

Gilmore ordered him to lie on the floor, and killed him with a bullet in the head.

Trying to lose the murder weapon in bushes outside, he accidentally shot himself in the hand. Gilmore returned to his car, hiding his bleeding hand in his pocket, but an attendant saw blood and called the police.

Gilmore was soon back in prison and entertaining a cellmate named Gibbs with a hilarious account of the homicides. A laugh a line. "I walked in on Bennie Bushnell, and I said to that fat son of a bitch, 'Your money, son, *and* your life.' The morning after I killed Jensen, I called up the gas station and asked if they had any job openings.

"Guess what my last request will be if they decide to hang me?" Gilmore asked Gibbs. "A rubber rope!" He bounced up and down to make sure Gibbs got the gag.

He stood on his head for several minutes, advising Gibbs, who was losing his hair, that it helps the blood circulate in the scalp and stimulates growth.

Gibbs was a good straight man, even with questions. "What if they gas you?" he asked.

"Then my last request will be for laughing gas!"

"If they decide to shoot me," Gibbs said, now well into the swing of things, "my last request will be for a bulletproof vest!"

If he'd had a gun with him and had known who was helping him in this double act, Gilmore would surely have shot him then and there. Wouldn't have waited for him to kneel or lie on the floor. Because Gilmore was laughing and joking and giving advice on hair restoration to a police informer.

Nicole blamed herself for Gilmore's murder spree, saying if she hadn't run away it wouldn't have happened. He said she wasn't to blame: he killed to relieve his murderous rage and it didn't matter a damn who the victims were.

As a firm believer in reincarnation, he wondered if, after his death, his ghostly victims would confront him seeking revenge. The closest he came to expressing remorse was to concede that the men probably didn't deserve to die "at that point in their lives."

He described his life, in a letter to his mother, as lonely and frustrated. He admitted he had led an evil existence but wanted to stop being evil.

At his trial, prosecutor Noall Wooton proposed to end Gilmore's evil life by executing him.

This was the prosecuting attorney's view of Gary Gilmore:

> "He's been convicted on two prior occasions of rob-
> bery. He served time for those. And he's learned some-
> thing because of that time. Do you know what that is?
> He's going to kill his victims. Now that's smart. If you
> are going to make your living as a robber, that just
> makes sense, because a dead victim's not going to iden-
> tify you. . . . Now he's also got a history of escape, three
> times from some sort of reform school and once from
> the Oregon State Penitentiary. Now what does that tell
> you? If you people tell us to lock Gary Gilmore up for
> life, whatever that means, we can't guarantee it. We
> can't guarantee that he won't escape again. . . . If he's
> ever free again, nobody who comes into contact with
> him is going to be safe, if they happen to have something
> he happens to want. . . . Now he's got a history of
> violence in prison. Even the other prisoners, if you tell
> us to send him to prison, cannot be guaranteed safety
> from his behavior. . . . Rehabilitation is hopeless. He's
> a danger if he escapes, he's a danger if he doesn't. He's
> an extremely high escape risk. He's an extreme danger
> to anybody. Without even considering all these factors,

however, I submit to you this: for what he did to Bennie
Bushnell and the position that he's put Bushnell's wife
in, he has forfeited his right to live any longer and he
should be executed, and I recommend that to you."

A rebuttal from Snyder for the defense:

> Mr. Gilmore is the type of person that needs
> treatment more than he does to be killed. He needs,
> I think, to be punished for what he does, and the
> law provides for that by a term of imprisonment.
> And I don't think Mr. Wooton's fears about
> rehabilitation, or [fears] that if he [Gilmore] ever
> gets out again [he will commit more violent crimes]
> . . . are founded. Mr. Gilmore is thirty-five years old.
> He is going to be incarcerated, if you will, for life.
> And although I suppose at some point in the future
> after many years he may be eligible for parole, that's
> a long, long ways away. I think he deserves the same
> opportunity, really, that Bennie Bushnell should have
> had. And I think and would strongly recommend to
> the jury that you award Mr. Gilmore his life. I
> would point out to you that in order to impose the
> death penalty, it does require a unanimous vote of
> all twelve of you. If one of you does not vote to
> impose the death penalty, then the sentence will be
> life imprisonment.

The jury voted unanimously for death.

When lawyers appealed his death sentence, Gilmore insisted on
putting his case in person before the Utah Supreme Court. He spoke
to them with his wrists and ankles manacled. "I believe I was given
a fair trial," he began. "The sentence was proper and I am willing
to accept it with dignity, like a man. I hope it will be carried out
without delay."

Waiting for their decision, he wrote to a former cellmate, "If
they've got the nerve to sentence a man to die, they should have the
balls to carry it out."

Four of the five judges agreed to his request. He chose a firing
squad rather than being hanged—and was the thirty-eighth of forty-
four condemned Utah prisoners to make that choice.

But he planned to escape the firing squad with Nicole's help. They had agreed on a suicide pact.

Like all celebrities, Gilmore received fan mail, much of it from teenage girls who thought he was cool; and collected enough Bibles to stock a motel. He was amused by a man's offer to change places with him, and doubted if his would-be benefactor would be around if he took him up on it. Movie producers wanted to screen his life, authors to write it, agents to hawk it. He was a hot property. Reporters jostled for inside information and TV celebrities wanted one-on-one interviews.

Gilmore's priority was Nicole. He went on a hunger strike, throwing food-laden trays at guards until they capitulated and let him phone her.

Leading religious lights pontificated on whether Gilmore should be shot. Monsignor McDougall had a more enlightened view, stressing that most of today's theologians oppose the death penalty because they believe it works unfairly against the socially and economically disadvantaged. Anyone who disagreed would be hard-pressed to mention one millionaire murderer who ever occupied a death row cell.

It wasn't clear if the Reverend Jay Confair, a Presbyterian, was for or against. On one hand he pointed out that "an eye for an eye" had been replaced by belief in love and rehabilitation. On the other hand, he stressed that Gilmore wished to die and did not want to be rehabilitated. He compared him with a terminal hospital patient who wanted the plug pulled but was being kept alive by machines.

Cline Campbell, the Mormon chaplain at Utah State Prison where Gilmore was held, thought it was kinder to kill him than condemn him to a degrading life in prison during which a man becomes more debased and hateful. He believed Gilmore would be better off dead, because then he would enter the spirit world where he could await his resurrection. "In the spirit world," said Campbell with surprising assurance," one would be more likely to find assistance than degradation."

Though Gilmore might still be worried that his victims might be waiting there to ambush him. However, he seemed in sympathy with the Reverend Campbell's outlook, and told Nicole he was embracing death to become less evil, more worthy, and as a final parole from unbearable life in prison.

Before Nicole visited him in the death house, the matron gave her a skin search but missed the Seconals inside a child's balloon hidden in her vagina. Gilmore took them to fulfill his part of the suicide pact. Soon after, they were both found in comas.

Nicole was taken to a mental hospital and Gilmore to the prison hospital, and both were revived.

Fellow prisoners greeted the returning Gilmore like a hero, with cheers and whistles. Looking weak and worn, he scowled at reporters' questions and answered one with an obscene gesture.

The night before his execution a guard brought him a big last meal of steak, potatoes, bread, butter, peas, cherry pie, coffee, and milk. He left everything untouched except the coffee and milk.

He kissed his younger brother, Mikal, good-bye, saying, "See you in darkness," and as Mikal was leaving called out, "Give my love to mom and put on some weight. You're still too skinny."

Two men, one twenty and the other ninety, asked Gilmore if he'd restore their sight by donating his eyes to them. "Call the young guy's doctor and tell him you've got them," Gilmore told his attorney, and asked him to let the old man down lightly. He was leaving his pituitary gland to his niece, who needed it.

Between eight and nine P.M. a local station played two of his favorites, "Valley of Tears" and "Walking in the Footsteps of Your Mind." People phoned Utah from all over the world throughout the night, and a woman in Munich, Germany, called repeatedly protesting Gilmore's imminent death, saying her husband had died in a concentration camp and "America is no better."

Gilmore had brief phone conversations with his mother and with singer Johnny Cash, who had himself been a prison inmate after a drug conviction.

While death penalty protestors huddled outside in the cold and his lawyers made their last-minute appeals, cameramen, TV and print reporters sat in hundreds of cars and vans in the prison parking lot, keeping the engines running to avoid freezing.

Inside, in the visitors' room, Gary Gilmore was having a ball. His Uncle Vern had brought a Robin Hood hat for the occasion and Gilmore wore it as he danced with his cousin to country music.

Chaplains Meersham and Campbell joined the party, and then his lawyers arrived with crackers and soft drinks. When they exhausted those, the guards brought cookies, coffee, Tang, and Kool-Aid.

A guard watched the curious celebration from his bulletproof glass-windowed booth overlooking the visiting room, puzzled how Gilmore could get high on Kool-Aid and coffee.

Gilmore had intended to face death buoyed by his own fighting spirits and so had canceled his order of a six-pack of beer, after a relative had urged him not to get drunk but to "forget the beer and think of God." But now he was accepting all the help he was offered, including some kind of speed smuggled in from the prison pharmacy.

Both of his attorneys had brought suits to change into in the morning. They'd left them in a locker. He approached each in turn with an offer of $50,000 for the key to the locker. He said in their clothes he could make an easy getaway. He was in remarkable physical shape, and not even the barbwire on top of the wall would stop him, he said. They both turned him down; and he didn't push it.

To show how fit he was Gilmore sparred with Stanger, a former member of Brigham Young University boxing team, and gave him a hard time.

At about one A.M. he was told a federal judge had postponed his execution. "Jesus fucking goddam Christ!" he spluttered, and threatened to kill himself if they wouldn't shoot him. While the state appealed the ruling, the warden gave orders to proceed with the sunrise execution as planned.

After a late-night supper of eggs, hamburger, and potatoes, Gilmore broke his promise to himself to stay sober and accepted two small bottles of bourbon that Uncle Vern had smuggled in under his armpits. Gilmore slipped into a small adjoining room to drink them out of sight of the guard on duty.

Four minutes before the scheduled time of execution, the warden said, "I'm going ahead: the stay has been vacated."

When guards arrived to take him to the firing squad, Gilmore put his arm around one, saying, "You're sort of a black bastard, but I like you." He accepted manacles around his wrists but put up a vigorous fight when they tried to shackle his legs, yelling, "I'm not ready to go yet!" More guards hurried in and overpowered him.

As Gilmore emerged from the prison, those cars not running to keep the occupants from freezing started up with a massive roar.

"Gilmore is wearing white pants and a black T-shirt," wrote Sam Anson in *New Times* magazine. "With the appearance of Gilmore the reporters become a mob, a herd spooked into a stampede. Camera lights tilt crazily up in the air as their bearers struggle to shift them into position. Producers are shouting orders. Directly in front of the prison building, Geraldo Rivera, attired in black leather jacket and jeans and looking cool, the way only Geraldo Rivera can look cool, is shouting into his mike, 'Kill the Rona segment. Get rid of it. Give me air. You'll be able to hear the shots, I promise!' "

Followed by what looked like a gold-rush crowd, Gilmore was driven to an until now secret site, an abandoned prison cannery on the 1,000-acre prison grounds.

Scores of sickos had phoned the prison hoping to earn $175 apiece on the firing squad. The warden had screened out those with "unhealthy motives," choosing five state policemen. They were hidden from Gilmore by a green sailcloth screen, but he could hear them talking.

He was loosely strapped into an old office chair with piled sandbags at back and sides and an old mattress to absorb any ricocheting bullets.

About thirty invited spectators watched him, and he looked at them with a bemused smile. Nicole wasn't there. He had invited her but she was still in the mental hospital recovering from her suicide attempt.

He chatted casually with the warden and Father Meersham, who held a cup of water for Gilmore to sip. He grabbed his Uncle Damico's hand as if to have a last Indian-wrestling contest. "Still think you can beat me, eh?" said his uncle. Gilmore asked him to take care of Nicole.

What do you say to a man about to be killed? Gilmore made it easy for them. He offered to leave his hair to his balding lawyer Robert Moody, with a "You need it more than I do." He shook hands with Lawrence Schiller, who intended to write the book about the life and death of Gary Gilmore, eventually written by Norman Mailer with a lot of Schiller's material in it. "I don't know what I'm here for," said Schiller. "To help me escape," Gilmore quiped.

When another attorney, Ronald Stanger, gave him a tearful hug while saying, "I can't believe how brave you are. I really admire you," Gilmore smiled, paused for a moment, and replied, "Play it cool."

Five volunteer marksmen, all state policemen, loaded their rifles. One bullet was a blank, to ease the conscience of all, though as Norman Mailer pointed out, the kick of a rifle firing a live bullet gives the game away.

Asked for any last statement, Gilmore, now looking drained and gray, said, "Let's do it."

Father Meersham gave him the last rites. The doctor pinned a circular white target on his black T-shirt, directly over his heart. A guard placed a loose-fitting black corduroy hood over his head. The priest made the sign of the cross. Everyone but Gilmore stuck cotton in his ears. The screen concealing the firing squad was removed. No one seemed to be breathing.

The leader of the marksmen whispered a count of three, and four bullets tore through the target, T-shirt, and Gilmore's heart. Blood ran down his shirt onto his white pants and his multicolored tennis shoes.

Gilmore fell forward held by the loose strap. Father Meersham was crying as he cradled Gilmore's head. Blood dripped from the priest's fingers onto the floor.

No one doubted it when the doctor said Gilmore was dead.

The warden phoned one word: "Completed." And an officer announced the show was over.

Gilmore's Uncle Vern was weeping as he left. He said afterwards, "It was very upsetting to me, but he got his wish. He died, and he died with dignity."

His cousin Brenda Nicol, who had responded to the imprisoned Gilmore's plea for one more chance and had encouraged his parole, now said, "Nobody in their right mind should have released Gary."

On the day of Gilmore's execution, January 17, 1977, Utah's Attorney General Robert Hansen said: "Capital punishment is symbolic of society's determination to enforce all of its laws. No death can be elevating, and there is much sadness when anyone dies, but I am infinitely more sorrowful about the two victims' families than the fact that Mr. Gilmore is no longer alive."

A nationwide poll showed 71 percent were in favor of executing Gilmore. When asked if they would like to watch his execution on TV, 86 percent said "No."

His eyes gave sight to a young man; his ashes were scattered from a small plane over the Utah Valley.

15

Charlie Brooks and Carroll Edward Cole
Lethal Injection

Charlie Brooks and Woodie Lourdes bound and gagged a Fort Worth, Texas, auto mechanic. Then one of them killed him by shooting him in the head. Neither admitted firing the fatal shot and the police couldn't determine which was the killer.

Lourdes plea-bargained and got a forty-year sentence. He could be free on parole in less than seven years. Brooks got a death sentence. He became the first person in the U.S. executed by the new "humane" lethal injection.

Shortly after midnight in December 1982, forty-year-old Brooks was strapped to his deathbed, a mattress covered with a sheet, on wheels, in Huntsville State Prison.

Although Dr. Ralph Gray and a team of medical technicians helped to prepare Brooks for death, prison officials then took over.

As he lay on the mattress he turned his head to look at his girl friend. He held her gaze and said, "I love you." Those were his last words.

He was given a lethal dose of sodium thiopental through a vein in his arm, followed by Pavulon and potassium chloride. He was officially dead in seven minutes.

"It was very peaceful," said Sheriff Darrell White, who watched the execution.

Not so, reported witness Bruce Nicoles, a UPI reporter. "There were two series of apparently involuntary efforts to breathe and a churning of his stomach muscles."

A third view was expressed by a student who had demonstrated outside the prison that night. "It's too lenient," he complained. "They've got to go painfully."

Dr. Ward Casscells, founder of Physicians Against the Death Penalty, objected to physicians helping in the execution. "Doctors have no business killing people," he said.

Almost exactly three years after Brooks' death by lethal injection in Texas, the same method was used to kill Carroll Edward Cole in Nevada. Cole became the fiftieth person to be executed in the U.S. since the Supreme Court revived the death penalty in 1976. Brooks was black, Cole white.

Carroll Cole learned at his mother's knees a murderous hatred of women. He committed his first murder at eight and blamed his mother for his becoming a serial killer; he admitted to a psychiatrist that he had murdered thirty-five people, all but the first women.

He murdered all the women, he said, as revenge against his mother. She was a prostitute who beat him and forced him to accompany her on her sexual escapades, threatening to punish him if he revealed to his father her liaisons with other men.

When he was eight a playmate teased him about his feminine-sounding name, Carroll, and in a rage he drowned the youngster. The murder was ruled an accident.

"At that point," said Cole, "I was primed. I made a mental commitment to get even with my mother, and things built up and became an obsession."

After several teenage run-ins with the law, he grew up a violent alcoholic, preying on women he picked up in bars. The urge to kill them was almost irresistible, and in 1960 he stopped a police car in Richmond, California, and asked the driver to get him off the street.

He was taken to Napa State Hospital where he was diagnosed as emotionally unstable. A doctor sent him to group therapy sessions, but he "couldn't relate" and so sat mum throughout the meetings.

Cole was released after ninety days and drifted, working at odd jobs and drinking himself into uncontrollable rages.

He checked himself into several more mental facilities. They kept him for a short while, then let him go. He admitted wryly that he was "the person who slid through the cracks in the psychiatric system."

Cole was briefly married to an alcoholic prostitute. She died while he was in a Missouri prison for trying to kill an eleven-year-old girl.

Out on parole in 1970, he returned to California where, the

following year, he strangled three women in two months. Hardly a year went by without more killings: three women in Dallas; one in Casper, Wyoming; one in Oklahoma City; and two in Las Vegas.

In 1979 he strangled his second wife, Diana.

Cole was convicted of strangling the three Dallas women, and after being extradited to Nevada was found guilty of slaying two women there, for which he was sentenced to death by lethal injection.

Most of his murders, he said, were committed after heavy drinking bouts and sex with his victims. He added, "I don't think I ever had any gratification. I was just left empty."

He didn't expect people to condone his crimes but wanted them to understand what compelled him to kill—the urge to somehow hit back at his mother. And he proposed a hotline people could use who were tempted to commit these "unnecessary crimes."

Saying he'd messed his life up so badly he didn't want to go on living, Cole declined to appeal his execution set for December 6, 1985.

Three fellow death-row inmates tried to stop his execution by an appeal before the Supreme Court, contending that Cole was incompetent and insane. They feared, apparently, that his execution would make theirs more certain.

Cole countered with: "Why prolong a despicable person's life who acted as judge, jury, and executioner to the people he murdered, without regard to the victims? I think my crimes deserve the death penalty." He admitted to being scared at the prospect of dying, but "sort of at peace, too."

He expressed concern because of the number of serial killers roaming the country and continued to press for a hotline for people with an urge to kill.

Most of his final day he watched TV, listened to the radio, played cards with the guards, read mail, and wrote several letters. He was calm and in good spirits. He ate a last meal of fried jumbo shrimps, French fries, tossed salad with French dressing, clam chowder, and ice cream.

A few hours before he was to die, he said confession to the Catholic chaplain and received Communion.

At 1:44 in the morning, four guards escorted the 47-year-old, slight, dark-haired Cole into the converted gas chamber at Nevada State Prison, lit by two overhead bulbs.

Warden Harol T. Whitley wanted witnesses to see that the prisoner arrived alive and well and under his own steam. Cole was more than that—he was willing to help. As soon as he reached the padded table on which he was to die, he tried to climb on to it. But he was too short and someone lifted him.

Among the twenty-six people watching him through windows were his friends Mike and Judy Newton, who had decided to write Cole's life story—and were here to see how it ended.

After guards had secured him to the table with eight straps, he turned his head and looked at his two friends. He said, "I appreciate this. How's it going?" He smiled and they waved to him, both on the verge of tears.

Cole's ear began to itch. "Please scratch my ear," he asked a guard. The man did. "Thanks," Cole said, looking the guard in the eye and disconcerting him for a moment with this human contact.

Outside in the below-freezing weather, about a dozen shivering opponents of the death penalty led by Rabbi Myra Soifer stood in the prison parking lot holding lit candles and praying for Cole, his victims, and his executioners. "We cannot ignore the departure of a life," said the rabbi.

Inside the prison one of the execution team lowered shades to hide Cole from witnesses while they prepared to kill him.

Three of the prison staff inserted intravenous needles in both arms and attached electrocardiograph leads to his chest. Just in case they couldn't find an arm vein, they were ready to insert a needle in a blood vessel in his leg—but this wasn't necessary.

A doctor stood by to help if something went wrong, but he would not take part in the actual execution.

At 2:05 A.M. the shades were raised.

Again, Cole turned his head to his writer friends and said, "It's all right. It's okay." Then he looked up into the lights.

A harmless intravenous solution was circulating through Cole's veins to keep them open.

Two executioners waited in an alcove. They each had a syringe containing a different poison which they were ready to inject through a tube attached to the needles in Cole's arms.

Nevada Prisons Director George Sumner, former warden of Sing

Sing, was supervising the execution. He told the warden to proceed.

The doctor surprised him by saying, "Wait a minute. There's no turning back once you start."

"I know," Sumner replied.

In turn, the executioners released the deadly chemicals that would destroy Cole's brain and paralyze his heart and lungs. He was to be the eighteenth and last man executed in the U.S. in 1985.

Cole closed his eyes as if the lights were too bright, coughed slightly, and looked like a man going to sleep.

Suddenly his body jerked convulsively. Once, twice, three times . . . and was still.

His heartbeats on the electrocardiograph machine read 00.

It had taken three minutes to kill him, though others estimated from twenty to ninety seconds.

"The first poison killed him in twenty seconds," said Sumner, "although it was not apparent to the witnesses."

One executioner said to the other, "What a humane way." The other agreed.

Las Vegas Chief Deputy DA Dan Seaton, who had prosecuted Cole, was also there to see him die. He said afterwards, "It was certainly a more merciful way to die than he allowed his victims. I feel good about this. It shows the system works."

Although Nevada Prisons Director Sumner judged lethal injection to be the most humane means of executing a murderer, his enthusiasm was qualified. "I believe the death penalty is a deterrent," he said. "But justice must be swift if it is to have any meaning." Cole had made it much swifter than usual by refusing to let lawyers appeal his case.

Even Cole's friends and future biographers thought that Cole got what he deserved as well as what he wanted. "We'll miss talking to him and knowing him," said Judy Newton. "At least we'll know he is away from his personal hell."

Cole's brain was removed an hour after his death. He had donated it to doctors to examine for signs of damage that might account for his frenzied killings.

But how could they expect to find in a brain destroyed by poisons the source of his rage against a mother he thought he was repaying for her cruelty each time he strangled a woman?

16

Bruno Richard Hauptmann
Trial by Fraud and Fury

"You think when I die it will be like a book I
close. But the book, it will never close."

—HAUPTMANN

"While I have no sympathy for Hauptmann, I
can't help wondering what would happen if it
were an innocent person on trial."

—ELEANOR ROOSEVELT

The kidnap-killing of the son of Charles Lindbergh, America's
great flying hero, was known as the crime of the century. It still is
fifty years later. Almost every writer researching the event concludes that it was a double tragedy: because they believe Bruno
Richard Hauptmann, the man executed for the crime, was probably
innocent.* Evidence recently come to light makes this even more
likely.

Hauptmann was offered a chance to escape the electric chair but
it had a catch-22 clause. He had to confess to the kidnapping and
describe how he'd pulled it off and killed the child. As he apparently
had no knowledge of the crime, his innocence was the death of him.

So—based on the evidence in this chapter—the baby's murder
was followed by Hauptmann's.**

As the first man to fly the Atlantic solo, Lindbergh was idolized,

*Especially Anthony Scaduto in *Scapegoat,* Putnam, 1976; and Ludovic
Kennedy in *The Airman and the Carpenter,* Viking Press, 1985.
**I am assuming the child was murdered, though he may have died
accidentally in a fall from the kidnap ladder.

and the kidnapping of his nineteen-month-old son, Charles, Jr., traumatized the nation. Psychics, amateur detectives, con men, and deeply concerned citizens volunteered to help search for the missing boy.

The distraught parents were willing to try almost anything. The kidnapper or kidnappers had left a ransom note and followed up with thirteen more. When Dr. John Condon, a retired Bronx teacher, offered to act as go-between, Lindbergh accepted.

Following the extortionist's instructions, Condon met him after dark in a Bronx cemetery while Lindbergh waited in a car outside. Condon handed over the $50,000 ransom and received a note from the man—who called himself John. It said the boy was on a boat off Martha's Vineyard, Massachusetts.

Lindbergh hurried there, but couldn't find the boat.

Six weeks after the boy's disappearance, on May 12, 1932, a truck driver discovered a child's badly decomposed body in a shallow grave nearly five miles from the Lindberghs' home. It was identified by the child's nursemaid, Betty Gow, and Charles Lindbergh. Chemists analyzed hairs from the corpse and souvenirs of the baby's hair kept by the child's grandmother, and found them identical.* Dr. Charles Mitchell performed an autopsy and diagnosed the cause of death as a fractured skull caused by external violence.

Millions mourned with the bereaved parents and eagerly awaited the killer's arrest.

Police reported the serial numbers on the ransom money, $35,000 of it gold certificates—and from time to time people turned it in, but none was traced to the extortionist.

During the next two years, although over a hundred people confessed to the crime they were all released as would-be suicides, mentally deranged, or publicity mad. The police were stumped, and still pressured by press and public to find the killer.

Two and a half years after the kidnapping, a filling station owner was given a $10 gold certificate by a customer. Gold certificates were strictly illegal—the government had withdrawn them from circulation—but banks were still accepting them. To be on the safe side, the man wrote the license number of his customer's car on the bill.

*Though Dr. VanIngen who had delivered the child said that if offered a million dollars, he could not identify the body.

It was one of the kidnap certificates and led police to the car's owner, a Bronx carpenter, Bruno Richard Hauptmann.

They found a $20 ransom bill in his wallet and $13,760 of the ransom money in his garage. The money, he explained, had been left in his care by friend and business partner Isidor Fisch, who had returned to Germany and recently died there of consumption. The unemployed carpenter said he had started to spend the money after learning of his friend's death, and then only up to an amount Fisch owed him.

At Hauptmann's murder trial in Flemington, New Jersey, an expert testified that a rail of the kidnap ladder had been made from a piece of the floor in Hauptmann's attic; seven experts agreed that his handwriting and the writing on the fourteen ransom notes were identical. Dr. Condon identified him as the man to whom he had given the $50,000 ransom money in St. Raymond's Cemetery; and Charles Lindbergh, who sat in a car outside the cemetery and briefly heard the extortionist calling out, said the voice was Hauptmann's.

History's most ballyhooed trial brought out the weirdos and the venture capitalists; not always easy to tell apart. One man did a brisk business in clippings of his own hair sold at $5 a clip, with a written guarantee that they came from the baby Lindbergh. Two big-city whores arrived, and outdid the local competition by promising a unique experience. One had a print or tattoo of Lindbergh's plane flying over Manhattan on a special part of her anatomy. The other had the same plane flying over the Eiffel Tower in a similar spot. Adventurous customers could take a round-trip ride from Manhattan to Paris, or vice versa, at a special no-frills price. The more serious-minded could buy miniature copies of the kidnap ladder. If the trial had lasted any longer, no doubt miniature electric chairs would have flooded the market.

Hauptmann was no angel. He was an illegal immigrant from Germany where he had a criminal record for housebreaking and armed robbery, which cost him four years in prison. He had climbed a ladder to rob the home of the mayor of a small German town. And he and a partner in crime had stolen food from women at gunpoint.

He had a clean record in America, but his friend and business partner—they shared profits from Hauptmann's investments and Fisch's fur trading—was discovered after his death to have been a shady character who dealt in hot money.

Hauptmann maintained a calm, almost detached manner during his trial, showing few signs of fear and rarely losing control under the relentless pressure and, at times, bullying tactics of the prosecuting attorney, New Jersey's Attorney General David Wilentz.

But the warden, Harry McCrae, knew that after some days in court Hauptmann wept in his cell. Afraid he might attempt suicide, McCrae provided paper spoons, forks, and plates. After Hauptmann had used them for his meals, the warden gave them to friends as mementoes.

Every day of the trial a mob of thousands gathered outside the court chanting "Kill Hauptmann! Kill the German!" The jury didn't need any encouragement. Expert evidence seemed overwhelmingly against him. He was found guilty of the kidnap-murder and sentenced to die.

Even prisoners at Trenton State Prison jeered and hissed at him when he was taken to a ground-floor death-row cell next to the death chamber. He was alone there. Several other death-row inmates were in cells on the floor above. Guards removed his shoelaces and belt, just in case he thought of hanging himself—though they left him his tie. As they were leaving, he asked for a Bible.

Two appeals delayed his date with death, but when his attorneys told him there was no hope for a third, he broke down.

A New York newspaper tried to tempt him with $75,000 to go to his widow and baby son if he would admit to the crime for which now he was certain to die. He refused the offer.

At the last moment the governor of New Jersey, Harold Hoffman, offered to save his life by arranging to commute the death sentence to life in prison, if only Hauptmann would admit to the crime. He said he had nothing to confess. He was innocent. He knew nothing of the crime.

A crowd of some two thousand gathered outside the prison despite the raw, damp evening of April 3, 1936, to be in at the kill. In case things got out of hand, 250 policemen and state troopers formed a barricade. Hauptmann had his supporters, as well as those who screamed for his death; and a fire truck was parked outside the prison's main gate with water hoses ready to cool off hotheads. Overhead, guards with bayoneted rifles patrolled the prison's floodlit roof to frustrate any free-Hauptmann mob, or lynch-Hauptmann mob, that might spring from frenzied elements in the restless crowd.

Several men had been electrocuted during the almost fourteen months Hauptmann waited for his turn. Each time, he heard the eerie noise, like a strange howling wind, as executioner Robert Elliott started the dynamos—the sound of death on command. Hauptmann could hear the dynamos being tested now for him, while his head was shaved and he changed into denim pants, white shirt, and felt slippers.

Outside, newsreel cameramen filmed the anything-for-a-laugh crowd. Each time a flashbulb went off, they whooped and cheered, almost drowning out the bells tolling in nearby churches to announce evening services.

Witnesses entering the prison to observe Hauptmann's execution were searched by guards looking for hidden cameras. Anyone who objected wasn't allowed in. Those who got in were not to say a word once Hauptmann appeared. The warden threatened to throw out anybody who broke the no-speaking rule. He wanted absolute silence to hear what he hoped would be a last-minute confession.

The silent witnesses sitting in ten rows of chairs watched two clergymen enter the brightly lit death chamber followed by Hauptmann. He walked briskly to the chair, his pale face set in neutral. He said nothing. His only movement was to shake his head as if the leather cap was uncomfortable. Then a guard put a mask over Hauptmann's eyes.

Executioner Elliott stood at a control panel several feet behind the electric chair. He turned a wheel and it lit up bulbs on the panel. Hauptmann's lips were forced open like a test pilot's at high speed. His hands grabbed the chair arms fiercely and turned blood-red. Three times the dynamos accelerated to a banshee-like howl, slowed to a drone and then silence; silence broken only by a clergyman saying, "I believe in one God the Father Almighty, maker of heaven and earth, and of all things visible and invisible . . ." The other clergyman bowed his head, apparently shocked speechless.

No fewer than six doctors put stethoscopes to the corpse before one announced the obvious. A guard held up a clock. It was 8:47 P.M.—an efficient three-minute execution.

Though Hauptmann hadn't spoken, he had left a statement in German. Translated, it read: "I am glad that my life in a world which has not understood me has ended. Soon I will be at home with the Lord, as I am dying an innocent man. Should, however, my death serve the purpose of abolishing capital punishment—such punishment being arrived at only by circumstantial evidence—I feel that my death has not been in vain. I am at peace with God. I repeat, I protest my innocence of the crime for which I was convicted. However, I die with no malice or hatred in my heart. The love of Christ has filled my soul and I am happy in Him."

Suspecting Hauptmann had been framed, New Jersey Governor Harold Hoffman did something unique in U.S. history—he borrowed police records of the case and launched his own criminal investigation independent of the New Jersey State Police and the FBI. They clearly indicate that the state may have electrocuted the wrong man. Hoffman stored all this evidence in the garage of his South Amboy home. After his death it remained there, apparently unknown to everyone until recently when it was accidentally discovered and returned to the New Jersey State Police.

Attorney Robert R. Bryan of San Francisco, California, was allowed to obtain thousands of pages of this material, which include FBI reports on the crime of the century. Bryan was astounded at what he discovered.

For example:

> Evidence in Hauptmann's favor was suppressed by
> the prosecution, defense witnesses were intimidated,
> an almost-blind prosecution witness positively
> identified Hauptmann as being at the scene of the
> crime.

Bryan also discovered the following:

THIRD DEGREE

After Hauptmann's arrest, New Jersey State Police handcuffed him to a chair and beat him until he fell with the chair to the floor. One cop showed him a hammer. Someone doused the lights and hit him with the hammer on his shoulders, back of his head, and arm. Several men kicked him in the groin and stomach, yelling, "Where is the money?" "Where is the baby?" "We'll knock your brains out."

This, of course, is Hauptmann's account of his interrogation, but Dr. Thurston Dexter examined him and concluded: "He had been subjected to a severe beating, all or mostly with blunt instruments."

Although the prosecutor, David Wilentz, knew of the beatings, he concealed them from the jury and the defense attorneys.

An FBI memo reports an attempt by Bronx DA Samuel Foley to intimidate Hauptmann, saying:

> You have killed one baby and now you're going to ruin the life of another baby, your own child. I can see where the first baby you killed might have met his death through an accident. You might not have intended to kill it. Maybe there is some excuse for that. Now you are deliberately, in cold blood, fully aware of what you are doing, wrecking and ruining the life of your own child. Your wife is being held in the Women's Jail with a lot of prostitutes. She is separated from the baby. It has no one who loves it to take care of it. It may die of undernourishment. Your wife is hysterical. She will probably become an imbecile over the shock of this thing. [None of the account of Hauptmann's wife and child was true.] If you have any speck of manhood left in you, you will come clean on this and do one manly thing in your life. But I can see you're just an animal. You don't care what happens to your wife and baby. You don't care about anything. You're the lowest human being I ever had before me in this room and I've had a lot of bad ones. Why, the other night down at the police department, a mob were trying to get at your poor wife to hang her. That poor woman has to put up with so much from you.

The FBI memo concludes that "while Mr. Foley was making the latter few remarks, Hauptmann was shedding tears and appeared to be greatly shaken, continually crying out 'Stop, Stop, I didn't do it. I told you everything. I don't know any more.'"

IDENTIFICATION

Dr. John Condon, the eccentric, waffling go-between who handed the $50,000 ransom to the extortionist "John," stated that the man had a growth on his right thumb. Hauptmann never had such a growth. Condon said John was sick and coughing during the ransom negotiations. Hauptmann was extremely healthy at that time. Condon identified various individuals other than Hauptmann as the man he met in the cemetery, including Ernest Brinkert, believed to be an acquaintance of Violet Sharpe, the Lindberghs' servant who committed suicide just before she was about to be interrogated.

OTHER SUSPECTS

Violet Sharpe was still a suspect at the time of Hauptmann's arrest. Press reports and police witnesses for the prosecution at Hauptmann's trial misrepresented that she had always been above suspicion. The prosecution also concealed information supporting the possibility that the kidnapping was an inside job committed by some of the Lindbergh's staff.

EYEWITNESSES

Condon originally described the extortionist as eleven years younger, six inches shorter, forty-five pounds lighter, and having a much slimmer build than Hauptmann. This information was suppressed at the trial.

Amandus Hockmuth testified for the prosecution that he saw Hauptmann in a car near the Lindbergh home the night of the kidnapping. Hockmuth was later discovered to have such rotten eyesight that he was the one who described a filing cabinet with flowers on top as "a woman wearing a hat."

THE KIDNAP LADDER

Wood expert Arthur Koehler testified for the prosecution that a wooden side rail in the kidnap ladder came from a floor board in Hauptmann's attic. Yet several detailed searches by the FBI and thirty-seven policemen had failed to find anything evidential in the attic. It was only after the New Jersey police rented the Hauptmann home and kept all other observers out that they said they found a piece missing from a floorboard that had obviously been used as part of the ladder. The New Jersey police had every opportunity to saw off the piece of wood themselves and substitute it for a rung of the ladder. And from the way other phony evidence was collected, this seems not unlikely. Even the FBI was suspicious.

This FBI memo of May 26, 1936, was written almost two months after Hauptmann's execution:

> From examination of the information in the Bureau files concerning Arthur Koehler that the testimony given by him in the capacity of a Forestry Service U.S. Government wood expert relative to the wood used by the kidnapper to the effect that he traced the wood from a mill in South Carolina to the National Company, Bronx, N.Y., is not consistent with the evidence. The identification of the wood in the ladder, resulting in the opinion that wood in the attic of Hauptmann's residence was identical with that of the ladder, was developed subsequent to the withdrawal of the Bureau from an active part in the investigation and occurred *after* the New Jersey police had rented the Hauptmann residence. [The implication here is that what the FBI couldn't find, the New Jersey police may have faked.]

Also, the prosecution suppressed the fact that the supposed kidnap ladder would not support Hauptmann's weight.

SHOE PRINTS

Not only did the plaster cast of a shoe print believed to be that of John the extortionist not match Hauptmann's shoe print, neither did a shoe print believed to have been left by the kidnap-killer on the grounds of the Lindbergh home. This information favorable to Hauptmann was suppressed by the prosecution.

FINGERPRINTS

A fingerprint expert, Erastus Mead Hudson, M.D., found over five hundred fingerprints on the ladder believed used to kidnap Charles Lindbergh, Jr. from his second-floor bedroom. Not one of the fingerprints was Hauptmann's.

The FBI found fingerprints on various ransom notes and envelopes and identified them as made by "John" the extortionist and believed kidnap-killer. None matched with Hauptmann's prints. Yet, at the trial, Frank A. Kelly, New Jersey State Police fingerprint expert, testified that no fingerprints of any kind were found on the ransom notes.

HANDWRITING

Before the trial, experts said Hauptmann could not possibly have written the ransom notes. In court, the same experts said that writing on several of the ransom notes was unquestionably his.

HAUPTMANN'S DEFENSE

FBI agent E. A. Tamm sent this memo to his chief, J. Edgar Hoover: "In a discussion with Special Agent T. H. Sisk, on January 21, 1936, he advised me that during the course of the trial of Hauptmann at Flemington, New Jersey, he had approached defense counsel Edward Reilly and in a joking manner asked Reilly, 'why he didn't give up?' Reilly stated, 'he knew Hauptmann was guilty, didn't like him and was anxious to see him get the chair.' "

Reilly, Hauptmann's chief counsel, was charging $25,000 for his work. He was an alcoholic and suffering from syphilis. The drink and illness were very likely affecting his brain during the trial.

Reilly's associate, Lloyd Fisher, convinced of Hauptmann's innocence, was kept in a subordinate role by Reilly.

RANSOM MONEY

Hauptmann's explanation for possessing some $14,000 of the $50,000 ransom money was that it had been left in his care by a friend and business partner Isidor Fisch, who had died in Germany. Hauptmann said that Fisch had brought the money to him in a shoebox, and he only later discovered that it contained money. Another of Hauptmann's friends, Hans Kloppenburg, had seen Fisch deliver the shoebox to Hauptmann. But in a private meeting, prosecutor Wilentz threatened to implicate Kloppenburg in the kidnap-murder if he so testified. Intimidated, the friend did testify but cautiously avoided using the word *shoebox*.

Armed with this material, attorney Robert R. Bryan and Hauptmann's widow, Anna, are trying to clear Hauptmann's name. I asked Bryan how he got involved:*

Bryan: In late 1972 a Kenneth W. Kerwin contacted me, saying he had evidence indicating he might be the Lindbergh son who was kidnapped and supposedly murdered in 1932. He had read of our success in a number of murder cases using creative and unusual techniques. I contacted a former aide to Harold Hoffman, the New Jersey governor who was in office at the time of Hauptmann's execution in 1936. He knew of Kenneth Kerwin and said he was legitimate and he did not know, of course, whether he was the Lindbergh son, but he felt there was certainly a possibility and I should investigate it. He felt Kerwin was not a publicity-seeker or money-seeker but rather really wanted to know his true identity. So that's how I initially got involved. Three years later, in 1976, I had interviewed hundreds of people and conducted a wide-ranging investigation, not only in this country but in several other countries in behalf of Mr. Kerwin. We initiated an action against the FBI, seeking under the Freedom of Information Act access to whatever material the federal government might have concerning the Lindbergh case. Clarence Kelly was then director of the FBI; this was post-Hoover days. They agreed to open up FBI files which had never been revealed publicly. But it took about a year and a half for them to go through the files and delete out anything that might be confidential. In the fall of 1977 I started receiving over 34,000 pages of FBI files in Washington. At the time I didn't know Mrs. Anna Hauptmann. My client was Kenneth Kerwin. When I went through that FBI material, I was startled at what I discovered concerning Richard Hauptmann. I've probably tried around a hundred murder cases around the country, including a large number involving capital punishment. I've also handled a lot of civil rights litigation involving American Indians and black Americans in the South West, South Dakota and places like that. So I have seen injustice.

*In tape-recorded interviews on February 6 and March 24, 1986.

I WAS TOTALLY ASTOUNDED

But as I went through the FBI material in
Washington I was totally astounded at what I was
discovering that had never been made public. What I
realized, by the time I finished my review, was that
Richard Hauptmann had been a victim, victimized by
fraud, misconduct by the authorities, and of course by
a tremendous amount of public pressure against him. I
discovered in the files that it was clearly orchestrated
by the authorities, taking advantage of the anti-German
sentiment of the times—which was 1934, when Mr.
Hauptmann was arrested, and the trial in 1935.
[Hitler's heyday.] We even found indications that the
Hearst newspapers were directly engaged in fanning the
flames of prejudice, to make an example out of
someone, because there were a lot of kidnappings back
then. And that type of situation sold newspapers. I
realized the bigger issue growing out of this was that a
miscarriage of justice of monumental proportions had
occurred. It was shocking that the information I had
regarding this did not come from third parties, or just
my own investigations; but rather from government
sources, material that existed at the time of the trial,
certainly before the execution, and that the government
sat on that information. The authorities did not reveal
it publicly. They should have. Had they, Richard
Hauptmann would not have been executed, regardless
of the prejudice of the time.

LEGALIZED MURDER

For background purposes I wanted to talk with Mrs.
Hauptmann, who lives in the Philadelphia area. I
finally met her in 1981, the early spring. As we were
talking in her living room I mentioned the FBI files.
She suddenly almost turned white. "What files?" she
asked. I said, "The ones I discovered a few years ago
in Washington under the Freedom of Information
Act." She said, "Tell me about them. I haven't heard

about this. I know my husband was innocent, but the government withheld evidence?" When, several weeks later, I returned to the Philadelphia area, I brought some of the FBI documents with me. I've never seen a client as shocked as Mrs. Hauptmann was as she went through the FBI material. She even started crying, because she realized not only had a mistake been made but that it appeared that the judicial system had been used for a legalized murder. She asked me was there anything I could do to reopen the case for her husband. I said it would be difficult after nearly fifty years but I would be willing to try. She said I must do it not only for her and her husband, but for all those in the future facing the death penalty.

200,000 PAGES OF MATERIAL

So, in September 1981, I filed a suit in state court in Flemington, N.J., the scene of the original Hauptmann trial, to get access to whatever documents New Jersey might have similar to the federal material. The state up to that time had been resisting very vigorously—the Attorney General's Office and the State Police—public disclosure of the material they had. Their position was, and I have letters from them to this effect, that it was not in the public interest. Shortly after that, there was a tremendous public response, heavy coverage by the media, and we made appearances on a couple of T.V. shows like the "Today" show and "Good Morning America"; and as a result of that there was public pressure. Then it became political. The governor of New Jersey then entered an executive order requiring the State Police to open up their files to us. So they were opened up publicly. So, beginning in November 1981, we reviewed over 200,000 pages of material that until then had not been made public.

LYING WITNESSES

I filed a federal wrongful death suit at Newark, N.J. in October, 1981. The thrust of it was that Richard

Hauptmann was innocent and had been a victim of an unfair trial. We were seeking an opportunity to go to trial with a wrongful death action, in order to present all the newly discovered evidence from the FBI files. In the suit, I itemized samples of some of the new evidence we had of witnesses lying, and fabrications. As I discovered more evidence, I filed succeeding amendments to the complaints. We sued the state of New Jersey; David Wilentz, the original prosecutor; and surviving police officers who were directly involved in the cover-up and the fraud. I also sued the Hearst newspapers, and later added as a defendant Thomas H. Sisk, the principal FBI agent involved in the Hauptmann investigation and prosecution. Counsel for these various parties argued that Mrs. Hauptmann should have filed suit earlier and that the statute of limitations had run out, and that what we were trying to do was relitigate the case, which was true. They contended that since the jury had already said Hauptmann was guilty, there was nothing to litigate regardless of the new evidence we had. They also argued that the prosecutor, Wilentz, was totally immune from any civil prosecution or liability, based upon a decision by the U. S. Supreme Court. The Supreme Court did hold that a prosecutor is absolutely protected from any wrongdoing as long as this was within the parameters of his normal prosecutorial function, even if he commits fraud.

HAUPTMANN'S INNOCENCE

Eventually the lower courts ruled in favor of the defendants and dismissed the suit. We were not allowed to go to trial and present the new evidence. In a very lengthy opinion, the judge found exactly what the other side was contending. I appealed that. A three-judge panel at the U.S. Court of Appeals in Philadelphia in the summer of 1985 refused to reverse the lower court. I then filed a petition with the U.S. Supreme Court, which denied relief without opinion. The New Jersey material relating to Hauptmann had been held by Governor Hoffman, who came into office as New Jersey governor during the early stages of the six-week trial in 1935. The material was unknown to anyone except him. Even the governor's family didn't know it was sitting there, stored in his garage for years. I thought we already had an incredible case, but when I got into that material in 1985 I discovered things I never dreamt would be documented concerning the fraud, the wrongdoing, the innocence of Richard Hauptmann. I was like a kid in a candy store when I first started going through it. And we realized we had new grounds to seek relief for Mrs. Hauptmann in her quest to clear her husband's name.

At a press conference Mrs. Hauptmann and I had in Trenton in October 1985, I laid out examples of some of the material for the press to look at. The State Police and the Attorney General had stated the day before that there was nothing new in the evidence and it just proved Hauptmann guilty. That was a complete lie. I felt the documents could speak far better than anything we could say. So there they were. We are still going through the material very carefully. We hope we will finish the review by early March 1986, and we expect to initiate new litigation later in the year.

I have had for some time evidence in state and federal governmental documents which proves that Richard Hauptmann: (1) did not get a fair trial; (2) was innocent; and (3) that at least some who controlled the prosecution were aware that he was innocent. We are seeking two things: official recognition that Richard Hauptmann did not get a fair trial and that he was innocent. Mrs. Hauptmann is 87 years old. My purpose is to accomplish this while she is still alive.

STANDING HISTORY ON ITS HEAD

Our efforts have been very successful publicly, not only here but in Europe, based upon articles I receive and thousands of letters. But we will not be satisfied until we accomplish our goal officially. We want

history officially righted. I think Kennedy said
something about standing history on its head. That's
exactly what we've been doing all this time. I'm totally
convinced this is what's keeping Mrs. Hauptmann
alive. All these years she never remarried. She had one
goal, and is a woman of unshakable faith but very
limited means. She believed that someday something
would happen and the truth would come out. And
since she and I met, it is coming out.

Is the thrust of your belief in his innocence that he
couldn't possibly have been at the kidnap scene?
Bryan: Yes. I will give you an example. In this new
material we have discovered an affidavit. This is from
the governor's office. A woman who was on the
subway on March 1, 1932, [day of kidnapping] going
out to do an interview for a job in Mount Vernon,
which is north of the Bronx. She was an elderly
woman and needed help in finding her way. A young
man helped her. He was coming home from work. And
that man happened to be Hauptmann. Her name was
Frieda Von Valta, and she wrote that on the first day
of March, 1932, she went from Hoboken, N.J., to
Mount Vernon, N.Y., around five o'clock on an
advertisement in a German newspaper that in
translation said: Woman for housework. Good home.
Little family. Wages $40. And it gave an address in
Mount Vernon. On her way around Times Square, she
asked directions from different people. When one man
in the company of another man answered: "I will help
you to find the right way." she said: "They rode with
me after changing at 149th Street and after a while
they left the train in the Bronx around 220th Street.
[Hauptmann lived on 222 Street.] And one of the two
told me I had to change again to a streetcar at the end
station of the subway. When leaving me, he gave me
ten cents in case I should not get the desired position,
to be sure to have some carfare home, mentioning that
he has a mother in the homeland [Hauptmann did] and
somebody might do her a favor if she should be in
need." The deponent when seeing the picture of Bruno
Richard Hauptmann in the papers recollected his face

immediately as the man who helped her in the subway as described above, It was between 6:00 and 6:30 in the evening when he got to the Bronx. Then she says: "I was threatened by the Hoboken police in case I should go to Flemington to testify for Hauptmann." In spite of these threats, deponent went to Flemington to offer herself as a witness to the chief counselor Reilly "who refused me. It was there I met Pastor V. G. Warner whom I told my experience in an affidavit." So she actually went to the defense attorney Reilly, the one hired by the Hearst newspapers, and he rejected her and she was never used. This affidavit was signed and dated January 10, 1936. The last paragraph reads: "The proponent further says that from all the circumstances and the entire knowledge as related above she is convinced in her own mind that Hauptmann could not be the kidnapper of the Hauptmann child."

Would that time preclude him from reaching New Jersey that night?

Bryan: Yes. Because it's between six and six-thirty. You'd figure he'd have to walk home from the subway station and get his car, and then pick up his wife from work. There's no way he could make it in the time frame.

If you were the prosecutor, and that woman came to you with that evidence, how impressed would you have been—that she really identified Hauptmann?

Bryan: I can see where you could play devil's advocate and argue against it, but the totality of it when you have this and another piece of evidence and you start adding it up, it becomes convincing. We've got very strong evidence that Hauptmann was in New York that night with Mrs. Hauptmann. He picked her up after work. He always took the subway home, got the car, and drove to Frederickson's Bakery, picked her up, and then they went home. So our evidence is very clear that Hauptmann not only was not near Hopewell, New Jersey, the Lindbergh home on the night of March 1, 1932, but that he had absolutely no connection with it. Fingerprints of the kidnapper were discovered on the ransom notes. The authorities knew

of that for two or two and a half years, good latent
prints. It's clear from the documents they knew they
would have the right person when the prints matched
up. When Hauptmann was arrested—and this was not
made public—one of the first things the police did was
to fingerprint him. Those prints were rushed to State
Police headquarters in West Trenton and compared.
And they did not match. So that was suppressed. And
that was unknown at the trial. And it was, of course, a
key piece of evidence. Police officials were totally
convinced these were the prints of the kidnapper—and
they were not Richard Hauptmann's prints.

How could they be sure they were the kidnapper's
fingerprints?

Bryan: They came from ransom notes enclosed in
sealed envelopes.

Hauptmann ridiculed the kidnap ladder and called it
a musical instrument, implying he was a professional
carpenter who would have made a much better ladder.
Was there any evidence that he was a first-rate
carpenter?

Bryan: Yes, plenty, and the state police had it. Not
only the work he did, but when they ransacked his
home and took everything these poor people had—
much of which has not been returned to this day,
personal items they kept as souvenirs—there were little
inlaid musical boxes which Richard Hauptmann
made, very fine work. Mrs. Hauptmann still has
one; one of her most treasured items, a real mark of
craftsmanship.

Seven experts said that the handwriting on the
ransom notes was Hauptmann's.

Bryan: It's interesting what was suppressed at the
trial. The Osborns [father and son], who were the two
principal handwriting experts, were the ones who
brought in their friends, the other handwriting experts.
These were not people who were independently judged
as being the best. Osborn, the old man, picked the
others to come in and assist him; to corroborate, in
effect, his findings. Both Osborn and his son made
significant mistakes in their careers as handwriting
experts. After Hauptmann was arrested, the authorities

confiscated from his home a lot of papers with his writing. They also took a lot of samples of his writing at the police station and had him write out things. These were sent over to the Osborns. Young Osborn and his father reviewed the writing, and they had been working on this case for two and a half years. They made a lot of comparisons with many suspects. I discovered an FBI document in which the authorities were sitting around—because the fingerprints on the ransom notes did not match with Hauptmann's— waiting to hear from the Osborns. Osborn senior called and he asked to talk to Norman Schwartzkopf, head of the N.J. State Police, and Osborn said they had reviewed the material and "I hate to tell you this, but there are too many dissimilarities. The suspect you have [Hauptmann] is not the same person who wrote the ransom notes." Later, the Osborns were called back after some of the money was found, and they said "Look, we're sure we've got the right man, because he had a portion of the ransom money." Osborn said, "I'll call you back in a little while." In less than an hour Osborn called and said, "I've changed my mind. This man did write the ransom notes. I'm completely convinced." According to this FBI document, the detectives were all laughing about how easy it was to influence handwriting experts.

I employed a very well qualified handwriting expert, Gus Lesnevitch, who spent over nine hundred hours working on this case, using the original ransom notes, original writings of Hauptmann. And he found there was no way Hauptmann could have written the ransom notes. Too many inconsistencies, too many things did not fit in. Also, concerning the handwriting, Hauptmann was told how to spell words, so some of the characteristic misspellings that were used by some of the handwriting experts to support their conclusions that Hauptmann was the author of the ransom notes don't hold weight, regarding those misspellings. I've also employed, this past year, another handwriting expert from Palo Alto, California. Independent of the first one, she went through the material and looked at the original ransom notes and came to the same conclusion—that Richard Hauptmann could not have been the author. Also, both of my handwriting experts were concerned about the method by which the original experts went about arriving at their conclusions. The methodology, the way the handwriting samples were taken, would not even be considered in a court of law today. Probably the handwriting experts, other than the Osborns, didn't know there was anything questionable about the manner in which the samples of Hauptmann's handwriting were taken.

But didn't Lindbergh positively identify Hauptmann by his voice as the man who took the ransom money?

Bryan: Yes. Lindbergh was a great distance away and heard a voice in the cemetery the night the ransom was paid hollering to Dr. John Condon, "Hey, Doc!" or "Hey, Doktor!" Two and a half years later when Hauptmann was arrested, Lindbergh was brought into the police station and supposedly identified Hauptmann's voice. What we discovered was that he testified before a Bronx grand jury that he could not identify the voice. And yet, at the trial, the prosecution and police concealed that from the court, the jury, and the public. Then, he said unequivocally that it was Hauptmann's voice he heard the night the ransom was paid. And nobody outside of law enforcement knew he had previously made a contradictory statement. One could argue that in the two months between the grand jury appearance and the trial he changed his mind, obviously. What I discovered in these new documents —which is important on that point—is that between Hauptmann's arrest and the grand jury appearance, Lindbergh was taken to the police station and heard Hauptmann's voice [since hearing a voice at the cemetery]. There was no evidence available that Lindbergh had heard Hauptmann's voice before the grand jury appearance, until recently. It seemed that at first he said, "Gosh, I don't think I could identify the voice," and later when he heard Hauptmann speak after the grand jury meeting, he changed his mind. But we now know that shortly after Hauptmann's arrest, before Lindbergh went to the grand jury, he was taken to the police station, heard Hauptmann speak, and said, "That is not the voice." He goes to the grand jury and says basically the same thing. Then says just the opposite at the trial, which is shocking. It is incredible that somebody of his stature and influence would do that.

And defense attorney Reilly didn't pick it up?

Bryan: He did not know about it.

Didn't Dr. Condon do the same sort of thing?

Bryan: Condon did more. Condon went farther than saying, "I'm not going to identify him. I want to be sure." Condon took the next step and said, "You've got the wrong man." On another occasion Condon said, "He's the wrong size." On another occasion he said, "Maybe it's his brother." Hauptmann's brother was in Germany and had never been in the United States. And these statements of Condon's were unknown at the time of the trial outside the prosecution camp, that not only had Hauptmann not been identified by Condon, but that Condon said affirmatively, "He is not the person." We did discover that Condon was placed under a lot of pressure by the authorities. He was even a suspect. There is a document in which Condon took the Fifth Amendment, refused to answer questions.

He was a suspect because he volunteered to get into the act as a go-between for Lindbergh and the kidnapper?

Bryan: Yes, and because there was so much contradictory about his activities, his statements, his behavior.

Do you suspect him as an accomplice?

Bryan: No. He might have been; I may be wrong on that. But we do not. He was a bumbling, eccentric old man, who like so many involved in the case craved publicity.

Is Hauptmann's friend Hans Kloppenburg still alive?

Bryan: Yes. He was the man in December 1933 who opened the door to let Fisch in [with the shoebox assumed to contain the ransom money].

Kloppenburg was warned by Wilentz not to testify in court. How did Wilentz threaten him?

Bryan: They were going to implicate him somehow in the crime.

But if these men are innocent, why would they be frightened by such threats when a friend's life is at stake?

Bryan: He did go and testify, but before he testified he had been threatened. If you were Richard Hauptmann's friend and you know he is innocent, yet he is being prosecuted, wouldn't you be a little frightened that they might do the same to you too? It is scary. He courageously did not back down.

Have you any idea why Isidor Fisch, this dealer in hot money, would leave all that ransom money with Hauptmann, his friend and business partner, when he left the U.S. for Germany?

Bryan: I don't think Fisch wanted to risk the chance of being searched and have something like that discovered. Now, whether Fisch knew it was Lindbergh money is subject to debate. We do know he was dealing in hot money, and people who knew him whom I've interviewed give me two different reactions: either that Fisch, not knowing it was Lindbergh money when he bought it, but knowing it was hot, didn't want to be carrying it around—Hauptmann was a very trustworthy person. So what better person to leave his personal papers [and cash] with than Hauptmann? Some people who knew Fisch think that's all it was. Other people feel that Fisch was directly involved in the kidnapping and that was the reason he didn't want to be carrying it in international travel. It was very highly publicized that the authorities had the serial numbers of the gold certificates and such could be traced.

But Hauptmann himself had a criminal record in Germany, hadn't he?

Bryan: Let me explain. That was at the height of the Depression in Germany after World War I, in the early 1920s. Inflation was incredible. It took literally a wheelbarrow of marks to buy a loaf of bread. Unemployment was very high and Richard Hauptmann was like hundreds of thousands of young Germans drafted into the army—after the war left with nothing.

He was hungry and did steal. And years later when he proposed to Mrs. Hauptmann, as they sat on Riverside Drive overlooking the Hudson River; he said, "There's something I want you to know about me before you say yes, and that is that I got into trouble in Germany. I did it and I went to jail. And you need to know this about me." After fleeing Germany he came to the U.S. as a stowaway on a ship. He became a model citizen. And the authorities investigated Richard Hauptmann probably as closely as anybody ever had been, and found not one blemish in his activities. He didn't even gamble.

But his crime in Germany was armed robbery, and against women on one or two occasions, and he did go to prison for four years. So it puts him in a harsher light as a character than the picture of an honest guy whom Fisch thought he could trust with a large sum of money.

Bryan: I agree; you have to recognize what Hauptmann did in Germany was wrong. Not everybody who was hungry committed crimes in Germany after World War I. However, his record as a person who lived in the U.S. after that was exemplary. His greatest crime was being hungry and desperate.

With the reservation that his business partner and friend was a shady character dealing in hot money. So he still had a close associate, a business partner who was a crook.

Bryan: The evidence established that he was unaware that Isidor Fisch was a crook until after the guy had died and Hauptmann went around trying to recoup his losses. Then he discovered that Fisch had lied to him about a number of things. Now, I don't know if this was wishful thinking on Hauptmann's part or whether he did not want to believe when Fish was alive that he was a shady character, or whether Fisch was that good a con man to have conned Hauptmann. It appears pretty clear he was duped by Fisch.

Is it your assumption that prosecutor Wilentz was so convinced of Hauptmann's guilt that he was prepared to intimidate witnesses and suppress evidence to get a conviction?

Bryan: I don't know if Wilentz believed Hauptmann guilty. Obviously he was willing for the end to justify the means. I have affidavits in which he was offering to bribe witnesses and people who had information such as defense investigators. He participated in a fraud upon the court and jury. To get a conviction, it was clear he was willing to go to much greater lengths than would have been ethical and legal even at that time, including suborning perjury.

Isn't it true that Governor Hoffman doubted Hauptmann was the kidnapper or extortionist but believed he was somehow connected with the crime?

Bryan: That's not correct. That's the impression people have had through the years. However, in this new material we secured in October 1985, there is plenty of evidence that the Governor was convinced Hauptmann was not involved. Period. Now, what he said publicly and his beliefs as reflected in the files don't always coincide because he was obviously a politician. But we have documentary evidence that he was convinced of Hauptmann's innocence. As a matter of fact, the night he went to see Hauptmann on death row, afterwards he made a comment to some people— including Mrs. Hauptmann—that Richard Hauptmann was innocent. But that was not made publicly to the press.

But he could have meant innocent of murder or kidnapping or extortion.

Bryan: No, he was talking about the Lindbergh crime generally.

Do you also believe Hauptmann was completely innocent?

Bryan: Absolutely, without any reservations. And that is strictly based not upon wishful thinking, but on hard, cold facts, totally disregarding my independent investigation and looking strictly at the facts and evidence withheld at the time by the authorities which we now know of—in other words, the prosecution's evidence that was suppressed and Governor Hoffman's evidence that was withheld—based strictly on that, yes, Richard Hauptmann was innocent.

If Hearst was paying for Hauptmann's defense, why did the Hearst papers try to get him convicted?

Bryan: In essence they were trying to throw the case. The reason they were paying for his defense is very clear: they wanted an inside track to the defense camp. Something else I discovered in the state files is that Hearst had reporters with the defense virtually twenty-four hours a day. They even had a female reporter staying in a room with Mrs. Hauptmann. [Dorothy Kilgallen was one of three.] I discovered that Hearst was helping the prosecution. I have two telegrams between the prosecutor and Adela Rogers St. John. So here you have a situation of Hearst helping the prosecution convict this man. He is supposedly helping the defense by financing it. Hearst, having been inside the defense camp, gave the prosecution a direct line to the defense and they knew everything the defense was doing in advance.

Didn't Hauptmann's chief defense attorney, Reilly, only see him for about half an hour?

Bryan: Yes.

Isn't that incredible?

Bryan: It certainly is. He was too busy across the street from the courthouse in the Union Hotel drinking and cavorting with these different women he had with him, and with the press, than spending time with his poor client in jail.

Reilly was a syphilitic and alcoholic. A terrible attorney, obviously.

Bryan: Yes, he was called Death House Reilly. He was suffering from syphilis and doing some really crazy things. He was very erratic in his behavior. His comment to the FBI agent that he believed Hauptmann guilty, didn't like him, and was anxious for him to get the chair—I suspect this had some connection with mental problems Reilly was having because of the syphilis. It's hard for me to believe any trial lawyer, even if he harbored some belief his client might be guilty, would make a statement like that to an FBI agent. It's just incredible and insane. Reilly was not in a condition to be defense counsel in a case of such magnitude.

Do you think you would have liked Hauptmann?

Bryan: Very much.

How about the other defense attorney, Lloyd Fisher?

Bryan: There were things he could have done he didn't do, even though he believed until the day he died that Hauptmann was innocent. Fisher was a nice guy, but he was not willing to fight where it really counted—at trial. I can't imagine any good lawyer who has a strong sense of ethics sitting by in a murder case and letting a chief counsel behave the way Reilly did and remain mute. I do not understand it. At one point in the trial, Reilly conceded that the remains found were those of the Lindbergh child, and Fisher responded, "You've just conceded our client to the electric chair!" And he went storming out of the courtroom. Instead of walking away and abandoning his client when he was so angry, Fisher should have called a recess to have a hearing out of the presence of the jury. He should have said in essence to the judge, "Your honor, this man is on trial for his life. His rights are not being protected. What Mr. Reilly did is improper. He's not spending time with his client. He is under the influence of alcohol even in court and I ask that he be removed from the case." Fisher and the other two defense attorneys should have explained to Hauptmann that he was getting royally screwed. Unfortunately, they remained passive and mute, and their client died.

Has it ever happened during a murder trial that an assistant attorney got rid of his boss?

Bryan: Certainly it can happen. The lead defense counsel is not the boss of the other attorneys. Each attorney, even an associate attorney, has a primary obligation is to his or her client. I don't know if these lawyers were intimidated by Reilly, this loud city lawyer from Brooklyn, or whether they were overwhelmed by the mob and the whole hysteria of the period surrounding the trial. But that has always troubled me about those lawyers letting that type of thing happen and remaining silent.

The $100,000,000 damages you were claiming on Mrs. Hauptmann's behalf is irrelevant now, is it?

Bryan: It was kind of irrelevant at the beginning. In a wrongful death action you have to ask for damages. When I looked at it I thought, "Here we have the trial of the century." It's still recognized as the biggest criminal trial in the history of this country. If all of this is correct, then you have the greatest fraud in American jurisprudence. Since one of the bases for damages is not only to compensate the victim, but also to punish the wrongdoer—one should set damages commensurate with the magnitude of the wrong. The wrongs here are very large. But, from the beginning our position has been that we'll waive any claim to money if we can achieve those two points: in securing an official exoneration of Richard Hauptmann, an admission that the trial was unfair and he was innocent. The money is not going to help Mrs. Hauptmann. I don't want the money to be a factor in the New Jersey authorities saying: "We can't admit this because Robert Bryan is making this demand for money." So I've communicated to government officials that we will waive any claim for money, if the State of New Jersey will recognize that Richard Hauptmann did not receive a fair trial, and was innocent. Mrs. Hauptmann knows she doesn't have that long to live, so time and results are important, not money.

Could such a trial take place today?

Bryan: In my opinion, it could. I have handled cases in which the police suppressed evidence, and the truth was twisted. Certainly not in every case. But sometimes the police operate under the philosophy that the end justifies the means. This is especially true when they're certain they've got the right person and there's public pressure. Then there's a real inclination for this type of behavior to occur. Even if one believes in the death penalty—which I don't—it should not be used at this time because we have a very imperfect system. When you iron out the problems, when you have a perfect system, when you can be absolutely sure these people who are convicted are guilty, and prejudice is removed from the legal process, then at least there would be some logic for capital punishment. But until we have a perfect system we can't do it. And the Hauptmann case is very important in dramatizing that. The evidence against him seemed overwhelming, but now we know from government documents that it was a monumental fraud. He was a victim of fraud, corruption, and racism. That is why he died. But regardless of how successful I am, it's not going to bring back this poor man's life. This case dramatizes the horror of the death penalty, and why it is so wrong under any circumstances.

At the time of Hauptmann's trial, was it illegal for the prosecution to withhold evidence they had indicating his innocence?

Bryan: The rules then were not so favorable to the accused as they are today. However, the law then was as strong as it is now that trial by fraud is illegal and unconstitutional. What happened then was trial by fraud.

Today, would the prosecution have to supply evidence of the accused's innocence?

Bryan: Yes. The rules vary from state to state. For instance, in California the prosecution, in effect, has to almost completely open up its files in state court to the defense. In a lot of states that's not true. However, regarding evidence exculpatory in nature, that is bearing on innocence, the prosecution is mandated to make known to the defense. That wouldn't have made any difference in Hauptmann's case because the authorities were not playing by the rules. Our system is only as fair and effective as those who function within it. And when those in authority such as police and prosecutors bend the rules, then innocent people are going to be convicted and sometimes die. It happens today—maybe not on the massive scale of the Hauptmann case, but I know of a number of cases under modern-day rules where the prosecution has deliberately withheld or suppressed evidence which might have cleared the accused. This occurs because one is a target defendant, because of political reasons or public pressure.

Would a Dershowitz or a Lee Bailey have got Hauptmann off?

Bryan: Probably. Certainly combining information I

now have Hauptmann would have been acquitted. Mrs. Hauptmann had asked Clarence Darrow to represent her husband, but tragically he was too ill to enter the case.

Did any of the letters you've received indicate who the kidnapper or kidnappers were?

Bryan: We've had a lot of suggestions. There's a bootlegger theory, a gang theory, an Al Capone theory. I'll say this: A lot of the theories that have been floating around for five decades are full of more holes than Swiss cheese. We're conducting an independent investigation and now have a very clear indication as to who was involved and why it happened. But that is not complete yet. I hope this aspect of our investigation will be completed soon.

How have you financed your investigation?

Bryan: Unfortunately, I've had to do it myself. We get some small donations from the public, but make no solicitations. I don't want this to take on the tone of the purpose being monetary. Mrs. Hauptmann does not have funds, so I have financed it.

To be fair to Edward J. Reilly, he did object to the wood expert's testimony that a rung of the kidnap ladder was made from a floorboard in Hauptmann's attic, saying: "I don't know who cooked up this idea of trying to make this ladder and this board agree, but I don't think this jury is going to stand for that kind of evidence. This case it too perfect from the prosecution's viewpoint. . . . There isn't a man in the world with brains enough to plan this kidnapping alone and not with a gang."

He maintained that the kidnapping was an inside job in which Charles and Anne Morrow Lindbergh's servants were involved as well as those of her mother. He mentioned how Violet Sharp, a housemaid who had behaved very suspiciously, changed her story under interrogation, and faced with more questions had killed herself with cyanide; as well as Betty Gow, the baby's nurse; and the butler, Oliver Whately, who had since died.

Taking a leaf from Arthur Conan Doyle, he pointed to the suspicious behavior of the Lindbergh's dog that never barked at the time the intruder was kidnapping the child. And "who controlled the dog's movements that night? The butler."

Characterizing Hauptmann as "Public Enemy Number One of the World and "a man with ice water in his veins," Attorney General Wilentz asked that he be given "no mercy." Wilentz ended one harangue with, "He's cold, yes, but he'll be thawed out when he hears the switch!"

After the verdict of guilty and the death sentence, "cold-blooded" Hauptmann cried uncontrollably in his death cell.

While Attorney General Wilentz was convinced he had condemned a ruthless killer to death, New Jersey's Governor Harold G. Hoffman shared "with hundreds of thousands of our people the doubt as to the value of the evidence that placed Hauptmann in the Lindbergh nursery. . . . I do doubt that this crime could have been committed by one man."

Fifty years later and after the books and articles questioning Hauptmann's guilt and damning his trial as at least flawed and at most a fraud, I wondered if David T. Wilentz still felt confident he had sent the right man to the chair. I spoke with him by phone in 1984, when he was 88, yet still working—in private practice. He was reluctant to talk, partly because of a heavy cold.

> Warden Lawes of Sing Sing and Warden Duffy of San Quentin both were very much against capital punishment, partly because of their fears that innocent people were executed. I wondered, because there's still a controversy about Hauptmann's guilt, if you felt as they did? You recall, Hauptmann was a professional carpenter and he laughed at the ladder brought into court—the one said to have been used in the kidnapping. He said it was such a badly made ladder he couldn't possibly have built it. Was it badly made?
> *Wilentz:* That's ridiculous: we couldn't admit that and we didn't admit it. We had no proof that it was or wasn't. He just dismissed the contention of the use of the ladder. That was his way of denying he built the ladder. That's all there was to that.
> Your wood expert, Koehler, proved that part of Hauptmann's attic flooring was used for a rail of the ladder.
> *Wilentz:* That's right.
> And the assumption was that Hauptmann had both made and used it. But did you have any carpentry

expert say if it was professionally built or the work of an amateur?

Wilentz: I can't remember. That was so many years ago.

Hauptmann said Isidor Fisch gave him the ransom money and then returned to Germany.

Wilentz: That's ridiculous. He was dead.
[The kidnapping was March 1, 1932; the ransom money was handed to "John" on April 2, 1932; the corpse of the Lindbergh baby was discovered on May 12, 1932. That same day Isidor Fisch applied for a passport, intending to sail for Germany in July. He postponed his trip until December 6, 1933, and died of tuberculosis of the lungs in St. George Hospital, Leipzig, on March 29, 1934. A movie-theater cashier received a ransom bill from a customer on November 26, 1933. Hauptmann gave a ransom bill to a gas station attendant on September 15, 1934, and Hauptmann was arrested on September 19, 1934.]

Right. But did Fisch's relatives back up Hauptmann?

Wilentz: No, no. They denied it.

And there was no evidence he had done so?

Wilentz: Of course not. [There was evidence from Hauptmann's friend Kloppenburg.] The money, of course, went to Hauptmann.

Except, there's still about thirty thousand dollars missing, isn't there?

Wilentz: I don't remember. I cannot remember.

I know that Lindbergh was convinced Hauptmann was the killer.

Wilentz: Well, regardless of that, the jury convicted him. No use in going into that now.

But juries do make mistakes, don't they? Are you for or against capital punishment?

Wilentz: The truth of the matter is that I feel very lukewarm about it. I have nothing to do with the law. I am not for or against capital punishment as such. I have my doubts about it.

Would you say it's an open question, worthy of being discussed?

Wilentz: Well, it's being discussed throughout the goddammed world—so why do you ask me that?

Because a lot of people say we've got to have it; that
there's no discussion needed.
Wilentz: Oh, no, no. I don't say that at all.

A *Washington Post* reporter, Tom Zito, questioned Wilentz about
the civil lawsuit brought by Robert Bryan and Anna Hauptmann
in 1981 charging that the State of New Jersey and others "did
negligently and willfully deprive Richard Hauptmann of the right
to have access to exculpatory and other information, the right to a
fair trial . . . and deliberately withheld information that very likely
would have saved his life." "That's really ridiculous," Wilentz responded. "If during all these years that have elapsed since the trial,
there was anything then or now to give some justification to what
they say, I would not have been able to enjoy life the way I have."

Do police and prosecutors lose much sleep over faking evidence
or hiding evidence of advantage to the accused, especially if they
think they're guilty?
Did they lose much sleep over Barbara Graham after her execution in San Quentin's gas chamber?
They even lied about her after she was dead.

17

Barbara Graham
Dark Memory

Her gardener discovered Mabel Monahan in a closet of her Burbank
home. Although she had deep scalp wounds, she appeared to have
been suffocated by a pillowcase over her head, secured at the throat
with a torn strip of sheet.
Sixty-two-year-old Mrs. Monahan had been a vaudeville star of
sorts who retired after an injury. She lived alone, but still saw her
ex-son-in-law, a Las Vegas gambler who was rumored by the under-

world to skim gambling money and to have stashed away $100,000 of it in a safe in the Monahan house.

Hollywood columnist Louella Parsons called the killing a "thriller-diller" and rated it the best since Bugsy Siegel's demise. He had been a flamboyant Beverly Hills mobster with film-star intimates who ended as a blood-spattered corpse among the chintz chairs and sofa of a sixteen-room apartment. Parsons twittered that already three producers were bidding for the movie rights to the Monahan murder story, even before they knew the who, what, or why of it.

Police picked up a truckful of suspects and held four men and a woman among them for further grilling. The men were members of a larger gang suspected of many unsolved, brutal torture-murders. The woman was a surprise—an attractive twenty-eight-year-old brunette and mother of three young sons—a surprise until police checked her record.

Her full name, Barbara Elaine Wood Kielhammer Puchelle Newman Graham, told of five marriages, three of them bigamous.

Bigamy was by no means her only conflict with the law. When she was two her mother was sent to a reformatory for wayward girls at Ventura, California. Barbara followed in Mom's unsteady footsteps, attending the same alma mater twelve years later, in 1939. She had been characterized by the cops as "a lewd vagrant," having practiced prostitution in every Pacific Coast city from San Diego to Seattle. To the less censorious, such girls as Barbara who followed the fleet were known as "seagulls."

She twice ran away from the reformatory, and they finally let her go, at sixteen, to work as a cocktail waitress in seedy San Francisco joints, hustling drinks and leaving work with tanked-up customers.

Barbara was otherwise employed for a time giving birth to a son. Still a kid herself, she moved south and wandered L.A. streets with her one-year-old in tow until she landed a job with Emmett Perkins at his El Monte Club, luring men to gambling tables where they were fleeced and, on leaving, frequently mugged.

World War II proved a boom for business. Most of her friends were petty crooks who had weaseled their way out of military service or were on the run. Two such friends had been arrested for roughing up and robbing Sally Stanford, a well-known and even respected San Francisco madam. They asked Barbara to be their alibi. Even though she was in Chicago at the time of the crime, she could never say no to a friend.

She was nailed for perjury and spent a year in jail. That perjury rap through helping friends in need probably cost her her life.

Briefly married to a salesman in 1948, she worked as a nurse's aide until she was arrested on a bad check charge. A year later, now twenty-six, Barbara became a sailor's wife, but walked out after two months and soon after was arrested for prostitution.

By now, as one Barbara Graham aficionado noted, she was "as well known to the average Los Angeles cop as his badge number, and it was pretty much the same in San Francisco."*

She may have tried to go straight in 1951 when she married husband number five, Henry Graham; gave birth to a third son; and ran a small hamburger stand in Seattle.

But it wasn't easy. Mr. Graham used drugs and gave her easy access to marijuana and heroin. About this time she also met more shady characters, the shadiest of them all being Jack Santo.

Santo, a sadist known to cops as a great hunting companion—he hunted people and animals with equal zest—headed a freelance gang. When Emmett Perkins' gambling tables weren't paying off, he was Santo's first choice to blow a safe or help torture or kill any robbery victim who resisted. Their most callous murder-robbery engineered by Santo and executed by Perkins was to bludgeon to death with a lead pipe a man and three young children, then stuff their corpses into a car trunk on top of a still-living child victim.

Barbara Graham, of course, knew they were crooks; so were most of her friends. It is unlikely she knew they were killers, at least when she first joined them.

Despite her early years of poverty, neglect, and abuse, and her sleazy life-style and loose morals, she stood out from her circle of dope pushers and hookers. She enjoyed poetry and good music. Her hard-boiled veneer barely hid an insecure, frightened woman over anxious to please others.

She had an arresting personality in more ways than one, and some even detected beauty beneath her thick mask of pancake makeup and bottle-bleached hair. She was expected to go places.

According to the prosecutor at Barbara Graham's murder trial, Jack Santo and Emmett Perkins had offered her just that chance.

*Jack Leslie in his book *Decathlon of Death*, Tarquin Books, 1979.

They told her of a wealthy widow with a small fortune hidden in her expensive Burbank house. She lived alone, and they'd have no trouble scaring her into handing over money and jewelry. One look at Santo's ugly mug would do the trick. All Barbara had to do was get the woman to open her door and ask to use her phone. Once the door was open, they—and John True, a sometime deep-sea diver on the make—would take over.

The gang had been misinformed about the money. It was all in a bank. They got away with nothing and left behind a corpse stuffed in a closet.

John True not only escaped a murder charge but got off scot-free by appearing as the state's star canary. He testified how, when Mrs. Monahan answered the door to Barbara, the widow had been suspicious and reluctant to let her in to use the phone. At that, he said, Barbara grabbed the elderly woman's hair and fatally battered her over the head with a gun butt.

To indicate the fury of Barbara's attack, the prosecutor said the victim looked as if she had been hit by a heavy truck traveling at speed.

San Francisco and Los Angeles newspapers covering the trial no longer called Barbara "Seagull." She was now "Tiger Woman" and "Bloody Babs," a ruthless and amoral killer. Santo, Perkins, and especially True, though not cast in the same mold as Albert Schweitzer, were portrayed as having done their futile best to prevent the young woman's vicious, deadly attack.

Barbara's defense was that at the time of the murder she'd had a fight with her husband, who had walked out, leaving her alone with their young son. Santo and Perkins told her nevertheless to keep her mouth shut, not to testify, and they were confident that things would then go easier for the three of them.

But, insisting on her innocence, she took the stand. She called her husband, who was a reluctant witness. At first he couldn't recall what happened that night; then he remembered, Barbara was at home. But as a drug addict he did not impress the jury favorably: his testimony was so suspect they simply didn't buy it.

Without an alibi, it looked likely that Barbara Graham would join Santo and Perkins in the gas chamber.

During the trial a cellmate repeatedly offered to provide Barbara with an alibi, but only if she would admit to the murder, as proof of good faith or something of the sort. Barbara turned down the offer several times, but eventually in desperation admitted to the Monahan murder as the price for an alibi witness.

The cellmate was an undercover cop who had secretly tape-recorded Barbara's murder confession.

It's possible the jury might have sympathized with her explanation—she'd falsely confessed, hoping to save her life. But Detective Inspector Al Corrusa stymied that. He testified that Barbara had already been to prison for perjury, after providing a false alibi for two pals who pistol-whipped and robbed Sally Stanford. She was a legally proven liar.

The San Francisco *Examiner* sent its star reporter, Ed Montgomery, to report the trial. Montgomery, in his thirties, had won a 1950 Pulitzer Prize for exposing corruption in the Internal Revenue Service. He claimed that, for bribes of $1,000 and up, clerks in a San Francisco IRS office "fixed" income tax returns for California millionaires, saving them hundreds of thousands of dollars.

The FBI and Treasury Department ridiculed Montgomery's charges and challenged him to prove the "rumors." Montgomery did and in detail.

The government departments reluctantly admitted he was right and investigated.

Those among the guilty who didn't commit suicide went to prison for long terms.

In his work, Montgomery had made many friends as well as enemies on both sides of the law. He knew his way around underworld haunts and police headquarters.

One of his best informants was gangster Mickey Cohen, who seemed to have a tap on every criminal's phone on the West Coast.

While covering the trial for the San Francisco *Examiner*, reporter Ed Montgomery had no doubt that Graham was guilty as hell. The first broad hint that she wasn't came after the trial when he was interviewing Santo, who said, "Christ, I didn't think they'd convict anyone as innocent as Barbara." At the time, Montgomery put the remark down to Santo's perverse sense of humor.

That it wasn't in the least funny was revealed to the reporter by a young, resourceful private investigator, Carl Palmberg, hired by Barbara's new attorney, Al Matthews. Over time, Palmberg convinced Montgomery that the state was planning to execute an innocent woman.

In turn, Montgomery persuaded his newspaper to try to save her from the gas chamber, agreeing with his editor's proviso: "If I'm going to involve this newspaper in a crusade to save the most worthless whore in the world, it's got to be on nothing but the evidence."

During the trial, Montgomery thought Barbara Graham dull and colorless. In fact she was so physically and mentally exhausted by the trial that she had to be carried into the State Prison for Women in Corona, near L.A. She was also so weakened by drugs the doctor wondered if he could keep her alive for her execution.

He worked wonders, and when Montgomery first interviewed her in the prison her eyes had come alive and she was almost attractive.

She discussed a news account that compared her poor childhood with Marilyn Monroe's. "They were very much alike," she said. "We were both illegitimate. Both of our unwed mothers couldn't take care of us. Like Marilyn, I had a hundred guys tell me I was starlet material, but none of mine were in the movies. When you sleep with a hundred guys who aren't in the movies, instead of becoming a big star, you become a big whore."

Montgomery tracked down a woman who had wanted to adopt Barbara as a child. "One decent break and a little bit of love, and things would have been different," she told him. "Her own mother hated her and never missed a chance to drum it into her that she was illegitimate. The poor kid never had anyone who really loved her. And she was the most beautiful thing in the world. At thirteen she was like a doll, always so lively and full of fun. I only had her for two months. Her mother was being vindictive when she wouldn't let me adopt her."

Barbara was elated during Montgomery's second visit to the prison, having just seen her nineteen-month-old son, Tommy. She said she wanted him to be a brain surgeon or a scientist.

The reporter told her that, to arouse public support, his account would emphasize her early life—when she had been molested by foster fathers and forced by one demented foster mother to stand for hours with a raw onion under her eyes. Each time she wiped away tears, the woman hit her with a stick.

He was pleased to find that she was frequently seeing the Catholic chaplain Father Daniel McAlister. In his ten years at the prison he had taken part in sixty-five executions. "Without him I'd go crazy," she said.

She also found comfort in books, especially those on psychiatry and religion. She told her attorney, Al Matthews, she'd like to make use of her newfound knowledge by appearing on TV's "What's My Line?" She said, "I'd dress in a navy blue skirt with a white blouse with a ruffled neck, the kind that makes you look like a piece of candy. Then, when they hadn't come close to guessing my line, I'd say in a sweet little voice, 'I'm a whore.' "

" 'What's My Line?' doesn't pay enough," Matthews quipped. "We'll have to get you on a program where you can make a mint."

"I don't want that, even for $64,000," she said seriously. "I've already been turned into a freak. I don't want to go that route again. I want to be as normal as cornflakes when I get out."

She was driven from Corona to San Quentin for her execution. As the only woman prisoner there, she was locked in a cell near the psychiatric ward. From there she heard a man crying his heart out all night. It got to her, so she began to cry. She cried, too, when she missed her young son.

But she found ways of cheering herself up even when she couldn't sleep, by bursting into song at three or four in the morning.

Five days before her execution date, Supreme Court Justice William O. Douglas granted a stay, citing ineffective counsel and a coerced confession.

She had faith that Carl Palmberg, the twenty-four-year-old private investigator, would be the key to her freedom. He had volunteered his services and was enthusiastic about the evidence he had unearthed in her favor.

Three months after the stay of execution, Palmberg died unexpectedly of leukemia. When she heard the news, Barbara collapsed and was in shock for two days. She refused to eat, and survived for the next two months on a diet of vitamin pills.

The Supreme Court refused to review her case, or those of Santo and Perkins, and their executions were set for June 3, 1955.

"We're in here because we didn't kill enough witnesses," Perkins told Warden Teets. "Like that time in 1934 when I did two years for knocking over a gas station. I'd have been all right if I'd've killed all fourteen witnesses instead of four."

"How many should you have killed this time?" the warden asked.

"All of them. Every son-of-a-bitch that shot his mouth off in court."

"What about Barbara Graham?"

"She's okay. She's the only one I'd let live."

"She's the only one who's going to die," the warden pointed out. "All the others [members of the Santo gang] are going to live."

Perkins shrugged and said, "Well, that's justice for you."

He wouldn't say what the warden was waiting to hear and what Ed Montgomery now strongly suspected; that Barbara Graham was innocent of the murder.

Perkins claimed he wasn't scared to die, but that maybe Santo was right when he said having Barbara in this with them would keep them alive forever. She was their insurance. They didn't think the state would execute a woman and hoped to be saved along with her.

"You don't believe that," Montgomery told Perkins.

"I don't give a damn," Perkins replied. "I don't care if they drop the pellets now. But I can't let Jack Santo down. Anyway, what's so great about letting that blond whore live? She ain't no good to anyone."

Barbara was moved back to Corona. She lightheartedly described the group making the trip as "four uniformed men, one matron in a sundress, and little me in hardware."

She looked dull and indifferent when Montgomery next saw her. "The matrons like me better this way," she said. "They don't have to force food down my throat." Three days later he found her listening to classical records. On a third visit she was reading a book on Socrates. She had an above-average IQ of 114.

Montgomery was depressed. Although his newspaper's campaign had gained Barbara many supporters, it had not swayed those who could save her life.

"Don't look so grim," she told him. "It's not like they're going to kill anything much when they drop the pellets. They've killed most of me already. I don't want to be a crybaby. I really think I've gotten over the worst of it."

One night she dreamed she was dying and woke screaming. "My screams had all the night crew's hair standing on end," she said.

She asked for a parakeet for company, but was refused because her cell was "already too cluttered."

The night before her execution, she was driven in shackles the hot ten-hour journey back to San Quentin, in a black limousine formerly used by General de Gaulle on a state visit and General Eisenhower during his presidential campaign. She had a similar escort of motorcycle police fore and aft.

On arrival she was helped out, pale and dazed with fatigue, her crimson lipstick like blood on her pallid face. Montgomery thought that, as death approached, the dull, plain woman had grown into a frail beauty.

When she reached her cell she collapsed.

"I've never seen a human being in weaker physical condition," said the warden. "Nor one with more courage. She's barely conscious, but I got a smile out of her when I asked her for a cigarette —a reversal of the usual procedure." He told her, "Please understand this is difficult for all of us. We want to make it as easy for you as we can."

And she replied, "I'm awfully sorry you have to go through this, Warden."

The long-drawn-out torture that followed wasn't his fault.

On her last night she refused a final meal, settling for a milkshake. A dentist called briefly to ease a sudden toothache.

The governor was reported to be wearing a gray suit with matching face at a press conference that evening. He announced that he had received appeals for clemency for Barbara Graham from scores of people including brothel-keeper Sally Stanford and Catholic Archbishop Joseph T. McGlucken, but they had not changed his mind. She would die next morning.

Just before dawn she wrote a farewell letter to Ed Montgomery:

Dear Ed,

I'm writing this with the sun coming up. I can't see it, but I can see the sky getting light. I've just realized that it's summer. The two years I've been in prison are like one long night, with no seasons and no warmth, and I can't tell you how glad I am that it's over. I really don't mind at all, except that the closer I come to death, the more reasons there are to live, which I suppose is natural with someone who has led an utterly wasted life.

But what I want to tell you, the thing that hurts most, is that so much of my life was spent hating people. I can't remember any time as a child when I wasn't alone and afraid and filled with hate. But now, when this thing is happening, so awful that never in all my fears and hatreds did I ever imagine anything like this, I've stopped hating. I only think of the many

people who had no reason to care, but they did care.
This is the thing I'm taking with me. It's a big thing,
and I want you to always remember that you were part
of it.

Good-bye,
Barbara

She gave the letter to her attorney, who took it to Montgomery.
He was waiting outside the gates of San Quentin in his car where
he was to spend the night—wanting to be there, but not to see her
die. He recalled her last words to him: "I've thought of committing
suicide, but it's not because I'm a Catholic that I can't. No matter
what happens, make everyone understand that I wanted to live."

Father McAlister gave her extreme unction and returned a few
minutes before ten A.M. to say, "It's time."

"Thank God," she replied.

A wheelchair was in the next cell in case she was too weak or
hysterical to walk. But when the priest took her hand he was surprised at the feeling of strength in it and realized the wheelchair
wouldn't be needed.

"I feel good, Father," she said. "I don't feel any hatred. I feel only
pity for everyone who will have to live with what they're doing to
me."

She wore a beige suit and a crucifix around her neck.

As they were about to leave the cell, the warden opened the door
and said, "Governor Knight has instructed me to delay the proceedings."

"My God, why?" the priest asked.

When he explained it was a legal technicality, not a reprieve,
Barbara collapsed.

Twenty-five minutes later, the governor told the warden to go
ahead with the execution. Barbara had now recovered. Father
McAlister had walked with sixty-five other condemned prisoners to
their deaths, but never one with more courage. Even so, it took him
and another Catholic chaplain, Father Edward Dingberg, twenty
minutes to get the frail woman to within a few steps of the gas
chamber.

Her attorneys were still making frantic last-second legal appeals
to keep her alive, even while a guard and the doctor prepared her
for execution.

Just as Barbara reached the gas chamber, Warden Teets appeared from the next room looking sick. "Governor Knight has ordered another delay," he said.

"I can't take it," Barbara gasped. "Why didn't they let me go at ten? I was ready to go."

The death party waited in the room adjoining the gas chamber. Barbara sat in a swivel chair.

At 11:18 Barbara's execution was on again.

Sixteen guards, five police inspectors, and sixteen newspapermen had been waiting for almost an hour to see Barbara die. Ed Montgomery was still in his car. "I sat in my car all night and until after the execution," Montgomery said. "Although I'd covered several executions both at San Quentin and up in Nevada, I couldn't bear to see her killed."

They had wanted her to go barefoot, but she insisted on wearing slippers and even earrings. At the last moment she said to the matron, "I don't want to look at those people." So the matron put a mask over her eyes.

Speculating on the amount of poison gas about to be used, a reporter said, "I hear American Cyanide was up six points this morning."

As she appeared, her eyes hidden, the priests guiding her lightly by the elbows, another witness said, "Good-bye and God bless you, Barbara."

One observer thought she had achieved a strange beauty only because these were her last moments. Her dark brown hair, no longer bleached blond, looked soft and shiny.

What little could be seen of her face, the red lips and pale skin was accentuated by the black eye mask, giving the impression of an ivory cameo. It almost seemed to one writer seeing the two priests on either side of her that Catholicism had transformed this confused whore into a beatific martyr.

A less impressionable reporter saw a respectable suburban housewife with neat brown hair and a scrubbed face.

Guards took over from the priests and she trembled as she changed hands.

"Her two guards in their tan uniforms solicitously helped her into the chair and carefully strapped down her arms. As they bent to buckle her legs, she looked very fragile, almost beautiful," wrote Arthur Hoppe in the San Francisco *Chronicle*.

The smaller of the guards asked if the straps were too tight. She nodded and he loosened them slightly, then patted her lightly on the shoulder. The other leaned over and said, "Count to ten after you hear the cyanide tablets drop and then take a deep breath. It's easier that way."

She turned her head toward him and said, "How the hell would you know?"

The guards left, slammed the heavy steel door, and turned the airtight locks. Thirty-seven witnesses crowded the windows of the gas chamber watching her swallow nervously and wet her lips once or twice. Nothing happened for almost a minute. The gold wedding band on her finger flashed in the bluish light. Then, at 11:34, two cyanide pellets the size of mothballs dropped into a tank of sulphuric acid under her chair.

Reporter Arthur Hoppe noticed her small pendant earrings quivering nervously.

She took deep breaths and her head slumped forward. Seconds later she raised her head, then flung it back. She coughed a few times and her head sank and was still.

Her heart stopped twelve minutes after they'd strapped her in the chair.

As soon as her slight body was carried away, lunch was announced. Not too many of the witnesses were hungry.

It took three hours to clear the gas from the chamber, and the twin seats were taken by Santo and Perkins. As fifty-four-year-old Santo was strapped in, he grinned at the guards and said, "Take care of yourselves. Don't do anything I wouldn't do."

Without his dentures, Perkins looked much older than his forty-seven years.

The two men chatted together for half a minute, Santo doing most of the talking and Perkins nodding as if he had other things on his mind.

Santo died in six minutes; Perkins took a minute longer; both died as casually as they had killed.

"It was too easy," said witness Ed Cassidy, a Burbank detective. "They had it a lot easier than Mabel Monahan."

Not to mention the many others they had massacred.

The news reports and Ed Montgomery's futile attempt to save Barbara Graham weren't the end. Ironically, gossip columnist Louella Parsons' announcement of Hollywood interest came true, but quite unexpectedly.

Movie producer Walter Wanger suspected his actress wife, Joan

Bennett, of having an affair with her agent, Jennings Lang. He confronted Lang in a parking lot and shot him in the crotch. Wagner had done time for that and was traumatized by his comparatively easy prison stay. When he came out, he decided to expose the system, especially capital punishment, as the horror he believed it to be.

Ed Montgomery had submitted a sixty-page outline of Barbara Graham's life and death. Continuing his investigation after her death, Montgomery now was convinced the woman he first saw as a monster was an innocent victim. Wanger used the outline as the basis of a screenplay.

Susan Hayward played Barbara Graham. She got into the skin of the character by visiting women's prisons and sitting in the chair in the San Quentin gas chamber where Barbara Graham had died three years before.

The director, Robert Wise, watched an execution at San Quentin in an effort to ensure the film was authentic.

Hayward's performance had the director and some of the film crew in tears. It did not, however, make her an abolitionist. She said, "If somebody murdered the man I loved and didn't get the death penalty, I'd murder him myself."

Montgomery rated the picture "pretty factual," adding, "Oh, they Hollywooded the hell out of parts of it. But everything from the day she leaves Corona, the women's prison, to the execution in San Quentin is authentic as hell."

Clinton H. Anderson vigorously disagreed. He was Beverly Hills' chief of police and thought the film "brought what we felt was discredit on law enforcement methods and glorified a vicious criminal, Mrs. Barbara Graham, who had been executed by the State of California for her part in the brutal murder of an elderly housewife. The film purported to show that the Graham woman was innocent and that her conviction had been obtained by trickery. As a drama it was powerful enough to win an Academy Award for Susan Hayward, but in substance it was an unfair, untrue, and biased attack on police methods."*

Harlan Cooke, who had successfully prosecuted Barbara Graham, also damned the film as a distortion that omitted much of the trial evidence.

---

*Beverly Hills Is My Beat, by Clinton H. Anderson, Popular Library, 1962.

But emotions aroused by the film caused groups for and against the death penalty to demand what amounted to a retrial of the ghost of Barbara Graham. Under the new governor, Pat Brown, a state committee composed exclusively of lawyer-politicians listened to old and recently unearthed evidence to find out if evidence in her favor had been suppressed at the trial.

Cooke dropped a bombshell. He told the committee that she had confessed to Warden Teets before she was taken to the gas chamber. The warden was not available, having died at fifty-seven, some said of premature old age brought on by the strain of executing a woman. The doctor had called the cause a massive coronary.

San Quentin's Catholic chaplain, Father McAlister, told the committee that juries would never send anyone to the gas chamber if prosecutors didn't emotionally inflame them. Asked if Mrs. Graham had confessed to him the murder of Mrs. Monahan, he refused "to say what Mrs. Graham may or may not have confessed. The Confessional is not to be debased in this matter."

The next witness, Mrs. Nova, a San Quentin police officer, testified: "Barbara entered the prison at four in the afternoon. I was with her constantly from that moment until she entered the gas chamber late the next morning. Warden Teets saw her twice, each time for no more than two minutes."

A committee member asked: "Was anything said by Mrs. Graham that might be interpreted as a confession?"

"Nothing at all. There was no mention of anything relating to the murder."

Barbara might have confessed the warden during her earlier imprisonment at San Quentin—so the committee called for Mrs. Lorraine Mitchell, a woman police officer who was there at the time. She said: "Warden Teets insisted that I be present each time he or the prison doctor conferred with Barbara. I heard every word of each conversation. Nothing was ever said that could be construed as a confession."

Had John True, by changing his original testimony, traded his life for Barbara's? The public officials swore that True had not made any pretrial confession exonerating Barbara. But a subpoena produced such a confession.

Unknown to the jury that sent Barbara to her death, True had radically changed his original testimony to police interrogators. In his original statement, True said Barbara Graham was not involved in the planning or the execution of the crime. At the trial he reversed himself and described her in the house holding a gun on Mrs. Monahan while Perkins strangled the elderly woman.

More evidence of Barbara's innocence came from mystery writer Erle Stanley Gardner. He said Warden Teets had shown him a letter in Emmett Perkins' handwriting confessing to the Monahan murder. Perkins also admitted to the warden that, although Barbara had been traveling with the gang for weeks, she was not with them on the night of the murder.

"Why not clear her?" the warden asked Perkins. "In God's name, man, why not save an innocent woman's life?"

"She can go to hell!" he replied. "She had her chance and she blew it."

I said to Ed Montgomery during an interview on February 27, 1986: "What astonished me is that the warden didn't reveal this Perkins confession. It would have saved her life."

> *Montgomery:* Exactly. I've often pondered that. I couldn't figure out why he didn't. Another thing, Teets' assistant—Big Red they called him—went around telling people that Barbara Graham beat Mabel Monahan until her brains showed through her skull. That's a lot of bull. There was no such thing. She died of suffocation. They put the thing around her neck and garrotted her. Sure, there were two wounds above her forehead; the scalp was split; but the skull was not fractured. There were no brains coming out.

Why couldn't Warden Teets have given Perkins' written confession to Barbara Graham's attorney?

> *Montgomery:* I've often wondered about that. There were two defense attorneys. Neither one of them was worth a damn. They couldn't get your dog out of a pound.

What was to stop Teets from showing that confession to the authorities?

> *Montgomery:* Nothing.

Don't you think it's strange that he didn't?

> *Montgomery:* It is. During one of my last conversations with Perkins, I said he owed it to her to come forward and tell what he knew and get her out of there. He said he'd think about it and talk to Jack

Santo about it. And he decided if he was going to do anything he'd let me know. About a week before her execution, before she'd even been brought up from down south [Corona] to San Quentin, Friday about two P.M. I got a phone call from Warden Teets. He told me, "Perks wants to see you." I was president of the press club then and there was something very important on that evening, so I said, "Tell Perks I will be there at eleven o'clock Monday morning." "Fine, fine." Well, instead of quietly telling Perkins that I'd gotten the message and would be there, Teets phoned it up to the guard on death row and the guard shouted it the full length of death row. Perkins was in the second cell from the end, as I recall. Of course, right away everybody in prison knew what the hell was going on. And Santo was not aware until then that Perkins had called and wanted to see me. Perkins was going to carry it as though I'd come over to see him without his calling me. And Santo was livid with rage. He raised so much hell with Perkins when I got over there at eleven Monday morning. Teets went with me, and they brought Perkins down off death row to the special interview room for death-row prisoners, and we stood there talking through the screen to him. The first thing Perkins did was to cuss hell out of Teets. He said, "You silly bastard" this, that, and the other. "Didn't know any better than to relay a message that way in prison." And Perkins looked at me and said, "Everybody in this joint knows you're here and what you're here for and why I'm here. So I'm not talking." I got a little hot under the collar and chided him on a few things and said, "Perkins, the least you could have done is tell the DA, goddammit it, that Barbara was left-handed. Sure, she wrote with her right hand because at school they whacked her across the knuckles if she didn't, but everyone I talked to, everyone who knew her, said she was left-handed; that included the matron at the reform school she served time at." [The wounds on Mabel Monahan's scalp indicated they had been inflicted by a right-hander— probably Perkins.] I said, "She couldn't have pistol-whipped the woman the way they claimed."

Perkins said: "For Chrissakes, Montgomery, the old lady wasn't pistol-whipped. She was hit by her own cane." We didn't even know she had a cane. It turned out she'd been on the vaudeville stage as a skater, on the Orpheum circuit, had fallen and wrecked her hip and never skated after that and used a cane.

Why would Perkins worry about everybody on death row knowing he was talking to you at his request? After all, he was going to be executed. What had he got to lose? What could they do to him even if they knew he had admitted Barbara Graham was innocent?

Montgomery: He did tell me she wasn't pistol-whipped, she was hit with her own cane. That's when we found out for the first time that Mabel Monahan had a cane.

But why was Perkins so reluctant to talk to you after Santo and everyone else on death row knew he'd asked for the interview?

Montgomery: I don't know, except the code that you don't talk. You're going to die whatever you say and the other guys say, "My God, he kept quiet to the end."

The tough guy's code?

Montgomery: That's right.

Was Perkins under Jack Santo's control?

Montgomery: I never could quite figure it out, but if Santo wanted to blow a safe he'd send for Perkins; if Santo wanted to pull a particular kind of job he'd send for Perkins.

Why was Santo so anxious for Barbara Graham to die with them?

Montgomery: He was sore that she took that stand and testified. He said, "Don't you dare take the stand! If you don't take the stand they can't convict us of first-degree murder." She went ahead and took the stand in her own defense, and it was a big mistake, because she had once been convicted of perjury. They brought that out and it just destroyed her. And their case went out the window.

And Santo thought if she didn't take the stand he'd maybe get off?

Montgomery: That they'd all get off. He felt if she

didn't testify they couldn't convict anybody. But the thing that convinced me of Barbara Graham's innocence was the original confession of John True. He was in on the murder, but they dropped the charge against him before the trial started and he turned state's evidence. He took the stand and described in great detail how Barbara Graham pistol-whipped Mabel Monahan. As I said, she never was pistol-whipped—she was hit with her own cane, as Perkins admitted. But that didn't come out at the trial. Nobody knew she had a cane until long after Barbara Graham was executed. The night John True was picked up by the police, he gave a detailed statement and repeated it next day under oath for the Assistant DA for Los Angeles, who flew up to San Francisco. In that original confession True told how Perkins went into the bedroom, took a sheet and pillowcase off the bed, put the pillowcase over the woman's head, tore the sheet into strips, and choked her to death. In court, True said it was Barbara Graham, not Perkins, who did that. In the original confession, he told how he went down to L.A. and Burbank with Santo with some hot gold they stole off the mother lode up around Grass Valley. In fact, they killed a man up there and disposed of the gold on the black market. On the witness stand, True said he went down to L.A. to dive for abalone. He was a diver by profession. But at the time of the Monahan murder, abalone wasn't in season. He couldn't have gotten a job diving for abalone if he had wanted to. There's one conflict after another.

But had Barbara Graham been used to get Mrs. Monahan to open her door?

Montgomery: True testified how he stood alongside Perkins' car after Perkins had sent Barbara to ring the Monahan doorbell on the pretense of having to use a phone, and how Perkins instructed him, "The minute you see the light when the door opens, follow her in, rush over, and go in behind her." Now, I've gone there, long after the conviction and trial and all. You stand where John True says he stood and you can't see the front door. Talk about seeing the crack of light, you can't even see the door. The line of vision is such

that you just don't see it. In his original confession
True also told how they cased the place for two
evenings. Two of them sat in a car for an hour and a
half a block away and took off before people got
suspicious. Then the other car would come and watch.
They thought there was going to be a lot of money
there. Monahan's former son-in-law was a Las Vegas
gambler, and they thought he'd been skimming and
hidden big money in a safe in her home. And they'd
watch to see who came and went. Mrs. Monahan used
to go over to Gardena quite a bit to play poker. True
told in great detail how they cased the place and
decided which way to come and how to leave and all.
Yet, when he took the witness stand and testified, he
said he didn't even know there was going to be a
robbery until they pulled up in front of the place and
Perkins put a gun in his hand. That's the way the case
went all the way.

And the defense didn't have any of this material
from John True's original statements that would have
cleared Barbara Graham?

Montgomery: No. Hell, she had two attorneys paid a
total of five hundred dollars for all summer long until
the trial up until October: three months of pretrial
work. They didn't even have an investigator on the
case. Five hundred for two lawyers for six months'
work—what the hell do you expect? They didn't get
anything.

Where was she at the time of the murder?

Montgomery: She was in L.A. in an apartment with
her baby. I've talked to the woman next door to her.
There was no question. Barbara wasn't at the crime
scene.

Why didn't that woman testify for her?

Montgomery: She did. She gave a statement. They
discounted it.

Did you often speak to Barbara Graham on death
row?

Montgomery: Yes. They had her up at San Quentin
first, then they took her down to the women's prison in
Chino, Southern California. They brought her back just
before her execution at San Quentin. My boss then was

managing editor William Wren, perhaps the last of the
honest-to-god newspapermen in San Francisco. He said,
"You stay with it." So I made four or five trips to
Chino.

Did she admit if she was a member of the Santo and
Perkins murder gang?

Montgomery: No. She leveled with me on that score.
She said she'd get dolled up and go into the
Ambassador and pick up some guy with half a heat on
and a wad of dough—somebody from Texas or
somewhere—have a few drinks, and later on wind up
at Perkins' gambling joint called the El Monte Club.
And they'd fleece him. And she'd go back to town
with him and he'd think he was going to get something
at the hotel and she'd excuse herself to powder her
nose and leave out of a side door and go out to the
Biltmore and do it all over again. She said some nights
she made as much as a thousand bucks. So she made
no bones about that. And she had been a call girl, a
madam, a whatnot. She was very honest and frank in
that respect. But she didn't really know Santo. She did
know Perkins. And Perkins and Santo had worked on
jobs before. I have a picture of a woman with Santo
and Perkins and True, all at a nightclub. One of these
nightclub photos, you know, that they take? And here's
this girl right smack in the middle of it. I got it from
Mickey Cohen the mobster. And Mickey Cohen said,
"There's the gal that was with the boys that night." It
wasn't Barbara Graham. Of course, I got this a long
time after her execution. Most of the good stuff I
uncovered came after her execution.

If she wasn't involved in the murder, why did they
implicate her?

Montgomery: Well, there was a woman involved.
They did use a woman to gain access to the house. I'm
told it's this other gal whose name I don't think I
should reveal until some official action is taken toward
her. Because I could lay myself wide open. All I have
is Mickey Cohen's say-so, and Mickey's dead.

But why would Santo and Perkins want to finger
Barbara Graham rather than the real woman?

Montgomery: Because they were teed off at Barbara

Graham for testifying at the trial. They'd warned her to keep her mouth shut. John True was teed off in the first place because he tried to score with her and she'd have nothing to do with him. And Perkins—she'd do whatever he told her to do. She'd worked for him for a long time and all.

Where is John True now? I heard he drowned diving, when someone cut his air hose.

Montgomery: No. About two years after Barbara's execution, he was caught in a boat below decks in a collision on the Mississippi River and he drowned. His stateroom door jammed and he couldn't get out and he went to the bottom.

You've seen several people go to the gas chamber. How humane is it?

Montgomery: You have to think back to what Barbara said after they led her in there blindfolded the third time. Oh, that was awful, being led into the chamber and out again twice and then brought back a third time. How effective the stuff is I don't know. It seems that they're knocked out very quickly. The first whiff or so seems to put them under. But they're not dead for quite a while. That's why they have restraining straps, because there's muscular action, and all that is not at all pleasant. The first one I saw was up in Carson City, Nevada. Nevada was the first state to use the gas chamber, and the first man executed was a Chinaman.

Have you discussed your evidence of Barbara Graham's innocence with anyone in authority, and if so what was his response?

Montgomery: Frank Ahern, who then headed San Francisco Homicide and later became chief of police, was livid. He was enraged when he found out what John True had testified to, but they didn't care in San Francisco. It wasn't their case. It was all going on down in L.A. But when I said, "Frank, how in the hell could they let John True get up there and talk about going to L.A. to dive for abalone when abalone weren't in season?" Ahern said, "He didn't go to dive for abalone. He went to peddle hot gold." And I said, "Hot gold? What's all this about?" And then they told me about the original statement they took from True, and DA Tom Lynch let me have a copy of that original statement. Tom Lynch was the DA of San Francisco in whose office and in whose presence the statement had been made. Oh, and Inspector Corrusa of the San Francisco police, who died here a short time back, was the one who put her in Chicago when she went alibi for these two men who beat up Sally Stanford. And Corrusa said to his dying day that there was no doubt in his mind that Barbara Graham had nothing to do with the Monahan murder.

You once told me she was squeamish about the sight of blood.

Montgomery: Inspector Al Corrusa said that while she was working as a cocktail waitress in a bar on Market Street in San Francisco, a fight broke out, somebody got smacked in the nose and blood on his face, and she was through for the night. She couldn't get away from the place fast enough. Corrusa had arrested her three times and knew her very well. He was one of those who told me she was left-handed and was willing to swear to the fact. And he was the one who said she wouldn't tolerate violence and couldn't stand violence. When John True testified that Barbara pistol-whipped Mabel Monahan, Corrusa said that couldn't be: She couldn't bring herself to do it. And as I said, they eventually found she wasn't pistol-whipped at all, but was hit with her own cane.

Leslie Tusup was one of those who joined Ed Montgomery in the futile battle to save Barbara Graham's life. I interviewed him on February 3, 1986.

Do you go along with Ed Montgomery in thinking she was innocent?

Tusup: He was totally 110-percent convinced she was innocent. Where we differed was that we both believed she was innocent of the murder. I am not certain she might not have been somewhat involved in the crime that led to the murder. She was running around with these criminals, but Ed was sure she was never in any way involved with the crime, even to the way they got the door open.

So you think that incriminating her was a plot by the gang.

Tusup: Yes. I think they said, "We'll force the state to execute her in order to execute us—and they haven't got the guts to do that, so that will save us from execution." They felt that if they got her up front and got the death penalty for her as well, then that gave them a chance of being saved from the gas chamber, because if they commuted Barbara's sentence they'd have to commute them all.

Although California had already gassed two women, Spinelli and Peete.

Tusup: But not for quite a while. And the opposition to the death penalty was growing in California at the time. Barbara was charged with being involved in this one crime, but these other guys [Santo and Perkins and others] had killed seven people [at least] at different times and they were such bastards that public opinion was willing to let Barbara go in order to get them. But Barbara's execution plus the execution of Caryl Chessmann led to the abolition of the death penalty in California. Now it's back again [1986], although the courts are blocking its enforcement.

Wouldn't Barbara Graham's last attorney, Al Matthews, be the most likely to solve the mystery of her guilt or innocence? I tried to contact him, but he was in the hospital with a stroke. However, his wife, Emily, had been his legal secretary during the Graham appeal—had worked with him on it—and she spoke with me on March 2, 1986.

It's understandable why Barbara should pick Matthews. He had a reputation as a miracle worker who tackled "impossible" cases and saved innocents who seemed destined for the gas chamber. A fifth-generation lawyer, his uncle was a lawyer and his father a Dubuque, Iowa, judge, and many relatives in Ireland were judges or lawyers.

After a few years in private practice, Matthews took tests to become a public defender. His outstanding score, a 98.6-percent average, catapulted him into the big time. He was immediately appointed number-one deputy public defender, a job he held from 1947 to 1950.

Matthews started a unique organization, The Court of Last Resort, when he asked crime writer Erle Stanley Gardner to help him free William Marvin Lindley from death row.* Lindley had been convicted of a particularly brutal sex murder on eyewitness testimony and the evidence against him was overwhelming. But Matthews believed he was not guilty, and the appeal to Gardner—who read a transcript of Lindley's trial—moved the writer to petition Governor Earl Warren to free Lindley.

"I worked with Al on the Lindley case for two or three years," Mrs. Matthews recalled. "We couldn't prove he was innocent, but we raised so much doubt that his death sentence was commuted to life in prison. He lived in homes for the elderly after that and died in one of them. He was going to be paroled but he didn't want to be, because he had no place to go.

"Before Lindley, Al proved that a man sentenced to life imprisonment was completely innocent of the crime and picked up the guilty man. That happened in Sacramento."

Matthews was back in private practice when Barbara Graham was asked what attorney she'd like to appeal her death sentence. "I want Al Matthews," she said.

Knowing she was broke, he didn't charge a fee and paid for investigators out of his own pocket. I asked Mrs. Matthews if it was usual for an attorney to work for nothing.

> *Emily Matthews:* No, not common at all.
> He did it as a humanitarian?
> *Matthews:* Yes. Most people would take a public defender and let it go at that. But Al was now out of the public defender's office and back in private practice. Barbara knew of his history; that's why she wanted him.

---

*The Court of Last Resort consisted of crime experts—among them Al Matthews; Erle Stanley Gardner; Dr. Le Moyne Snyder, who was both an attorney and doctor of medicine; and detective Raymond Schindler—who donated their time and expertise to investigate cases of those they believed unjustly convicted of murder. Their reports were published in the now-defunct magazine *Argosy*.

Ed Montgomery contends that Santo and Perkins framed her.

Matthews: No question about it. They had a girl friend that had been running around with them up in Northern California. We've always felt she was the one, and they shielded her and framed Barbara.

I'm curious about who was looking after her baby son the night she was picked up by the police with Santo and Perkins.

Matthews: Her husband. He wasn't such an addict he couldn't take care of the baby. He was just a drug user.

Her priest implied that she never confessed to him that she'd committed murder.

Matthews: Yes. She was buried in hallowed ground by the Catholic church. They believed she was innocent. She wouldn't have been buried in hallowed ground if they thought she'd committed murder.

I presume she had a sense of humor and was joking about appearing on "What's My Line?" as a prostitute?

Matthews: Yes, I think she had a sense of humor. But she was quite a demure girl, really. She was very ladylike. She never talked vulgar or anything like that, according to Mr. Matthews. You know, it's interesting, but everyone connected with that case that testified against Barbara died, I can't say a violent death, but an unusual, unexpected death.

Why d'you think Mr. Matthews couldn't save her life?

Matthews: Because there was no one to testify as to her innocence, only Barbara herself. No one was at the scene who would say Barbara didn't do it.

He was sure she was innocent?

Matthews: He felt Barbara Graham was absolutely innocent. He still feels that way today. So do I.

Barbara Graham was no Mother Teresa. She ran around with vicious killers, and although Montgomery and Inspector Corrusa said she couldn't stand the sight of blood, she knew that many of the men she lured to Perkins' gambling joint were mugged on their way out. That didn't stop her. Yet, the evidence of John True's radically changed testimony, of the comments to Montgomery by Santo and Perkins, as well as Montgomery's investigation, suggest that California executed an innocent woman.

Why, after her death, did Warden Teets or the prosecutor lie—and say that she had privately confessed her guilt? Why did the warden suppress Perkins' letter in which he admitted to the murder?

California Governor Brown called Barbara Graham's execution "one of the most distasteful episodes in California history. It has been like some dark memory out of the Roman Colosseum."

Fate played a cruel, ironic trick on Barbara Graham. Santo and Perkins framed her thinking she was their passport to life. But the State was so determined to execute the two vicious murderers, it allowed Barbara Graham to be sacrificed with them even though there was doubt about her guilt.

18

Theodore Bundy
"Everywhere he goes, death follows"
The Homicidal Crisis Counselor

In almost any group, he'd be the last you'd suspect of any crime. Articulate, clean-cut, good-looking, and a law student active in Young Republican affairs, he was so concerned with others he worked as a Crisis Hotline volunteer and gave phone comfort to people in distress. Yet he had a saving sense of humor.

Too good to be true? He was. Lurking behind the friendly smile, steady gaze, and lighthearted banter was a psychopathic killer who savagely murdered and mutilated at least thirty and possibly over a hundred women in a killing spree across five states, from Washington to Florida.

He was arrested, twice escaped from custody, and made a third unsuccessful escape attempt from a death-row cell.

His last victim, thirteen-year-old Kimberly Leach, was a Lake

City Junior High student. More than two thousand residents of her small town signed a petition in favor of executing Bundy.

"Many who signed said they'd like to sign twice and would pull the switch twice," said a nurse whose daughter was Kimberly's classmate. "Our town has not been the same since Bundy came here. Now, if our children are a few minutes late getting home from anywhere, we almost panic."

Lake City may get its wish. Found guilty of murdering Kimberly as well as two young women at Florida State University, Bundy has been sentenced to die in the electric chair.

To get an expert's opinion on Bundy, I interviewed criminologist James Sewell. He investigated murders for which Bundy got the death sentence. I spoke with him on January 10, 1986; and a week later I interviewed one of Bundy's attorneys, Vic Africano, to get a defense viewpoint.

Jim Sewell: Ted Bundy's been killing for a long time. He was raised on the West Coast in the Seattle, Washington, area and probably was responsible for at least double-digit murders out in Washington, Oregon, Utah, and Colorado. He had been convicted of an attempted kidnapping in Salt Lake City of a woman, Carol DaRonch. After he'd started his sentence, he was then bound over to stand trial for murder in Colorado. He escaped while he was awaiting trial, twice; the second time was December 31, 1977. He made his way from the Aspen, Colorado, area to Michigan; from there through Atlanta to Tallahassee where he arrived in early January of 1978.

The morning of January fifteenth—Now, part of this is supposition and part hard fact—we know that sometime after two o'clock on that Sunday morning Bundy entered the Chi Omega sorority house. During the course of the next hour and twenty minutes he murdered two women and left two for dead. He probably entered by a back door; there was a combination security lock on that door that had a tendency to jam.

He went up to the second floor in the living quarters. Again, supposition, he probably scouted the area because that's Ted's MO. He doesn't let himself get boxed in. He went from door to door down the corridor and probably entered a couple of rooms before he found one with somebody in it.

The first victim he struck with an oak club and strangled. The second, he did the same thing to and then he entered the room of two women together and did the same to both of them. He was interrupted in that last episode, probably by women who had just arrived home from dates, and he heard noises and decided to run. He fled down the front staircase and out the front door of the sorority house. He was seen by a woman who woke up the sorority president and asked why there had been a man in the house.

While the two women were talking, another victim, Karen Chandler, stumbled out of her room, and they turned to ask her if she had seen a man and realized she was bleeding. They called the hospital. The hospital called the Tallahassee police department, and the Florida State University police at about 3:23 A.M. The first police officers arrived on the scene at 3:26.

Now, my involvement at that time: I was sergeant with the Florida State University police in charge of administration, and was also public information officer for the department. Standard operations were for me to be notified of any major event like that. So I was the first administrator notified and I was at the sorority house fifteen minutes after my notification. So I got to deal with the bodies and the blood.

I got there at 3:50; my chief and the chief investigator got there within another twenty or twenty-five minutes. The sheriff and some fifteen people were also there. While we were talking, about four-thirty or quarter to five, we got another call to another assault that had taken place nearby. The woman we found, Cheryl Thomas, was Bundy's primary victim. That's pretty much the way things went down there.

Some time later, in early February, Bundy left Tallahassee in a stolen van and went to Jacksonville, where he attempted to pick up a girl named Leslie Parmenter. Leslie went to junior high there. Bundy

parked at a parking lot across from the school and
saw Leslie. She was about fourteen and probably
looked eighteen, particularly physically. Bundy
tried to get her in the van, and luckily Leslie's brother
turned up at the time and chased Bundy away.
Bundy had alleged that he was an investigator for
the fire department and that his name was Richard
Burton. Interestingly enough, Leslie's father
was a homicide detective for the Jacksonville sheriff's
office.

Bundy left there and went to Lake City, spent the
night at the Holiday Inn there, and next morning
kidnapped Kimberly Leach. We don't know how he
got her in the van, but he got her in the van. Her body
was found about a month later in the woods near Lake
City.

Bundy came back to Tallahassee for a couple of
days, stole another car, and fled west. He got a room
in Pensacola and parked in an alley at a strange hour,
like three in the morning. A Pensacola police officer,
David Lee, saw the car and fell in behind it. Bundy
decided to move. David ran the tag through the
Florida Crime and Information Center computer. It
came back that it was a stolen tag. David pursued him,
got him out of the car, there was a struggle. Bundy
fled. There was another struggle and David managed to
take him into custody.

For a couple of days we didn't know who he was.
He claimed his name was Ken Misner. Ken was a
former FSU track star and Bundy had ID belonging to
Ken. He'd apparently stolen it with a number of other
things during his time here. After a day or so Bundy
decided to identify himself. He had been added to the
FBI's Most Wanted list a couple of days before but we
hadn't run his prints yet, so we didn't know who he
was until he said, "I'm Ted Bundy and I think
somebody's looking for me."

He was indicted here for two counts of murder and
three counts of attempted murder on the basis of the
Tallahassee cases, and one count of murder for the
Kimberly Leach case. In July 1978 he stood trial for
the Tallahassee portion of cases. In the summer of

1979 he was tried and convicted of two murders and three attempted murders, and in January or early February 1980 he was tried for the Kimberly Leach murder and was convicted of that.

He's got three death sentences right now here in Florida. The clemency board has just ruled and has not granted him clemency. The warrant has not yet been signed. His appeals have been through the state system. There are appeals pending in the federal system, but Governor Graham has not yet signed the death warrant.

Then he could appeal to the U.S. Supreme Court?

Sewell: Right.

So it could be several more years at least.

Sewell: I'm planning on this being a lifetime career. I think it will be a while before Ted's executed.

Do you think he will be?

Sewell: I think so.

Were you at his trial?

Sewell: He cross-examined me. Ted examined me during the pretrial hearings and then I was under cross-examination in the trial stage. During the Tallahassee case I was more an administrator and less an investigator. But during the Lake City case I wound up doing part of the investigation to identify one of the murder weapons. I testified in the murder case of Kimberly Leach. So I was at the second trial and I think Ted learned from that. I think he had better counsel. Victor Africano was his principal counsel during the Lake City trial and Vic kept him under tighter rein than he was kept in Miami, so he didn't get involved as much as being both a defense attorney and the defendant.

What was your impression of Bundy as his own attorney?

Sewell: He didn't learn the first lesson you learn in law school: that if you're on trial you don't use yourself as your own attorney.

When he was questioning you, what was your impression of him?

Sewell: I don't think he was that good. Ted's a very intelligent young man, but a lot less intelligent than he would like people to think. His IQ tested at roughly 125. That's above average, but he tried to appear more of an intellectual than he is. He obviously was a challenge. He's got an innate animal intelligence.

Some talk of his hypnotic effect on others. That was an explanation of why a prison employee tried to help him escape recently. Remember he cut through two bars?

Sewell: Sure. I think that's crap. Ted's a con man. Ted's a sociopath. He's able to con people and make them believe he is one of their friends and that they're helping him, and how innocent he is. But I don't think there's anything as far as a real hypnotic spell that he placed people under.

Then he conned one of the guards to help him escape, did he?

Sewell: Sure. I think a combination of being able to convince him and being able to offer him pay was the kind of thing that will do that.

His defense is that he's entirely innocent of all these crimes.

Sewell: That's been his defense: that he's not involved.

What's the psychiatric view of him?

Sewell: That he's probably classically a sociopath. During part of the Tallahassee pretrial, Dr. Cleckley, who wrote *The Mask of Sanity,* was brought in; and Cleckley, after examining Bundy, was pretty well convinced he was a sociopath.

Under the M'Naghten Rule, that's no excuse, because he would know what he had done was wrong.

Sewell: There's no question in my mind that Ted Bundy knew what he was doing was wrong.

Might he be excused under the Durham Rule?

Sewell: I don't think so. I don't think Ted Bundy's crazy. He's a sadist. Ted is not crazy in terms of the law. A sociopath is not mentally ill. It's a mental disturbance, not mental illness. There's a fiction book out called *The Red Dragon,* by Thomas Harris. Thomas wrote the book *Black Sunday* about a terrorist

seizing the Goodyear Blimp to blow up the Superbowl.
And *The Red Dragon* is one of the best books on a
serial murderer. He probably had a lot of help from
the FBI Behavioral Sciences Unit, because of some of
the stuff that's in there, and there's a lot of vying at
times for who at the FBI gave him the most
information. The protagonist in the book is an FBI
expert on serial murderers—a contract agent, not a real
agent—and he is asked by a newspaperman if he
considered this serial killer to be a sociopath or a
psychotic, or was he mentally ill, or how would
he define him? And the protagonist said he would
define him as a monster. He's an aberration, not
within our realm of understanding. And I think Ted
Bundy is a monster. I don't think he's mentally ill in
the way we think of a psychotic, or of the normally
disturbed person. His disturbance is far too deep.
He's a cold, calculating killer. There's no question
in my mind that Ted Bundy has been killing since he
was a teenager. There is no question in my mind
that, except for the fact that he made mistakes, he
would have continued killing if he had escaped from
Pensacola or from any other place. And that he
would continue to do it and would continue to enjoy
doing it.

Do any psychiatrists claim they could rehabilitate
him?

Sewell: None I know; none I respect.

A book was written, *The Only Living Witness,* in
which Bundy cooperated and speculated about the
murders. "If I were the killer," et cetera. A very
strange thing to do.

Sewell: Ted talked like that a lot. When we
interviewed him in Pensacola for the first time, he took
part in a lot of that type of conversation. He said, "If I
was the one who killed Kimberly Leach I would look
for her body in" such-and-such location, or "I would
not want to find it because it's so horrible what's been
done to it."

Was he giving you the right location?

Sewell: Yes. He never told us where it is, but he came real close.

Can you speculate what Bundy would say if you asked him, "What do you think of serial murderers who mutilate and kill?"

Sewell: Yes. I think he probably would have opened up as to why. I think there was a time when Ted would have done that willingly. I think there was a time when Ted would have admitted to having done the crimes. I'm not sure it still exists, but there were at least two points during the process when Ted basically offered a deal to talk more openly in exchange for things like being able to return and spend his time in a Washington facility instead of in Florida.

Washington would have been more comfortable.

Sewell: Sure, and would have been right close to his family.

And perhaps he thought he could escape more easily from Washington.

Sewell: That's always a possibility with Ted.

Could he still make a deal?

Sewell: Not now. At that time there was [a chance]. Any Florida governor willing to say "I'm going to let Ted Bundy out to go to Washington" runs a grave political risk. Ted Bundy's an emotional issue in the state.

When you thought he might have talked openly, was that in the early days when a woman colleague of his whom he'd phoned wanted to see him?

Sewell: That's right.

Do you find it strange that a serial killer should have worked for Crisis Hotline, in an organization to help people?

Sewell: That's not different from other murderers. Edmund Kemper is a classic serial murderer out of California. He killed his grandmother and grandfather while a teenager and spent time in a mental facility and was allowed out.* During the course of the next several years he killed six young women hitchhikers,

*"I just wondered how it would feel to shoot Grandma," he told authorities.

then killed his mother and his mother's best friend. Now, the first two killings weren't serial. The hitchhikers were, though. Kemper, I think, was an auxiliary police officer; he was into some of the social service type of things. John Wayne Gacy, the Chicago serial killer, was also into things designed to help people. He was known as the community clown because he'd dress up in a clown's costume to appear at children's events. I don't think it's atypical. It's one further way for them to disguise themselves. Ted was not only working at the Crisis Hotline, as documented in the book by Ann Rule, [*The Stranger Beside Me*] he was involved in a weight-prevention program that the governor of Washington put together; and he was involved in political campaigns.

And, of course counseling distressed people is one way for a sadist to get close to cruelty and hear about it.

Sewell: Sure.

Are you for or against capital punishment?

Sewell: I believe capital punishment is a viable alternative in any case of homicide.

How about killings in the heat of passion?

Sewell: They aren't a recidivist problem. One of my first dealings as a police officer was with a group of killers in Jacksonville who robbed mom-and-pop grocery stores and shot people afterwards for fun. Those guys deserved to die. They could not accept social mores. They did not believe the things we believe. There's no other way to control those kinds of people. And society has both a right and an obligation to destroy mad dogs.

A chaplain at Starke Prison characterizes death-row inmates there as warm, loving persons; or depraved. How would Bundy be perceived?

Sewell: If he wants to project it, he could be perceived as a warm, loving person. Anybody who knows the depravity of the offenses Bundy committed would not believe it. He showed when he was doing crisis counseling on the phone that he could convey the image of being warm and comforting. I think his standard method of operation where he enticed women to come into his car also conveys that; because obviously he could sell himself as something he wasn't. He did two back-to-back kidnappings in Washington where he approached women only a couple of hours apart with his arm in a sling, saying he had a broken arm and needed help in putting his canoe into his Volkswagen, and was able to convince some fairly astute women that he needed help.

There's a new rule in California allowing psychiatrists to interview condemned killers on death row. It's confidential. The killer can tell the psychiatrist anything, and the psychiatrist can only testify if the information is favorable to these condemned men. According to one psychiatrist, these men are so frank and outspoken about murders they committed—some still unknown to the police—and so graphic and bloodthirsty in descriptions of their victims' futile pleas for mercy, that he says, although fellow psychiatrists may ridicule him, he thinks these men are evil. Would that tie in with your calling Bundy a monster?

Sewell: Yes. I think Ted Bundy and many other serial murderers are evil incarnate. I realize, like that psychiatrist, that if I stand up as a criminologist and say there's such a thing as evil incarnate, many of my colleagues wouldn't understand. It's not scientific. Those same criminologists have never had to pick up a dying girl. There is evil incarnate, and I think Ted Bundy is one, Edmund Kemper is one, and John Wayne Gacy. Those people exemplify what we're talking about.

FOR THE DEFENSE

Victor Africano was one of Bundy's defense attorneys. I spoke with him on January 16, 1986. Mr. Africano, did you approve of Bundy collaborating on the book *The Only Living Witness*? [by Stephen G. Michaud and Hugh Aynesworth.]

Victor Africano: I had nothing to say about it. Any major criticisms of the book?

Africano: The conclusions they (the authors) drew that he was guilty. I disagree.

You argue that Bundy says he is innocent; but even *if* he is guilty, unrefuted psychiatric testimony says he must have been crazy at the times he committed the crimes; that is your argument, isn't it? That's what the two authors of the book quote as your argument.

Africano: That's not exactly what I said. I did not say "unrefuted psychiatric testimony," and if I did that's not what I meant to say. What I believe I said during the penalty phase was that if he was guilty of this crime, the crime he had been found guilty of—I'm paraphrasing—then obviously the man had to be crazy.

It's like a catch-22. For Bundy to be found *not guilty* by reason of insanity, he has to plead *guilty*.

Africano: Yes. When someone pleads not guilty by reason of insanity, one admits the acts but says I did not know the difference between right and wrong at the time.

And Bundy refuses to do that?

Africano: He refuses to admit the acts.

But doesn't he also refuse to plead insanity regardless of whether he committed the acts?

Africano: No, that was my argument, not Mr. Bundy's. It's my opinion that if in fact Mr. Bundy did these things as two juries have found, then he must have been crazy. I said that without admitting my client was guilty, because I still professed his innocence. But based upon the decisions of the two juries, then this man, if in fact guilty by the two jury verdicts, had to be crazy.

In her book *The Phantom Prince,* Elizabeth Kendell quotes her record of a phone conversation with Bundy in which he virtually confesses to murder by mentioning a consuming force that on occasions he couldn't resist.

Africano: If you want to question me on the basis that it's going to have some scientific or legal merit and you want to have my viewpoint, that's fine; but if you take dribs and drabs from books by people who have touched Bundy and are out to make a buck out of their interpretations—

This woman lived with Bundy for several years.

Africano: I know who she is. She's out to make a buck and so are the authors of *The Only Living*

Witness. I don't take what they say. Don't ask me questions based upon what someone like that said, because my opinion is that they are out to make a buck, which is their constitutional right. But I'm not going to answer questions on the assumption that what they're saying is true and correct. Do you know where I'm coming from?

My question is a legal one. Is what Elizabeth Kendell reports as a recorded conversation held over the telephone—she says in the book that she took a pencil to make notes because otherwise she wouldn't remember it accurately—is that conversation admissible in court?

Africano: I wouldn't think so.

The two writers Michaud and Aynesworth conclude their book *The Only Living Witness* in these words: "By his own lunatic testimony Bundy likes death row and is unconcerned about his prospective execution." Do you have any response to that?

Africano: The times I've seen Mr. Bundy, he doesn't profess any liking for death row and he certainly is not unconcerned about the prospects of an execution. As I said, they're writing conclusions. They took a different tack from the others.

Though he did cooperate with them, didn't he?

Africano: As far as I know. I wasn't there when it was going on, but I was aware that it was going on.

How many more appeals can you make on Bundy's behalf?

Africano: The next court is the U.S. Supreme Court. If there's no reversal at that level, then you start back down at the district court level in the federal system. You hope to get back to the Supreme Court, but on different grounds.

And that could be several more years?

Africano: Yes, sir.

Do you believe in capital punishment?

Africano: No, sir.

Not even for serial killers?

Africano: I don't think I'd have any problem in seeing a life being taken if it was taken at the scene of the crime. Somebody walks into a store, and in an exchange of gunfire while they were brutally murdering a teller, their life is taken. With that I have no problem. When the system gets involved and they go through all the procedures, safeguards, and what have you, and the heat of passion has subsided as far as society is concerned, I think better things could be done with these people. Study them scientifically to see what causes them to do this, so perhaps something useful could be known about these types of people. If you saw a common thread in their genes or chromosones, and youngsters could be tested when they show similar signs—and be given help; I think we as a society are intelligent enough to do that.

In a Miami *Herald* report, Bundy had appealed the sentence on the grounds that the judge . . . because of pretrial publicity had erred in finding the murders "especially heinous, atrocious, and cruel." The judge said, "There's no merit in this argument. The victims were bludgeoned, sexually battered, and strangled. The circumstances are more than sufficient to uphold the trial findings." Why d'you think Bundy would say such crimes aren't atrocious, et cetera?

Africano: I didn't make that argument and I haven't discussed it with him. As far as I'm concerned, they were. Those words (that the crimes were not atrocious] did not come out of Bundy's mouth. They came out of the mouth of the lawyer arguing against the death penalty.

And he may have been grasping at anything?

Africano: Certainly. In my case, certainly if the young lady, the Leach girl, who was killed—in a theory advanced by the state—it was "especially heinous, atrocious, and cruel." My argument was that there was no proof that it was, because there were a number of different ways that she could have left the junior high school and wound up in that hog pen in the same condition, without the crime being especially heinous, atrocious, and cruel. And it's up to the state to prove those elements beyond and to the exclusion of every reasonable doubt. There are other theories inconsistent with the state's hypothesis. Perhaps that was what was being argued down there.

If Bundy is executed, do you think they will have executed an innocent man?

Africano: I'm defending the man. I'm ethically obligated to advance the cause of his innocence.

If a man you represent admits he has committed the crime, are you legally bound to reveal this?

Africano: Absolutely not. Everything that passes between an attorney and client is privileged. Your burden is to challenge the proofs of the prosecution. But you cannot advance any defense if you are aware your client is guilty. You can't put him on the stand and have him say, "No, I'm not guilty," or parade a thousand alibi witnesses who are going to perjure themselves and say he was around the corner when this whole thing happened. You cannot do that. But, notwithstanding what he may tell you, you are not bound to reveal that. As a matter of fact, you would be disbarred if you do.

On the other hand, must the prosecution help the accused if they have evidence in his favor?

Africano: The rules, especially in Florida, as far as what the government is required to give the defense, are probably the most liberal in the country. It would be very hard, although not impossible, for the state to suppress evidence. Certainly, if they had somebody else's fingerprints on the knife and said they were the defendant's fingerprints, that would certainly be a violation that's very hard to do. Most of your law enforcement people, your prosecutors, play by the rules. I say most. There are some that don't. What little I know about it, if Sacco and Vanzetti and Richard Hauptmann were prosecuted today, they'd get a fair trial. I don't know what the outcome would be, but I think they'd get a fair trial. Because of the carnival atmosphere in those days and even since, in the Sam Sheppard case, the courts are more aware that you have to control the press and what happens in the courtroom.

As a defense attorney, if the accused admits to you that he's guilty of the crime but insists on pleading innocent in court, you could give up the case, couldn't you?

Africano: To the defense attorney, it does not matter what his client tells him as far as his guilt or innocence is concerned. Because he is not legally guilty until the state proves his guilt beyond and to the exclusion of every reasonable doubt. Only then, in the eyes of the law, is he guilty. Factual guilt is . . . I don't want to use the word *immaterial* because that would offend society and the public; but for the legal system, as far as convicting that person, it is immaterial.

At a Board of Clemency hearing for Bundy, attorney Willie Meggs urged Florida Governor Bob Graham not to overturn the double death sentence, saying, "This was a brutal crime, a savage crime, an animalistic crime. People in the area lived in terror until Bundy was caught." Meggs' assistant, Jack Poitinger, said Bundy may have killed more than a hundred women and "is like the plague —everywhere he goes, death follows."

Bundy wasn't present. He had written from death row in Starke Prison, "To allow any hearing to take place without any representation or input from me will make it a sham and a farce. My sincere best wishes for all of you for a joyous and loving Christmas, Peace, Ted Bundy."

Suspecting this was another of Bundy's delaying tactics, Governor Graham moved the case forward by signing the black-bordered death warrant for Bundy to be executed on March 4, 1986.

Bundy's new attorneys, Polly Nelson and Patricia Douglass of Washington, D.C., asked the U.S. Supreme Court to block his scheduled execution. The court did so. A week before Bundy was to die, the justices postponed the event until they had time to consider a formal appeal on his behalf.

His attorneys then asked the U.S. Supreme Court to overturn his murder conviction because his constitutional rights had been violated when testimony from a hypnotized witness was admitted in his trial.

They questioned the use of hypnosis on Nita Neary, a sorority sister who testified that she vaguely recalled seeing a man leave the house after Margaret Bowman and Lisa Levy were murdered. She identified Bundy in a photo lineup after seeing his picture in newspapers, and a year later identified him in court.

And—his attorneys claimed—because he had not been allowed to confront his hypnotized accuser, he had not been given an opportunity to argue that a witness against him whose memory had been sharpened by hypnosis had violated his rights under the Fifth and Fourteenth Amendments.

Additionally, they said his constitutional rights had been violated by the exclusion of jurors opposed to the death penalty.

The high court denied Bundy's appeal 7-2, with Justices William Brennan and Thurgood Marshall [opponents of the death penalty] dissenting; and Governor Graham signed a new death warrant setting Bundy's electrocution date for July 2, 1986.

Sixteen hours before he was to die, the 11th U.S. Circuit Court of Appeals in Atlanta granted Bundy an indefinite stay.

Interviewed by Richard Holmes, dean of the University of Louisville [Ky.] School of Justice Administration, for a book on serial killers, Bundy said: "Killers are very rational people. The more people they kill, the better they get at disposing of bodies. . . . You only find the bodies that a serial killer wants you to find. There's plenty more you'll never find."

Eight years after the Florida murders, I asked Jim Sewell how he feels about the fate of the now thirty-nine-year-old Bundy.

"Part of me says Ted Bundy shouldn't die," Sewell replied. "The other part of me is the police officer who saw those victims, who dealt with the two injured women, who had to notify the parents that their daughters were dead. That part of me wants to watch Ted Bundy die."

If Bundy tunes in to radio station WAPE in Jacksonville, he can hear the unambivalent views of a disc jockey known as The Greaseman.

The morning John Spenkelink was to die in the electric chair, The Greaseman held the mike to what sounded like sizzling bacon, saying, "That's for you, John!"

Once, The Greaseman greeted death-row inmates with, "Good morning, you maggots. Are you up yet? You'd better enjoy the sunrise. There aren't many left for you."

The Greaseman believes he speaks for most Floridians—and maybe most Americans—when he says of people like Theodore Bundy: "Let them babies burn!"

John Cheever gave a writing class for Sing Sing prisoners, and his subsequent based-on-fact novel *Falconer* quotes a guard's-eye view of the death-row crowd.

"They murder," said the guard, "they rape, they stuff babies into furnaces, they'd strangle their own mothers for a stick of chewing gum."

He didn't add: "Of course, some may be innocent."

19

Gallows Humor

Gallows humor is alive and well in the death rows of America. While some go screaming or traumatized with terror, many go with a smile and a quip, and some even die laughing. Jack Sullivan, at twenty-three, went to the Florence, Arizona, gas chamber with a big grin and a cigar between his teeth. At the last moment he handed over the cigar, but he kept the grin until the gas hit him.

As he sat in the electric chair, Frederick Wood said to the witnesses, "Gents, this is an educational project. You are about to witness the damaging effect of electricity on Wood. Enjoy yourselves."

Either the gas chamber isn't soundproof, or there was a lip-reader among the witnesses who watched Lloyd Anderson executed. As the cyanide tablets dropped into the sulphuric acid under his chair, Anderson looked at the faces at the windows and said, "The same to the rest of you guys."

In Sing Sing, the day before he was to be electrocuted, a prisoner was taken to a holding cell in a large circular room where he could hear radio or phonograph music. Prisoners called it "the dance hall," the walk to the chair "the last mile," and the chair itself "the hot seat." They referred to electrocution as "frying" or "burning," and whenever a man got a reprieve, they'd say "the burner is out of a fee."

Those going to die and those waiting their turns often play it cool. One man on his way to his execution called out to a death-row neighbor, "See you tomorrow."

"You'd better not," the other responded. "Ghosts spoil my appetite."

If they are neither sullen nor obviously scared, killers seem to psych themselves up with an almost pathological emphasis on the sunny side of things. Boy Van Winkle killed a policeman in a gun battle and was himself paralyzed with a bullet in the back. He was carried into court on a stretcher, found guilty of murder, and sentenced to death. The twenty-six-year-old Van Winkle looked almost pleased. "When you die young," he said, "you make a good-looking corpse."

At times the humor is hysterical or insane. On his way to his murder trial, Kenneth Neu sang and did a fair imitation of Fred Astaire. Neu had been discharged from the army as psychotic. He claimed he was kicked out because of his affair with a colonel's wife. Although he had a record of mental illness and had been treated in the Georgia State Mental Home, state psychiatrists put him through thirty-three days of tests and interviews and said he was fit for trial.

Neu's defense was that in resisting a homosexual's advances, he had fatally smashed the man's skull with an electric iron. In his death cell he entertained the guards by singing and tap dancing. He also composed two songs. One was titled "I'm As Fit As a Fiddle and Ready To Hang"; the other, "Oh You Nasty Man," he dedicated to the hangman.

Was Neu insane? A psychiatrist for the defense testified that he was; that his brain was affected by cerebral syphilis. But the defense psychiatrist was obviously outgunned by psychiatrists for the prosecution.

Warden Lawes of Sing Sing was amused by many death-row inmates who seemed to have adopted Albert Schweitzer's reverence for life and claimed they never even killed an insect. Lawes remarked that it was unfortunate they hadn't developed this respect for life a little earlier.

But Lawes was impressed by the gentleness and care many condemned men gave to stray birds that flew into their cells. In fact, some, like the Bird Man of Alcatraz, were given permission to breed canaries. The warden who took over from Lawes, Wilfred Denno, put an end to the canary breeding when he found that the birdseed the men used contained poppy seeds whose plants produce—opium.

The night before he was gassed, Wilson de la Roi played on a harmonica "I Want a Pardon for My Daddy," and "I'll Be Glad

When You're Dead, You Rascal, You." His last request was for some Tums, "because I think I'm about to get gas in my stomach." He entered the gas chamber smiling.

About to face a firing squad, James Rodgers' last request was for a bulletproof vest.

One prisoner almost had his foot in the gas chamber when the phone rang and he was given a reprieve. A fellow death-row prisoner wanted to know how he felt when he thought he was about to die. "Did your ass twitch?" the other man asked. "Hell," he replied, "it jumped clean out of its socket."

Murderer Chuck Appel had an acute sense of humor and timing. He was about to be electrocuted for killing a New York policeman. Executioner Robert Elliott had already put the hood on Appel's head when he said, "Elliott, you are about to serve a baked Appel."

Roger DeGarmo, nicknamed "Animal," tried to auction three of the five invitations he was given for personal witnesses at his execution in Huntsville, Texas, before dawn on March 12, 1986. Three strangers who wanted to see him die bid up to $1,500. But prison authorities wouldn't go along with his scheme, telling the condemned killer he'd left it too late.

For coolness under pressure Elliott gave the award to a woman, Irene Schroder. She and her lover had killed a state policeman during an attempted robbery. Shortly before she was to die in a double execution—with her lover as her partner—her only concern was for him. "Please tell the cook to fry Glenn's eggs on both sides," she told a guard. "That's how he likes them."

For grace under pressure, no one beats the anonymous young man about to face San Quentin's gas chamber. He had asked Warden Clinton Duffy to bring a small bottle of whiskey to help him go to his death like a man. Duffy liked the young man and broke the rules by bringing the drink. As they walked together to the gas chamber, Duffy surreptitiously handed over the bottle. On these occasions, Duffy, who was a compassionate warden, was often deeply upset. He was now. The young man glanced at Duffy and gave the drink back, saying, "You need it more than I do."

For welcoming their own execution, few match Walter Jankowski. He had killed a guard during an abortive prison break. Now as he was escorted to the electric chair, he ran from the guards—toward the chair. And kissed it. "I was never so happy to see anything," he explained to the astonished guards as they strapped him in. And although he cried, they were tears of joy. Jankowski had been dying painfully from tuberculosis and regarded his execution as an end to suffering.

The last laugh goes to an Englishman about to be hanged. "See that cloud up there?" he said to the hangman and witnesses. They followed the direction he was pointing and saw through a window in the roof of the execution chamber a large cloud. "In a few minutes I'll be sitting on that cloud," he told them. "And then I'll spit on the lot of you!"

20

Executioners Talk

Albert Pierrepoint, Britain's longtime hangman, with some three hundred corpses to his credit, regarded his job as sacred. He believed too many murderers were reprieved; that reduced his take-home pay, of course. And, when questioned, he thought it perfectly okay to hang the insane.

Giving evidence before a British Royal Commission on Capital Punishment [1949–1953], the chauvinistic hangman said the only awkward moment in his long career was when a spy—"he was not an Englishman—kicked up rough. He went for everybody." He dived at Pierrepoint with his head, then fought with everything he had. Finally, he had to be strapped to a chair in which he was carried to the gallows.

Pierrepoint spoke proudly of the many English murderers who maintained the stiff-upper-lip tradition to the very end. Another expert witness agreed with Pierrepoint, adding, "English people take their punishment better than foreigners."

The British hangman was never short of assistants. An average of five people a week applied to the prison commissioners for the job of executioner. Anyone considered suitable was given on-the-job training as an assistant hangman, then put on a list of those qualified for the work.

When Pierrepoint retired, an assistant, Harry Allen, took over. He squeezed the work in with running a pub. Allen noted to his surprise that "the calmest man at an execution was the condemned man. Right until the end he was buoyed up by hope that he would be reprieved."

Allen scorned foreign practices, explaining why: "I have studied methods used abroad, like the guillotine and the electric chair, and I can say that our system is best."

Apparently he had not read the letter from Jessie Dobson, a Recorder of Britain's Royal College of Surgeons, published in a 1951 issue of *The Lancet,* a distinguished medical journal: "The procedure employed in judicial hanging has been, and maybe still is, an uncertain means of causing instantaneous death." She described how the bodies of thirty-six criminals were dissected after hanging, and pathologists found that in ten of them the hearts were still beating. In two cases the heartbeats continued for five hours. In one case they lasted over seven hours.

A lot depended on the man on the other end of the rope. Louisiana's hangman Johnston, who operated at the start of this century, had a terrifying reputation. With an average of one homicide every other day in New Orleans alone, he was kept working overtime. And he enjoyed scaring those he was about to hang with graphic accounts of hangings he had botched.

Robert Elliott, known as "the gentle executioner," perhaps because he didn't seem to enjoy his work, was official executioner for New York, New Jersey, Pennsylvania, Massachusetts, Connecticut, and Vermont.

His most haunting experience was just after he had executed a wife killer in Pennsylvania, and the phone rang. A reprieve? "I was transfixed, frozen, horrified," Elliott recalled. Only a few days before, he had seen a movie in which an innocent man was pardoned minutes after his execution. As the phone rang in reality, so this film scene flashed through his mind. Had he too killed an innocent man? It was a wrong number.

When Britain abolished the death penalty in 1965, hangman Harry Allen went back to running his pub full-time. He regretted the good old days, feeling that murderers are better off dead, for their own good as well as society's. But the loss of his job may have saved his life if not his sanity, judging by the fate of his predecessors.

Hangman Jack Ellis ended it by cutting his throat; Thomas Billington murdered his wife and three children; and H. Critchell retired, complaining bitterly of his "shame" and "the harm it has done to me no doctor can remove." James Berry became a religious fanatic, and another published obscene books that got him six months in prison.

The American executioner Robert Elliott found relief from his work by puttering around his Richmond Hill, N.Y., garden. He received hundreds of letters threatening his life after he executed the anarchists Sacco and Vanzetti. And one night a bomb almost destroyed his home. The state helped him to rebuild it.

But the warden at Sing Sing rarely opened his mail without finding a job application from a would-be executioner. When Elliott died in 1949, there was an avalanche of applications, one in five of the letters from women.

Two widows vied with each other for the job. One who described herself as having plenty of nerve and the ability to repair her own radio felt confident she could quickly learn the "little trick" of electrocution. If the warden turned her down she asked him to find her a "nice honest husband." She didn't want him to choose one from the prison population, though.

Her rival had worked as a nurse but would like to be an executioner because it was odd and different. She said she was in perfect health, didn't have any bad habits, and "I am not hard-hearted, neither am I chicken hearted."

One applicant modestly requested a one-shot execution, needing the $150 fee to send his son to college, and another man was seeking cash for a dowry to marry off his daughter.

A midwestern farmer boasted of his prowess at killing, although he claimed to be a big man with a big heart. He listed his victims as Germans during the war, chicken and cattle on his farm, a man who attacked him and whom he killed in self-defense. All he needed, he told Warden Lawes, was a crash course in killing by electricity and he promised that the man he killed would stay killed. He hoped to hear from the warden by return mail. He did. No thanks.

For chutzpah, sex murderer Rudolph Pleil leads the pack. Offering himself as hangman, he told the mayor that his qualifications were in a well on the edge of town in Germany. Police went there and found a strangled corpse. After his arrest, Pleil said, "Every man has his passion. Some prefer cards. I prefer killing people." He proved his point by killing himself in his cell in 1958.

On the other hand, the softhearted—some might say the soft-headed—and the suicidal offered themselves as sacrificial substitute lambs. One man was willing to take anyone's place in the Sing Sing electric chair if the warden would pay his fare to the prison. A seventy-year-old, ailing would-be martyr was willing to replace a young man destined to die, saying the younger man might prove worthy of a second chance.

A married man with children said he'd switch places with the next man in line for the chair, in return for lifetime support for the family he'd leave behind.

A father made an emotional appeal to the warden to let him die in place of his son. He felt he'd neglected the boy and was to blame for his fate.

Of the voyeurs eager to watch an execution, perhaps the most sneaky excuse came from a henpecked husband. He explained that his wife nagged him nonstop day and night, made jokes at his expense, and ridiculed him in front of others. He had been seriously tempted to kill her three times, he told the warden, and feared he might not be able to resist a fourth provocation. Watching an execution, he speculated, might deter him from turning murderer.

Here was the warden's big chance to prevent a murder! He didn't take it. He wrote back his opinion that watching another executed was no antidote for murder and that his correspondent should try to break his wife of nagging to avoid breaking her neck.

Today, Florida, with some twelve hundred homicides a year, leads all thirty-eight capital punishment states in numbers executed: Two hundred and forty-one prisoners were waiting for the chair in 1986. Since 1976 Florida has executed sixteen men and given six clemency: one killed in 1979; none in 1980, 1981, or 1982; one in 1983; eight in 1984; three in 1985; and three in the first half of 1986.

Until 1923, Florida hanged its murderers on county courthouse lawns. When the electric chair replaced the gallows, county sheriffs pulled the switch. None of them volunteered for the task and many needed stiff drinks before and after. They lobbied the state to give the job to someone else, citing among other reasons the death threats they received after every execution.

The state agreed to advertise the job, and in 1941 a WANTED,

EXECUTIONERS ad appeared in local papers. The work paid $150 a time, not bad for unskilled labor requiring merely pulling a switch. After screening out fanatics and freaks—pinpointed by their bizarre applications—and political extremists of right and left, the state chose a slight, elderly man from Tampa.

Wearing a black hood and using an assumed name, he pulled the switch for several years until a Jacksonville resident took over. By 1964, when executions halted nationwide, the two men had electrocuted 197 prisoners.

When death penalty laws were upheld by the U.S. Supreme Court in 1976 hundreds applied for the job of executioner. Three were chosen. They carry on the tradition of secrecy, wearing black hoods for the execution and not revealing their identities.

Harry Singletary, Florida Department of Corrections assistant secretary for operations, keeps a waiting list of those who have applied to watch executions. No one is ever refused permission. For family members with a relative who was the murderer's victim, it "completes the grief cycle," says Singletary. "For a policeman, it may mark the end of a case."

Patrolman Tommy Weathington had seen J. D. Raulerson kill a fellow policeman, Michael Stewart. Weathington watched Raulerson executed and "just felt relieved. I waited for it for almost ten years. I saw him kill a police officer who was a friend of mine."

Florida Representative Willie Logan found it much worse than he expected, saying, "I didn't think they would actually burn, like meat."

A Vietnam veteran, now a law school graduate, wondered how an execution would differ from death in combat. "There is a significant difference," he said afterwards. "In battle, you are in a high state of stress, trying to survive. In the prison atmosphere it's going on before you. You get up and walk away, and what was a man is just a lump of flesh without spirit. Some witnesses were overwhelmed. But I was somewhat prepared for it."

County Commissioner Maxie Carter, Jr. has watched two men executed and neither experience bothered him. "It needed to be done," he remarked. "I'm 110 percent for capital punishment. I don't know what would happen to this country without it."

Intending to join the college students, professors, attorneys, policemen, businessmen, and an insurance agent who have seen executions is a baseball umpire who hopes watching an electrocution will help him complete a novel he is writing.

Public Defender Richard Jorandby had a more compelling motive. He felt he had to stand by two clients to the end.

"The ritual was the worst thing," he said of the walk from the holding cell to the execution chamber, the last words, the black face mask placed over the condemned men, the hand motions of the black-hooded executioner. "I could just see somebody standing there saying the gods are appeased. I was very depressed. I kept waking up in the middle of the night. It's important that I never forget the horror."

21

To Kill or Not to Kill
Experts Argue

Alan M. Dershowitz is known as a "lawyer of last resort," brought in to appeal after a case has been lost at the trial. He has represented former CIA agent Frank Snepp; socialite-millionaire Claus von Bulow; and destitute Jack Henry Abbott. As well as being an outstanding, controversial trial lawyer and TV personality, Dershowitz teaches at Harvard Law School. Every week about ten prisoners on death rows phone Dershowitz, asking him to save their lives.

I interviewed Professor Dershowitz on January 25, 1986.

In the case of murderers condemned to life imprisonment or awaiting trial who escape from custody and kill again—Theodore Bundy, for example —what would you do if you represented them? With such men who seem compelled to kill but don't plead insanity, would you have no compunction in trying to free them?

Dershowitz: Under no circumstances would I free such a killer. I believe very strongly in confining killers like that permanently and making it impossible for them ever to be free again. Moreover, in certain circumstances they ought to be isolated from the general prison population if they pose a threat to the prison system. I think when a person has killed, the burden of proof rests heavily on that person to demonstrate by a high preponderance of the evidence that he or she is prepared to be free. So I have no compunction about making that kind of confinement permanent.

Would you defend such a person?

Dershowitz: Of course. I would defend anybody charged with any crime, no matter what the circumstances.

If you defended a compulsive killer, there's a good chance you would get him free.

Dershowitz: There's a very, very slight chance I would get them free, and if I did it would demonstrate that the adversary system is working. There are many, many people I have defended who, when I wear my other hat as citizen, I would not like to see free. The same thing would be true if you asked a surgeon, "Would you try to save the life of a terrible serial killer, knowing that if you saved that person's life the likelihood is that he might go free and kill again?" I don't see any conflict between my personal views as a citizen about a matter and my professional obligations to defend anybody.

Don't you think you have a moral responsibility to society as well as to your client, especially if you suspect he is dangerous?

Dershowitz: The only reason I suspect he's dangerous is because he's told me that he is or, of course, the record of his dangerous or deadly acts, in most cases. And I've learned that in confidence. Anybody choosing to be a lawyer, particularly a criminal lawyer, must realize that he is the only person in the world whose job is to unequivocally defend that person. I see no conflict between the very special role and responsibility I've been accorded and my generally conservative and tough views on crime, which lead me to want many of the types of people I defend to be locked up. No, I don't see any conflict.

So, if a hypothetical surgeon saved Hitler's life in 1930, you'd be in sympathy with the surgeon.

Dershowitz: If I were presented with a Hitler who I knew was a Hitler, I would probably kill him and not do it as a lawyer, but as a citizen, an individual. I hope I'd have the courage to kill him. If, however, I had to lure him into my office as a lawyer, I don't think after doing that I could continue to practice law. I would have violated my trust as a lawyer and prevailed as a human being. I used to have dreams at night when Mengele was still alive that he would call me and ask me to represent him. And the dream would always end with uncertainty as to whether I would represent him, turn him in, or murder him. There are occasions when one's obligations as a human being prevail over those as an attorney; but if they happen, one can't do it as an attorney. One has to do it as an act of civil disobedience.

What do you think you would have done if confronted by Mengele?

Dershowitz: I've no idea. It depends. Since Mengele was not a continuing danger at the time, had he been captured in the United States by the United States, and had nobody else been willing to represent him, I think I would have been there to represent him.

Can I propose a scenario for you as you do for your students at Harvard? This is it. You know or strongly suspect that your client is guilty of one or more horrendous, sadistic murders. During the trial, which you appear to be winning, you get persuasive information that if freed he intends to murder your wife, or mother, or child, or you. What would you do?

Dershowitz: Many things, ranging from killing him myself. If it were a proximate case of self-defense I would be entitled to do that. That's the maximum I would do. The minimum would be to immediately leave the case and turn him in to the police. There's a legal obligation to disclose to the police a future crime, a stated intention to commit a future crime by a defendant. So that poses no conflict at all for a lawyer. There's an obligation to disclose the information and turn him in. I tell my client that in advance, by the way.

Gerry Spence had that problem. He was prosecuting

a man who had blown up and killed one of Spence's friends. And while in prison that man was ordering murders that were taking place. And he was also threatening Spence.

Dershowitz: I don't think lawyers should ever become involved in a case where in any way, as prosecutor or defendant, they know the people involved; or where any kind of personal aspect is involved. If a murderer killed any member of my family, my response would range from probably in an emotional way trying to harm him, and certainly doing everything I could to try to help him be prosecuted. I'm entitled to do that. I would not be his lawyer.

In your book *The Best Defense,* you say the criminal justice system is corrupt. Are you involved in any major attempts to make it less corrupt?

Dershowitz: Oh, sure, I speak out probably on a daily basis, trying to expose the corruption of the system. I take cases very deliberately which seek to expose the corruption. I teach daily about the corruption of the system. I suspect I spend more of my life dealing with the corruption of the legal system, probably more than anybody in the country.

Have there been any changes as a result?

Dershowitz: It's hard to know. I certainly think I've helped to keep the system a little bit more honest. When I appear before a judge these days, I have a sense that he knows the decision in the case is not the end of the road if I feel there has been corruption as I define it; and that I certainly will expose it.

Have you ever seen murder victims?

Dershowitz: Oh, sure. I've represented murder victims.

Mutilated victims?

Dershowitz: Sure. Right now I'm representing victims of a murder in a lawsuit against the alleged killers who have not been brought to justice.

I ask that because many people against capital punishment have not seen murder victims.

Dershowitz: Oh, of course.

Have you ever witnessed an execution?

Dershowitz: No.

Do you support the argument about to be presented to the Supreme Court that it should be mandatory to spare the life of a prisoner on death row who goes mad while awaiting execution?*

Dershowitz: I've never been tremendously sympathetic to distinguishing between people who go mad on death row and a wide variety of other reasons why people might be spared execution. On the other hand, being a strong opponent of the death penalty, I am happy to support any distinction which will cut down the death-row population. It's, of course, an irony that if a person goes mad on death row he then should theoretically be treated, restored to sanity, and executed. Plainly we're not prepared to do that. In some respects, many normal people probably should go mad when faced with the barbarity of execution. But I certainly support the argument, as I understand it; and that is the attempt to limit the number of people to be executed in this country today.

Do you believe Richard Hauptmann, executed for the kidnap-murder of the Lindbergh baby, was innocent?

Dershowitz: I know the whole case very closely. I believe that doubts have been raised about several people in this country who've been executed for murder, but I'm not an advocate of their innocence necessarily. I don't think one has to take the position that they are necessarily innocent in order to conclude that the process by which they were found guilty and executed was grossly unfair. I would include in those categories Sacco and Vanzetti, and the Rosenbergs, and Hauptmann, and numerous others without necessarily believing beyond a reasonable doubt in their innocence. I am absolutely convinced that the process of justice was absolutely unfair. And that's my job, the process of justice and not necessarily the ends of justice.

The prosecuting attorney for the *In Cold Blood* case said to the jury: "The next time they go slaughtering, it

*In June 1986 the U.S. Supreme Court ruled 5–4 that it is unconstitutional to execute an insane killer.

may be your family. I say to you, some of our enormous crimes only happen because once upon a time a pack of chicken hearted jurors refused to do their duty." The two men were hanged, as you know. A quarter of a century later, in 1984, Duane West, that same attorney, said: "Those two guys were scum and they needed to be executed. I would have gone up and pulled the lever on those guys." And even Hickock's defense attorney, Harrison Smith, said, "I'd say the executions were warranted in this particular case if they ever are warranted." Do you sympathize with their attitude?

Dershowitz: Absolutely not. I think the prosecutor should have been prosecuted himself and disbarred for that kind of argument. I think that's an outrageous distortion of justice. It makes it impossible for a jury to see justice done. In most civilized states in this country, that conviction would have been reversed for a new trial and the prosecutor would have been subjected to disciplinary proceedings. We have a case here in Massachusetts right now where a prosecutor is being subjected to disciplinary proceedings for comments far, far less incendiary than that one.

But those killers did imply or say to Capote that they intended to kill again if they were freed.

Dershowitz: I'm not suggesting for a moment that I have any brief for those killers. I certainly wanted to see them in prison for the rest of their lives. But I think a prosecutor of the kind you described, and the statements he made, does more to distort the process of justice in this country than most criminals.

I told Duane West what Alan Dershowitz thought of him.*

Duane West: This is where I disagree with Professor Dershowitz and a lot of these bleeding hearts. He's the kind of guy that says it's murder for the state to execute somebody who's been convicted of murder. I don't know if he's made that statement, but there are

*I interviewed attorney Duane West on February 14, 1986.

people who say, "Oh, that's murder!" To me, that's ridiculous. This is something that's done by the state after they've given every, every, every possible out, in every way, shape, and form. And I think it's a bunch of garbage that we're saying the prosecutor can't get up and tell the jury what's happened, saying, "Hold on! You can't inflame the passions of the jury!" Well, all that was done was to tell the people the facts. And there's some point in time when the public is going to stop putting up with this crap that's been going down over the last twenty some years, the way we're thinking only of the poor defendants in these cases. And we've gone overboard, and we've got to get back absolutely to some common sense in the prosecution of the criminals. To make that outrageous statement: "We're going to prosecute the prosecutor," is a bunch of garbage. These guys that live in ivory towers—

He's also a practicing attorney.

West: And I'm sure he's made a good living pushing these ridiculous, idiotic positions about prosecuting the prosecutors when they're up there trying to convict murderers that slaughtered a bunch of people. I don't have any sympathy for him and any use for those kind of folks at all.

I think his argument would be that murder is barbaric but so is executing murderers; that Smith and Hickock should have been sentenced to life without any possibility of parole.

West: That's a myth. You show me any place where a prisoner's been kept in jail without parole. It's just not happening.

How about The Bird Man of Alcatraz, Stroud?

West: The simple fact is that a fantastic number of murderers who are sentenced to prison in turn get out and kill someone else. The public has got to be protected against that sort of thing.

The argument I think Dershowitz and others might make is that if you imprison murderers for life it gives psychiatrists a chance to study them, to find out what makes them tick, and possibly discover ways of preventing potential murderers from becoming actual killers.

West: We don't have the money available in this country to do that. And I don't think psychiatry is an exact enough science to do that, anyway. If science could help you put your finger on the exact thing causing murder, that would be great. But I think it's an impossibility. I've worked in mental health for a long, long time, and psychiatry is not an exact science. You get six psychiatrists in a room and you get six different opinions as to whether a person's safe or unsafe, and how they're going to react.

But don't you think it's unfair that, with hundreds on death row sentenced to death, only a handful are picked out to be executed?

West: I think it's a failure of our justice system. I don't think there's anything unfair about it. People say, "Do you favor capital punishment?" and I say, "Hell, we haven't had capital punishment in this country, for the simple fact we've got the legal system screwed up because of these ridiculous technicalities." There's no common sense anymore in the administration of justice.

D'you think it would be just if everyone on death row was executed?

West: They've been sentenced that way, and that's what ought to happen to them. If we were actually executing these people, it would put some fear of God in these people who are going around killing people. But as it is now, there haven't been enough people executed under our capital punishment laws to really be a deterrent. My God, when the Supreme Court can't even decide something except on a five-to-four decision, how is the cop out there on the beat expected to make a decision that stands up in court? It's ridiculous what we're doing with these highly technical things.

What about the case of Hauptmann and the Lindbergh kidnapping? A California attorney working for Mrs. Hauptmann has got FBI files of the trial that were hidden for years and other documents; and he says the trial was a sham, that witnesses were intimidated and the police corrupt.

West: I've seen a little about that in the press. The contention was rejected by a court recently, wasn't it?

He's got more material and he's presenting it again in the spring.

West: Well, they do about anything in California. That's one of the problems with the system: Any kooky idea that comes out of California gets adopted by other jurisdictions. [He laughed.] I don't know whether they're going to get that old gal out of there, or recalled, but I think that's probably a good idea.

Who's that?

West: Rose Bird, the Chief Justice of the California Supreme Court. [She's against capital punishment, and holding up executions of prisoners on California's death row.]

Do you think one method of execution is more humane than another?

West: We hang people in Kansas. To me, killing people is killing them, and I don't think one is any more or less humane than another.

Although the electric chair came into being because hanging was too often botched.

West: I think probably the electric chair came into being because it was promoted by the electricians' union.

You're cynical about these things.

West: I would say if you're going to hang somebody, that surely a guy ought to be able to get the job done. We have people hang themselves every day with a piece of sheet in the jail cell. If they can do it, surely a guy being paid ought to be able to get somebody hanged.

Do you think any innocent people have been executed?

West: I've never read of a case or known of a case where it was proven to my satisfaction that some were executed who were not guilty. Maybe it has happened. It's possible. In the case I dealt with [the murder of the Clutter family by Smith and Hickock], it sure as hell didn't happen.

If a reputable psychiatrist had testified that they didn't know what they were doing was wrong, that they were insane at the time, could they have avoided the death penalty?

West: If there had been one psychiatrist who said yes, they did know what they were doing and one who said no, they didn't, I think the jury would have convicted them. If all the psychiatric evidence said no, these people absolutely have no conception of right or wrong whatsoever, then I think there might have been a possibility. I doubt it, frankly, because I think the public's got a lot more sense than the psychiatrists.

And it's rare to get psychiatrists to agree in court.

West: That's right. It's such a damned inexact thing. We had a situation in this country not terribly long ago: Some guy and his wife were having problems and she went home and lined up the kids and shot one of them. The jury brought in a verdict of not guilty by reason of insanity and sent her down to the state hospital. Well, she's out already. And it's weird. I don't think she should be running around loose. Any lady that lines her kids up and shoots them is obviously not in her right mind.

She shot *one* of them?

West: She was prevented from shooting the others because her husband or somebody rushed in and grabbed the gun away from her. But the point is, she's already out and trying to regain custody of the kids she lost. And our court system is so damned screwed up, they say, "Unless you show that she might be a problem, you ought to turn her loose." To me, the public is entitled to protection; and because we've got things so screwed up, these people who are in fact guilty of first-degree murder—the one surefire way of guaranteeing the public is protected is to execute them.

What do you think of the insanity defense?

West: It's used by a lot of people when they're not truly insane, unless you say that anybody who commits a crime is insane.

But it's a very small percentage that gets off with the insanity plea.

West: That's true. And, of course, Kansas has a tough insanity rule. But we're all fouled up here. A person shouldn't be innocent by reason of insanity. They're guilty by reason of insanity. We had a guy in the same situation as Lee Andrews who did some hatchet murders several years ago, killing his parents. And they turned him loose in nine months saying he was cured. I disagree with that. I think society has to have protection.

Has he committed any crimes since?

West: I don't know.

His defense was insanity, was it?

West: Yes. And he was in a mental institution for nine months. We had a spree a year ago in the northern part of our state where these people came through on the Interstate. They'd been down to Florida to kill some people. They killed a couple of people, maybe in Arkansas. They came through here and stopped in a little old roadside stand by I70 and killed the clerk, shot him down in cold blood, and then the sheriff's deputy stopped the car because it was speeding. They jumped out and shot him, but they didn't kill him. He got on the radio and they chased them. And they went into a little town and drove up to a little elevator, took a couple of guys hostages, shot another fellow then, but didn't kill him. Then the officers chased them and they went up the road and just stopped, pushed those two hostages out the back of the pickup, and shot them dead and drove on down the road into a farmhouse. The officers surrounded the farmhouse and they had a shoot-out. Luckily, one of the desperadoes got killed—a shame they didn't shoot them all—but anyway they were convicted in a court of murder. And, of course, the girl claimed she didn't have anything to do with it. There were four altogether and three were convicted. Now they've shipped them back. I think one of them's gone to Arkansas to stand trial there, and he said, "I'll be around to haunt you forever!" And that's true. Those people in the area, there's no way they're ever going to feel safe again, as long as that son-of-a-bitch is alive.

Is it likely they'll get away with life imprisonment?

West: This guy here in Kansas, of course we don't have capital punishment anymore. Down in Arkansas, luckily, they do, and I hope they get him down there and stretch his neck. There isn't any reason why we ought to put up with those people.

Is there a strong movement in Kansas to restore the death penalty?

West: Yes, and that'll probably be accomplished after our current governor goes out of office. He can't succeed himself; and after he goes, I think the new governor will sign capital punishment into law. They're talking about capital punishment only if you kill a guard in prison or a law-enforcement officer. That's garbage as far as I'm concerned, because my life is just as valuable as theirs and I think that's unfair. Although, you can't have control in a prison where you have no punishment. Because these guys in there for life can kill anybody with impunity if they want to and say, "Ha!Ha!Ha! What can you do to me? Give me another life sentence?"

Just put them in solitary.

West: That's right. It's a laugh.

I'm interested to know you're not disturbed at the thought that Dershowitz thinks you should be prosecuted.

West: I don't have much respect for Mr. Dershowitz, frankly, with some of the wild ideas he's put out.

He wants to make the criminal justice system less corrupt. He thinks it's very corrupt.

West: Well, that doesn't have a damned thing to do with corruption. I certainly want to make the criminal justice system less corrupt, too. But I want to be sure the judges are honest, the prosecutors are honest, and so on. But standing up in front of a jury and telling them the facts about a case, that's not being corrupt. If that's his definition of corruption, I feel sorry for him.

No, I think his view is that you got the jury emotionally inflamed by saying they personally would be guilty of whatever might happen in the future if the two men were not executed.

West: I think my statement was that the only way we could be sure these guys never walk the land and kill someone else is to convict them of this crime. I forget just exactly the language.

"Chickenhearted jurors" doesn't ring a bell with you?

West: No.

You don't disassociate yourself from that feeling, though, do you?

West: No. I think it's a matter of duty. The whole idea of the jury system is to bring in a verdict of guilty when people are guilty. In this case they had to make up their minds whether they were going to sentence them to death or not. That's what they were asked to do. Now there's some question as to whether you can even exclude people from the jury who don't believe in capital punishment. I don't agree with that at all. I don't think that's fair to the public.

With one juror like that considering a capital crime, you could never get a death sentence.

West: That's exactly right, and I think it's grossly unfair. The reason the legal system is falling into disrepute with the public is because of the kind of garbage that people like Dershowitz have put out. I think it's absolutely ridiculous.

22

What Shall We Do with Our Murderers?

What does imprisonment for life mean? Three years or less for some. More than half the convicted murderers released from state prisons in 1983 served less than seven years behind bars, according to Bureau of Justice Statistics released in 1986. The median time served on a life sentence was eight years and seven months.

Psychiatrist Karl Menninger stressed his lifelong opposition to capital punishment when I spoke with him twelve days before his ninety-second birthday on July 19, 1985. Menninger is cofounder of the famed Menninger Clinic for the mentally ill.

I reminded him that the *In Cold Blood* murderers Richard Hickock and Perry Smith had told Truman Capote (their Boswell) that, had they escaped the hangman, they would have hitchhiked across America killing and robbing.

Menninger: That's what they said one day. You don't know what they thought the next day.

Capote knew them for three years. In the case of serial killers who say they enjoy killing, and who threaten to murder more if they escape from prison or custody, what do you think should happen to them?

Menninger: You mean *be done* to them? You don't mean *happen:* I'm not God.

Yes, be done to them by the authorities?

Menninger: I think they should be detained, don't you?

How about those who say they intend to escape?

Menninger: Then I'd detain them again.

In the meantime they may have tortured and killed people.

Menninger: Yes, that's quite a problem. What's the next question? You know that question isn't answerable by me.

I know. It's very tough.

Menninger: I don't consider it tough. That's not a real question.

Would you oppose capital punishment for such men?

Menninger: I'm not a killer for any reason. I don't believe in killing. So I'd be against capital punishment for anybody.

Would you imprison them for life?

Menninger: I don't know. I'd have to examine them.

Do you think the public should see executions?

Menninger: Yes. If you're going to do it, you ought to see it.

Do you agree that the most difficult problem is with serial murderers who kill because they enjoy killing?

Menninger: They're hardly ever caught, you know. Most of them are never caught.

When they are caught, shouldn't they be executed?

Menninger: No, I'm not for executing anybody.

When they are caught, should they be imprisoned for a complete lifetime?

Menninger: I don't know that without examining them. I don't feel comfortable with your kind of generalizations.

Do you remember Albert Fish, the man who killed and ate children?

Menninger: Oh yes, in New York.

I spoke with the psychiatrist Frederic Wertham, who examined Fish—

Menninger: I used to know Wertham.

Wertham told the court at Fish's murder trial that Fish was obviously insane. But Fish had been in mental institutions; and psychiatrists from those places testified that Fish was not insane.

Menninger: Well, I'm not going to stand in judgment of psychiatrists I never saw.

So your point is that nobody should be executed, whatever they do.

Menninger: I think that's the wrong way to put it. You're making it extreme like saying, "Everything in America is mixed up, so let's get rid of the country!" I don't like these extreme statements. They don't help me in thinking. I can see how they may be helpful to others.

I'm writing a book which describes in greater detail than other books do how murderers die, what their lives are like on death row awaiting execution, and what the executions are like. Do you think the public should know that?

Menninger: I thought once it would be a good publicity idea. I think the world ought to quit killing people, shooting people, piling up ammunition.

But is prison the answer for killers? The prisons are already overcrowded.

Menninger: The Senate just passed a law to make more guns available. D'you think that will help?

No.

Menninger: No, of course not.

Don't you think, though, the more informed the public is, the better?

Menninger: I don't know. We know more now than
we used to. Do you think we do any better?

In some cases we do, in some we don't. But I can
see you're irrevocably against capital punishment.

Menninger: I've always been against it.

Philosopher professor Hugo Adam Bedau of Tufts University is
one of the leading advocates of the movement to abolish the death
penalty. Bedau has held a Carnegie Fellowship in Law and Philosophy at the Harvard Law School and has taught philosophy at Dart-
mouth, Princeton, Rutgers, and Swathmore. He is editor of *The
Death Penalty in America*. With sociologist Michael L. Radelet of
the University of Florida, Bedau is working on a Project on Innocence to be published in the *Law Review* in late 1986. They claim
that out of some seven thousand people executed in the U.S. since
1893, twenty-five were innocent. I interviewed both men in January
1986.

Hugo Bedau: The metaphysics of evil apart, I think
that in a society such as ours for crimes of terrorism,
crimes of multiple murder like the Bundys of the world
commit, recourse to the death penalty is unnecessary
and undesirable.

But how about serial killers who say they will kill
again if given the chance and who do escape and kill
again?

Bedau: Not very many of them escape, and some we
know tell a fantastic series of lies about the crimes they
have done. As for the rest, our job is to see to it that
they either don't escape, or if they do, that they don't
carry out their threats.

Theodore Bundy escaped and killed two young
women and a thirteen-year-old girl.

Bedau: No doubt he did and it constitutes a tragedy.
But he is not an implacable embodiment of
metaphysical evil. I don't find that a helpful way to
view it. He's not a ministering agent of some criminal
government, like an Eichmann. He's simply a human
being. And our job, confronted by his kind of behavior,
is to come up with something more imaginative, more
effective than simply putting him to death. I don't

want to make an exception in his case, even though I am appalled and infuriated and disgusted with the predicament he presents to us. I'm infuriated that I and others have to spend our time dealing with cases of this sort, and yet I see no alternative I'm willing to stomach.

Have you ever witnessed an execution?

Bedau: No, and I haven't any desire to. I've also never had an opportunity, but if I had I think I'd probably turn it down.

Here are some of New York Mayor Koch's arguments in favor of the death penalty: "An MIT study based on 1970 murders concluded that one stood more risk of being murdered in an American city than an American soldier risked being killed in combat in World War II. If other countries had our murder problem, the cry for capital punishment would be just as loud as it is here. I dare say," says Koch, "that any other major democracy where 75% approximately of the people supported the death penalty would soon enact it into law." Incidentally, of people polled by the Los Angeles *Herald* about the Hillside Killings, 94 percent were for executing the killer.

Bedau: I'm prepared to believe all that. So what?

Murders are on the increase.

Bedau: That's not true in the United States.

They increased by three hundred percent in New York City in less than twenty years, from 1963 to 1980.

Bedau: That's true. An important question is the extent to which the bulge in the murder rate in the U.S. during the period was owing in part to the tremendous bulge in the baby boom that came of age as teenagers and in their early twenties in that same period. The bulge has now moved on, not because of capital punishment, not because of the effectiveness of the police, but because of the aging factor. Those young men now are in their forties, and the crimes being committed twenty years ago are not typical of their behavior today. Criminologists have studied the question of the role of the death penalty both on the statute books and as actually employed during this century in the U.S., quite exhaustively. With one or

two exceptions, they have concluded that there is no
evidence to substantiate the claim that the disuse or the
decline in use of the death penalty is a factor in the
rise of the murder rate.

You say that a study of seven thousand executions in
the U.S. from 1893 to 1971 uncovered that eight
innocents were executed. Are you sure they were innocent?

Bedau: I hardly claim the role of final judge. All I
can do is report what I and others think. In the nature
of the case, once a person is executed there is no forum
in which that issue can be settled with the kind of legal
conclusiveness that the issue of guilt or innocence has
when we have a trial court or appellate court that can
face the issue for the *living* defendant. So we're
reduced to having historians and philosophers and
social commentators do the best they can. I simply
submit to the world the research that my colleague
Michael Radalet and I are now bringing to completion.
We've reexamined the data and have not changed our
minds about any of the cases I identified twenty years
ago. Meanwhile we have extended our survey and our
research methods enormously and have tripled the
number of cases where we believe an error in execution
occurred to twenty-four. The real issue is this: What is
the argument in favor of a system that makes
correction of error impossible as the death-penalty
system does, as opposed to an alternative system of
imprisonment which allows to some extent the
correction of error?

But I think that in the years you list twenty-four
innocents were executed, more than that number of
imprisoned murderers escaped and killed again.

Bedau: I think that's true. The errors of the parole
or custody system make it possible for persons to put
others at risk and to kill. Any system is going to be
flawed. Therefore, we have to face what system it is we
are prepared to embrace. There are fundamentally
three choices. One is the system in which we avoid all
possible errors of parole and custody, by killing all
those who are put behind bars for these crimes. Kill
everyone. Another system, the one I favor, we kill none
of them. The third system is the one we have and that

apparently most Americans want, where we pick and
choose. We've been doing it throughout history and
have the most difficult time trying to make out a line
of reasoning which shows whom we should permit to
live in this case, with a lesser punishment than death,
and in that case, execute. I do not think we have found
a *system* which enables us to make rational those kind
of choices. That the parole system is not perfect seems
to me an argument of no great weight, unless you're
prepared to take the extreme view. Mayor Koch and
all defenders of the death penalty I've met very
carefully avoid taking the bull by the horns and
agreeing, yes, every person convicted of murder is to be
put to death, no ifs ands or buts. Now that is too
heroic for the stomachs of most of the defenders of the
death penalty in the United States.

What would you do with a murderer in the Midwest
named Hopkinson? He was in prison on trial for
murder and while there directed others outside to
commit more murders for him.

Bedau: I'd try to stop him. I cannot really believe
that the satanic power this person had was so great
and overpowering that the minds of law enforcement in
the Midwest area were totally baffled. It sounds like
Dr. Moriarty straight out of Arthur Conan Doyle
books, and I don't believe that crap.

He had weak-willed people outside who were on
drugs and he paid them to kill for him. How about the
guard who recently gave Theodore Bundy a file to try
to escape from death row and he got through a couple
of bars before he was stopped?

Bedau: Bundy and others like him are not
cannonballs rolling loose on the deck of society, as
your anecdotes are bringing out. These people need
help and they manage to corrupt others around them.
That suggests that the evil, if you so wish to designate
it, is rather broadly spread throughout our society. It is
not confined to unique individuals who are beyond the
pale of humanity such as the Bundys, the Eichmanns,
and whoever else you wish to name. I swear Eichmann
could not have begun to accomplish the sins for which
he was tried without the help of thousands and

thousands of good Germans, as we all know. And you've just pointed to a couple of other good Germans in the pay of our criminal justice system who have allowed themselves to be corrupted, to assist in these things. I don't look at it with complacency or indifference. But putting people to death here and there seems to me not to have any connection with the scope of the problem. All we get out of that is the satisfaction that whoever else may do whatever they may do, Bundy won't do it again. Under certain conditions, where self-defense is our only recourse and violence is needed in that situation, I can fully understand the police shooting, or a citizen killing someone. I don't think we need to set up institutions of government to run society to do that as well.

Koch denies that capital punishment cheapens human life. On the contrary, he says that when we "lower the penalty for murder it signals a lessened regard for the value of the victim's life."

Bedau: There is some point to this hoary metaphor the mayor uses. For those who find it appealing, the problem is, Where do you draw the line? It's very easy to say we'll draw the line at multiple murders. As a political matter I would be happy tomorrow to see the U.S. Government and every state that hasn't abolished the death penalty agree that the death penalty would be limited to all and only those capable of multiple murders, and where the multiplicity starts at two, I would regard that as a great step forward down the path that I think we will ultimately reach, which is the total abolition of the death penalty. Very few other Americans are prepared to go this far, so you find the enthusiasm for the death penalty strung out all along the spectrum from a small number who favor killing them all to a small number at the other end like me, who favor killing none; with the bulk of the population distributed helter-skelter in between.

Have you taken any special interest in the guilt or innocence of Richard Hauptmann who was electrocuted for the Lindbergh kidnap-killing?

Bedau: I can remember as a boy when that crime occurred. I was living in California then. I have read the standard books on it, including the very telling recent volume by Ludovic Kennedy, and find his account imaginative and compellingly convincing.

Are you convinced of Hauptmann's innocence?

Bedau: I didn't need Kennedy's book to have grave doubts, but I think it has done more to reassemble and restate the evidence than anything else I have read; to make the verdict in that case appear, as I believe it is, utterly unfounded and wrong. What a proper scenario is for the crime is very unclear.

I next spoke with Professor Bedau's fellow researcher on the Project on Innocence, Michael Radalet.

Radalet: Thus far we've documented about 350 cases this century in which an innocent person has been either convicted of homicide, or convicted of another crime for which he received the death sentence.

How many were executed?

Radalet: We're carrying twenty-five cases this century in the U.S.

How do you determine they were innocent?

Radalet: Most often it's the state's admission of error. But the state doesn't admit error after the person's been executed. When it's a simple conviction, usually it's a pardon or someone else is convicted, or someone else confesses. If there's an erroneous execution, typically there's new evidence that comes to light after the execution. We believe most people looking at the evidence would conclude that the person was probably innocent.

Is the most dramatic case maybe Hauptmann?

Radalet: Yes. Another classic is Sacco and Vanzetti.

Who were the real killers?

Radalet: Unknown. But there's substantial evidence from another confession in the Sacco and Vanzetti case, from a member of the Morelli gang. That gang was involved in several holdups, especially in Providence, Rhode Island, which is not far from where the crime for which Sacco and Vanzetti were executed occurred.

I think the strongest feeling that pro–capital
punishment advocates have is against serial killers like
Bundy who can escape and murder after they've been
imprisoned. And who do escape and kill again. They
outnumber your innocents probably several times. How
do you feel they should be treated?

Radalet: First of all, Bundy escaped from two little
cells that were in essence local jails.

He also made an escape bid here in Florida from the
death house, where one of the guards gave him a file.
He was almost on his way.

Radalet: Well, almost. It's true that in August 1984
he did have a hacksaw and did go through a couple of
bars there, one inch by about a quarter of an inch steel
plates that are on the window. The probability of his
getting out of that prison [Raiford], even if he'd made
it through the window, was about zilch. It was
essentially more a suicide attempt than anything else.

You mean they'd shoot him trying to escape?

Radalet: Certainly.

I spoke with a man who saw two of Bundy's victims,
and he said that as a policeman seeing prisoners on
death row he felt sorry for them and could understand
the attitude of abolitionists. But having seen Bundy's
victims he feels the men should be executed. If these
brutal killers who apparently are, to use a
non-psychological term, evil or twisted are likely to
escape and kill other innocent victims, why shouldn't
they be painlessly and swiftly put to death?

Radalet: First of all, they're not going to be
painlessly and quickly put to death.

As painlessly and quickly as possible. The delay is
because of the appeals they make to avoid or delay
execution.

Radalet: Right. But I don't think it's possible to
quickly and painlessly put people to death. The U.S.
Supreme Court has said you can kill these folks, but
only given certain steps and routines. So the probability
of cutting the delays much below eight years . . . Well,
we're not ever going to do that. That's holding out
hope for a system we can't have. If you want to get rid
of somebody like Bundy for fear that he might kill

again, two points: The pain of the death penalty is not the last ten seconds of the guy's life. It's not whether you get a jolt of electricity; it's not whether you get your spine broken. It's the anticipation. It's seeing your family go through the anticipation of your dying. The second point is that, given how we're not going to be able to hang these folks on the courthouse lawn, on the first oak tree we come across—if Ted Bundy was going to escape he would escape now. He can sit around passively until they get around to killing him or try to get out. We can build prisons that are secure enough to keep the most violent type of prisoners there. People don't escape from death row in Florida.

Never?

Radalet: One person escaped in 1978. He was recaptured within a few days, without killing again. I'm also against the death penalty on a cost-benefit analysis. There might be benefits in the individual case, but the question for us as citizens is not whether person X or person Y should or should not be put to death. It is whether we as taxpayers should support the system. It's the system of capital punishment we've got to take or leave.

Here's one answer, from Los Angeles Mayor Tom Bradley. He's quoted in the L.A. *Times* of January 9, 1986. "I've seen far too many people killed, I've seen far too much violence in our society. I see some of it today with people who have no compassion, no concern, no idea of the consequence of their acts. So they would rather kill at the blink of an eye, go into a store and pull a robbery. And when somebody doesn't move fast enough, they blow them away. I believe that the death penalty is necessary and I support it. There's got to be some way that we remove them, that we separate them from you and me and the rest of our society . . . those who take the lives of innocent people. Otherwise all of us will be living in a jungle with no security, no protection."

Radalet: He's into societal protection. How do you read that? As a general deterrent?

No, I don't. Because statistics have been argued for years and they're not persuasive either way.

Radalet: Once you execute one person, he'll never kill again?

That's right.

Radalet: So the question is whether you want to kill a hundred to get at the one who might or will indeed kill again? With all the appeals courts, and all the attempts to be fair, looking into the person's background and record and motives—with all those protections, the likelihood of innocent people being executed is very low. How many were executed in the U.S. last year? There were some twenty thousand murders, and I imagine some hundreds sentenced to death. How many of those were executed?

Radalet: Last year there were eighteen.

Do you believe any of those were innocent?

Radalet: I think at least one was, James Adams of Florida. There's another one, James Baldwin of Louisiana.

Let me give you a situation. The man had four life terms for murder with no chance of parole. So he was in for ever. He persuaded a woman to join him in the prison chaplain's office where he strangled her. What can they do to him? There's no death penalty in that state.

Radalet: To be pragmatic, I'll give you that one. I would like to see how many of the 1,600 people on death row today are in that situation. I bet 99.9 percent are not.

But don't you agree that if a man kills under great provocation, in a rage or during a violent quarrel, he rarely gets the death penalty?

Radalet: Rarely, but they sometimes do. There are some people convicted of homicide even though they might be crazy. The Freddie Goode case in Florida is a prime example of killing the mentally ill. [He was executed on April 5, 1984.] In the Goode case, he tried to argue not guilty by reason of insanity and tried to fire his attorney. Goode then said: "No, I'm not insane. Having sex with children is the way it should be done." The judge let him act as co-counsel. He got on the stand and spent a couple of hours saying how much fun it was to have sex with little boys.

A lot of people would want the death penalty for that alone.

Radalet: Of course. And if you read how the guy talks about his crimes, you think, "My God, horrible, horrible!" Another case is that of Ernest Dobbert, executed in Florida in 1984. Dobbert had a jury recommendation of life imprisonment. The judge overrode it and sentenced him to death anyhow. The override provision is the quickest way I know of to increase the probability of innocent people being executed.

[Dobbert was condemned to death for the 1972 beating and choking death of his nine-year-old daughter. He was also found guilty of killing his seven-year-old son, torturing an eleven-year-old son, and abusing his five-year-old daughter. "I think this was the most cold-blooded case I have ever worked," said Police Lieutenant James Suber of Jacksonville. Michael Radalet had appealed to Governor Graham to halt the execution in a petition signed by the University of Florida's eleven criminology professors. The group issued a statement: "There is no credible scientific research that supports the contention that the threat or use of the death penalty is or has been a deterrence to homicide." Governor Graham said Dobbert's execution might be a warning to other abusive parents: "Ernest Dobbert has been executed because of his brutal actions toward his own children. I hope that this indication of the seriousness of child abuse will be an example of the value which the people of Florida place upon the lives of infants and young people in our state."] A juror in the Dobbert case said the reason they voted for life was because they weren't sure that Dobbert had intended his victim to die. His victim was his kid. He was a child abuser. So there was a serious question there about criminal intent. So the jury voted yes for conviction, but no for death. But the judge overrode it and they killed Dobbert.

How many states allow the judge to override the jury's recommended sentence?

Radalet: Three. Florida, Louisiana, and Alabama.

You've made it quite clear you're against the death penalty.

Radalet: To be concerned about the execution of

innocent people, you have to be against it. Although
the pro–capital punishment people are no less
concerned about the execution of the innocent than I
am.

What would you do with thrill killers who commit
multiple murders and are not judged to be insane?

Radalet: In the U.S. you can build properly
administered prisons that would reduce the probability
of future dangers to a minuscule level. Some of them
will kill again, there's no question about that. Some of
them will always kill again, and that's a cost.

23

Do We Convict the Innocent?

1893. Mississippi. Eyewitness testimony helped convict
Will Purvis of murder and he was sentenced to death. In
what must have seemed to him an act of God, he survived
the hanging when the knot slipped. After five years in prison
he was pardoned in 1898. The deathbed confession of the
real murderer in 1917 cleared Purvis of the murder conviction.

1898. Massachusetts. Jack O'Neil was the last man hanged
[January 7, 1898] in Massachusetts. The gallows was replaced by the electric chair the following year. O'Neil
claimed he had not killed Hattie McCloud, but said, "I shall
meet death like a man and I hope those who see me hanged
will live to see the day when it is proved I am innocent."
They didn't have long to wait. A few months later a dying
soldier who had been fighting the Spaniards in Cuba admitted he had murdered Hattie McCloud, and signed a confession.

1901. Florida. Instead of J. B. Brown's name on the execution warrant, someone had goofed and written the name of the jury foreman. The baffled authorities led Brown from the gallows back to his cell. His sentence was commuted to life. In 1913 the man believed to have been his accomplice in murder made a deathbed confession saying he had falsely implicated Brown in the crime. Brown was freed in 1929.

1907. Alabama. After serving four years of a life sentence for first-degree murder, Bill Wilson's "victim" turned up alive. Wilson was pardoned by the governor and indemnified.

1907. New Jersey. John Schuyler was saved from execution and pardoned when the real murderer confessed.

1908. Virginia. Ernest Lyons had spent three years of an eighteen-year sentence for second-degree murder when the supposed victim was found to be alive in North Carolina.

1911. Wisconsin. John Johnson had served eleven years of a life sentence for murder when in 1922 someone else confessed to the crime.

1913. Georgia. Leo Frank. He was convicted of murder and sentenced to death on the lying testimony of the real killer. Although the governor commuted the death sentence in 1915, it did not save Frank's life. A mob lynched him.

1915. New York. Less than an hour before his execution, Charles Stielow was reprieved. Three years later he was released from prison when the murderer confessed.

1925. Kentucky. Condy Dabney had spent a year of his life sentence for murder behind bars when the "murder victim" was discovered to be alive. Dabney was pardoned.

1925. New York. Edward Larkman was sentenced to death for murder. Two years later the sentence was commuted to life, and two years after that another convict confessed to the crime. Larkman was pardoned in 1933.

1926. Texas. Anastarcio Vargas' head had been shaved in readiness for execution in the electric chair when a look-alike confessed to the crime. After investigating, the judge cleared Vargas, whose sentence was commuted to life. In 1930 he was pardoned and given $26,500 compensation.

1927. Pennsylvania. Jerry Weeks was sentenced to death for killing his sister-in-law and her three children. When he was being strapped into the electric chair, Salvation Army chaplain Fred Goddard said to him, "You have a few more seconds of this life to live. No earthly power can save you now. With your last breath, tell me the truth. Are you guilty?" Weeks replied, "In the name of my mother in heaven, I am not guilty." A moment later Weeks was executed. The executioner, Robert Elliott, eventually became a strong opponent of capital punishment and said his belief in Weeks' innocence was the main reason.

1928. Massachusetts. The night Cero Gangi was to be executed for murder, a witness identified Gangi's employer, Samuel Gallo, as the murderer. Cero was reprieved and Gallo charged with the crime. Both men were then tried together. This time Cero was acquitted and Gallo found guilty. After the witness left the country, Gallo faced another trial, and was acquitted.

1928. Alabama. Louise Butler and George Yelder had served two months of their life sentences for murder when their victim was found to be alive and well in another county.

1930. New York. Pietro Matera was sentenced to death for murder, but Governor Franklin Roosevelt reduced the sentence to life. Matera had spent thirty years in prison when the real murderer's wife, Adalgisa Lo Cascio, confessed on her deathbed that she had fingered Matera to save her husband's life. Matera was freed from prison in 1961.

1934. Massachusetts. It was a close call for Clement Molway and Louis Berrett, Boston taxi drivers accused of murdering an employee of the Paramount Theater in Lynn. Eight eyewitnesses swore that the two men were guilty. Then Abraham Faber, who with others had been sentenced for other murders, admitted they had killed the Paramount Theater employee, and that the two cabdrivers were completely innocent. Molway and Berrett were exonerated, freed, and paid compensation. Hosea Bradstreet, the jury foreman, said, "Those witnesses were so positive in their identification it was only natural we should be misled. This trial has taught me one thing. Before, I was a firm believer in capital punishment. I'm not now."

1940. New York. Louis Hoffner, after being sentenced to death for murder, had his sentence commuted by Governor Dewey in 1955, when he was freed and paid compensation for fifteen years of false imprisonment.

1945. U.S. Army Private A. B. Ritchie was sentenced to hang for murder on July 1, 1945, when another man confessed to the crime. Ritchie was pardoned in 1947.

1954. Massachusetts. Santos Rodriguez had been in prison three years and three months after being found guilty of murdering a woman. Then another prisoner confessed to the crime, saying he had waited until after his mother had died before admitting to the crime. Rodriguez was set free and given $12,500.

1954. Pennsylvania. Paul Pfeffer was given a twenty-years-to-life sentence, when John Roche confessed and established Pfeffer's innocence.

1963. Washington, D.C. Just minutes before he was to be executed, Charles Bernstein's sentence was commuted. Two years later a police investigation proved Bernstein was innocent. He was released and pardoned by the President.

Most of these innocents, fortunately, survived. Nobody knows how many have been executed.

Doubtless, most if not all of them were poor. U.S. Supreme Court Justice Hugo Black believed there "can be no equal justice where the kind of trial a man gets depends on the amount of money he has." The Court seemed to have remedied that in 1963, when all states were required to give poor criminal defendants free counsel.

What is that worth? Stephen Gillers, professor of law at New York University, gives some idea:

> James Messer, a poor man, was charged with murder. The first lawyer appointed to defend him begged off, citing community outrage at the crime. So did the second. A third lawyer adopted a low-key strategy: He made no opening statement, called no witnesses, did not object to evidence, and engaged in only cursory cross-examination. At the sentencing hearing following conviction, he did not ask the jury to spare Messer's life, did not offer mitigating details inviting mercy, and hinted that execution was appropriate. Messer is now on Georgia's death row.*
>
> In 1985 Messer claimed his lawyer had been ineffective. He lost the case.

24

Paroled—To Kill Again

Poor men convicted of murder rarely escape death row. The rich buy their way out.

New York Times reporter Tom Wicker gives a vivid example in John Young, who spent ten years on death row before he was executed in 1984.

As a child, Young slept in the same bed as his prostitute mother who was murdered beside him at the age of eight. He was left alone in the world, and to support himself he became a child prostitute. Three people who survived his attacks were willing to appear at his

---

*In a *New York Times* article in 1986.

murder trial and recommend life in prison rather than death. But Young's court-appointed attorney called none of those witnesses—and Young got death.

That attorney was later disbarred for drug abuse. It's virtually certain that a Dershowitz, a Lee Bailey, or a Gerry Spence could have saved Young's life.

Clinton Duffy, San Quentin's longtime warden, agreed with Wicker that only the poor end up on death row.

Another opponent of capital punishment, Michael V. DiSalle, a former governor of Ohio, believes the cause of most murders is a disordered childhood "in which habits of conduct are formed without proper guidance, affection, or correction."

To which Stanton Samenow, who has evaluated and counseled criminals, responds: "They seize upon any hardship in their lives, real or made up, to justify their acts against society. A man may describe a savage beating by a maniacal father, but he never tells what he did to provoke such treatment.

"All that can be done with the worst of sex offenders, especially those who prey on children, is to lock them up or execute them, and I don't much care which. I am not so heartless as to insist that a man or woman pay with his or her life for a crime committed in the heat of passion or under great momentary stress."

Author Jacques Barzun supports capital punishment, too, saying: "The uncontrollable brute whom I want put out of the way is not to be punished for his misdeeds, nor used as an example or a warning; he is to be killed for the protection of others."

But why, say abolitionists, kill the killers? Why not imprison them for life? Because they may escape, or kill while in prison, or be patroled only to kill again, say death penalty advocates.

It happens.

In 1931 murderer Bob Harper escaped from a Michigan prison and killed two people. He was recaptured—and killed the prison warden and his deputy.

In 1936, according to J. Edgar Hoover, an unnamed prisoner who had committed two murders was given clemency. He subsequently murdered two more people.

In 1939 murderess Louise Peete was paroled. She shot and killed a woman and was believed responsible for killing several other people.

George Fitzsimmons, a New Yorker, murdered his parents and was found not guilty by reason of insanity. Psychiatrists eventually decided he was no longer dangerous and he was released from a mental institution, going to live with an aunt and uncle. He told psychiatrists he loved them like his own mother and father. He fatally stabbed them both. Investigators then discovered that Fitzsimmons had named himself as the beneficiary of the life insurances of all four victims.

In 1951 Joseph Taborsky was sentenced to death for murder. At a new trial in 1955, he successfully claimed that his brother, who had been the chief prosecution witness, was insane. He won his appeal and his freedom. For several days in 1957 Taborsky terrorized people in Connecticut. He was caught again, found guilty of another murder, and sentenced to death. Before his execution in 1960, he confessed to the 1951 murder.

James Lockhart murdered a fellow resident in a Georgia state-subsidized home for former mental patients. Psychiatrists called him "a severe schizophrenic with a very poor prognosis for marked improvement" and he was found not guilty of the murder and sent to a mental institution. Four years later he was released and soon afterwards was arrested for another murder.

Edgar Smith was convicted of killing a fifteen-year-old girl in New Jersey. He insisted that he was innocent. Eventually he was set free. Six years later he was arrested for attempting to kill a woman, and admitted he had killed the teenager.

Frederick Wood was paroled from Clinton State Prison after serving seventeen years of a twenty-year sentence for second-degree murder. Free for less than a month, Wood killed a man in a New York hotel. After his arrest he confessed to four more murders.

After Rhode Island abolished the death penalty, a man serving a life sentence there for murder killed a guard. There was no law to punish him for that second murder.

Elmo Smith was imprisoned for brutal sexual assaults on women. He was released despite protests of law-enforcement authorities. Less than a year later he raped and sadistically murdered a sixteen-year-old girl. He was executed in Pennsylvania in 1962.

In 1966 Charles Yukl strangled a young woman and mutilated her body. He was paroled after five years in prison. Two years later he strangled another woman.

Joseph Morse, twenty-three, killed his mother and crippled sister, and while awaiting trial killed a third person. "I can't change because I can't benefit by experience. If I were to get out of here I'd probably kill again," he told Truman Capote, who was taking part in a TV documentary being filmed on San Quentin's death row.

Henry Jarrette, twenty-six, escaped from a Georgia prison where he was serving time for two murders. In stealing a car, he stabbed a young man to death.

Richard Marquette was sent to prison for life for murdering and dismembering a woman. After twelve years he was paroled. A year later he decapitated a woman. Two years after that he killed and dismembered a third woman. He was arrested and sentenced to— a second life term.

After wounding a tourist in Hawaii in an unprovoked sniper attack, Robert Miller was committed to a state hospital. After six years he was given leave. In 1979 he returned to Waikiki Beach with a rifle and shot seven people.

Joseph Bowen, in prison for murdering a policeman, killed a prison warden and his deputy in 1975. He is reported to have laughed when sentenced to two life terms. In 1981 he led rioting inmates in taking thirty-eight hostages.

Steven Judy gave the jury fair warning at his murder trial. He had been found guilty of raping and strangling an Indianapolis woman and of drowning her three children. "You better vote for the death penalty," he told the jury, "because I'm gonna get out one way or another, and it may be one of you next, or your families." They took him at his word. He was executed on March 9, 1981.

Jack Henry Abbott, in prison for murder, was freed on parole only to murder again in 1982.

While on parole for murdering his high school girl friend, Jimmy Lee Gray raped and suffocated a three-year-old girl. He was executed in Mississippi's gas chamber in 1984.

Paroled rapist and murderer Dennis Janson, thirty-five, tried to rape and murder another woman he had taken out on a first date. He was sentenced to eighteen years in prison.

The day after his wife, Charlyce, left him in 1964, Robert Nicolaus took their two-year-old daughter, Heidi, and two children from a former marriage into a field where he shot them dead. "I thought it was the best way to send them to heaven," he told detectives.

He was sentenced to death, but the California Supreme Court ruled that although sane at the time of the crime, he could not understand the enormity of the crime; consequently, the sentence was reduced to from five years to life in prison.

Superior Court Judge Albert Mundt advised state prison officials: "I am satisfied that this man has and will continue to have a state of mind which makes him a danger to society." He recommended that Nicolaus should never be released on parole.

In 1977 he was released on parole.

In 1984, say police, Nicolaus began following and threatening his former wife. They say he blocked her car in an alley in February 1985 when she was with her three-year-old daughter, and shot her. Charlyce identified her former husband as her assailant before she died in the emergency room of University Medical Center, Sacramento.

In the summer of 1984 an FBI spokesman said, "We're caught up in an epidemic of homicidal mania and it's going to get worse before it gets better."

Perhaps that's why many Americans support the death penalty despite all the persuasive arguments of the abolitionists on humane, psychiatric, religious, pragmatic, and statistical grounds.

A nationwide poll by Media General-Associated Press in 1985 showed 84 percent of Americans favor capital punishment, and 42 percent support it "to protect society from future crimes that person may commit."

About the same time a Gallup Poll showed 72 percent for the death penalty, but it would decline to 52 percent if life imprisonment without possibility of parole were certain for convicted murderers.

In the same poll, 56 percent thought lethal injection to be the most humane method of execution; 16 percent, the electric chair; 8 percent, the gas chamber; 3 percent, the firing squad; and 1 percent, hanging.

What are the answers? Here's the view of Ramsey Clark, a former Attorney General, strongly against the death penalty:

> In America we have cultivated crime and reaped a
> bountiful crop. Crime is the ultimate human
> degradation. A civilized people have no higher duty
> than to do everything within their power to seek its

reduction. We can prevent nearly all of the crime now suffered in America—if we care. Our character is at stake.

If all of our research and learning about human behavior, if all the teaching in our great universities about medical science, mental health, psychiatry, psychology, sociology, hereditary, and environmental influences has any applicability to real life, here in corrections it has an immense and critically important role. Yet, divorcement of all those lessons and skills from the people who need them is almost total.

If America cares for its character, it must revolutionize its approach to corrections.*

Meanwhile, U.S. Supreme Court decisions about who on death rows should die and who should be spared has spurred Justice Thurgood Marshall to complain about "this court's own special contribution to the arbitrariness and freakishness that continues to characterize the implementation of the death penalty."**

*Ramsey Clark in *Crime in America*, Simon and Schuster, 1970.
**Justice Marshall was referring to the inconsistent rulings of the U.S. Supreme Court on March 20, 1986. Then by a five-to-four vote the justices decided to spare the life of murderer Davidson James while considering a formal challenge to his death sentence. On the same day they voted five-to-four to let Roy Allen Harich die, even though his appeal raised the same issue as James'—whether excluding opponents of the death penalty from juries in capital punishment cases stacks the deck against the defendants by producing a "conviction-prone jury." [Harich was spared temporarily by a federal appeals court in Atlanta.]

Get the Inside Story—
It's Stranger than Fiction!